Veritas

The Captain's Redemption

To Sandy
Thank you for your
support
I hope you enjoy
my best

28/5/22

In Partes Ignotas: Book One

Veritas
The Captain's Redemption

By
Lenny Montgomery

evertype
2022

Published by Evertype, 19A Corso Street, Dundee, DD2 1DR, Scotland. www.evertype.com.

First edition 2022.

A catalogue record for this book is available from the British Library.

ISBN-10 1-78201-100-5
ISBN-13 978-1-78201-100-2

Poem on p. 307 excerpted from "Invictus" by William Ernest Henley, 1897.

Typeset in Plantin Light and **Nic** by Michael Everson.

Cover design by Jennifer Demeter.

Dedication

To the memory of Leonard Nimoy—
without his portrayal of Spock in *Star Trek*,
my interest in science fiction would not have been captured
and this book would not exist.

And in memory of my great-uncles:

Able Seaman Joseph Hull Montgomery,
killed in action aged 21, Crete, 27 April 1941,
on the HMS *Wryneck*, Royal Navy

Trimmer William Guthrie Montgomery,
killed in action aged 33, North Atlantic, 11 March 1943,
on the SS *Empire Lakeland*, Merchant Navy

They, like my characters, served their country on ships.

Acknowledgements

My thanks to:

My parents, John and Marion, who taught me to read
and write at an early age and encouraged my writing.
Dad, for being a good wall off which to bounce ideas
and characters, and not minding the random and sometimes
odd questions, and mum, who knows random things
such as the average volume of a teaspoon
without having to look it up!

My best friend, Laura Gilbert, whose excitement to read
the finished novel kept spurring me on when work and life
got in the way of my muse, and for some great ideas—
which I used, of course!

Contents

Veritas

The Captain's Redemption

1

The Impact of Dreams

"**K**eep her steady!"
"I can't, sir! We've lost power—the helm's not responding!"
"Try it! All hands, battle stations! We are under attack." The
captain stopped and drew a breath before continuing, "Good
luck." Slowly, he thumbed off the intercom and turned back to
his chair. Noticing the bridge crew were looking at him, he
nodded. "You heard me. We don't stand a chance."

At that moment, a double salvo shook the ship. It seemed as
though their attackers knew they were unable to return fire and
used every ounce of their force against them. An alarm sounded,
followed by a shout that the shields were failing.

"Captain?"

The captain shook his head as he turned to the Helm.
"Surrender is not an option." There had been no need to ask
what she was trying to say. He turned to the communications
officer. "Send a signal to headquarters!"

"Aye, Captain." The communications officer's hands moved
swiftly over his control panel. "I can't raise them—on any
frequency!" He paused a moment, listening intently through his
earpiece. "Sir, the alien ship is hailing *us!*"

"Answer them! Get them on the screen." He turned to the
viewscreen, at last face to face with their attackers. "I am Captain
Stephen MacAlpin, of the United Earth Ship *Wryneck*. We are
on a peaceful mission."

"You are out of time; in a moment you will be boarded. I am
waiting, Captain MacAlpin. Give me your unconditional
surrender and I will not destroy your ship."

The captain's voice was quiet when he replied, but all the bridge crew heard every word. "I will *never* give you that!"

"You will all die! You have one of your Earth minutes left. What do you say, *Captain?*"

Keeping his eyes on the screen, Captain MacAlpin spoke clearly. "Computer, begin auto-destruct sequence." He drew a deep breath and switched internal communications on. "This is the captain speaking, for the last time. In one minute, this vessel will self-destruct. I am sorry, but you all know our orders—they're not to get the ship."

The explosion that followed lit up space for what seemed an eternity and then all that was left was the dark void of space; debris hanging on nothingness.

•

Tiberius MacAlpin sat bolt upright in bed, bedclothes all over the place; pillow on the floor, hair all tousled, sweat on his brow, palms clammy, his breath coming and going as fast as if he had run a marathon. Someone had screamed; it took a moment to realize it had been himself and that was what had woken him.

The door opened at almost the same time and a quiet voice initiated the lights to come on low in the room, showing Tiberius that his girlfriend, Lashinda Davis, was standing by the bed, as he woke every night to find her, taking his hand gently. "Hush," she murmured. "Is it the same dream?"

"Did they hear me?"

She shook her head. "No, baby. No-one knows; no-one but me." She smoothed the hair back from his damp forehead. "Is it the same?"

He nodded, but then shook his head. "It is, but every time there is a little more. He's trying to tell me something."

"But no-one knows what happened. Your father died when you were just a little kid."

"I never knew him. Mum was pregnant when he left for the last time." He glanced at the cabinet beside the bed.

Lashinda lifted the photo-frame and looked at it for a moment. "You are like him."

He sniffed. Tears trickled down his cheeks, tears no-one would ever see but her. Only she would ever see him as vulnerable as this. "I used to open the wardrobe and stand on a stool to stroke his uniform, dreaming of being big enough to wear it. I remember the day they came to tell mum he was dead; they brought his medals. I didn't know why she was crying or why she held me until she bruised my arms."

Lashinda put her arm around him and caressed his tousled hair.

"I knew from *that* day, all I wanted was to be like him. Mum told me about his ship, and I wanted nothing more than to have one of my own, but I never told her. Then one day, when I was sixteen, she caught me in dad's uniform—posing, parading in front of the mirror. She knew then and hasn't forgiven me for following him into space."

"You mustn't think like that. She will have guessed, even perhaps understood. The dreams are making your imagination run wild."

"I *saw* him! Something terrible happened, and no-one will tell me what. They say it is a closed file; why do they not want me to know? Space was everything to dad. That's why I have such an unusual name. Mum told me, dad loved this ancient show that was on television in the twentieth century, and it made him fall in love with space. Mum knew I would follow him, why does she hate to see me in the same uniform?" He pulled away from Lashinda and buried his face on his arms.

Lashinda slid off the bed and picked up the pillows. She rearranged the dishevelled bedclothes and made him lie down. She sat on the bed beside him, her long, slim legs tucked under, and began to sing an old African lullaby that her mother used to sing to her when she could not sleep.

2

"Congratulations, Captain"

The chirp of an incoming transmission sounded in the receiver implant in his ear, followed by the clipped, precise tones of the communications officer assigned to the admiral's office. "Lieutenant Commander MacAlpin, report to Admiral Kehoe immediately."

Tiberius raised his wrist to his mouth. "Acknowledged. I'm on my way." He spoke into the transmission implant on the side of his left wrist. "What have I done?" he wondered aloud. A call to see the admiral usually came with more notice than this, at least for a lowly lieutenant commander. If he were a commander or captain, it would not be such a surprise. He raised his hand again, giving Lashinda's call sign. "We'll have to get that coffee later. I've been summoned by Kehoe."

After a moment's silence, "Is everything all right?"

"I don't know. I just got the call."

"Let me know, Tibby."

"I will." He signed off and hurried towards the admiral's office. 'Immediately' meant he should have arrived there by now, but he could always pretend he had been further away than he really had been. Being a self-assured young man, when things happened out of the ordinary it did not normally bother him, but this sudden summons by the admiral did concern him. He was sure he had been behaving himself lately. There had been a time when he was a little wild, but his promotion to lieutenant commander seemed to have cured him of needing to attract attention, and he could think of nothing that would have caused anyone to report him to High Command.

It was with mixed feelings that he presented himself in the ante office. He nodded coolly to the communications officer who had contacted him—a thin, harassed-looking young man whose expression said that things had not been going according to plan this morning. He moved along and flashed a winning smile at the admiral's secretary, a woman of about his own age. "Any chance of seeing you later?" he asked, a cheeky grin on his face. "Do you want me to tell Lashinda?" she replied swiftly.

He laughed, shook his head, and walked on. The security guard outside the main office glanced at him as he came up. "You're expected, sir." She tapped the security panel and activated the door.

He nodded his thanks and stepped in through the door, snapping smartly to attention as he saluted. "Reporting as ordered, ma'am."

Admiral Leandri Kehoe looked up and returned the salute. "Sit down, MacAlpin. The others will be here directly, but I wanted to speak to you first." Seeing the apprehension in his face, she laughed. "At ease. You're not in any trouble." She smiled as he visibly relaxed. "How's promotion suiting you?"

"I like it, ma'am." Tiberius wondered where this was leading. He noticed she looked less fearsome when she smiled.

The admiral was a tiny South African woman, but everyone knew she was the most relentless and efficient admiral in the whole service. A word from her could start, stop or prevent a war, and junior officers, seniors too for that matter, quaked in their boots when she raised her voice. She was neat and pristine, her long iron-grey hair tied back severely in a tight bun and barely a touch of makeup on her tanned face, bar the dark cherry-red lipstick she always wore. She saw Tiberius looking at her and smiled again.

Tiberius reddened, realizing he had been staring at her. "What was it you wanted to talk to me about, ma'am?" he asked, finding his voice again.

She nodded. "I have a strange proposition to put to you, but the others are here now." The intercom at the door sounded and she called out "Enter!" and the door slid open to reveal three officers without. "Come in, please."

Tiberius rose to his feet, standing to attention, as the officers entered and took their seats in the chairs that had been placed ready for them. Two of the officers he knew by reputation only but the third was Captain Xander Galen, his commanding officer—a man he greatly admired.

"At ease, MacAlpin." The admiral indicated that he sit down again.

Captain Galen glanced across and smiled reassuringly. He could read some tension in the younger man's face and bearing. Naturally, he would be feeling nervous being summoned before senior officers in this manner.

Admiral Kehoe touched the intercom button on her desk. "Please inform Fleet Admiral Morgan that he can come up now."

There was a brief interval and then, as the door opened again, all five officers rose to their feet and saluted.

Fleet Admiral Caden-Zhu Morgan returned the salute and bade them sit with a small gesture of his hand. He, despite being close to retirement age, still had a strong military bearing and seemed to fill the room with his personality as he favoured the assembled officers with a warm smile. He gave Tiberius a fatherly clap on the shoulder as he passed him to take a seat beside Admiral Kehoe behind her desk.

Leandri Kehoe nodded. "Go ahead, sir," she invited.

"I am not sure how much Kehoe has told you, MacAlpin, but I am certain you will be wondering why you have been summoned in this fashion. How much has Galen told you?"

"Nothing, sir."

Xander Galen interrupted. "I apologize, sir. I had every intention of discussing this with MacAlpin." He coughed and paused a moment. "You will be aware, of course, that I was recently hospitalized for some time."

Morgan nodded. "There is no need to apologize, Captain. I am aware of your circumstances."

Tiberius glanced across at his commanding officer. He had visited Xander in the hospital but there had been nothing to suggest his CO had anything important to discuss.

Fleet Admiral Morgan was continuing. "You all know the story of the prototype ship the UES *Wryneck* of course."

"Yes sir, my father was her captain." *No-one talked about the Wryneck. Why was he bringing it up?*

Morgan nodded. "Just so. Then you will perhaps be aware that the schematics have been re-released in the last few years and a second ship, identical in all details to the *Wryneck*, has been built? She is almost ready for launch; Captain Galen was to have been her commanding officer but, due to health issues, he is stepping down from active service."

Tiberius looked shocked. "I didn't know any of that."

"Something else you've not discussed, Galen?"

Xander reddened. "I'm sorry, sir. I should have said something. Perhaps I was hoping that by saying nothing it would prolong my time in command—although I step down voluntarily."

"Understandable," Admiral Kehoe commented. "At least you are not leaving the service, but instead joining my staff. We need to keep good officers for as long as we can."

Tiberius turned back to Morgan. "If Captain Galen is not to command, then I presume my new commanding officer will be Commander Ross? He is the first officer."

"Normally, that would be the case," Morgan replied. "I have spoken to Commander Ross and he will be promoted to captain in Galen's place on the *Victorious*. You are being transferred to the new ship."

"Oh? I will be sorry to leave the *Victorious*. If I am permitted to ask, why, sir?"

The senior officers looked at each other and Kehoe nodded. "Because of the nature of the mission the new ship is to undertake; we want you on board the *Invincible* as commanding officer."

Tiberius gasped audibly and then appeared to cease breathing, his face first turning very pale and then reddening slowly. "CO?!" he managed to blurt out. "*Why*?!"

"The nature of the mission demands it." Admiral Kehoe paused and then continued, "Now, the reason for this may hurt you at first—I am fully aware, of course, of your loyalty to your father."

Tiberius' shoulders stiffened. He knew many called his love and loyalty for the late Stephen MacAlpin misplaced. It was common knowledge that the case regarding the destruction of the *Wryneck* thirty years ago had been closed pending further inquiry and that charges of cowardice, gross dereliction of duty and manslaughter had been brought against the *Wryneck*'s captain, stating that he had acted hastily in ordering the self-destruction of his ship and that he had not given his crew a choice; they had not been given the option of abandoning ship before she exploded but instead all had perished along with their captain and their ship. Tiberius always maintained his father must have had good reasons for his actions—some said that only being four years old at the time, his father would have appeared a hero to him, and he did not understand how serious it was. Knowing what many said about his father, he had refused to allow that to sway his determination to enter the service himself and to wear the same uniform of which his father had been so proud. Despite being bullied all through school, and as a cadet, and the shame of discovering that his father's name was not on the list of captains with illustrious careers which the cadets studied, he had overcome the difficulties, including being informed by one tutor that the name MacAlpin would work against him, and promotions and postings would not come his way; that he would be a jinx on any mission.

Tiberius, who felt the anguish of these gibes and insults deep down inside, vowed he would make his mother proud of him; he would honour his father's memory by fighting his way to the top if he had to. He excelled as a cadet, winning distinction in sports and in the classroom. Within a year of graduating, Ensign MacAlpin got his first deep-space mission and found himself serving under the command of Xander Galen—a fine officer, but a very private man. There were stories about him; some said he had a terrible secret, something he never spoke of. Xander had served with Tiberius' father, and he took the young ensign under his wing. Taking a personal interest in his training, he saw him work hard and promoted to lieutenant by the end of that first mission.

Tiberius forced himself to focus on what was being said as Admiral Kehoe continued speaking, pushing the file, at which she had been looking when he arrived, across the desk to him.

"New information and allegations have come to light which made reopening the case a necessity. Another examination of the final log entry Captain MacAlpin transmitted confirmed that the *Wryneck* was indeed capable of penetrating further into unknown space than any of our current ships—that was the reason for the prototype—and that is another reason why so much time has elapsed. We did not have any material, any eye-witness statements, of the things they saw along the way. No ship, except the *Wryneck*, has been able to make a trip like that, until this new one. It has therefore been decided that the *Invincible* will make her maiden voyage to the very spot where MacAlpin ordered the *Wryneck*'s destruction." She turned to Morgan and nodded, giving him his turn to speak again.

The fleet admiral stood up and held out his hand. "Congratulations, Captain MacAlpin. You will receive your rank officially in a ceremony this evening and will also receive your orders to take your new command in due course."

Tiberius stood up and shook Morgan's hand. "Thank you, sir," he said, almost in a daze. He turned and shook Kehoe's hand as she stood up.

Kehoe nodded. "Dismissed, Captain."

Tiberius saluted, turned smartly on his heel, and marched out of the room. He waited until he rounded the bend in the passage before letting his shoulders slump. He leaned on the wall and let out a long breath, almost like a whistle. Hearing footsteps coming down the passage towards him, he stood upright and continued walking slowly until he heard the footsteps come around the corner and the voice of his old commanding officer hailing him. He stopped and let Xander catch up.

Xander Galen, at sixty-eight years old, was still a handsome man. His dark hair was thickly threaded with grey, but his brown eyes were still as sharp as a young man's. Some were surprised that he was still only a captain but those who knew his record knew he had been promoted late because of refusing to take promotion above commander, not wanting to leave the ship and captain he served with at the time, and then he had been missing in action for ten years. On his return to service, he continued to turn down promotion until the death of his commanding officer in battle when he had finally accepted the promotion to captain but, over the years, turned down other offers; preferring to remain on active duty. Now, though, there was a noticeable pallor in his cheeks, a slightly drawn look, and fine lines becoming visible around his eyes. It was known, of late, that he had been suffering bouts of ill health and there was a chance he might retire.

It had, however, come as a shock to Tiberius that Xander had decided to retire from active duty and accept a desk job in the admiral's office.

Xander seemed to guess what was going through Tiberius' mind and he smiled. "I'm sorry I sprang that on you so suddenly," he said. "I had only fully made up my mind this morning. I was finally persuaded that I might manage to scrape a few more years if I stood down."

"*Scrape?*" Tiberius looked keenly at the older man. "Come on, Xander. You're only sixty-eight—you've heaps of time left."

Xander shook his head. "Not heaps—I only wish that were true. I am heading for retirement age anyway, but that last visit of mine to the hospital showed up some things I would rather not have known—funny how advanced we are in this day and age, even medically, and there are still some things that cannot be cured."

"I don't think *funny* is the right word there." Tiberius' tone was gloomy. "I'll miss you, I've got used to you as CO and I like to think we're friends."

Xander laughed. "You sound like me. That's why I'm still only a captain at this age. Don't make the same mistakes I've made, son, and don't refuse a promotion for the sake of friendship. If they think you're good enough for the job, don't turn it down. Friendships will survive, your career won't if you jeopardize it." He paused and looked at the younger man's gloomy face. "We are friends; just as I was your father's friend. I owe you that—for him. I have helped you when I have been able to, but I will not be here for you forever. It is Kehoe's indulgence that has given me a desk job—that I have not been retired completely. I swore years back that I would die in uniform, and I intend to do so."

"Don't talk about dying!"

Xander laughed again, softly. "Why? That is one of the few things that is certain in this life; we are all born, and one day we will die. The only thing that is not certain about either is when; not one of us knows how long we have been given. Your father was a few years older than you when he died, and I do not think I will reach seventy-five. I got thirty more years than I expected." He broke off, as though he was about to say something else but stopped himself.

Tiberius waited, wondering if Xander would finish his sentence and then changed the subject. "I'm not looking forward to tonight."

"Why ever not? You should be thrilled to be captain of your own ship. It is what we all dream of. I am delighted for you; you will be an excellent captain."

"I'm just thinking about what might be said. Everyone knows the story. For me to be given the new ship and that mission— well, there's bound to be talk."

Xander smiled. "Of course there will be talk. There always is. Do you not wonder how much talk there was about my having been your father's best friend? He was called a coward, a traitor. Think for a moment what impact such allegations had on his friends, those of us who stood by his reputation and made every effort to defend his name and his honour. I sponsored you as a cadet, for his sake. You are so like him, especially now. Looking at you, I see him and know that everything I have done for you, everything I taught you while you served with me, has in effect helped wipe away some of the dirt stuck to his name. You are a fine officer; he would be proud of you—just as I am and as I will be this evening watching you receive the same rank as your father. You are his exact image and because of this, you must not mind what anyone says about him—about you. High Command believes you to be worthy of promotion, and that you are worthy of commanding the *Invincible* on this mission that could be the greatest voyage into deep space since your father made the same journey. This could clear your father's name and could finally vindicate him; to show that those of us who trusted him, and believed in him, were not fools to do so. You must *never* give up believing in him. If you honestly believe he is innocent of the charges that were laid against him, you must *always* believe in him. If you return from this mission with absolute proof that the accusations were correct, then I know you to be strong enough to accept it. But, if you obtain proof he was falsely accused, that his name has been slandered all these years, then I know you will present the evidence and his account of what happened in his stead—the chance he did not get because he died." He leaned against the wall as he finished this long speech, his face growing a little more wan.

"You're tired," Tiberius said. "Let me see you home." He put his hand under Xander's elbow and assisted him along the passage, slowing his stride to match the older man's slower steps. They reached the door from which shuttle taxicabs went between the HQ and the living accommodation around the perimeter of the base.

When they reached the officers' private apartments, Tiberius activated the door controls and saw Xander safely inside. "Promise me that you'll rest. I want to see you tonight, for father's sake. I know he would want you to be there."

Xander nodded and smiled. "I promise." He waited until the front door shut and then went through into the bedroom and shrugged off his tunic before sitting on the edge of the bed to remove his boots. He lay back against the pillow and sighed heavily. It went against the grain not to tell Tiberius the full story. But he had sworn he never would; it would only make things harder. If he found out, then he would have to tell but he was not going to volunteer the information. For the sake of those years of friendship with Stephen MacAlpin, he could not.

3

"A tall ship and a star to steer her by"

Tiberius left Xander's quarters in a daze. The events of the morning had taken him completely by surprise and he did not quite know what to make of what had occurred. He walked back to the large glass-domed atrium which was filled with people busy coming and going. Stopping in the centre by a large water feature that glowed with ever-changing fibre-optic lights as the water flowed in its constant cycle, he sat on one of the marble seats set into the base of the feature and raised his wrist to his mouth and gave Lashinda's call-sign and waited until her voice responded in his ear. "Can we get that coffee now, Lash?" he asked, trying to keep his voice from giving anything away.

"Of course. What's up? You sound tense."

"I'm at the fountain. Want to go to the usual place?"

"I'll be there in ten. I have something to finish off before I can get away."

"I'll be waiting." He smiled at the sound of a kiss in his ear and knew she had kissed her transmitter to make it sound that clear. "Love you too," he added as he ended the transmission.

The usual spot was a coffee bar in the open plaza outside HQ. Tiberius was waiting there when Lashinda came hurrying up. "Sorry, I didn't have a break coming up. I had to beg for one, that's why I had to finish what I was working on; to have a good reason why I could take a break." She leaned over and kissed him. "I can stay as long as it takes to drink a large latte—slowly."

He returned the kiss and smiled. "I'll order." He returned a short moment later with a latte for Lashinda and a strong black coffee for himself.

When they settled, Lashinda looked at him. "What's up? You were called to see the admiral. Is something wrong?"

"No, nothing is wrong," Tiberius replied slowly. "I had a shock, that's all. I'm not supposed to say anything."

She looked long and hard at him but did not press for an answer even though deep down she wanted to know.

After a long pause, Tiberius took a deep breath and told her. He knew he could not keep it from her.

●

Xander glanced at his reflection in the mirror and silently thanked God that his illness did not show in his face, he just needed time to get used to it. Perhaps there was a wee shadow under his eyes, but no-one would be looking that closely, he hoped; at least not this evening. All eyes should, tonight, be on Tiberius. There would be surprise, shock even, at the news. Surprise would be an understatement. Even shock would not quite fit the bill. People would be stunned—Tiberius was young. Perhaps, he thought, young was not the right word—many got their first command around that age. Inexperienced in command was a better term. Tiberius was thirty-four, with a wealth of experience, but not in command. The fact that it was the newest ship alone would be enough to wring a gasp from those assembled. Jealousy even. He knew there were some who were due for promotion and would feel overlooked, maybe even jealous. And, above all, there was the story of the *Wryneck*, and her destruction on Stephen MacAlpin's order.

●

The hall was packed, filled with the hum of many voices. It was not every day a new ship was commissioned and the secrecy regarding its launch fired everyone's imagination and they were all agog to hear the news. The hall looked out onto dry dock but shutters across the windows shut out any glimpse of the new ship for now and excitement was rife with many speculations flying around the room.

The crew of the UES *Victorious* trooped in. Captain Galen and Commander Ross first, with Tiberius just behind them. Those closest to the group as they entered saw that Xander was looking tired, although there was nothing in his demeanour or lack of spring in his step to give any hint to it. They took their seats, and Ross leaned over to his commanding officer. "Any idea what is going on, sir? Is it to do with those meetings you've been attending?"

Xander nodded. "I'd be lying if I said I had no idea. And yes—all those meetings." Some of the meetings had been legitimate meetings with Admiral Kehoe and the Admiralty Board. Others, he had told them were meetings—but were actually of a different nature. Appointments and consultations with doctor after doctor, specialist after specialist, trying in vain to find a treatment. He had not the heart to tell Ross. Ross had been one of his protégés and he had not hesitated to recommend him for the first officer's position on the *Victorious*.

Beside Ross, Tiberius was nervous but just about managing to hide it. He felt Ross looking at him and studiously stared at the toes of his highly polished boots. He knew Ross knew something was going on but did not want him to ask any questions.

A crewman leaned forward and asked Xander if he knew what was going on. Xander smiled slightly. "You'll see," he responded, leaning back in his seat. He was unable to prevent a sharp gasp from escaping his lips as a stab of pain went through him as he leaned back.

Ross turned and looked at him and seemed about to speak but then stopped himself. *No. If there was something wrong, he would have told me.*

Just then the doors at the back of the hall opened and the senior officers came onto the platform and took their seats. They sat talking amongst themselves while the buzz of expectation rang around the hall. Admiral Kehoe had not arrived yet, and the proceedings would not get underway without her. There were still ten minutes to the scheduled start, and everyone knew she would arrive exactly one minute before time. After what seemed ages, the door opened, and Admiral Kehoe entered with Fleet Admiral Morgan, and they took their seats. A bell sounded to mark the half-hour and complete silence fell as Admiral Kehoe stood up. She looked around the crowded hall at the sea of faces before her; some old, some young. "We are all here for the same reason," she began. "To open a new chapter in our history—a wonderful, exciting chapter. To launch a new ship and a new step in starship design. Also, today we honour the long and dedicated service of one officer and mark the start of what we hope will be the long and distinguished career of another. We will begin with by revealing the new ship." She turned to Fleet Admiral Morgan. "Over to you, sir." She sat down and Morgan moved to the lectern.

Xander shifted slightly in his seat, feeling a little uncomfortable—it seemed his retirement from active service was going to be announced in public—this would cause a stir and he hoped Ross would not be upset that he had not told him. And he had not told him the *Victorious* was to be decommissioned and the crew transferred to the new ship, and Ross would remain first officer, while Tiberius was promoted over his head.

Ross leaned over. "You okay? You seem a bit restless."

Xander nodded. "Just a bit stiff. These chairs are not so comfortable after a while."

The fleet admiral began to speak. "Thirty-four years ago, a prototype of a new ship was launched—and sadly lost on her maiden voyage. Today, we remember the *Wryneck* and her lost crew as we launch her sister ship, the *Invincible.*"

A gasp rang around the room as though a single sound as Morgan pressed a button on the lectern and the shutters over the big glass windows, looking out onto dry dock, slowly raised and the new ship was finally revealed.

The older officers, who remembered the launch of the *Wryneck,* looked at each other. She was exact in every detail; the blueprints had been followed to the letter. Only the name was different.

Xander thought of his friend, Tiberius' father, who had commanded the fleet's newest ship and, on her first voyage, had to make the decision that no captain ever wanted to make—to destroy their ship, wiping out every life on board. On launch day, they had sat side by side, eager to see their new ship, just as he was sitting now only younger and excited by the prospects of the future. He guessed Tiberius would be thinking of his father too, the man he had never met and the disgrace that surrounded him, no-one knowing whether it was deserved or not—knowing that, in one way, he bore his father's shame just for being his son.

Morgan turned to look out of the window at the new ship, massive and beautiful against the dark sky.

Tiberius leaned forward. The first glimpse of his first command and excitement bubbled up inside him. She was his ship. Sleek and streamlined against the sky, all he could think was of how beautiful she was, and he fell head over heels in love. He had longed for a ship of his own, since he was a boy, and she was stunning.

There was a long silence as everyone looked, as though spellbound. Then Morgan turned back and broke the spell, as it were, by speaking. "Along with commissioning of this ship, we have to announce the decommission of another."

This caught everyone's attention and every commanding officer in the room was afraid for their ship. "Not my ship!" went through their minds.

"But that will be later," Morgan continued. "Firstly, there are a couple of items we must go through. Kehoe, I will hand back to you." He stepped back and gave her a little bow as she moved back to the lectern.

"Long service to the fleet must be rewarded," Kehoe announced, "Especially when it is drawing to its close. In this case, however, this career draws to a close from active service only. This officer has chosen to retire from active duty and accept the position of my chief of staff."

Everyone looked around, wondering who it was. Many older officers still held a field position, and any one of them was due for retirement from active service. Ross suddenly experienced a sinking feeling at the bottom of his heart. That's why he had been offered the *Victorious*. Xander was retiring. It must be his health; he had recently been hospitalized; everyone knew that. It had to be serious for him to contemplate leaving the *Victorious*. And Xander had said nothing to him. He glanced across at Xander sitting beside him.

Xander's cheeks reddened, and he looked down at his hands. He should have told him. He had not even needed to guess why Ross was looking at him.

"Captain Galen, please join me."

Kehoe's voice brought him back to the present. Xander stood up and marched up to the dais, mounted the steps and stood facing Admiral Kehoe, side on to the people watching. He saluted smartly.

"Captain Galen, your career has spanned five decades and has been filled with success, promotions, and medals. Your name is ranked among some of our finest captains, and they teach our cadets about you. It will be with mixed feelings that you take on your new role and it is with great pleasure that I award you the Long Service Medal for fifty years' service." She stretched up and pinned the medal onto his tunic. Then she picked up rank pins. She reached up and attached them to the collar of his tunic. "It is also a pleasure to promote you to Rear Admiral."

Xander's pale cheeks flushed as the room erupted into applause. He had not expected promotion. He saluted again.

"Thank you, ma'am. I appreciate the opportunity to continue serving for as long as I am able." He returned to his seat and Ross leaned across and was about to speak. Xander shook his head. "Not now," he said, looking him right in the eyes. "I'll tell you the truth, later. I promise."

Admiral Kehoe turned her attention back to the room. "I know you will all be intrigued to find out who the *Invincible*'s captain is, and who is being assigned to her crew. She is fitted for deep-space missions and designed to be away from base for a greater length of time. It has been decided that the *Victorious* will be decommissioned, and the crew transferred to other vessels. Some of you may find yourselves aboard the new *Invincible*."

Ross turned directly to Xander then. "I'm not getting the *Victorious*?" he mouthed. "They offered and I accepted!"

Xander shook his head, in shock. He was glad he had not had to tell Ross that. He knew Ross had been offered the command and was stunned to hear his old ship was to be taken out of service, the chance wrested out of Ross' hands. Ross would be a good captain, but he had refused promotion time and again to remain serving with Xander. Just as he himself had with Stephen MacAlpin. Now that he was to leave active service, Ross could be forgiven for deciding that the time was now right to accept a command of his own. He could hardly believe Kehoe had made a U-turn like that.

Kehoe looked around and then continued. "Now, I am sure you are all desperate to learn who has been given command of the new vessel. A lot of thought has gone into this, due to the nature of the *Invincible*'s first mission which, at this moment, is still classified."

Ross was listening, his heart beginning to pound. Maybe that's why he was not getting the *Victorious*? Had they decided to give him the *Invincible*?

"Lieutenant Commander MacAlpin, step forward."

The gasp that shot around the room sounded as though charged with electricity. Much more of a gasp than for Xander's retirement being announced, or at the decommissioning of the *Victorious*.

As Tiberius headed for the dais, Ross rounded on Xander. "You knew?!" he hissed. "They are giving her to MacAlpin? After what his father did?!"

"Quiet!" Xander snapped in response. He was watching Tiberius receiving his new rank. "I am proud of him right now;

give him a break. He has suffered so much because of what his father was charged with. What if everyone was wrong? Let him have this moment. I know you are disappointed, but they must have reasons. We can discuss it afterwards, in private." He turned away, looking up at Tiberius shaking hands with Kehoe and saluting. He felt a stabbing ache in his chest. Tiberius was the image of his father and watching him brought memories back; memories that threatened to overwhelm him.

Tiberius flopped weakly onto his chair as he re-joined the group. He was still flabbergasted by what had happened; even though he had known about the promotion in advance, it had not fully sunk in until he was on the dais. Looking around from the dais and seeing the equally stunned faces looking up at him was when it began to really hit him that all this was true. His head was swimming and barely even felt Lashinda reach across and hug him, and never saw the look Ross shot at him. His hand was clasped warmly, and he raised shocked eyes.

It was Xander who had taken his hand. "Well done, kid. You deserve it. You will make a fine captain."

Tiberius shook hands numbly and did not even bother to point out that, at thirty-four years old, he was not a kid. He no longer heard the remainder of the speech from Admiral Kehoe. Part of him was so shocked that he could not believe it was true while another part wanted to scream and jump up and down. He had longed for this with all his heart—to command a starship, just as his father had. Like his father's friend, Xander; like all his heroes over the years. Those special, privileged men and women he had idolized as a child. He was not stupid; he knew the entire room was in shock. He knew there were many who knew his father all those years ago, and some who entered the service on the tail end of the tragedy. It did not take a genius to know that there were mixed feelings—predominantly surprise and shock. But some would be wondering why, when he had been condemned as a coward and a murderer, Stephen MacAlpin's son had been given the new ship—essentially the same ship as the prototype his father had destroyed thirty years ago. An untested ship, the only records available being the weekly regulation logs that had been submitted to Headquarters before that fateful day. He barely heard Admiral Kehoe announce the moment the ship was to be christened and only jumped up when Xander leaned over and hissed to him to stand up.

"A tall ship and a star to steer her by"

Admiral Kehoe pressed a button on the lectern and, in the best age-old tradition that even in the twenty-ninth century was still adhered to, a bottle of champagne was swung and broken against her hull. Her voice rang out clearly, "I name this ship *Invincible*. Good wishes to all who serve with her."

There was a loud cheer that rang round the hall, ringing in the rafters. Whatever everyone was feeling, it was a splendid sight to behold a new ship and to be present at the commissioning. Silence fell as the vessel, manned by a specially chosen crew, slid silently from her docking bay and out of the big doors which slid open for her, and out into the darkness of space, running lights pinpointing her location as she turned and made for the general moorings and then applause rang out combined with some younger members of the crowd whooping loudly.

"And all I ask is a tall ship and a star to steer her by."

Admiral Kehoe summed up all their thoughts with these words and Tiberius smiled softly. He had heard those words from the Masefield poem many times before and he quoted another line under his breath. "It is a wild call and a clear call that may not be denied." That summed up his own feelings; why he had followed his father's footsteps, against his mother's wishes. The call his father had felt called him also and he had dreamed of little but having the command of a starship for himself. It could not be denied.

Then one of the officers, an old academy classmate of Tiberius' raised a cheer for the new ship's equally new commanding officer. "Three cheers for Captain MacAlpin!" The cheers were given, and Tiberius hung his head, blushing. The blackness that surrounded his father's memory did not shame him, he had always fiercely maintained that he was innocent. But, right now, it was very much on his mind. He only had to look at Commander Ross' face to know exactly what he was thinking. He knew Ross had expected to take over from Xander one day, and to have that promotion, that chance of the captaincy he dreamed of, snatched away from him. He could have been left the *Victorious*. Tiberius did not know why that was not the case. There was nothing wrong with the *Victorious*. Why could Ross not have been given that command? Instead, he would have a first officer who resented him—if Ross was assigned to that position. His mind was a whirl and he felt as though he could not think straight any more.

The proceedings ended when Admiral Kehoe announced that the postings for the crew assigned to the new ship would soon be found on the screens in the main plaza and dismissed them. Everyone stood to attention as the senior officers withdrew and then, with much talking, the hall was vacated.

The plaza was a wide-open area, flanked by cafés and small shops, like an old railway station or shopping precinct. At one end, high up on the wall, there were screens on which postings and other information were displayed.

On the way out of the assembly hall, Tiberius put his hand on Xander's arm. "Would you grab a coffee with me? You too, Ross. We should talk."

Ross looked at him. "I have duties to attend to so, please, excuse me." He strode away.

"Forgive him," Xander said. "You know as well as I do what is wrong. I will talk to him."

Tiberius nodded. "It's a shame. We have served together long enough. I thought he liked me, but I don't need him to like me, just to do his duty."

Xander put his hand on the younger man's shoulder. "He will do that; he is a good officer. Now, that coffee."

They crossed to one of the small coffee shops, sat down at a table and placed their order via the table-top ordering system. When the coffee arrived, Xander leaned back in his chair and sighed. "I needed this, I was getting thirsty in there."

Tiberius nodded. "Xander, how much did you know? Before the meeting with Kehoe, I mean. Did you know that I was getting the *Invincible*?"

"I knew." Xander sipped his coffee. "I was to have been given the command, but you know that I am dying; I have a few years left at best."

"Don't say that!" Tiberius interrupted, his face pained.

"It is true. There is no cure—not on Earth. And I am too old to start chasing around the Universe seeking a cure which may only be a myth." Xander smiled kindly. "It is part of life, son. You will make a good captain. Do you remember that time Ross and I were both injured in that attack that put us in sickbay for three months? You took command of the ship, negotiated a truce with the people that attacked us and set up a trade agreement. All the crew reports said how good you were. I was impressed and immensely proud of you." Xander looked down at his coffee as he swirled the liquid around in the bottom of the mug before he looked up. "You are like your father. He was an excellent officer and one of the best captains I ever served with, despite what is said now. As you know, I refused a command of my own many times so that I would remain serving with him."

Tiberius sighed. "Ross will make it hard for me. He should have a command."

"Ross will behave as he ought," Xander replied. His tone boded ill for Ross if he should behave in any way that was unacceptable in his position. "I will talk with him. You must understand, it was always assumed that he would get the *Victorious* after I retired. And then, on hearing it was to be decommissioned, the prospect of a new ship to command would thrill anyone. You're not the only one to dream of it. We all do—every one of us."

Tiberius sighed again. "I always looked up to him—I just feel that it won't be the same anymore."

"Of course it won't. You will be the captain and he must take orders from you. But also, he must help and advise you. That is *his* duty. That is assuming that he has been posted along with you; perhaps your crew will all be new." Xander finished the last mouthful of his coffee and leaned back again. "Time for another? Or perhaps you should go and join a certain young lady who has been sitting by the fountain waiting for you ever since we left the hall."

Tiberius glanced round and saw Lashinda sitting waiting patiently. He waved to her, beckoning. "She can join us for one more."

Lashinda hurried across and sat down. "Latte, please," she said as Xander tapped at the order screen.

4

A Fight—An Apology

That night, Tiberius tossed and turned in bed, plagued by his dreams. He always had been, even in his earliest childhood he had woken crying in the night as the bad dreams frightened him. And, once again, the same dream he had been having recently occurred.

•

"Keep her steady!"

"I can't, Captain! We've lost power to the helm."

"Try it! All hands, battle stations! We are under attack." The captain stopped and drew a deep breath before continuing. "Good luck." Slowly, he thumbed off the intercom and turned back to his chair. Noticing the bridge crew were looking, he nodded. "You heard me. We don't have a chance."

At that precise moment, a double salvo shook the ship again. It seemed as though the enemy ship knew they were unable to return fire, and they used every ounce of their power against them. An alarm sounded, followed by a shout that the shields were failing.

"Captain?"

The captain shook his head as he turned to the Helm. "I am not considering surrender at all. That is not an option." He had not needed to ask what she was trying to say. He turned to the communications officer. "Send a signal to headquarters."

"Aye, Captain." The communications officer's hands moved swiftly over his control panel. "I can't raise them—on any frequency." He paused for a moment, listening intently through his ear-receiver. "Sir, the alien ship is signalling *us!*"

"Answer them—get them on the screen." He turned to the viewscreen, face to face with their attackers at last. "I am Captain

Stephen MacAlpin, of the United Earth Ship *Wryneck*. We are on a peaceful mission."

"We know who you are—only too well, *Stephen*," the alien responded. "You did not think that we would not come after you?" The tone changed. "You are out of time—in a moment you will be boarded. I am waiting—give me your unconditional surrender and I will not destroy your ship."

The captain's voice was quiet when he replied, but everyone on the bridge heard every word. "I will *never* give you that!"

"You will all die! You have one of your Earth minutes left. What do you say, *Captain*? Will you save your crew by surrendering yourself to us? Your crew will not be harmed if you come of your own free will."

Keeping his eyes on the screen, Captain MacAlpin spoke clearly. "Computer, begin auto-destruct sequence." He took a deep breath and flicked on the ship's intercom. "All hands, this is the captain speaking—for the last time. In one minute, this vessel will self-destruct. I am sorry, but you all know our orders. They're not to get the ship."

The explosion lit up space for what seemed an eternity and then all that was left was the dark void of space; debris hanging on nothingness.

•

Tiberius moaned and thrashed his legs which were tangled up in the sheet, soaked with sweat.

His father's face swam before his eyes, in close-up as it were, and he saw the resignation in his eyes as he raised them— seeming to look right at him. *I had no alternative—no choice. Forgive me.* That was the last message headquarters should have received, but it had never been sent. Tiberius could see his father's finger over the transmit key on the command chair's touchscreen. The light would have turned green if the message sent. It was still not green when the ship exploded seconds later.

He woke screaming. This time, however, he smothered it in the sweat-soaked pillow. He did not want anyone to know—they might take his ship away before he even got the chance to command her. He groped for his glass of water, took a gulp and lay thinking about the scene that played out in his head. It was so vivid, and he compared it with the last time he had seen it because seemed there was more this time. The alien attacker had called his father by his first name and said he knew who he was 'only too well'. What had his father done that would make the aliens come after them, demanding his surrender? And why had he preferred destruction and death despite the crew being promised safety? He could not understand that. Did it mean his father was hiding something? Something some of the crew might have known about? Had he killed them all, and himself, to hide something he had done? His father's words 'forgive me' were playing on his mind. Why did he need forgiveness? Was it just because he was carrying out his orders to destroy the prototype rather than let it fall into alien hands? There was something else too—something he could not yet work out; something missing. He closed his eyes and tried to picture the scene again.

There was a tap at the door and the lights came on softly as Lashinda let herself in. Tiberius had called her when he had woken up. "Tibby, are you okay?" She sat on the edge of the bed and looked around. She took in the dishevelled sheets, the pillow on the floor and the stale smell of sweat. "Another nightmare? Go and shower. I'll strip the bed."

Tiberius got up and headed for the shower. When he returned, wrapped in his dressing-gown, the bed was re-made and Lashinda was at the coffee machine. "Get into bed; I'm making you cocoa."

He slipped under the sheets and cuddled down until she came over with a steaming mug. "There was more this time," he said, sitting up and wrapping his hands around the mug. "It is like I am gradually seeing more of the picture. I am scared, it looks like he is hiding something." He looked up. "What if they were right?"

Lashinda sat back on the edge of the bed. "What if they were wrong? You don't know what happened. You only *think* you are seeing what happened through your dreams."

"I know I am! Why don't you believe me?"

"I do believe you; just don't let your imagination run wild. When you wake up in the morning, think back on it and write some things down. Not now, not while you are still upset."

"Something is worrying me; something wrong with the scene. I can't work it out. I *know* there is something I don't see that should be there."

"Drink your cocoa and go back to sleep." She stroked his hair and kissed him on the cheek. She watched as he drank the cocoa and then took the mug. As he lay down, she pulled the sheets up, tucked him in, and bent to kiss him again.

He slipped his arms out from under the sheets and wrapped them around her neck, pulling her down and kissing her. "I love you, Lash."

"I love you too. Now, go to sleep. I'll stay here until you do."

•

When he woke, a little later than his usual time, Tiberius lay staring at the ceiling for a while and then he remembered. He had dreamed it again, and this time there had been something that bugged him. Something that should have been there, but he could not work out yet what it was; what should he be able to see when looking at that scene? It must be important, or he would not have that feeling. The absence of whatever it was had to be staring him in the face and he knew it. He sighed and got up, dressing quickly in his new uniform. He did not get his usual breakfast from the selection he had in his little kitchen but headed instead for the plaza. He wanted something substantial— something he did not get very often. He went to his favourite café and ordered coffee with a bacon and egg roll.

Xander walked past just then, and Tiberius called to him, touching the order pad again to place an order for black coffee and pancakes which he knew the older man had without fail for his breakfast—pancakes with bacon and maple syrup. Xander came across and joined him at the table. "I see you have already ordered for me," he said, nodding at the holographic receipt, hovering over the order pad.

"I need to talk to you, about father."

Xander was silent as their order arrived and he put exactly half a spoon of sugar into his coffee. "Why?"

"Why shouldn't I? Are you hiding something?" The moment he said it Tiberius regretted it and was sorry he had raised his voice at his father's old friend. "I'm sorry."

"It's all right. I understand how you feel—especially now."

"I need to know!" Tiberius took a deep breath and added, "My dreams—they are of nothing but that day. The first time it was just the ship exploding, then the next I saw inside—just before the explosion. Then the third time, the scene seemed to be re-enacted for me. Each time, there is a little more information. It seems almost like father is trying to tell me what happened."

Xander took another sip of his coffee, and his hand shook a little as he set down the mug. "I'm sorry, Tiberius. I cannot tell you anything about that day—I was not there. Obviously, as I survived."

Tiberius looked at him for a long moment and then understanding crossed his face. "*Now* I know what was missing in my dream last night. You were not there. You were the *Wryneck*'s first officer—how come you weren't there?"

Xander curled his hands around his mug. "I should have been beside the captain. I'm sorry. I cannot tell you anything."

"Cannot? Or will not?!" Tiberius' face grew red. "I know you must know something. You were my father's first officer, how come you were not there to die with the others? What is the secret? Is it that *you* were the coward and escaped somehow, leaving my father to die, and be blamed with all those deaths?"

Xander's hands shook, and he knocked his mug over as he shoved his chair back and stood up. "You have said more than enough, Tiberius. I understand that growing up without your father was a struggle—but lashing out at me is not going to get you answers and will just hurt us both."

"Then tell me!"

"I cannot." Xander's voice was quiet. "I understand your dream is upsetting and that you do have a right to know what happened. It does not give you the right to make such accusations. I stood by your father through thick and thin—always. All the years we served together. If I tell you that it was not my fault that I was not there, would you believe me? If I had been, you know I would have died at his side—his friend, as always. Many times I have wished I had died with them—to be the only one left never stops hurting." He turned on his heel and walked out of the café.

Tiberius watched him leave, too angry to call him back. Angry at himself for calling his friend and mentor a coward—angry with Xander for not telling him the facts.

●

That evening, Tiberius stood on the balcony outside his quarters, a glass in one hand and the other tucked around Lashinda's waist.

"You're quiet tonight," Lashinda said softly, resting her head on his shoulder. "Is something wrong? You look broody when you should be happy."

Tiberius looked up at the dark sky; a cushion of black velvet encrusted with millions of diamonds—stars beyond stars, and the swirling shimmer of the Milky Way wafting its path across the heavens. "I fell out with Xander. I called him a coward, asking him why the *Wryneck*'s first officer was not there to die alongside his comrades. I was pretty mean and didn't call him back when he walked away."

Lashinda looked at him. "Don't hurt him, Tibby. He has been your mentor—your guide. He will have a reason why he can't tell—what if he had to take an oath of silence? You know how hushed up this whole affair has been. You need to go and see him—you've left it all day. You can't leave it until tomorrow—he was your father's friend and has *always* been yours. Call him—go and see him tonight."

Tiberius sighed, knowing she was right. He called Xander on the communication chip in his wrist but there was no response. "He won't answer. I'll go along and see if he is in. Goodnight, Lash. Thanks for making me see what a fool I am."

She kissed him. "Tell him you're sorry. Play chess like you used to—anything. Inside, he will understand why you got mad. Finding out what happened to your father means a lot to you. But you can't hurt him just because he's there and you're angry. That's unfair."

Tiberius nodded and left. When he reached Xander's apartment, he pressed the buzzer. He waited a while and then pressed it again. Then he knocked and leaned his head on the door and called "Xander? I'm sorry I was mean to you. Please, talk to me."

There was a long silence and then the door opened and Xander stood there. "I wondered if you would come. But I thought you would not."

"Lashinda made me realize I was being an idiot," Tiberius replied. "My arrogance..."

"Come on in then, don't just stand there," Xander interrupted softly, shutting the door behind them. "I feel I do owe you *some* explanation as to why I cannot tell you what you want to know." He led Tiberius through to the living room and waited for the younger man to sit down and then sat on the sofa opposite. "The events that led up to your father destroying the *Wryneck* are shrouded in secrecy—I had to swear that I would not speak of what happened."

"Did he do wrong? Please, you *must* tell me that!"

"I neither condemn nor condone any action your father took," Xander replied. "I cannot tell you, but whatever he did, he was *always* my friend and my commanding officer."

"You were not there. Where was the first officer?"

Xander looked down at the ground. "It was a long mission—things happen."

"Were you wounded?"

Xander shook his head again. "I was wounded early in the mission, along with your father, but I was well again by then. I just cannot tell you anything more."

"I don't see you in the dream, and you said you were not there. Where were you when the *Wryneck* was destroyed?"

Forced to respond, Xander shook his head. "Please, I'm tired. Don't ask me any more questions, I can't answer them. If you want to know anything else, you must ask to see the files. I wish to God I had been there! Whatever happened, your father needed a friend when he made that decision. I was his first officer—his best friend; I should have been at his side."

"Then why weren't you?!" Tiberius' face grew red. But he was not angry with Xander now, not even when he would not answer. He was angry with himself for pushing his father's friend.

"I was unable to be there, through your father's choice," Xander replied quietly. "I do not know if he knew then what he would do and wished to spare my life or if he was mad at me because I challenged his authority on a decision. I was left behind on the planet."

Tiberius stared at him. "You were *abandoned*?!"

Xander shrugged. "If you want to put it like that; I suppose that is what it was. Of course, Stephen didn't call it that. Tiberius, you must promise not to ask me anything more. All I will say is that I was left behind, supposedly to follow through with something we had been working on—they were to come back for me. The next thing I knew was that the *Wryneck* had left orbit and the people of the planet seized me, handcuffed me, and marched me off to prison. I was there for years before our government was able to trace me and negotiate for my release. Your father's log, stating where I was, must not have reached headquarters." *If he ever sent it*, he thought.

"*Prison*?!"

"I do not want to talk about it. It was not pleasant."

Tiberius looked at Xander for a long while and then nodded. "I will demand to see the files. I can see that whatever happened disturbs you."

Xander stood up and went to look out of the window across the dark city, the bright lights twinkling below. "I want you to go now. I accept your apology—I understand why you were angry.

I sympathize, but it reminds me of things I want to forget. Please leave me. I will talk with you tomorrow."

Tiberius stood up and turned to the door. "I am sorry. Sorry that I hurt you and that I have made you remember. All I ask is that you try and think what it is like for me—not knowing. Trying to find out but being told it is secret—the files classified. If you only knew." He did not look back, so he did not see Xander's face. If he had, he would have known that his father's old friend knew and understood more than he realized.

With the door closed behind his visitor, Xander dropped into a chair. Burying his face in his hands as he drew a shuddering breath that wrenched out a sound like a sob—eerily loud in the silence of his apartment.

5

A Mother's Fear

Tiberius headed to the plaza the next morning to see if crew postings had been announced. He had yet to meet his new crew, and something inside still hoped Ross would be transferred to another ship but, since the *Victorious* had been decommissioned and the rumour was that the crew all, or at least most, had been transferred to the *Invincible*, the likelihood of Ross not being transferred was slim. As Xander had said, he was a highly experienced officer, with many years in space, the last five being spent as the *Victorious*'s first officer. It would be odd if that were not considered.

There were three screens, bearing the registration number of the *Invincible*—UES 1987—but still no postings so he turned away with a sigh. He was eager and impatient to meet the crew who would be serving with him on the new ship—the first time he could call them 'his' crew. There was a footstep behind him, and he turned to see Commander Ross coming up and he flushed slightly, knowing what he had been thinking. He liked Ross and had been shocked to see him so angry that he had been given the captaincy. "Hey." He hoped that came over as light-hearted as he tried to make it.

Ross nodded in response, too much a professional to ignore him. "No postings yet?"

Tiberius shook his head. "Not even yours." He paused and then added, "If you have been transferred away, I will demand it changed. I want you on the *Invincible*." He went a little pink; he had not thought that earlier but just now it was as though he realized he would have felt the same if roles had been reversed.

Ross looked at him. "Better the devil you know?"

Tiberius shook his head. "Let me be frank with you. I saw your face, the anger in your eyes. You expected to take over from Xander—I understand that. It's not my fault that they chose me to command the *Invincible*. For some reason, they want me despite my lack of experience. I've hardly ever even taken the centre seat as you have. I need a man like you to keep me right. You have the experience—you have been at Xander's side, his second in command for some years."

Ross looked at him and nodded. "You are right, I was angry. I've wanted a command of my own for years but my loyalty to Xander prevented me from accepting a posting. When I saw him being retired from active service with a promotion and an award for long service, I saw my chance; my right, as I saw it, to take his place. I see you, naturally, as too inexperienced to command a ship like the *Invincible*. Perhaps I have a duty to see you make a good job of it." He turned, faced the younger man, and held out his hand. "Forgive me and accept my friendship and guidance. I will do my duty to you as I did for Captain Galen. You will find me as loyal as I was for him."

Tiberius took the proffered hand and his grey-green eyes danced. "Thank you. I needed a boost like that. To know someone is on my side in all this. If you help me to be a good captain and stay with the *Invincible* to the end of this mission, I will recommend you for your own command, and insist you take it if need be! If you can help me to be half the captain Xander was you will have more than earned your turn." He looked at Ross. "I mean it. Do we have a deal?"

Ross nodded. "We do. I am sure that, after the way I reacted to the news, I am the last person you would wish to have at your side, giving you advice."

Tiberius grinned a sudden infectious smile. "I would be lying if I denied that, but I changed my mind, for Xander's sake. I know you are friends, and he would be upset if we did not get on. I respect him too much to let him down like that. He has been like a father to me—as I never knew mine, he took his place at times when I most needed a father figure.

Ross put his hand on Tiberius' shoulder. "I understand. You do not need to explain. I have accepted your offer, and I too will do my best not to let Xander down."

Ross walked away and Tiberius watched him go. His heart felt lighter now as he knew he had done the right thing by speaking, by telling Ross that he needed him on the *Invincible*—that he needed him as Xander had. Surely that is what would have happened anyway? What would be the point in having an untried captain with an inexperienced first officer? High Command would not do that, especially if the rumours were true and that the *Invincible*'s first mission would be in deep space, further than the *Wryneck* had gone. He turned away from the screens and went to a quiet space by the fountain and called his mother. She was not happy he had followed his father into space. Losing her husband when her son was only four years old had made her cling closer to the child than perhaps she might have. Deep down, she must have known which way his path would turn. The little boy had idolized the memory of the father he had never known. Born while his father was away, he knew him only from photographs and stories. So he had avoided telling his mother the news until now. He was the same age his father had been when he left, and the same rank. He was the image of his father and it would bring back the day thirty years ago when the news of Stephen's death had been brought to her. He loved his mother dearly and was loathe to upset her. But he had to tell her.

His mother answered after a moment or two. "Tiberius? I thought it was your call-sign. I have not heard from you for a while. How are you?"

"I'm fine, mum. Can I come and see you? I have another assignment and will be going away soon."

"Of course. Come for dinner. Are you bringing that nice girl you are friends with?"

"Mum, we're not *friends*, she's my girlfriend. And no, I am coming alone this time. I want to talk. I'll bring Lashinda another time. Just before I go away—if I can." Tiberius told her that he would be over before 19:00 and signed off. He debated going out of uniform and then steeled himself. She had to know and to see him in a captain's uniform sooner or later; tonight would be the perfect opportunity.

That evening, Tiberius took a shuttle cab to the city suburbs where his mother lived and pressed the buzzer on the door. He wore a greatcoat over his uniform—he did not want her opening the door and having a heart attack. He smoothed down the coat and tweaked his cap straight while he waited.

Bethany MacAlpin opened the door with a smile. "Tiberius." She tiptoed to kiss him as he bent his head for her. "You are so grown up."

"I am thirty-four, mother. You act like I'm still a boy."

"I know, I'm sorry, but I do not see much of you now. You've been away and I had not seen you for five years and now you've been so busy I've only seen you a couple of times." She put up her hand and patted his cheek. "Come in and take your coat off, son."

He followed her into the living room. While she went to fetch coffee, he took off his coat and stood in front of the fireplace, his hands clasped behind his back so she would not see the rank insignia as soon as she came in.

When she returned, she pulled over a small table and set out their cups with a coffee pot, cream, and sugar. She looked up and saw him standing just like Stephen used to. "You look so like your father—you could be him." She drew in her breath and then asked, "What is your news?"

Tiberius did not move for a moment and he did not speak either. He watched as she began to pour the coffee and he stepped forward, letting his sleeves come into view. "I was promoted, mother."

She looked up and her face went white. Her son looked just as his father had thirty-four years ago when he had stood facing her in this very room—looking so proud in his new uniform. She remembered it as if it were yesterday. He had stood there, looking so pleased. He had got what he had dreamed of—a command of his own. A new ship, he told her, his hands on her swollen belly, feeling baby Tiberius moving in her womb. She remembered his laugh, saying the baby was excited by his news too. Then almost in a daze, she had heard him say it was a prototype, a deep space mission ship, especially designed to go further than ever before. They would be away for a long time, eight years at least.

"I have been given command of a new ship. The first of its kind since the *Wryneck*—a deep-space vessel."

"*No!*" She shook her head. "No! No! No! I can't! I can't look at you. You look just like Stephen. You even used almost the same words."

"Mother." Tiberius' voice was gentle. "You have known for years that I wanted this—that my sole ambition has been to be like my father."

She looked up. "That does not make it any easier. I don't want to lose you as I lost him. I lost him as soon as he put on that uniform. It was his whole life! And you, his son—you are the image of him, now you wear the same uniform."

35

Tiberius sat beside her on the sofa. "You knew that when you married him; he was in uniform even then and he made no secret of his ambition. You have told me you even used to tease him, calling him 'Captain'. You always knew I would go. From the day you found me climbing on a chair to try on his cap, you knew. You saw me stroking his tunic in the wardrobe. I never knew him, but I feel sometimes that I do because I have a photograph of him and, when I look in the mirror, it is his face that looks back at me. He would want me to do this. I *will* find out what happened to him and I *will* clear his name."

Bethany smiled sadly. "You have his determination; he would be proud of you. I wish the truth would come out."

"I need to know," Tiberius told her. "Something happened and it is a big mystery, and I don't like it! They say father did wrong— I must know. Even if he did do wrong, I must keep faith with him." He remembered the lines of a poem, written hundreds of years ago during a great war—*if ye break faith with us who die... we shall not sleep.* "I must let him sleep," he said suddenly. "If he did wrong, I need to know what he did. If he was framed, I must find out who did it and see that they are punished for what they blamed father with." He did not tell her that he was afraid there was more to the story now it transpired that Xander had allegedly been abandoned by the captain and then thrown into prison. But why would Stephen MacAlpin desert his best friend and first officer on an alien planet, leaving him to endure many years of imprisonment? Another thought crossed his mind. What if Xander had lied to him? He could not bear that thought. The man who had been there for him and, in his late teens, standing in place of his father, and not just because Tiberius was his godson. His middle name was Alexander for his father's old friend—a long friendship remembered, as promised. His mother had told him once that one of his father's letters to her, not long before he was born, had asked her to name the child after Xander if it was a boy. He had said he owed him. Tiberius wondered how much, and why that seemed to have changed. Pounding in his mind was Xander's voice, telling him he had been abandoned. He came back to reality with a bump as his mother pushed a cup towards him.

"I *am* proud of you, Tiberius. Just as I was proud of your father. Whatever happens, you will always have my love and support."

Tiberius smiled. "Thanks, mama, that means so much."

After dinner, Tiberius returned to his apartment and sat at his desk with a mug of coffee. He woke the computer and sat staring at the screen for a long time, planning a message for Admiral Kehoe, to request a meeting. He recorded his message and then played it back. "Erase." He started again and it took him an hour to get it right. One hour and three mugs of coffee. He played back one more time and then sent it. He leaned back and sighed. There were two ways that message could be answered—an affirmative, or a negative. He hoped Admiral Kehoe would understand why it meant so much to him to know the truth. He headed for the shower and then bed. Tomorrow could be a busy day for him. Starting with being called to the admiral's office, or so he hoped despite dreading it too. She was a tough nut to crack; a very strong-willed professional woman used to having her way and having her commands obeyed.

As he curled up under the covers, he allowed his mind to run over the events of the evening; especially of his mother's outburst when she saw the captain's rank on his sleeves. Pain, buried deep over the years; the pain of a lost love and the sharp reminder of it at the sight of Stephen's son at the same age. He woke when the computer chimed, letting him know he had received a message. He touched the face of his watch to see the time. 05:15? He rolled over and buried his head in the pillow and tried to ignore having heard the sound.

It chirped again, and then again. He realized after a moment that the incessant sound was not an incoming message but a call. He stumbled out of bed and punched *respond*. "MacAlpin!"

Admiral Kehoe's face filled the screen. "Don't just give me audio, MacAlpin! I want to see you."

Tiberius tapped the key to open a visual link. "Good morning, Admiral," he said, knowing he still looked half asleep while she appeared not to have been to bed yet or had been up for hours; either way, she looked as fresh as a daisy. He knew he would look as he felt—someone awakened from sleep.

Kehoe smiled. "Woke you, did I? Anyway, I got your message. I want to see you in my office at 07:00, without delay."

Tiberius looked at her and then nodded. "Yes, ma'am." He opened his mouth as though to ask a question, but she held up her hand.

"Save any questions you might have and ask me later."

Tiberius blinked as the call ended and the screen went blank. *That was odd.* He looked at his watch again. 05:30—no point in going back to bed. He had to be at the admiral's office at seven precisely. He sighed, made some coffee, and then curled up on the couch for a while, reading through a list he had begun to make of things he would talk about with his command team. When he finished his coffee, he showered and dressed. It was now 06:30 and he headed out, taking a shuttle to the HQ complex.

It was exactly two minutes to seven when he arrived in the outer office and the duty officer looked up. "Good morning, sir. You're to go straight through."

Tiberius went on and at exactly 07:00 he pressed the buzzer and was admitted. On the way, all kinds of thoughts ran through his mind. Had his message been too demanding? Would she understand why he had to see the file? Why he had to know.

Admiral Kehoe did not look up from her screen. "Sit, MacAlpin." A pause and then, "You have been asking questions."

"Yes, ma'am."

"Questions you have been warned not to ask." She turned then and looked at him.

"Yes, ma'am." Tiberius got the distinct feeling that he could be in trouble.

"I see in your message that you request to see the files. At around the same time, I received a message from Rear Admiral Galen informing me that you were persistently demanding the truth; even going so far as to challenge his courage and loyalty."

Tiberius bit his lip. "He told you that? I told him I was sorry."

"He told me that too, but you cannot say things like that. *However*, it does not appear he is too angry with you and requested I permit you to see what we have on file."

Tiberius held his breath.

"I warn you—you will not find all the answers you seek. There will be many left unanswered. There are more reasons than one why the events surrounding your father's death are top secret. We do *not* know the answers; the people who could give us those answers are dead. All except for Galen and he has not told us what he knows—if anything. He told us only that he was left behind on the planet to finish some work they had begun—to be collected at a later time. He was arrested by the planet's government and imprisoned and your father never returned for him. The rest, as they say, is history. Your father never submitted

38

a final log, not even stating what was happening—what he was about to do."

Tiberius gnawed his lip again. He knew that whatever his father intended to do, that last log should have been submitted. What if it had been, but had been hidden? Was there something in the log that explained his reasons? It must surely have given information as to why Xander was not on the ship; and that he was on the planet, and to explain why he was left behind. Could it be that those in charge had deliberately hidden the truth all these years and laid the blame on Stephen MacAlpin who was unable to defend himself?

Admiral Kehoe rested her elbows on the desk and looked at Tiberius. "I will permit the access you desire, but not until you have launched. You have duties to attend to, new crew to meet and work alongside to prepare for your mission. If you get access now it will become the only thing you desire. It is obvious you feel deeply about it and your loyalty does you credit." She paused and the unspoken *even if it is misplaced* was pretty clear to Tiberius.

He nodded, understanding.

"Dismissed. Oh, and do not tell anyone you have the files. It is not necessary."

Tiberius stood up. "Yes, ma'am. Thank you. You are right that it is important to me. More so now than ever before." Turning to leave, he paused and looked back. "Crew assignments—I know they are to be posted today and that it basically is the entire crew of the *Victorious*, but I understand there are to be some changes. May I request that no change is made to the first officer? I want Commander Ross at my side for my first command. We have worked together, and his experience will be valuable to me."

Admiral Kehoe looked up. "Commander Ross submitted a transfer request."

"When?"

"Just after the commissioning ceremony. I have not yet authorized it."

"That was before I spoke to him then, Admiral. I have since talked with Ross and have told him that I want him on the *Invincible*. He said he would be glad to be first officer. So, could you not authorize it, please?"

Kehoe nodded. "I was going to deny his request anyway. You are right, his experience will be invaluable to you. Use what skills you learned from serving with Galen—he was a fine captain."

As she turned back to her computer, Tiberius knew he was dismissed. He saluted and left the room.

6
Crew Postings

Xander was still not used to being addressed as 'Admiral' and catching sight of himself in his new uniform still startled him as did the salutes from lower ranks passing him as he headed for the plaza. He joined Tiberius at the younger man's favourite café. It was lunchtime and the crew postings were finally to be announced that afternoon. Xander sat down and greeted Lashinda who was there too. A few moments later, Commander Ross joined them, apologizing for being late.

"You're not," Tiberius told him. He tapped the table-top screen and the holographic menu appeared.

Lashinda picked sushi and Ross a pasta salad, while Xander chose grilled rainbow trout and rice, and Tiberius ordered a favourite of his—fried chicken with fries and corn on the cob. They submitted the order and then settled back to talk while they waited for their meal to arrive.

Tiberius turned to Ross. "I told Kehoe that I want you as my first officer; she told me you already requested a transfer."

Ross reddened. "That was before you spoke to me. I will speak to her."

"I already have, and your request has been denied."

Xander looked at Ross. "You asked for a transfer? Before being assigned?"

Ross nodded, still red in the face. "I expected the captaincy after you, sir. When I heard them announcing your retirement, I knew I had a chance to follow my dream of commanding the *Victorious*, then her decommissioning was announced so I guess I expected to get the new ship, but MacAlpin was promoted over my head. I was angry and jealous. I have had more years of experience—even of command. But that is past now. I am sorry that I was angry. My duty is to follow orders, whatever they are; and I will do just that."

"I need your experience and your friendship." Tiberius met Ross' eyes and smiled.

No-one said anything else just then as their drinks arrived and it gave Ross time to recover himself.

Xander looked around at his companions and held up his coffee mug. "To a new era for all of us."

They clinked their mugs. "A new era!"

Tiberius sipped his coffee. He desperately wanted to tell them he had been granted permission to see the files, but he had been told not to, although would probably tell Xander later.

Their meals arrived and they settled down to eat. Soon, the three men were swapping stories of their various postings, and Lashinda asked them lots of questions. She was ground-crew and had never been in space apart from a shuttle run to a star-base. They all had stories from when they were young ensigns, and they laughed over how similar some of the stories were.

The younger officers ordered dessert but Xander declined, ordering another coffee instead.

Lashinda stated that she was thinking of applying for officer training. "I love my work, but I don't know if I want to be stuck on Earth or on a star base for the rest of my career, especially as you are going to be away so long, Tibby."

Tiberius looked at her. "I'll be glad to see you do that. But you are a computer technician, and that is an important job. If I talk to the admiral perhaps?"

"No." Lashinda shook her head. "You're the captain. You could not be seen to be in a relationship with a member of the crew, and it would seem like you were looking for favours. Not professional."

Xander looked at them seriously. "She is right. It will have to be a long-distance relationship—as so many are. Keeping in touch will not be an issue."

•

In the admiral's office, Kehoe and her team were going over a list of the crew who were transferring from the *Victorious*. The personal files were pulled for each name. Notes were made; some names erased, and others were added.

Admiral Kehoe looked up. "Now the first officer. MacAlpin has requested Ross. He wants his expertise." She pulled the file and tapped the screen. "Ross, Kirbie Samuel. Born in Gold

Coast, Australia. Age thirty-seven—seven years old when the *Wryneck* was lost. Only three years older than MacAlpin."

"Only three years more experience than MacAlpin," one of the officers commented. "Were Ross' parents not lost when the *Wryneck* was destroyed?"

Kehoe nodded. "Yes, and he would have been on board too had he not been ill and left at home with his grandparents at the last minute. It is thanks to food poisoning he is alive today." *And he hates MacAlpin because of what his father did,* she added inwardly. All crew who were affected in some way by the loss of the *Wryneck* had been questioned about their feelings. Some had been brutally honest but only she knew that, however, and if anyone found out and asked her reasons, she would have no answer. She pressed the intercom and called her aide in and instructed her to transmit the lists to the screens in the plaza. When the others had gone, she looked at her copy of the list and read each name over and over. It was a good crew; Galen had trusted them when he was captain. There were some alterations, some of the *Victorious* crew would find themselves transferred to other ships, while some serving with other crews would find themselves transferred to the *Invincible*, with the 'Untried Captain' as some were calling Tiberius already.

Officers, remembering the day they got their first command, did not call him this. They had all been untried in that situation and they sympathized with him for being landed with what could only be termed a high-profile command.

•

Tiberius leaned forward and tapped his account details into the table-top screen and took the receipt chip it spat out. "The postings should be up soon," he said. "Shall we head that way? I am eager to know."

Xander and Ross nodded. "You will be keen to meet them," Xander said. "You'll need to decide on your department heads."

Tiberius tried not to look panicked, but he knew there was a lot of work involved. He had worked with all the *Victorious* crew but making these decisions had never been a task of his. "I will need their files," he said. "I will know most of them, and what their strengths are, but the *Invincible* carries a larger crew than the *Victorious* so there will be lots of new faces."

Xander smiled. "Don't worry, you have Ross to assist you. And I am to give you any help you may need in preparing your ship and crew. You were my protégé, after all. I want to see you

43

succeed, for your sake—and your father's." He added the last quietly, almost as though he did not want to be heard.

Tiberius nodded and drew a deep breath. "Sorry. I am okay now—panic over. I just don't want to mess up right at the start. Everyone would make those 'I told you so' noises."

Xander shook his head. "You need to develop a thicker skin; you *have* to forget everyone else, and their opinions. They do *not* matter, you don't have to prove yourself to *anyone*. You would not have been given this position if no-one thought you could do it—High Command is not stupid. I know you care about the opinions of others—you always did. Hold onto a little of that, so you do not brush people off, but you *must* not care so much about what is thought of you. You are the captain. It matters not if your crew like you—only that they respect you for your rank, and the kind of man you are. If you are yourself and do your job to the best of your ability, then they will respect you. Even despite the unknown of the past which you fear will always haunt you. He paused and finished off his drink. "Okay?"

Tiberius nodded. "Thanks, Xander." He stood up. "I will do my best."

Xander stood up too and clapped him on the shoulder. "I know you will. Let's go and see the postings. I want to know how many of my old crew are to be with you."

When they reached the plaza, it was crowded. The crowd was thickest around the screens where the *Invincible*'s postings were displayed. One of the crew looked around. "Here's the captain, with Galen." Heads turned at her words and the crowd parted like the Red Sea for Moses and formed two lines on either side as the officers walked down.

Tiberius took out a wafer-thin device and touched the screen. He looked up at the main screen and waited for the connection to be acknowledged and then downloaded the new crew roster. He glanced at it and then spoke quietly to Ross.

The *Invincible*'s new first officer nodded and then turned around. "All crew members must board the *Invincible* by 16:00 hours. The captain will address you then."

As they walked back past the lines of officers and crew, Tiberius nodded to the ones who caught his eye and smiled at him as he passed.

Xander watched, feeling proud. Plunged suddenly into a command he had not expected quite so soon, Tiberius was coping well, as he had known he would. He knew the younger man felt he had a lot to prove. Years of anguish at hearing his father's name spoken of not as the hero he had thought him to be had hurt the boy and, now a man, Tiberius had to defend his belief in his father's honour—it meant that much. And Xander was only too aware of that.

Leaving the crowd behind them, they parted, with Tiberius and Ross heading off to prepare to board the *Invincible*. Lashinda returned to work in the big computer labs and Xander made his way to his office to start his new desk job.

7

Settling In

Tiberius let himself into his apartment and looked around before going to his desk to check the computer for messages. There was one from his mother, reminding him to visit before he left for space.

He replied, telling her he would. There were two days before the official launch with the captain and crew on board and he began to pack his bag. There were a few personal items he would never leave behind—his father's photograph and uniform. He had so much to live up to; the honour of his father to defend. His father's memory meant everything to him, and he intended to find out exactly what had happened all those years ago. He folded the tunic carefully and laid it in the case and then lifted down his father's cap. He held it in his hands for a moment and then put it on top of the tunic. He picked up his own cap and put it into the wardrobe; he would wear his father's cap instead of his own. The uniforms had not changed much in thirty years, and the cap had not changed at all. It was only worn on official occasions, but it would mean a lot for him to wear his father's. He picked up the flat disc Admiral Kehoe had given him; it contained all the information about his father's case, and he had been told not to look until they left the station. He looked at the computer. She would not know.

He slid the disc into the computer and a moment later the computer asked if he wanted to proceed. He took a deep breath. "Abort." He would obey her for now. "Eject." He removed the disc and tucked it into the bag. There would be time enough to see what it contained. Part of him was fearful—afraid that all those rumours were true. Something niggled at him all the time, and that was Xander's reluctance to talk about what had happened. He had managed to find out that he had been imprisoned on the planet for whatever reason and was not on the ship. There was something not being told, and it worried him. Had his father *really* abandoned his first officer and friend, leaving him to be incarcerated for something he had not done? Was it something his father had done and Xander had paid the price? The last time he had dreamed, it had seemed like this was the case.

He stepped out onto the balcony and looked out across the city. "I can't believe you would betray Xander! You were friends for so many years, I cannot ignore that." But, deep in his mind, there were always the same questions. The same uncertainty. Not knowing was worse than if he found the stories and theories were true. His father, for some unknown reason, had destroyed his ship, killing every member of the crew—even knowing he had done this for no reason other than to cover up a crime would be better than not knowing. Or would it? He did not know. He could not know until he had the facts before him and could make his own judgement. Until then, he had to cling to his belief in his father's innocence and to his own fight to clear his name.

He sighed and slammed his palms onto the railings of the balcony in frustration. He knew his search for the answers would haunt him until he had the truth at his fingertips and could accept the past.

•

Xander sat at the desk in his new office. He was beginning to settle into the desk job he had dreaded while a serving officer on active duty. He leaned back in his chair and looked around the room for a few minutes and then reached forward and touched the centre of the top drawer which slid open easily under his fingers. He lifted out an old-fashioned picture frame and looked at the photograph it contained for a long time in silence.

It had been taken the day Stephen had been promoted to captain and was given command of the *Wryneck*. They were both in it. Captain Stephen MacAlpin and his newly assigned first officer, Commander Alexander Galen. They were both smiling and Xander sighed, remembering that day clearly despite the passage of time. They had been enthused with the same sense of adventure of being sent on the first mission of this kind. A new ship, going further than humans had ever ventured, deep into the very darkest depths of space. Neither of them would have believed it if anyone had told them Stephen would not return and that, of four hundred plus crew members, only Xander would survive. That no-one would know why—and if there were answers out there, they were concealed, and the case closed despite never being resolved. They had made such plans for a great future; how they would finish their careers together, spending their old age with their families and watching the careers of their children and grandchildren with pride.

Grief welled up in his throat. "Damn you, Stephen! *Why*?!" he cried suddenly and threw the photograph across the room. It struck the wall and fell to the floor with a crash as the glass shattered. At the sound of breaking glass, he was struck with a sudden stab of remorse and got up from the desk, kneeling on the floor and holding the shattered frame in his hand while carefully picking up the broken glass. He was so wrapped up in his own feelings that he did not hear the door open and never saw Admiral Kehoe step into the room.

"It hurts, doesn't it?" she said quietly, guessing what he had done. "His betrayal of all you both believed in—the betrayal of your friendship."

Xander looked up, ashamed to be found in a moment of weakness. He saw her hand extended and allowed her to pull him to his feet. He went back to the desk and laid the broken frame down. "Yes, it hurts. I can't believe it still. The truth…"

"Cannot be told," Kehoe finished. "One day, perhaps, but not now. You know that. You will not break your oath?"

Xander drew a deep breath and shook his head. "I will keep my promise."

"Even when he asks you?"

He nodded again. "He will find out one day; you have given him access to the files."

"Not full access. There are some things it is best he does not find out. At least not yet. He must establish his own career on his own merits; *not* on those of his father."

"He has been given a hard task," Xander responded. "To follow in the footsteps of a man he admires as a hero—whose memory is shrouded in secrecy. He does not know the truth and yet we give him an identical ship and give him the command and send him to the same region of space? Don't forget Tiberius is like a son to me. I saw him through his studies and took him onto my crew. I nurtured him—encouraged him to strive for a captaincy. I tried to be to him the father he never knew. Don't we owe him something?"

Leandri Kehoe listened without a word and then nodded. "We owe him a chance to forge his own career." She tapped the photograph. "He would be proud of his son, I do know that."

Xander sighed. "If only there was a log that explained what happened; even just one that explained why he chose to destroy ship and crew without a moment's thought."

She looked at him. "Some things will never be known." She turned to the door. "If the truth is meant to be told then it will be."

Xander watched her leave and then looked at the shattered photo in front of him. "Why did I do that? Why am I so angry with you?" he asked, looking down at the face of his friend in the photograph. He tipped the broken glass into the waste-bin under the desk and slipped the photograph back into the drawer. He would get it repaired later.

•

Tiberius entered his new quarters on the ship and tossed his bag onto the bed. He sat down at the desk and woke the computer. He slid the wafer-thin information disc the admiral had given him into the computer and waited until the list of files it contained appeared on the screen. He studied the list and saw a sub-file named LOGS. *Good, there should be something here.* He touched the screen and the first file opened. There was a routine log in it and he listened to it, hearing his father's voice for the first time. He bit his lip for it was just as emotional as he had imagined. There was nothing in the log to hint at anything untoward and the next three logs were the same. Just routine.

He touched the fourth one and the computer's artificial voice informed him, "Access restricted. Please enter authorization code."

"I don't have a code."

"Access denied. This file carries a security restriction."

Tiberius swore under his breath. Admiral Kehoe had given him access, but obviously,only to the files she deemed necessary. What were they hiding from him? It had to be that. These logs must contain something—the truth perhaps. He tried personal logs. They were all restricted, but for some of the older ones. One of them contained Stephen MacAlpin's delight on hearing he had a son, and Tiberius asked the computer to play it.

"I look forward to the day I can meet him." Stephen's words brought tears to Tiberius' eyes. His father had died four years later without ever meeting the child he spoke of with so much happiness. That brought it all home with a vengeance—his father had never had the chance. He ran his hand over his eyes and was angry with himself when he found his hand was wet. He blinked angrily and began to search through all the files. All the ones he could access ended about a week before his father's death. No records, or if there were then they must be the ones that were restricted. He slammed his fist on the desk, realizing he had been tricked into keeping silent by being made to believe he had been given access. He tried another log and listened to his father talking about the photograph Bethany had sent of their new son. "She says he looks like me, but I don't know. He's bald and wrinkly with a screwed up red face. I thought I was better looking than that!"

Tiberius heard his father laugh and knew he had been more than happy and was glad that he had at least seen photographs. He listened for a while longer and then could bear it no more and tried the restricted files again.

"Access denied!"

And again. "Access denied!"

He thumped on the desk in complete frustration and then began to dictate an angry message to Admiral Kehoe, venting his fury at being refused access.

There was a buzz at the door and Commander Ross entered. "Captain," he began and then broke off as he saw the message on the screen. "You haven't sent that?"

Tiberius shook his head and Ross leaned over his shoulder. "Discard message," he instructed. Then he leaned on the desk and looked at the younger man. "Don't put yourself in the wrong, Tiberius, however you feel about this. You think I don't understand? I do—I would give anything to know what happened. We all would. My parents were on board the *Wryneck*. I never saw them again. See, I do understand."

"I understand too why you must hate me, because of my father."

"Don't be silly—I don't hate you. You are not your father. I just want to know the truth one day. My parents were good friends with your father. I met him, even though I was only a young kid at the time. I find it hard to believe he would condemn his entire crew to death without giving them a choice. No, there *is* something more, and making Kehoe mad is *not* going to help in *any* way." He clapped Tiberius on the shoulder. "Now, I came to take you on your first official tour of the ship and then you need to address the crew."

Tiberius looked up. "That part is scaring me. They will all be judging me."

Ross leaned forward and shook him, not ungently. "Of course they will! You are a new captain; this is your first command. But you are better than this—you have wanted this *all* your life— what others think and say must *not* matter or it will destroy you."

"Xander said the same thing," Tiberius admitted.

"He always gives you sound advice. You do not have to face them yet, you will speak to them from the bridge. Now, pull yourself together and come with me." Ross straightened up and went to hold the door open for his commanding officer.

Tiberius sat on the captain's chair on the bridge after the long tour around his new charge. She was a beautiful ship, fitted out with every new piece of technology and comfort for the crew; designed primarily to spend even longer away from the base than ever before. He could imagine his father's excitement all those years ago at being given such a charge. The newest ship in the fleet with a mission never before undertaken—the pride of High Command. Entrusted with a prototype ship, a new crew, and an important mission. A trust betrayed? He heaved a deep sigh and looked around the almost deserted bridge. Most of the crew were not due on board for a few hours yet so he had time to compose what he would say in his mind. The last thing he wanted was to come over as green as he felt. He turned as footsteps approached.

It was Ross. "The department heads are assembled in the briefing room, as you requested." He smiled. "Don't look so scared, you will be fine. You know them all already."

"*That* is what I am scared of—they all know me." Tiberius stood up. "Lead on."

•

That evening, Tiberius went back down onto the base to take Lashinda out for one last date before he left. They had dinner together at their favourite restaurant and then went to see a film. It was a comedy, supposedly, but Tiberius was not sure if it was the film itself, or his preoccupation with his thoughts, which stopped him enjoying it.

They walked hand in hand back to Lashinda's apartment and neither of them spoke much but, as she punched the access code into the panel by the door, she looked around. "Coffee before you have to go?"

Tiberius nodded. "Thanks, that would be nice." He followed her in and went out onto the balcony looking out across the city. He could hear her bustling around in the little kitchenette as she made the coffee. He listened with one ear as she continued to chat away. It was a one-sided conversation, but he was content. The more she talked, the fewer questions he had to answer.

"Tibby?"

He realized she must have asked him a question. He turned and came back inside. "Sorry, I was looking at the city."

Lashinda was standing by the sofa with two mugs of coffee in her hands. "You've not been listening to a word I've been saying," she chided. "What's on your mind? Do you want to talk?"

Tiberius sat down and looked at her as she put the mugs on the table. "I'm sorry, I was thinking something out. Something I need to tell you."

She looked at him. "It's because you are going away, you want to break up with me?"

Tiberius shook his head. "No! Not that! I love you, Lash—you have been my rock. I don't know how I would have got through the dreams if you had not been there. Yes, I am going away for several years."

"Eight years."

"Lash, don't make it any harder than it already is!" He put his hand into his tunic pocket and drew out a little blue box. He pushed the coffee table aside and went down on one knee in front of her. "Lashinda, I love you. I know I am going away for eight years, but will you wait for me? Would you do me the honour of becoming my wife?" He looked down for a moment as he opened the box to reveal a ring. "Will you marry me, Lashinda?"

Lashinda realized she was holding her breath and looked down at the ring, noting that it was gold with an emerald set in a small cluster of diamonds. Emerald—her favourite jewel. She nodded. "Yes, I'll marry you." She watched as he slipped the ring onto her finger. "It fits, how did you get the size right?"

"I pinched one of your rings last time I was over."

She laughed and leaned forward to kiss him, cupping his face in her hands.

"I brought champagne,"Tiberius told her when his mouth was free for a moment.

"Let's take it along to Xander's apartment. We need to tell him the news and he will want to celebrate with us." She looked down and held out her hands to pull him up. She smiled. "I know you want to share this moment with him too."

Tiberius' rather cheeky smile hit his eyes. "I think he will be happy."

In a few moments, they had collected the champagne and glasses and took the short shuttle ride to where Xander Galen lived. Tiberius rang the buzzer. After waiting a few minutes, he rang again and then knocked at the door. Another long moment and then Xander's voice came over the intercom. "Who is it?"

"It's me."

"Tiberius, it's nearly midnight—no, come on in!"

There was a beep and the door opened. Tiberius and Lashinda went through into the living room, just as Xander came in through another door, tying the belt of his dressing-gown.

Tiberius immediately looked contrite. "You were sleeping? I'm sorry."

"It's all right. Now, what's up?" Xander sat down in his deep armchair and leaned back.

Tiberius felt bad for waking him, he did look very tired. "We wanted you to celebrate with us. Lash and I, we just got engaged."

Xander's tired face lit up. "Truly?"

Lashinda held out her hand to show the ring. Xander smiled and took their hands in his. "I am so happy for you!"

Lashinda smiled and pulled her hand away as she saw that Tiberius wanted to hug the man who had stood in place of his father through many important times of his life. She went to sort out glasses for the champagne.

Tiberius gave Xander a big hug. "I am sorry we woke you, but I wanted you to be the first to know—to share our happiness. You have always been like a father to me."

Xander returned the hug warmly. "I don't mind being woken, I am glad to share this time." He laughed as he heard the *pop* of the champagne being opened. "You came prepared!"

Lashinda came across and held out glasses and then picked up hers.

Xander stood up. "Here's to you both. I wish you joy." He raised his glass and they touched theirs to his. He smiled as

Tiberius put his arm around Lashinda. "You'll be telling your mother tomorrow? You know you have to see her before you go."

Tiberius nodded. "Yes." He sounded subdued. He knew her feelings would be mixed. She did not want him to go, and she would remember being left behind only to wait in vain.

Xander looked at them and smiled softly. "Will you listen to an old man's advice? I've never married, as you know, but that's not because I did not want to—I did. But in this life, relationships are hard—make it work. Love is tough—it's not supposed to be easy. Tiberius, you are going to be away for a long time, find time for each other, even over the distance. Always call, write to each other; even just a quick call before you lay your head down to sleep. Both of you—remember that. I wish I had."

Tiberius turned and saw the sudden sadness in Xander's face. He understood—life had dealt him many blows: lost love, the death of his oldest friend, years of imprisonment and then hearing after his release of the loss of his ship and crew. How much regret and pain he must keep buried deep inside? "I swear it, Xander. I will keep her close despite the distance, she means the world to me."

Lashinda smiled. "You care about him, that is obvious. I will not hurt him."

Xander returned her smile, trying to bury a little more of his own pain in their happiness. There was a lot of which he never spoke.

8
Missing Pieces

The following evening, Tiberius was glad to escape back to the *Invincible* after a difficult visit to his mother. The visits got harder every time. He hid away in his quarters and lay on the bed in the darkness. He wanted some peace and just to be able to close his eyes for a moment.

He seemed to only have closed his eyes for the merest instant when the door buzzer sounded, and Commander Ross looked in.

"You wanted me to let you know when all the crew were aboard."

Tiberius sat up and rubbed his hand across his face.

"You okay?"

Tiberius nodded. "It wasn't easy saying goodbye to mum. She made it extremely hard and I'm just feeling a bit down. She still hasn't let herself move on and blames me for breaking her heart again."

Ross looked sympathetic. "Family! She'll be okay and I guess she is secretly proud of you. Now, you've got a new family to meet. The *Invincible* family. I know you're nervous about their preconceptions, but you are a confident officer, just be yourself."

Tiberius agreed and followed him from the room, after a quick glance in the mirror to smooth his hair and straighten his tunic.

When they reached the bridge, Tiberius took a deep breath and turned on the ship-wide intercom. "This is the captain. I want to take this opportunity to welcome you all on board the *Invincible*. Most of you know me already and all of you know who I am and what this means. I ask that you all try and accept that High Command have their reason for this, and I will do my utmost to live up to their faith in me. Some of you are surprised

I was given this command, because of who my father was. No-one is more surprised than I and all I ask is that you do your duty and give me a chance, and I will not let you down. MacAlpin out." As he switched off the intercom, he turned and saw Ross looking at him.

"Well done. You did just fine."

Tiberius sank back in his chair and closed his eyes. "I could feel them looking at me. As though they could see me through my voice. That was so hard. So many people are angry with me because of my father."

Ross frowned. "Stop it! If you keep thinking like that it will control you. You have your own career to forge; focusing on the feelings of others will destroy you, as I've said before."

Tiberius looked up. "You, of all of them." He stopped and turned red.

Ross turned away for a moment and then looked back and met Tiberius' eyes. "Yes, some would say I have more reason than most to hate you for what your father did. Your father died and I cannot discount what that loss means to you, but I lost *both* parents. But it was your father, *not* you. Don't talk like that again—you don't know the answers."

Tiberius sighed. "It is hard, but I'll try. It will be easier when I know what happened."

Ross nodded, understanding. Although his parents had been killed in the destruction of the *Wryneck* there was no stigma attached to their deaths, and their names appeared on the memorial. It was Stephen MacAlpin's actions that carried the stigma, and Tiberius, through no fault of his own, bore the weight of that shame and the pain of knowing his father's name was not included on the memorial to the lost crew of the *Wryneck*. Ross knew that had to hurt and he felt very sorry for Tiberius and vowed silently to make things as easy for him as he could by being the best first officer he could be.

•

They were not scheduled to leave for two days and everyone had one last night ashore, so the ship was quiet as Tiberius went for a wander through the deserted corridors. In two days they would leave for their voyage, watched by hundreds of eyes as he took his brand-new ship out of her docking bay, venturing beyond the space doors into the darkness—into the unknown for the first time as captain of his own vessel.

It was fear that made him pace the lonely corridors in this way. Not a fear of the unknown though. If that frightened him—the idea of heading into the dark unknown void of space—then he would be staying on Earth! It was not even a fear of the future—but an overwhelming fear of the truth. Something was making him uneasy; perhaps the reluctance of the senior officers to allow him access to the files, as though something was being concealed. Log entries locked by encrypted security codes. There was something wrong; he knew it, and it scared him. He thought back to his childhood, trying to think if there were any signs that his mother knew anything. He remembered she rarely spoke of his father and grew angry if her son asked too many questions. She had got upset when he put his father's uniform on. Was that because it made her remember him, or was it because she was ashamed of the uniform? He did not know any more. She had only struck him once when he was fifteen.

They had been at a dinner party at HQ—in Xander's honour if he remembered rightly. It would have been a year after his release, so was probably when he was given a medal for bravery. He had been upset at hearing some officer speaking badly of his father and he had accused his mother of not defending his father's name and honour, so he had; stamping his foot and yelling at the officers. She had boxed his ears and apologized to the group. Tiberius still did not know whether it was real anger toward him or anger at herself which had made her raise her hand to him—she never did again.

He shook his head. The truth had a way of coming out—he knew that. He had to be strong and prepare himself for whatever form the truth took. The truth was not always pleasant, and everyone had warned him about that. Only one thing scared him more, and that was his dreams. How would he cope with waking in the night without Lashinda to comfort him? In the close confines of a starship, everyone would hear him scream. As captain, he could not afford to show any weakness—especially in his situation. Mental affliction was one of the phrases which appeared often in the few reports about his father's death which he had been able to access, and they had debated the possibility that he was mentally afflicted at the time, either mad or ill, and this had been the cause of the tragedy. Tiberius knew he could not afford to wake screaming amid dreams that seemed to be showing him the events of the past; that would not look good on his record. Lashinda had always managed to protect him from anyone knowing and he wondered if he should talk to the doctor. Perhaps he would have if the ship's chief medical officer was the one he already knew, but the *Victorious*'s CMO had not been assigned to the *Invincible*, and the new one was a rather serious-looking woman, perhaps around his own age or a year or two older. He would need to get to know her before he could open up on a personal issue. Her record was outstanding—she was a skilled and highly-respected surgeon who had even written a couple of books and manuals which were used now to train new medical recruits and he could trust her with his life and the lives of all those on board, but not with this yet. He made his way back to his quarters and looked at the time. It was not quite midnight although it felt later so he had not been pacing the corridors for not as long as he had thought. He woke the computer and called Xander. If he were awake, he could always talk to him. Xander had been there for him as much as possible as he grew up and at the very least was just a call away—he had helped Tiberius through his teenage years and had been trusted enough to be the first port of call for every bit of girl trouble. Xander knew him well, and any advice he could get from his father's old friend was always taken on board and had saved him from heartbreak on more than one occasion. Perhaps it was too late to call—Xander was so often tired these days.

A moment or two later, Tiberius' computer beeped, and he turned to see Xander's face on the screen. "Did I wake you?"

"No, I've not gone to bed yet. Is something wrong?"

"I'm on the ship alone. Maybe I'm just letting my mind run away with me, but there is one thing I would like advice on. Can I come over?"

Xander smiled. "Of course. We should make the most of this time. I will not see you, not for a long time."

Tiberius had an uncomfortable feeling that Xander had been about to end that sentence quite differently and he felt a chill run down his spine. "Perhaps we should use this time to be honest with each other."

Their eyes met and Xander nodded. "Perhaps you are right—I will try and answer any questions you might have. I'll see you shortly—I'll get some beer out."

Tiberius smiled, they always found it easier to talk over a relaxed drink, ever since he had been old enough. Growing up, he had called Xander 'Pappi' and it had only been when he turned eighteen that he had begun to call him Xander. "I'll come right away." He ended the call and pulled his boots back on, headed out of his quarters and took one of the small shuttles back to the base and then caught a cab out to Xander's apartment.

Xander was waiting at the door, having heard the lift coming up. He greeted the younger man with a smile and held the door wide. "Come on in."

Tiberius went through to the lounge and sat on the couch. Xander joined him after a moment and handed him an opened bottle. "Something is troubling you; you sounded a little strained. Is everything okay?" He sat down opposite Tiberius and opened his own beer. "Pre-mission jitters?"

"Something like that," Tiberius confessed. "I'm scared. Not of the mission. It is the past that troubles me from time to time; about what happened thirty years ago."

"You know I can't..."

"I wasn't going to ask. It is just the dreams. I told you before that they trouble me at times. I can cope with the dreams themselves, but not with waking up screaming. Not on a ship where everyone will hear me."

Xander watched his face. "You should have told me they troubled you that much. Ask engineering to soundproof your quarters; that will give you some sense of security."

Tiberius nodded.

"Are you prepared to tell me about your dreams? What do they contain that has you wake screaming?"

Tiberius took a sip of his drink and sighed. "I see the bridge of the *Wryneck*; I see and hear what happened before the ship was destroyed. But there are pieces missing."

Xander sighed. "And you think knowing some of what occurred will prevent the dreams from troubling you?"

"I want to know one thing, to help me understand."

Xander ran his hand over his face. "I can't tell you, you know that. Please do not leave with bad feeling between us. I remember your last question, asking about my absence from the bridge. I told you I was not there; I was on the planet. I ended up a prisoner. I do not know why."

Tiberius met his eyes and knew he told the truth. "Xander, when I called; you said you would not see me for a long time. But you paused. You were going to say 'again', weren't you? Don't you think I have a right to know if you really are dying?"

Xander looked down at his hands.

"*Pappi!*" Tiberius had not called Xander that in sixteen years. "I am going away for eight years and you don't think it important to let me know there is every chance I will never see you again? You can't do that to me! Father left no explanation—you *can't* do the same!"

Xander shook his head. "Tiberius, calm down. I have said nothing because I did not want to hurt you. Perhaps I was wrong." He stood up and went to his desk and took a disc from a case and gave it to Tiberius. "My log entries. I did not give them all up. I kept some, in the hopes of learning the truth one day. As to my condition, there is no cure and I will keep you informed, especially when it begins to deteriorate. For now, the only real sign is that I get tired easily. Death is a natural part of life—it is easier to accept that."

Tiberius went to the window and stood looking out. He heard Xander's footsteps and felt his hand on his shoulder. "I can't accept it."

Xander sighed. "Do you think I want it like this? I don't want to die this way—we both have to be strong." He clapped the younger man on the shoulder. "You have the strength and the courage to complete this mission. Have you received your full orders yet?"

"Not yet. I know part of it is to find out what happened all those years ago and that scares me."

"And you are being sent without knowing the truth as far as it is known." Xander watched Tiberius' face. "You just need to accept the situation as it is and do your job—your duty. High Command does not need to justify its actions to you. They give orders and we obey."

Tiberius nodded. "I know. I just needed to talk about it."

"I understand. Life is an unknown—perhaps the greatest mystery in the universe. It unfolds daily and we cannot anticipate what it will bring us. It is up to us to deal with the situations as they reveal themselves. Now, it is late, and I am tired—get a blanket and make yourself comfortable on the couch. I'll go with you tomorrow to see Kehoe to get your final orders." Xander smiled. "Feel better?"

Tiberius took the final swig of his beer and nodded. "Yes. Thank you."

Xander made a move to clear up the bottles but Tiberius stopped him. "Go and rest—you look so tired. I'll clear away. Sleep well."

Xander nodded and headed for the bathroom. Tiberius heard him cleaning his teeth as he put the bottles into the recycling bucket. He heard the bedroom door close and went to the linen cupboard and pulled out a blanket. He kicked off his boots, curled up on the couch, tucking the blanket around himself. He rested his head on the cushions and allowed his eyes to close.

9
Pending Evidence

Xander's apartment was on the top floor and the rising sun flooded in through the uncovered window and fell across the sofa. Tiberius stirred and lay for a moment, wondering where he was and then remembered and rolled over and sat up, pushing back the blanket, and looked at his watch. It was early but still later than his usual time because of being up late the night before. He ran his hand through his reddish hair and yawned. He got up and went into the small kitchen to make some coffee. Xander liked fresh coffee and had a machine that produced it almost as quickly as making instant coffee. Tiberius sniffed appreciatively as he waited for it to be ready. He let himself out onto the balcony and looked out over the city as he drank a large mugful. Twenty minutes later he returned to the kitchen and began to hunt out eggs and bacon. Xander would appreciate waking up to find scrambled eggs, bacon, and coffee ready for him and it would not take long for the smell of cooking to wake him.

Xander came out of his room, rubbing his eyes, just as the last of the cooking was done. "Smells good." He sat down at the table, accepted a cup of coffee and sipped it with a sigh.

Tiberius dished up and put the plates on the table. "Do you think Kehoe will give me full orders?" He reached over the table, passing the salt to Xander.

Xander sprinkled his eggs with salt and pepper and was silent for a moment. "I would not worry too much—it will not change whatever happens. Mind what I said and accept what must be."

Tiberius nodded. "I have made up my mind to accept it. I know it will make it easier for me if I do." He ate a forkful of his eggs and sighed. "I just hope I can find the answers I want—that I need."

"Don't spend too much time thinking about it. This is your first command. You cannot afford to let yourself be distracted by a preoccupation—even over something so important."

Tiberius looked up. "Are you afraid of me finding out?"

Xander shook his head. "Not at all. I too would like to know what happened. I have years of my life to explain—lost years." He went quiet and Tiberius took the opportunity to get up and make some fresh toast.

Tiberius looked at Xander as he put the toast rack back on the table. "I know what it looks like, but do you think my father abandoned you? Your friendship meant a lot, didn't it?"

Xander looked up then. "It meant everything to both of us. I don't understand what happened, but I believe there was a reason for what he did. I never questioned his decisions."

"I will find out what happened, Xander. I promise. Will you promise to still be here when I return?"

Xander looked up and met Tiberius' eyes. "I cannot promise that, but I will try to be."

"I am just scared of not finding anything out." Tiberius gnawed his lip for a moment. "Finding out that logs have been encrypted means something is being hidden and I don't like it one bit!"

"You worry too much." Xander reached for the coffee pot and poured another cup. "The truth will out. That might just be a saying, but it is true. Whatever the truth is, we will find it. Patience is a virtue is another saying, and I suggest that you find that virtue, my son." His voice was kind as he spoke. He knew how much finding the truth meant to Tiberius—how much it meant to him too. He had been patient for twenty years although the patience had come at the price of always knowing that something had happened and had been covered up.

Tiberius looked up at the clock on the wall. "I need to go, just let me clear up for you."

"Just shove it all in the washer and I'll put it away tonight when I get back in." Xander got up and headed for the bedroom. "I will meet you at my office. Thank you for making breakfast." He smiled as Tiberius began to clear the table.

•

After clearing up, Tiberius headed back to his quarters on the *Invincible* to shower and change into uniform. He sat on the edge of his bed and pulled on his boots, making sure his uniform trousers fell neatly over the highly polished sheen of the boots. He glanced at himself in the full-length mirror before he closed the wardrobe door. He smoothed his hair back and put on the peaked cap that was part of the dress uniform. He checked his reflection again and nodded with satisfaction; it would not do to present himself to the admiral with anything out of place. He took a shuttle back down to the base and made his way to the admiral's office. He stopped at Xander's office first and knocked at the door. Xander came out, pulling his cap straight. "Ready, Tiberius?"

Tiberius shook his head. "Not really, but I don't suppose I will ever be more than I am now. As you said, I have wanted this for a long time."

Xander laughed. "Good man. Let's get your orders. She knows I am coming with you."

They strode together, their boots ringing on the floor. Tiberius pressed the buzzer at the door, and the admiral's aide showed them in.

Admiral Kehoe looked up. "Admiral Galen, Captain MacAlpin, come in." They saluted and she waved a hand to the chairs that were positioned in front of her desk. "Sit down, gentlemen." She touched the screen of the desktop computer. She looked at the screen for a while and then turned to Tiberius. "Are you happy with your bridge crew? There was much deliberation over the appointments."

Tiberius nodded. "I am satisfied, ma'am, I am glad to have faces I know around about me. It would make a long mission like this harder if all of us were newbies on the bridge."

"I agree with you there, although I must admit that my initial wishes were for an entire new crew for the *Invincible*. You have a good friend in Admiral Galen, and the fact that I listened to his advice speaks volumes to my respect for him. He has always spoken highly of you and I hope you understand your obligation to him."

"Believe me, ma'am, I owe Admiral Galen a lot more than that. I appreciate that he spoke out for me. I will do my best not to make him regret his recommendations." Tiberius looked at them both and twisted his fingers in his lap under the cover of the desk. Xander saw this out of the corner of his eye and looked studiously ahead of him so he would not draw attention to the only sign of nerves Tiberius was showing.

Kehoe pulled open a drawer in the desk and took out a buff file with a red stamp across the front. Tiberius recognized the file as the one that had lain on the desk during that first meeting. The CLOSED stamp had a line through it and a new stamp read PENDING EVIDENCE.

Tiberius looked up, meeting her eyes. "You've opened it?"

Leandri Kehoe nodded. "If you can provide enough evidence to make re-opening the case worthwhile, then yes. Your father was a fine officer and I think we owe it to his memory to show him for what he was once and for all—hero or coward."

Tiberius gnawed nervously at his lip. "The files you gave me were mostly encrypted. How can I find the truth if the evidence is being hidden from me?"

"You will be supplied with the key at the appointed time. Accept that and ask no more."

Tiberius nodded. "Thank you, ma'am. Now, is the mission solely to discover what happened to the *Wryneck*, or is that just a part?"

Kehoe sighed. "You are persistent." She tapped the screen in front of her and then pressed a button on the desk and a panel of the wall slid away, revealing a large screen. "This is a recording of the last full communication we received, before the logs began to peter out."

Tiberius and Xander turned and faced the screen as the admiral instructed the computer to play. The date of the transmission came up on the screen and it was about two months before the *Wryneck* had been destroyed.

The admiral glanced at MacAlpin as the computer asked another question, *audio or visual?* "Well? Do you want to see him?"

Tiberius held his breath for a moment and nodded. "I need to see him sooner or later."

"Play visual." The screen went dark for a moment and then changed to show the inside of the *Wryneck*'s captain's quarters and showed Stephen MacAlpin sitting at his desk.

I'm a bit concerned about not receiving clear instructions. Commander Galen and I are interpreting the last orders to the best of our understanding. We have been summoned to the planet to meet with the council and its leaders. The people seem friendly enough and I am looking forward to this first contact. We have not made contact with many new aliens on this voyage as this region of space is vast and seems to host very few inhabited planets. We have worked hard to be granted this audience—at first they seemed hesitant about welcoming visitors.

Tiberius watched his father on the screen and understood why older officers looked at him in a particular way—it was like watching himself on the screen.

On the recording, Stephen MacAlpin sighed and leaned his chin on his hand, his elbow resting on the arm of the chair. *Commander Galen warns me to be careful—I think his few more years of experience makes him wary where I am excited for any opportunities for first contact. I will, of course, listen to his advice.*

Tiberius glanced at Xander. "Did he?"

"Listen?" Xander replied. "On most occasions. There were times when he called me 'over-cautious' or thanked me for my input and went with his own plan anyway. Captain's prerogative."

Tiberius turned to the admiral. "Did my father not report on the meeting with the planetary council? That would be a major event, especially if these people were wary of outside visitors."

Admiral Kehoe shook her head. "Not the expected full report. Just a log entry that the meeting went ahead as scheduled. Nothing to say if it was amicable or if anything happened to precipitate the events which occurred afterwards, leading to his decision to destroy the ship and crew. If we could find that one log entry, it would explain so much. It would tell us why Commander Galen was left a prisoner in their hands, with no apparent effort being made to secure his release, and why, ultimately, the *Wryneck* was destroyed. He should have sent it just before the end."

Tiberius looked at Xander. "This life was everything to my father—you told me that. Something happened and it either happened the way it seems, or there has been a major cover up on the part of High Command. I *will* find out!" He looked up at the recording where the admiral had paused it. His father's face filled the screen. He could see the sincerity in his grey-green eyes. He could not believe this man was a coward and a murderer, and that his logs were cleverly fabricated to cover up some crime or misdemeanour. He shook his head. "I will find the truth—whatever it costs."

She smiled slightly. "Do you want to watch the remainder?"

Tiberius shook his head. "I have seen enough. Will you grant me full access to the files you have given me?"

The Admiral looked at Xander and then nodded. "You will be given that access. There are notes you will need to see if you are to understand and there are files on the hearing into the incident." She paused and then added, "Had he lived, there would have been a court-martial, a hearing and perhaps even a trial. He was charged with gross negligence, gross misconduct, and manslaughter. Had he been there to defend himself the verdict may have been worse." She switched off the screen. "I will send you the access codes. Dismissed."

Tiberius stood up and saluted before marching smartly out of the office. It was not until he reached the plaza and sat on the edge of the fountain that he relaxed and let out his breath slowly as though he had been holding it all that time. It was hard to allow the realization to sink in that he had been successful and that he had been granted access to the casefile. It scared him too. He wanted to know but, at the same time, it terrified him. Footsteps approached and he looked up to see a woman in uniform bearing the insignia of the admiral's office.

She held out an information chip. "Your orders, Captain MacAlpin. The launch time has been set for 14:30. All personnel must report for duty no later than 10:00. At 13:00 you will proceed to the Bridge and the mission will be officially launched over the ship's communication system. At 14:30 precisely, you will be given official clearance and you will give the order for the *Invincible* to leave dock." Her manner was almost regimental and there were no flaws in speech or delivery. Admiral Kehoe liked everything super-efficient, and her office was mostly staffed by the very latest in artificial intelligence. This android was the top model in the range. Efficient, methodical; programmed to do a specific job but also capable of human communication and interaction.

Tiberius held out his hand and took the chip. "Thanks." He allowed his fingers to brush the android's hand. *She even feels real.* He was surprised.

"You are welcome, Captain." She saluted and headed back to the main entrance of HQ.

Tiberius watched her walking away as he slipped the chip into the pocket of his tunic. He sat for a while longer, listening to the calming sound of the constant running water. He loved this fountain and always sat in this particular spot. He loved the way the water flowed constantly, a classic image of peace; one of the few things in the HQ complex that was not run by technology—

except for the lights. At night it was lit up, the water flowing all different colours, shimmering as it fell into the basin. The first time he had sat here he was fifteen years old with Xander beside him. Xander, still pale and emaciated from his long imprisonment, telling him about his father; the sound of the water a backdrop to Xander's soft voice telling him stories of their service together, but nothing about his death. Now he knew Xander had not been there, that he had not known of his friend's death until after his release; that must have been a shock, but he had taken time to sit with Stephen's son and talk to him, to try and help him to know him. *It is no use thinking like that,* he told himself. *The past cannot be changed.* He stood up and headed back to the ship and was just going down to his quarters when Ross came along.

"Where were you last night, Tiberius? I came to find you—a chance to meet the command team."

"Sorry, I went to see Xander—ended up sleeping on his sofa."

"Did it help?"

Tiberius nodded. "In a way. On the other hand, it made me realize just how long we will be away."

"You'll keep in touch."

"I know—it's not that. It's the distance if anything happens."

"It is no use thinking like that. No matter how you think or feel, your whole heart must be on this mission. All eyes will be on you—some wanting you to fail because of your father's story. Whether you like it or not, you are a high-profile officer—with a high-profile command. Admiral Kehoe will be watching. Do you not understand?"

"Understand what?"

"Don't be daft, man. You mean you haven't worked it out yet?"

"What are you talking about?! Worked what out?' Tiberius opened the door to his quarters. "Come in. If there is something I should know, tell me."

Ross followed him in and faced him across the desk. "Your crew has been hand-picked, especially the command team. Doesn't that tell you something?"

"I am new to command?" Tiberius said, watching Ross' face.

Ross shook his head. "Have you not seen their files? Did you really think the Admiral would let me transfer away from the *Invincible?*"

"What *are* you driving at, Kirbie?!" He could shake the first officer.

"The crew, each and every one of them, is connected to the *Wryneck*. They all had a family member serving on the ship under your father. A family member who died—*because* of your father."

Tiberius turned pale. "I saw all their files but there was no mention of this."

"Kehoe did not want you to know then. Those notes must have been deleted from the personnel files you were given."

Tiberius ran his hand through his hair. "Why?!"

"I can't answer that; I am not even supposed to know." Ross looked at him. "Afraid of them? Do you think they have all grown up with hatred for your father? The same hatred Kehoe has? She took quite a rap thirty years ago over the whole affair; she was in charge of the mission and there were many questions asked which she had to answer because your father could not. I am not saying she was involved in a cover-up..."

"But she had good reasons? Thanks, Kirbie."

Ross smiled. "You don't need to thank me. I am not against you, and neither is the crew. We will all benefit from finding the truth. Now, I'll come back in half an hour. It's time you should meet the command team. Take a short break and let what I've told you sink in—you'll be able to face them then. We're on your side and all looking forward to this voyage—it's not every day we are given a new ship!" He smiled and left the room, leaving Tiberius more than a little stunned by what he had been told.

It did worry him. Every crew member, connected to that one moment thirty years ago—thrown together for what reason? Did they know, or was Ross the only one who knew or had worked it out? And why would High Command do this? Was it only Admiral Kehoe, for some reason? A personal grudge: a vendetta against a man who could not defend himself against charges? *It's not fair*, he thought. *Is she hounding me because of my father's supposed crime?* He took the information chip from his pocket and put it into the little storage space in the desk which was revealed by touching a small dip in the surface and the top slid open—a touch in the same place slid it closed. He stood up when the buzzer sounded at the door and Ross looked in. "Ready?"

Ross nodded. "Yes, they await us in the officers' lounge." He walked beside Tiberius and the gathered officers stood to attention and saluted as the captain entered the room.

Tiberius' cheeks grew hot. He was still not used to this. "Please, sit down—Ross told me this would be an informal occasion."

"He knows," Ross told them. "I told him—about the connection we all have."

One of the female officers looked up. "We are on your side, Captain. You cannot be held responsible for what your father did—was supposed to have done. Even if he did something wrong, it is not your fault."

One of the males nodded. "We do not blame you for the loss of the *Wryneck* and our family members—we were all children. Whatever reason High Command has for placing us all together, it is not because we have signed anything to say we are against you. Nothing has been said, we all worked it out."

Another young officer chimed in. "You are proud to be given the captaincy. Each and every one of us is just as proud to serve on this new ship and to serve with you as our captain. We all swore an oath of loyalty and service. What kind of officers would we be if we pick and choose which commanding officers are worthy of our loyalty? Any captain would hate it. Make no mistake, though, not all of the crew will like you, but they *will* respect you."

Tiberius sat down, nodding. "I appreciate your honesty. Thank you." He accepted a drink from the officer who had just spoken. "I don't suppose you will allow me to apologize for what my father did? I promise, whatever else this mission is about, I *will* find the truth. I will either clear his name or be able to accept what happened and lay the ghosts." He raised his glass. "Here's to a successful voyage and to finding the truth." They touched glasses and his officers introduced themselves around the table.

•

The next day, Tiberius stood by the command chair and looked around the bridge. He glanced at the big window and could see all of the senior officers gathering for the official launch. The ship had been through her naming ceremony, but this was to be her official launch from the dock—the start of her new mission. In a short while, he had to give his very first command as the commanding officer of the *Invincible*. He scanned the faces lined up at the window and frowned. There was one missing. He could not give the command to leave the dock if Xander was not there. He looked around the bridge again and nodded. Everyone was in place, waiting. He opened the intercom from the ship to the lectern where Admiral Kehoe stood, looking very official in full dress uniform.

Kehoe pressed the button on the lectern. "Captain MacAlpin, is your ship ready?"

She is. But I am not. Xander was not there—it would be bad luck to leave without him there to bid them farewell. Tiberius knew she was waiting for an answer. "Yes, ma'am. We're all ready." He turned and looked around at the others. "This is it." He looked back at the window and saw Xander slipping into a place beside Admiral Kehoe. He heaved a sigh of relief—now they could go!

After a short address, Admiral Kehoe gave a nod and Tiberius sat down in the command chair and put his hands on the arms and tried not to let anyone see him stroke them gently. He loved the affinity he felt with his ship. *We can do this, girl.* He drew a deep breath and tried to stop his heart pounding, wondering if everyone would be able to hear it. "Helm, nice and slow, move us out." His first official order as the *Invincible*'s captain. "Permission to leave, ma'am?"

"Permission granted, Captain."

The big bay doors opened, giving them their first glimpse of the blackness of space beyond the station. The *Invincible* slipped between the doors and the cheers and applause of the assembled officers back at the station sounded over the intercom.

It was official; their mission was underway. Tiberius looked out of the big screen window and wondered what the next days and weeks would bring as he watched the space dock fade away in the distance, leaving them in darkness, surrounded by myriad stars.

10

Launch Day

Everyone stood watching as the *Invincible* slipped silently through the doors of space-dock. They saw her clearly for an instant; an elegant, streamlined silhouette against the blue-black, diamond-studded velvet expanse of space beyond. But only for an instant; as soon as she had passed through, the doors began to close as slowly and silently as they had opened.

Xander coughed and realized he had been holding his breath, he had forgotten anyone else but himself was standing there. Having been in this position himself, he knew the dangers and hardships Tiberius would face during the long voyage; not just the hardships presented by the unknown of space, but the trials and tribulations of a new command. He would discover the loyalty of his crew and learn that loyalty and respect cannot be bought and that not all of the *Invincible*'s new crew members would like him. Rarely would anyone ever be liked by everyone; that was life, and he knew Tiberius was not naive enough to believe otherwise. He heard someone speaking and he came back to earth with a jolt.

It was Kehoe. "Penny for them?"

"Are they worth that little?" Xander looked round. "We've not used the penny for five hundred years."

She laughed. "A figure of speech, Galen. You seemed so far away, as though part of you was longing to be aboard her."

"Am I *that* transparent?"

She shook her head. "No, but I do know that look. The look of a starship captain who is not ready to give up active duty. You would *still* be out there."

He interrupted her quickly. "Don't, please. I am still trying to come to terms with it. I would give anything to be back on the bridge and not tied to a desk and enduring endless medical examinations."

There was no answer to that—she understood. His life would be much more regulated now. She knew he had been told there was little chance of a cure and only strict routine, tests and experiments could give him any relief as the disease progressed. But not even she knew he had signed up to a research programme, giving his consent to be used in tests as scientists studied the disease and searched tirelessly for a cure. He knew he was dying, and he had but one desire and that was to still be alive when Tiberius returned. He had to believe it possible even though inside he had little hope, but he did want to know the truth of what had happened to his best friend all those years ago.

The bay doors had finally closed, shutting out the darkness beyond, and the assembled officers were dispersing. Xander looked around and saw they were almost alone. "Did you tell him?"

Kehoe knew what he meant without having to ask. "What point was there? He will find out for himself. I gave him access to the case files, but they will be of less help than he hopes. Many of the records were lost."

"Covered up, you mean."

"You cannot prove there was a conspiracy; if it was part of a big cover-up then it was ordered from the top. You know the trouble you will find yourself in if you make accusations like that."

"My testimony? Was that *lost* also?"

"Your testimony was of little use. You could only vouch for MacAlpin's character up until that point in time. You spent the rest of that time in prison on the planet and were only released ten years later. You did not even know they were all dead. What you had to say had little bearing on the case. Your appearance after your ordeal gave more fuel for the case against him. You acknowledged that he sent you, despite knowing it was a hostile situation on the planet."

"Any unknown situation is potentially hostile—it goes with the job!" Xander cut her off. "I refuse to believe that Stephen knowingly sent me into danger—to destroy me." He turned on his heel and strode away, unable to listen to any more. He had an unshakeable feeling there had been a cover-up and that Kehoe was aware of it. A conspiracy to disguise the truth and leave the dead Stephen MacAlpin condemned as a coward and mass-murderer. The blood of hundreds of souls had been laid at his door and he was unable to defend himself or to tell the truth of what had really happened, and their cries for justice echoed over the decades as the events were pushed aside as though it had never occurred.

He returned to his office and sat down at the desk. He pulled open the drawer where he had placed the photograph with its broken frame. The cracked glass seemed to symbolize his feelings—a friendship shattered like the glass, Stephen's son the one thing reminding him of the man with whom he had sworn brotherhood. Now, even Tiberius was gone; gone to make his career among the stars, carrying the weight of his father's supposed crime on his shoulders. He laid the photograph on the desk and rested his head down on his arms. "*Why*?!" He remembered the fear he experienced every day in prison; the waiting, hoping that every new day would see his friend coming to liberate him, and the heartache every day that passed without hearing anything. His captors had not been gentle with him and he had been beaten often and forced to spend days in the dark with his hands locked behind him in heavy metal cuffs. Every day that passed dragged him deeper into despair. As each day eventually blended into one, he lost track of time and it had been a great shock to learn on his release that ten years had passed, and that Stephen was dead.

"Why did you do it?"

"*Xander, you have to believe me—I didn't do it.*"

It was like a whisper, but it seemed so real, so audible, that Xander sat up and looked around. "Stephen?"

There was no response of course as his mind was playing tricks. He looked down at the photograph of his friend. "I want to believe it. Tiberius keeps having dreams where you seem to be showing him what happened. I keep thinking you are speaking to me." He rubbed his eyes and stood the broken frame upright. "I am not ashamed of you, Stephen. I'll not hide your photograph any more. Forgive me." He laughed slightly. "They'll think I'm mad if they catch me talking to you." He sighed and pressed the touchscreen interface set into his desk.

The holographic screen popped up, hovering over the desk. "Hello, Rear Admiral Galen," said the pleasant female voice he had chosen for his computer. "You have two hundred and seventy-seven new messages in your inbox."

"Oh, delete them all!" Xander gave a light laugh.

"Are you certain, Rear Admiral? There are seventy-five marked urgent; two are marked personal, and two hundred are past their deadline."

"Delete messages past their deadline."

"Complying. Would you like me to read your personal messages to you?"

"No! You know I always read them myself!" He laughed a moment later, realizing he had snapped at his own personal computer interface settings. He ran his finger down the keypad and opened the first of the personal messages. It was from Tiberius—a recorded message before he had left. The second was also from Tiberius; sent just moments after launch.

It was short: *I am glad you were there. It would have been bad luck to go without you watching. Thank you.* That was all. He went back to the recorded message and listened again, smiling. "Save message. Now, give me the urgent ones in order of importance." He leaned back in his chair and settled down to his first full day in the admiral's office.

11
Xander's Testimony

Tiberius left Ross in charge of the bridge and headed for engineering. The chief engineer, Lieutenant Commander Konane Akina, was a tall, broad-shouldered man with tanned skin. He looked up as the captain came in. "*Aloha,* Captain. Want a grand tour?"

Tiberius nodded. "Would be the perfect opportunity while Commander Ross has the Bridge so, yes, please." He was wondering how to broach the subject of which he had come to speak. He listened as Akina showed him around the state-of-the-art engineering. "It is amazing—it makes the *Victorious* look quite primitive! A question, Chief. Can you make modifications to personal quarters? Mine for instance? Explain the soundproofing to me. I mean, can anything be heard from room to room?"

Akina shook his head. "Each room is fully soundproofed, for crew privacy."

"So a shout for instance?"

"Would not be heard unless the intercom was open? Correct."

Tiberius smiled. "So, in your opinion, there is no need to work on the soundproofing?"

"Not at all, sir. It is the best there is. Like everything else on the *Invincible*. She is an excellent ship."

Tiberius nodded and thanked Akina for the tour and headed off, making his way back to the bridge. He was happy to hear that no-one would hear him crying if the dreams returned. Without Lashinda, he had to cope alone, and he was not sure he liked the prospect. He paused and changed direction and he made his way to the infirmary to meet the new chief medical officer. He wished the *Victorious*'s doctor had been transferred;

he had always trusted him, and he did not know the new one, but he would give her the benefit of the doubt. He looked in and saw Doctor Rivkah Malachi sitting at her desk, looking over crew medical records. She looked up when she heard footsteps and smiled. "Captain MacAlpin, we have not met properly yet."

He shook her outstretched hand and smiled. "Welcome aboard." He glanced at the screen and made a face. "You are studying me?"

"Familiarizing myself. I was reading the psychiatric report—the most recent one. Everyone connected with the *Wryneck* has an extensive report."

Tiberius looked at her and then nodded. "Of course."

"I was studying yours closely," she went on. "Your father's story has had a profound impact on you from childhood." She touched the screen. "I see a reference to dreams, would you care to tell me a little more? The report is not helpful; stating only that you suffer from these dreams. There is nothing there to tell me how it may affect your performance as commanding officer."

Tiberius reddened. "So you have decided they affect me? Isn't that a little presumptive?" He found her dark eyes compelling and looked at her, almost unable to look away. She was a handsome woman, her face friendly and warm.

She shook her head. "The word 'suffer' is used in the report, and comments on the likelihood that this could affect performance. It would be better for both of us if you were honest with me. If you do not wish to go into details of the dreams, then I will not press you. I am sorry, you came to meet me, not to be interrogated."

Tiberius nodded and decided to answer her. "They trouble me from time to time and do affect my sleep but do not affect my ability to perform my duties as commanding officer of this ship. If a time comes when they do begin to have an adverse effect, I will come to you for the necessary medication to aid sleep. That is all you need to be aware of at this time. Am I clear?"

"Perfectly, Captain. So long as you are aware that my position as chief medical officer means I have the responsibility for the wellbeing of *every* crew member in my hands and that includes my commanding officer."

He knew exactly what she meant. Only the CMO had authority over the captain should the need arise. He nodded. "I think we understand each other."

She switched off the screen. "You know I am the only member of the crew with no connection with the *Wryneck*?"

"We're a psychological project?!"

She shook her head. "No, Captain, but it *would* make an interesting study. Do not read more into this voyage than there actually is."

"If Kehoe wanted to make a study of the effects, or supposed effects, of what my father did, this would be just the way she would plan it. A neutral doctor, in the position of being able to observe each of the crew." Tiberius struggled to keep from getting angry.

"Don't make yourself angry over something that is not true."

He closed his eyes and sighed. "I'm sorry. I should have learned by now that getting defensive isn't going to help." He turned away and went to the door.

Doctor Malachi watched until the door closed and turned the screen back on and added the words 'touchy' and 'defensive' to the captain's profile. She entered in a note that he was holding a grudge, perhaps even subconsciously, against Admiral Kehoe. She had not lied to him; her role did not include profiling the crew, but it was an interest of hers and it was worth making a note of anything that could potentially affect the performance of the ship's CO.

Tiberius headed back to the bridge, wondering why he had allowed himself to get defensive. He warned himself to be careful; it was almost as though he had a target painted on his back. A high-profile command—Stephen MacAlpin's son—it all added up to being a nightmare for him. He stepped onto the bridge and sat in the command chair for the first time since leaving space-dock; he had been roaming the ship since he had seen the dock doors close, shutting them away from sight.

Ross held out a tablet. "You have not looked at the mission brief yet, sir. May I suggest that you take a look now?"

Tiberius stopped him with a smile. "Of course, you wish to know what our orders are—where we are heading. I'm sorry, I was excited to see the ship at work. I got a tour of engineering and had a chat with the new CMO—she seems an efficient doctor. She had read my profile already."

"One of the top of her field to ever come out of Jerusalem. Her recommendations and awards are phenomenal. Her grandmother was one of the people instrumental in finally bringing peace to the Middle East. I read her record."

Tiberius grinned. "Nothing but the best for us, eh, Kirbie?"

Ross returned the smile. "I won't press you, but Helm really does need a direction."

"Helm, steady as she goes. Keep on this heading until I give the order. Maintain current speed."

"Aye aye, Captain."

Ross looked around and was pleased to see everyone going on with their work, quietly and professionally. He sat down in his chair at the captain's right hand and touched the arm of the chair. The arm opened up to display a screen where the first officer could see all the necessary readings; speed, heading etc. He busied himself while he waited for the captain to read the official orders.

Tiberius sat a while, looking around the bridge at his officers. They were working silently unless communication was necessary. In fact, the only two talking quietly together were the chief science officer and his assistant who were putting some charts together at the captain's request and they were comparing notes as they worked on compiling accurate records. After a while, they gathered up their work and headed off to a lab where they would have some more instruments to work with.

As the door closed behind them, Tiberius leaned back in his seat and opened the file containing the orders and notes for the mission. He opened the first document which was officially welcoming him aboard as captain. He marked it as read with his thumbprint in the corner and then opened the next document. His father's picture met his eyes. A black line was drawn through it and a red question mark superimposed over his father's face. The document was headed 'what did happen thirty years ago?' He went a little pale and stood up. "Ross, take over but come and see me in my Ready Room when I send for you." He turned and disappeared through the door at the far side of the bridge.

Ross immediately took the centre seat, wondering what was up.

•

Tiberius sat at the desk and opened the second document again. There was a brief outline building a timeline of known events and positions and a few notes from Stephen MacAlpin's last logs. Notes from the hearing followed; these notes were more extensive, and he read them closely. He could see his father had not been condemned outright—everything had been looked at. One note interested him; commenting that the absence of the first officer's testimony meant they were unable to make a ruling. It seemed that only Xander's testimony would have swung it either way. A note below stated that it was filed as an "Unsolved Mystery" and could be reopened at any time should new evidence be uncovered. That made him wonder why the buff file in the admiral's office had borne the red stamp CLOSED rather than UNSOLVED. He moved onto the next file. This one was an amendment to the case notes, the inclusion of Commander Galen's testimony. There were two items in the file; one was a text file, and the other an icon marked audio/visual, and his finger hovered over this icon.

A signed testimony and an interrogation; that was all they had needed. Would Xander condemn his father, even unwittingly? He was almost too scared to find out. They had waited years for the testimony of the only member of the *Wryneck*'s crew who could give them an idea of what had happened. Xander was missing for ten years and spent the time immediately following his release undergoing intense hospital treatment. Notwithstanding the fact that the news of the death of his best friend and the entire crew must have been upsetting, he had made his testimony.

Tiberius held his breath and then tapped the icon for the video link. He leaned back in his chair and watched the screen. It was uncanny to sit there, watching Xander, still a relatively young man, thin and haggard from his ordeal. It was as though he were watching him—in the flesh, his clear voice answering the questions put to him. He wondered where he had plucked up the courage to speak to the court. The exhaustion and illness in his face were clearly visible and he was not requested to stand. A medical orderly sat beside him, with the authority to stop the questioning if it got too much for him.

The questions were simple at first, mostly about what he remembered of the mission and the events leading up to the imprisonment. Xander answered clearly, although his voice was tired. He told them he had been sent ahead to learn about the people with whom they were to make contact.

"Was there anything to make you believe Captain MacAlpin was up to anything?"

"No, nothing. I was following his orders as usual. There was no reason for me to be worried or to doubt them."

"What about the meeting? Did that take place as planned?"

"Yes. Steve—Captain MacAlpin and I attended as arranged. It went well. They were a strange people but there was nothing to make us concerned."

"Were you ever separated, during your time at the meeting?"

Xander shook his head but then nodded. "For a little while, yes, but not for long."

"In your opinion, Commander Galen, could this mean that something happened to change him? Something that would make him abandon you and destroy his ship—murdering the entire crew and taking his own life?"

Tiberius' heart almost skipped a beat as he watched.

Xander took his time, his hands tightly clenched. "Captain MacAlpin's loyalty to the service and to his friends and colleagues is unquestionable—I do not believe that anything would have shaken this—he would rather..." He paused, and the presiding officer looked up.

"He would rather what, Commander Galen? Rather die? That surely is what we are trying to determine here. Something, somehow connected with meeting these people, caused a once loyal officer to abandon his friend and first officer, and destroy an entire ship and crew."

Xander shook his head. The medical orderly put her hand on his back.

Tiberius clenched his fists. They had forced Xander to put words in their mouths, twisting his testimony to look as though he had incriminated his best friend, allowing them to say he had condemned him himself. He could not take his eyes off the screen as he watched the scene continuing. Xander was leaning forward, his face buried in his hands, clearly understanding what had happened.

The orderly looked up and spoke for the first time. "No more questions please, Commander Galen needs to rest." She stood up, helped Xander up and steered him to the door.

Tiberius stopped the recording and leaned back in his seat, rubbing his hand across his face. He understood now why Xander would not tell him what happened. He restarted the video and watched it again, right to the end this time. He saw Xander being guided from the room and saw the senior officers putting their heads together. He felt he was holding his breath and his fists were clenched as he waited to hear their final verdict.

The officers debated and argued for some time—some appeared in favour of clearing MacAlpin. "Galen doesn't know what happened," one of them pointed out. "I think that is clear."

"Look at what happened to him," another argued. "MacAlpin deserted him. He would still be in that prison now but for his captors using him as a hostage!"

The presiding officer nodded. "I will close the case. If fresh evidence comes to light it can be reopened. I dislike doing this to an officer of whom we have always spoken so highly. But a result is required—I am ruling gross negligence manslaughter with a wilful and reckless disregard to the life of his crew, and a disregard to the duty of care he owed them as their commanding officer. Case closed; pending further evidence."

Tiberius switched off the video as the officers stood up to leave the courtroom. "That's how they did it. They forced Xander into incriminating my father—although barely—and then they wrote him off." He sat for a long time, almost stunned, and then pulled himself together and touched the screen to open the third file.

This one was his official orders. There was a star chart and a list of coordinates. He looked at them for a while mulling over the familiarity of the charts—he had gone over them so many times before that it was as clear as if he had been there himself. He opened the final document, knowing he would find the answer inside. He read it to the end and his eyes opened wide. He knew they were going to the same area of space, but it was even more clear now that their mission was the same; to contact the same people, and to find out what had happened all those years ago. He pressed the button on the desk and asked his first officer to come in.

Ross arrived a moment later and took a seat.

"You will be wanting to know what our mission is." He touched the screen again and looked at the mission brief. "Our mission is to take the *Invincible* back into the region of space where the *Wryneck* was lost. We are to make contact with the alien world my father met—to negotiate for the same treaty."

He paused and Ross leaned back in his chair. "I get it; they have sent us to find out what happened thirty years ago and, if there is anything to discover, they want it to be us who find it."

Tiberius nodded. "Yes, and I don't know what I am feeling right now. It's finally sinking in although I knew the general idea from the start."

"Shock, I expect. It's not at all surprising in the circumstances. You would *never* have imagined they would send *you* to find out what happened to your father!"

Tiberius agreed with a sigh. "I should have—they kept talking about it. And the deliberate choosing of me as captain, instead of your experience."

Ross smiled. "We've been over that. I am content to use that experience to assist you to be as good a captain as your father was. If he was innocent, we'll show them—together."

Tiberius' eyes lit up as he smiled, seeming to finally understand that he really was not alone in this. "Thanks, Kirbie, that means a lot. I kind of felt alone; I must remember that I am not. Come on, shall we go and spring our destination on them?"

They both stood up and Ross stepped aside and allowed Tiberius to precede him as they returned to the bridge. The bridge crew looked around as they took their seats in the centre of the bridge. Tiberius settled back in his chair and crossed one leg over the other. "I expect you are all wondering about our destination, and why so much mystery has surrounded our mission." He paused and then went on. "We are to go to the Tamoran System." He saw their faces. "Yes, Tamora. To the last known position of the *Wryneck*—the *exact* location. Our mission is to uncover and solve a thirty-year-old mystery. Xander Galen was held captive by the Tamoran government; he suffered greatly at their hands and was used as a hostage after ten years a prisoner. I believe these people, or at least their leaders, know exactly what happened to the *Wryneck* and why. I am convinced there must have been something that occurred at the meeting with the Tamoran Council. Oh, and we also have to secure the trade deal they were sent to obtain." He turned to the Helm and gave her the coordinates from the mission brief. "Moderate speed—we have four years each way! We might have an ultimate goal, but we are all going further into deep space than we have been before. We would not be true to ourselves if we ignored this chance to explore." He leaned back in his chair. "Let's do it." Something deep inside him was thrilled at their assignment. Excited that, despite every other feeling inside, he had been chosen to lead the search for what happened to cause his father to destroy his ship.

12

Thoughts of the Past

Tiberius stretched out on his bed that night, his hands tucked under his head. He had a lot on his mind and sleep eluded him, nor could he rest easy. He was troubled by what he had learned from the files, and he was missing Lashinda. He closed his eyes, fighting wakefulness. He must have drifted off to sleep because he started awake sometime later and sat bolt upright, wondering what had woken him. He listened for a moment, but all was silent. Then he realized he had been dreaming; that must have been what woke him. It had not been the usual dream. His mind had been occupied with thoughts of Xander and his testimony and the dream had been of Xander chained up in an alien prison, waiting for his friend to come and rescue him—only to wait in vain. He reached for the bottle of water which stood on the shelf at the head of the bed and took a long drink before getting up and wrapping the blanket around his shoulders. Going to the computer, he recorded an entry in his private log and then opened his messages. One was from his mother, telling him to be a good boy. *When would she remember he was in his thirties?*

There was also a message from Lashinda; just a brief one saying she loved him and good night. He smiled and replied. He leaned back and began to record a message for Xander, telling him of the files he had seen. "I understand why you could not tell me—you would have had to say they put words in your mouth. You were not well enough to testify and they took advantage of you. I *will* find out what happened. I promise." He paused and then, "Send message." He sat back and began to study various reports.

The computer pinged fifteen minutes later, and the computer informed him that he had a communication. "Open message."

It was from Xander and was short. *If you can find the truth then I can die happy and your father will rest easy.*

"Stop talking about dying!" Tiberius responded.

Death is inevitable. I do not fear it. I only fear not knowing why.

There was a long pause; about twenty minutes before the computer cheerily informed him of another message. He opened it and saw it contained a file.

They do not know I kept this.

Tiberius clicked play and heard his father's voice. *I am worried about our meeting with the government—things are not what they seem. I can feel it.*

Another message from Xander popped up. *That was from his personal log—they never found it. I will not give them more ammunition.*

Tiberius tapped audio and asked, "What did he mean?"

Xander's voice was quiet, as though he had been afraid of being asked. Text had been easier. "About things not being what they seemed? I don't know but he was apprehensive about the meeting. That's all I know—something alarmed him; they would say he knew something was going to happen. Perhaps even that he knew I was to be arrested. They already said he betrayed me, and I cannot fuel the fire further. He was my friend, I knew him; he would never betray me. Not like they said he did."

"Xander, I want you to tell me what happened in prison—one day! I will not ask you now."

"One day, but not now. Good night."

Tiberius leaned back for a while and allowed this piece of information to process. His father had been worried. He tried to analyse the tone of his voice in the recording. He *had* sounded worried, but not scared. Whatever it was that he worried over had not given him cause to be afraid. "Save file," he told the computer. "Location—encrypted file JUSTICE."

When the computer informed him that the file was saved, he stood up and went to make some coffee. That was a luxury he permitted himself—real coffee. Not the gritty instant stuff that came from the beverage machines located in each of the crew quarters and in all the recreation and dining areas. In his quarters he kept a filter coffee-maker—his work allowed for few indulgences. This was one he could not do without. He closed his eyes as he took a sip and leaned back in his chair.

•

Back on Earth at Fleet HQ, Xander sat at his desk for a long time after the screen faded before he got up to fetch water and the pills he had been prescribed. He knew he should go to his apartment and try to sleep. His doctors told him to take care of himself, but there were many times sleep eluded him, and he ended up staying at his desk for long hours; not always working, sometimes he just sat there. He was glad Tiberius had seen the recording of the hearing—he *had* wanted to tell him, but the memories it evoked were far too painful. Prison, loneliness, pain. He shook his head, trying to shake off the memories and looked at his wrists. Twenty years had faded the scars left by the heavy chains with which he had been held captive. He shivered, remembering the helplessness—locked in a tiny, dark cell and chained to the wall by his wrists and ankles. On rare occasions when he had been taken from his cell, his face had been covered and hands at his elbows had guided him as he shuffled his shackled feet, trying to keep his balance. Those occasions were shrouded in pain and he remembered little but being strapped down and poked and prodded; bright lights shone in his face— his eyes always covered. He remembered frantic efforts to break free before needles pricked his arms and he passed out before finding himself back in his cell, chained up to the wall. He buried his face in shaking hands. Twenty years after he was released, it still haunted him. It dawned on him then, clearly, for perhaps the first time that they were unable to find a cure because his illness was not caused by his ten-year imprisonment, although the hardship and suffering would have contributed to it considerably. Perhaps there was no cure because no-one had thought of looking for other answers. The needles and experiments—the disease which was slowly killing him was caused by the aliens who had kept him prisoner. He winced, rubbing his arm where the needles had penetrated his skin. "No! Stephen, please don't let them find out that you left me to this on purpose," he whispered, looking at the photo on the desk. "You didn't betray me. *Please* don't let that be the truth." Quite upset now, he got up and went to lie down on the couch under the window, to try and rest a bit; maybe if he just closed his eyes for a spell. He was asleep in moments, his tired body finally giving in and letting him rest.

He awoke after a few hours and stretched, stiff from being curled up on the couch rather than in his bed. He rubbed his forehead and looked up as footsteps approached. He smiled when he saw it was his android aide.

"I saw you sleeping, Rear Admiral. I know you sleep for only a few hours at a time, so I have kept looking in on you—here is your coffee." She held out a steaming mug.

Xander took it gratefully as he swung his legs to the floor and sat upright. "Is anyone else around, or have I managed to avoid discovery?"

"It is 03:54, Admiral. You are the only one here. Do you wish me to summon a shuttle cab? I believe you would benefit from a few more hours' rest in your own bed."

He knew she was programmed to attend to his welfare needs, but it did feel nice to have someone care about him. He nodded. "Thank you. Have one here in ten minutes." He sipped his coffee and watched the android leave. You could swear she was human; the way she moved and walked was just like a human woman. *Great progress has been made in robotics*, he thought. He found himself watching the way her clothes moved on her hips, and his cheeks reddened. He could not remember when he felt like that the last time, feeling his heart beat a little faster. His work had always left little time for relationships, and then the long imprisonment. Well, he had never thought he could fall in love again, not after the experiments the aliens had performed on him. And she was not even a real woman, but he knew he had not felt this way over the sight of a female form for a long time.

He was finished with his coffee and had splashed water on his face by the time she returned to tell him the cab was waiting. He picked up his greatcoat and left the office, leaving the android to see to the lights and locking up. On arriving at his apartment, he let himself in and undressed quickly. He knew that sitting down for a rest would be fatal; he was so tired that he would just fall asleep. When he got into his bed, he was asleep almost as soon as his head touched the pillow.

Later when he woke again, he rolled over and looked at his watch. He frowned at first and closed his eyes before opening them again and re-focusing on the glowing numbers on the watch face. He had not been dreaming. It did say 13:47—he was late; by almost five hours. He tapped the chip communication device in his wrist and gave the call sign for the admiral's office. When she answered, she did not sound angry, just concerned. "Are you all right?"

"I'm sorry, I only just woke. I can be there in half an hour. I forgot about the meeting."

"Take the day off, Galen. We all agreed you would have some bad days and your work is not to be bound by regulations and timetables. If you have slept so long, then that is good for I know sleep is not easy for you. Get some more sleep or go for a walk. You can report in tomorrow."

Xander thanked her. He did feel better for the rest and suspected that his aide had already reported that he had worked late. That was confirmed a short while later by the arrival of the HQ's medical officer who was an old friend of his. When the buzzer sounded and the visitor announced his identity, Xander smiled slightly and told the computer to unlock the door and let the doctor in.

The doctor came through to the bedroom and saw Xander lying curled up against the pillows. "How do you feel?"

"Just tired. I overslept and was late for work. They've told me to take the rest of the day off. I was thinking about getting up and trying to do something." Xander sighed. "I don't seem to have the energy."

The doctor held his wrist and was quiet for a moment and then smiled. "You just need to take it easy when you get tired. Let me have a good look at you."

"They won't find it, you know, Clark." Xander watched as the doctor fastened the medi-reader to his upper arm. It was a small computer device that could read all the body signs through the skin without the need for thermometers and other gadgets. It also did away with the need to take blood samples for so many things, of which Xander was glad. He hated needles but put up with the important ones that he had to have.

"Find what?" Clark Tierney asked. He watched the readings as they came up and made some notes.

"A cure. They won't find one. They aren't looking for the right things." He turned his head on the pillows and sighed. "It was caused by the experiments when I was in prison." He shut his lips tightly, having said more than he meant to.

The doctor said nothing but patted Xander on the shoulder as he removed the device. "You know we will keep on trying. I would like you to come into hospital soon for some more tests. If what you say is true, then we should take more blood samples and test it for anything and everything—things we know about and things we don't. I'm worried about you, Xander; why did you never say anything? You were freed twenty years ago—did you not know or guess?'

Xander shook his head. "No, I just accepted what the doctors said then—that deprivation and the beatings had broken my health."

"They believed it to be cancer at one stage."

Another shake of the head. "I never believed it. Had it been, there are lots of treatments now. I have flashbacks to the torture. It is obvious they caused it, but I do not know why." He sighed and Dr Tierney saw him look utterly dejected for a moment.

The doctor took a moment to pull the sheets straight. "Try not to let it get you down. I'll look in on you later—and arrange a date for you to come to the hospital." He smiled as Xander curled up under the sheets. "We'll have a darn good try to find a cure—don't give up hope."

"And don't pretend, I beg you." Xander's voice was quiet. "I am dying—there may be no cure. I can accept it. Please don't mollycoddle me."

Tierney nodded. "I won't pretend. But all I will say is that where there is life there is hope and you're not dead yet!" His Irish accent strengthened as he spoke. He was from Limerick and maintained the strength of his accent despite not having been home for over fifty years.

Xander laughed. "Your bedside manner is atrocious."

The doctor shook his head. "No, it's not—your sense of humour is." He was pleased to see Xander laugh, he had looked so tired of late. Anyone who knew him best was aware of the adjustments he had to make—his promotion and new role, keeping a close eye on his conditions and watching his young friend, Tiberius, head off into space on a long mission to the same area of space where his best friend and crewmates had perished. His emotions were, understandably, all over the place right now. "I'll leave you to sleep—I'll call later to see how you are feeling." Clark clapped Xander once again on the shoulder and let himself out of the apartment. He went back to the hospital via the admiral's office to give her a report.

•

Xander felt much better when he woke again. He got up after a while to make some coffee and pulled on his dressing gown and went to stand on the balcony, looking out over the city as he sipped his drink. He wondered if there were any more tests they could do; he had endured many tests, examinations, and blood tests over the years, and no-one had even remotely hinted at anything alien. Was that because nothing showed up? Or was it because anything strange had been discounted, just triggering tests for known diseases? The hospital had categorically stated that it was not cancer, at least not any form known to them, but said it could be a new one. He did not agree—he never had. He had always known it was connected to his captivity but had never registered its significance until now. But he knew now; his illness and subsequent death would be a direct result of whatever these aliens had done to him. If only he knew what they had done. He only had the sounds and feelings to go on, the pain and terror. He had never seen them touch him, never saw what they used. He sighed as he looked over the dark city, its many lights twinkling in the darkness. There was always the niggling question in his mind; had Stephen left him there, a prisoner condemned for testing and death? His death had only been avoided by the fact that the planet's government had needed a hostage and he had been a controversial prisoner, because of the events surrounding the *Wryneck* and her crew. He remembered nothing about the day of his release but being dragged from his cell, hooded and chained, half-carried to a shuttle and a long flight before being dragged into a bright room, still hooded and hearing lots of voices as he was forced to kneel. He remembered a gentle hand on his shoulder and the hood being removed. He had looked up slowly into the face of one of their own officers and saw the concern in her eyes. He had fainted then and had found himself in hospital when he woke. He had hardly been able to believe he was free.

He shook himself as though trying to shake off the feelings and memories, finished his coffee and went back into the apartment and rinsed the mug before going to his computer and sitting down to some work he could do from home. There were some files he wanted to trace which would be easier here than from the office.

13
Examining the Reports

Tiberius woke to the sound of his computer announcing an incoming message. He sat up and rubbed his eyes before he got up and went to the machine. There was a message from Xander with some files attached. *Keep these quiet; it is not known that I have them. They are some of the log entries which have never been acknowledged.*

Tiberius opened them up and had a quick look before responding, begging Xander not to risk getting into trouble on his account. He saved them into the file he was compiling and then went for a shower and dressed before heading to the bridge to start another day.

They had just returned to their original course after a month-long detour to map a previously unknown star system with a large asteroid field close to their original flight path and they had been ordered to make the survey. The chief science officer was busy now in the astrometry lab with his team making up the requested charts and Tiberius was making a start on his report for HQ. It was their first big exploration under his command, and it excited him; the exuberance showed in his voice as he recorded his report.

He tapped the touchscreen on the arm of his chair and studied it for a while and then glanced at Ross on the seat to his right. "A job well done. The charts are going to be very useful in the future—and we were here first."

Ross nodded. "You coordinated the mission perfectly. My official log will reflect that."

Tiberius blushed slightly, remembering how he had thought Ross would be difficult to work with. "Thanks, it does mean a lot." He paused for a moment and then glanced up again. "Are there charts? Of the Tamoran System? The *Wryneck* was there for mapping too. They had been in the area for some time before they met with the council—that seems to be when everything went pear-shaped."

Ross nodded and leaned over to the arm of the captain's chair. His fingers tapped rapidly for a moment or two and then he swiped the screen a couple of times with his thumb before straightening up. "There, sir." He always called the captain 'sir' when they were on duty—he was a consummate professional and would never dream of calling him by his first name as Tiberius insisted when they were off duty. "These are detailed charts and some in-depth reports on the various planets. You will be interested in Tamora itself." He tapped the screen again. "And this is the detailed report on Tamora which your father wrote."

Tiberius pressed a button on the arm of the chair and the screen tilted so he could read it better. "Thanks, have astrometry collate all the information we have on Tamora—the planet, its people and environs. I want to know *everything* there possibly is to know. There must be some information about them that has been missed. Something that will tell us the truth about what happened."

"Yes, sir. I will go and speak to them now."

Tiberius looked up and smiled. "Thanks, it will be a great help. I'll read this report of my father's."

Ross paused and looked down at the captain. "Don't let it become an obsession. The search for the truth will destroy you if you allow it to be the only thing that matters to you. You will put the mission, your life, your ship and the lives of your crew in jeopardy if you allow that one desire you have to take control."

"I won't. I promise. You worry about me too much."

"That's part of my job." Ross turned away and left the bridge to carry out his appointed task.

Tiberius settled back in his chair and read the report his father had made after his first encounter with the Tamoran people. He read slowly and carefully, looking for any clues—any tips that would be of help to their mission. He knew his father had been wary of these newly discovered aliens so, surely, he would have left some form of a clue in a detailed report. The report was clear and concise and contained every detail that had been obtained once the *Wryneck* made its first contact with them. The most obvious underlying emotion was excitement—he could see that clearly. A new, intriguing species of aliens to learn about—it must have thrilled the *Wryneck*'s captain.

But there was a subtle change after a while; a hint of threat and menace crept in when Stephen MacAlpin introduced the idea that there were some things about the Tamorans that worried him. *Things are not entirely what they seem. I have not been able to put my finger on it to my satisfaction. Unlike other worlds we have visited, they seem reluctant to welcome us—there is a tension in the air. It concerns me but I have orders to follow, and I will carry these out to the best of my ability.*

Tiberius drew a breath. He knew it. Either there had been a hostile situation and death had been the only way out, or there had been a conspiracy and the crew of the *Wryneck* had been led into some form of a trap and the only way to save the Fleet's prototype ship from the aliens had been destruction—but why death for every member of the crew? A ship could be destroyed without loss of life—they could transfer to another ship or abandon her in the life-rafts or even be left on the planet while their ship was blown up. Tiberius could see the options. None of them pointed to why they all had to die, or to why his father had killed his entire crew, and himself, leaving only the first officer alive. He knew Xander had not been on the ship when the self-destruct order was given. But why everyone else?

He could find no reasons—no explanation. He opened another report and studied it intently. This one documented the first actual meeting between the captain, the first officer and the leaders of Tamora. Stephen MacAlpin described the silence with which they were greeted and the strange sensation that they were being scanned by the aliens although they had no devices with them. The aliens' eyes were described as cold and piercing—a stare that seemed to penetrate to their very marrow or seemed to. He also described them as looking like a fish's eyes, only a kind of silvery-gold colour. *The eyes of someone who can read your innermost thoughts and feelings without physical contact. They are cold and intense, and they frighten me.*

Tiberius felt his heart skip a beat. His father had been afraid. Did he destroy the ship and crew for fear of what these people might do? He continued to read.

They looked at us for a long time. They never spoke while they appeared to be taking mental notes on our appearance. It seemed hours before their manner changed and we were invited to sit down. Commander Galen seemed a little more shaken than I was—I wanted to ask him what he had felt, what he had experienced—but that would have to wait till later; I couldn't ask while our hosts were present. Suffice it to say that Galen was pale and kept his hands clenched in his lap—was this to keep them from shaking? I looked at my own hands and understood—I instinctively clenched mine too. I tried to catch his eye, but it was as though neither of us dared to look at the other while we were not alone. But he was afraid too. We are used to the unknown; it is a part of our job, and we have all known fear— but never like this.

Tiberius drew a breath and looked at the official files he had received from Admiral Kehoe. He had been right—there was no mention of this encounter in the files, and he did remember the admiral telling him there was no record of that first meeting with the Tamorans. But there *had* been a detailed report which had been removed from the rest of the files and then hidden. He was certain now, that something terrible had happened and that was the reason Xander would not speak of it. Fear was mentioned in the report—a fear they had felt simultaneously. Had Xander been tortured by the aliens at this point, he wondered? Had they been tortured together and somehow Stephen escaped and destroyed the ship to prevent any more of the crew being harmed? What if death had been the only escape? But if that was so, why would he leave his best friend suffering at the hands of the aliens? Surely, he would have tried to help him—or even to kill him rather than let him endure whatever was being done to him. He touched the screen to switch it off and gave the order for their necessary course change; the change that would take them to Tamora. As he leaned back, he wondered how much apprehension would mingle with the excitement at the prospect of visiting a new world—one they had only read about—and one which meant so much to all of them. The planet symbolized the loss of almost an entire generation of their families. Each of them would experience mixed feelings over the intervening months as they travelled toward the planet. He tried hard not to think of it too much. If he was not careful, as Ross had told him, it would become an overwhelming obsession, encompassing every thought, word and deed. He gave himself a mental shake and turned his attention to various reports which had pinged up on the screen for his attention.

14
Serenity

Admiral Kehoe glanced up as her aide looked in and informed her that Rear Admiral Galen had just entered his office. "You asked me to let you know."

"Thank you. Tell him to come and see me."

The aide left and gave Xander the message. He had been expecting a summons and he hurried there immediately, presenting himself with a salute.

"Sit down, Galen." Kehoe waved at a chair in front of the desk. "Are you feeling better?" She knew he had been off quite a bit throughout the last month.

Xander nodded. "I have been permitted to return. I must apologize for my repeated absences; I have had a lot of hospital visits."

She shook her head. "You were offered this position with the full understanding of your situation."

Xander thanked her and sat still, waiting, feeling there was something else besides a polite enquiry about his health.

"Two months ago, and a number of times early last month, certain encrypted files have been downloaded; meaning the encryption network has been hacked into."

"And this involves me how exactly?" Xander was wondering why she was telling him.

"They were hacked and downloaded from your workstation."

Xander was silent for a moment. "You will, of course, have evidence of this?" He was not going to deny or admit any part of this unless she knew for certain.

"I do but, oddly enough, it has only been on days you were absent due to your illness. After the first infiltration, I had your office watched and your workstation monitored. I suspected you at once due to the subject of the files."

"In that case, it cannot possibly have been me."

"Your terminal was accessed remotely by someone who is skilled in hacking. How skilled are you? Please hack into this file." She pointed to the screen and stood up. "Take my seat and let me see how good you are. This file has the same level of security as the copied files."

Xander felt his palms sweating as he sat behind the desk. He sat for a long while, staring at the screen, and then shook his head. "We are wasting time. I do not know where to begin—code breaking was never my strong point."

She nodded, hearing the sincerity in his voice. "I believe you." She paused as he returned to his seat and she resumed hers. "I do not believe, however, that you are entirely innocent in this. The files that were stolen were extremely significant in the MacAlpin case—ones for which I had not authorized the release. Part of me says I should not be suspecting you, as you are very reluctant to talk about those days, but I am not entirely certain."

Xander held his breath for a moment. "I have not hacked into any encrypted networks." He told the truth. He had not, but Serenity had. She had carried out his instructions; downloading the most important files while he had the best alibi—he had been in the hospital, undergoing more tests and had been monitored 24/7. "I also fail to understand why you have deemed it necessary to monitor my terminal—there should be no reason to do so if there is nothing to hide in the case files. You have stated categorically that there was no cover-up; no files removed or tampered with. If this is true, why are you treating me as a suspect?" \

Admiral Kehoe looked at him. *He is not an easy one to fool.* "You are aware of the sensitive nature of the case and there are some facts which, should they come to light, would have serious repercussions. Honesty, integrity, loyalty—they would all be called into question. No-one involved would be exempt. How would you like to keep going over it? Reliving those days?"

Xander watched her face. *I do anyway. Those years are never far from me. And what about Stephen's integrity and loyalty? His honesty?* "Don't lie to me. It is not me you are trying to protect— it is yourself, your own reputation. You were the officer commanding the operation and it was your order that sent us to Tamora, that had us meet the Council. Your orders that left me in a Tamoran prison for ten years. I suffered things I will never put into words, all because I was a pawn in a game of power and politics. Ten years is a long time to go on hoping and praying for rescue. And then to find my crewmates are all dead? Don't you *ever* dare to pretend to me that you even care for one moment! Four hundred and twenty-nine men and women died when the *Wryneck* exploded, and they are not even on your conscience. Never a day will pass when you spare a thought for those who died, and what happened to them was covered up—on your orders!"

"You had better stop now. You have said more than enough—including accuse me of treachery and murder. We all know it was not I who gave the order for the *Wryneck* to be destroyed. It was your friend, the friend who left you to rot and suffer in an alien prison. No, don't say anything—you are supposed to keep yourself calm. Return to your office and take your medication and let's forget this conversation ever took place, Rear Admiral." She dismissed Xander with a look.

The Android, Serenity, came in from her desk in the outer office when she heard his chair creak as he sat down. "Good morning, Rear Admiral." She scanned him with her strange eyes—almost human to look at but not quite. "You are unwell? Your heart rate is too high, and your cheeks are flushed."

"I'm okay, Serenity. I just spoke my mind to Kehoe, and it left me feeling stressed. I'll take my pills and I'll be fine." He took two tablets and swallowed them with some water Serenity poured from the jug on his desk. "Thank you for your concern. Now, I have a job for you. Search this office, and yours, from top to bottom. Every piece of furniture, the coffee maker, the computers, *everything*. Look for something that should not be here. A bug—a tapping device. I have a feeling you will find one."

In her office, Admiral Kehoe took her finger off the button on her intercom. "No, he is not a fool. I know it was you, Galen. You took those files and I just have to prove it!"

Half an hour later, Serenity straightened up from kneeling on the floor with her head under Xander's desk. She held out a flat disc with a blue light flashing on it. "You were under surveillance?"

"Seems so. Can you deactivate it?"

"Of course." Serenity's quick fingers unscrewed the back of the device and there was a blue flash and she looked at him with a smile. "A metal framework and electrical circuits have their uses."

"You short-circuited it?"

"Well, put it like this, Admiral, the next time this device is activated, they will get a shock, literally. I think they will not bug your office again."

Xander laughed. "Well done, Serenity. I'll let you access my computer now. I want you to find out if any messages—anything at all—are being either tracked, or a secret copy being sent to anyone else."

The Android pulled her chair around and got to work. "Is this because of the work you had me do?"

Xander nodded. "It is me they suspect, not you."

"It will not be long before they realize. You were in the hospital and the files needed a computer expert to hack into them. Who better than an Android? We are, at the basic level, just computers."

"Things are beginning to fit together in my mind, and it worries me," Xander told her. He stood up and went to make himself a coffee. As he prepared it, he thought over his talk with the Admiral. He was no fool and it had finally dawned on him that Admiral Kehoe either knew something or had been heavily involved in whatever it was that had happened those thirty years ago and was now involved in a cover-up on a massive scale. He worried about Tiberius and the crew of *Invincible* being sent to the same place. He had a horrible feeling that, somehow, Admiral Kehoe was responsible for his imprisonment and torture. Maybe not in so many words, she may not actually have ordered it, but it was because of her, he just knew it—which also meant the deaths of his friends and comrades were down to her too. He told himself to keep calm; that the truth would come out and he must not let his grief and anger get the better of him. He did grieve deeply for them—ten years of hoping they would come for him, only to then find they were all dead. Even twenty years further on, the pain was raw. He clenched his fists as he waited for the water to come to the right temperature. He had another reason for being angry; his doctor had told him that he was on borrowed time, that he could not say how long there was left before this unknown illness claimed him. They suspected at least a year, but it could be shorter than that, he was afraid to hope it would be longer. They could not even tell him what effects he would suffer as it progressed. Yes, he was frightened; not knowing what to expect scared him. He was not afraid of dying—he never had been. If you were, you did not go into space to face all manner of unknown perils. It was knowing he was dying and not knowing how he would be at the end that scared him. He had expected to die every day in prison and the one thing he feared the most was being alone at the end. He shook himself and poured the hot water which was ready now. He looked over his shoulder at the Android bent over her work at his computer. "Serenity." He paused as quickly as he had begun.

She looked up. "I have put an encryption block on your terminal; it will act as a jammer and any attempt to read, or intercept communication will fail, and it will alert you to activity."

Xander smiled. "Thank you. Are you up to a little more work?"

"Of the same kind?"

"Yes, I need more proof—memos, logs, anything from the time the *Wryneck* left for space, to the time HQ say they lost contact."

Serenity nodded. "Yes, sir." She returned to her office and began to set up the same security as on Xander's computer.

Xander watched her go with a smile. He had always thought Androids were just robots, in humanoid form, able to interact with others, but unable to think or feel anything that was not in their programming. Perhaps they were so, when they were first developed, but now they were capable of more than before and there was a loyalty he had noticed in Serenity. She would do anything he asked of her, not because he was her superior, but because she wanted to serve him. He had seen the eagerness with which she performed tasks for him, and how she did care about him, always making him coffee, ensuring he took his medication and kept his appointments with the doctor. He took a sip of his coffee and finally got to work on what he had been about to start when Kehoe had called him. This last encounter and the subsequent discovery in his office had taught him something; that Admiral Kehoe was dangerous, and he could not trust her.

His computer beeped and there was a message from Tiberius, checking he was okay. *I worry about you. Please tell me the treatment is going okay—and I'll try not to worry so much.* He sent a response, telling Tiberius not to fuss; that he was touched by his concern. He still could not tell him the truth, however—he could not bear Tiberius to be burdened by that while he had enough on his plate with the mission. He tapped "send". A moment later there was another beep, heralding another message. This one was from Serenity. Some files were attached to the message and he knew she had found something.

Is it bad? He acknowledged receipt.

Her response came back in seconds. *Read for yourself and judge.* She appeared in his office a moment later. "There are more, this is just the start. Read them and then take a break. You are supposed to be taking things easy."

Xander smiled. "You really care."

"I am programmed to serve you. If you keep to a routine, then your illness will be more manageable."

"I do appreciate it. The way you have everything under control—it does help."

Serenity smiled. "I am yours to command."

He watched her go back to the door and smiled to himself. These Androids were so advanced; would it be possible for them to develop feelings? He got the distinct feeling that Serenity's loyal service had something else at the bottom of it. Could the Android be in love with him? As far-fetched as it sounded, he began to realize the truth. Her care was that of a wife and it touched him. She was a machine, a computer—nothing but an array of circuits. But she had developed an affection for the man she was to serve. Right now, in the midst of all this uncertainty and everything that was going on with Kehoe, he felt warmed to know there was someone he could talk to; to reach out to when his illness progressed. He felt light-headed all of a sudden—he would not be alone. Serenity would be with him. He knew that for certain as if she had told him so herself and he was suddenly not so afraid any more. He glanced up when he saw she was still in the doorway. "Do Androids eat?" he asked.

"We do not need to, but we can if we wish. Our system turns anything we ingest into electricity which boosts function, much in the same way as for yourself only ours is not a chemical reaction." Serenity waited, wondering why he asked.

Xander nodded. "In that case, will you have dinner with me tonight? I have a desire for companionship."

She smiled. "Would you like me to make a reservation? Or are you asking me to your apartment?"

Xander blushed. "Am I that transparent? Make a reservation somewhere nice. We'll go out of uniform. Do you—"

"—have clothes other than uniform? Of course. I will surprise you." She headed back into her office and, out of sight, gave a twirl. She had always been told that, as artificial intelligence, she had no ability to love—it was not in her programming. But she was a new Android and their programming had been enhanced to make them much more human than ever before. She knew what she felt for Xander Galen must be love, and it seemed he felt something too. He had said he wanted companionship. He must be lonely; he had no family—never having been blessed that way. He was older now and dying; of course he needed someone. Her kindness and attentiveness to him must have drawn him towards her although she had not intended it. She realized they must have done what she had heard humans call 'falling in love'. If she could make him happy, to ease some of the loneliness and pain, then she would have her reward. She began to look at various restaurants where they could go and not be bothered by too many younger officers and chose somewhere off base and in the centre of the city. Less chance of anyone talking about them too.

Xander settled down to his work with a lighter heart. Having been told by the doctors that they could not tell him how long he had left, he had decided that he was not going to let life pass him by any more. He was going to live his life to the fullest and enjoy the time that remained to him. He did not look on Serenity as an AI but saw her as a colleague; a friend and now, someone he had fallen in love with. There were those who would question him; perhaps even rebuke him—they would say it was wrong. They would point out that she was a robot; an artificial being, a computer—her organs and brain nothing more than circuit boards; but who were they to say an Android could not think and feel—their programmes were so much more enhanced than even just a few centuries ago. He was older now, and terminally ill. He did not feel the urge to start a family, and, in fact, he could not— the alien experiments had put paid to that. He just needed to love and be loved by someone special, someone who would be with him in his last days. To know he would leave behind someone who would miss him when he was gone meant something. He wondered if she felt the same—he thought she did. Her reaction when he asked her out had not been of surprise—she had not hesitated or found an excuse. She had accepted immediately, almost as though she had been eager to accept. Could she have been waiting for him to ask?

He began to prepare a small message for Tiberius, telling him how things were. *You will be pleased to hear your advice is not falling on deaf ears. I know you were worried that my illness will preoccupy me too much—at first, perhaps it did.* He went on to explain that the doctor had been unable to give him a definite time left to him. *I could not just wait—it could be a matter of weeks, or it could be months, even years. I don't want to go through it alone, and I have no-one while you are gone. You have been like a son to me, and I hope I have been a good stand-in for your father. So don't be mad when I tell you that I am going to enjoy the time I have left. I am in love, with someone who returns my feelings. I no longer fear facing death alone.*

Enough, you can judge his reaction better by saying no more. "Send message." After that, he had some meetings and was away from his office most of the afternoon. When he returned, he smiled slightly as he saw the light flashing on his work station. "Open message." As he had expected, it was from Tiberius.

I thought I told you to stop talking about dying! But, hey, I'm delighted!! It's the last thing I expected you to say. Who is it?! Do I know them?

Xander's reply was short. *Serenity, my Android aide.*

The reply was a long time in coming back. On the *Invincible*, Tiberius sat, stunned, staring at Xander's message. He had expected that response even less than hearing that Xander was seeing someone. He thought for a long while and then answered it. *I wish you all the happiness in the Universe and then some. I feel better knowing you have someone who cares. Really, I am glad, Pappi. You deserve someone good in your life.* He knew the reply would please his old friend, the only man in his life who had tried to stand in, as best as he could, for his father.

Xander smiled when he saw Tiberius' response. He did not need the younger man's approval, but it felt good to have it, knowing Tiberius cared and was happy for him meant more than he realized.

That evening, when he reached the restaurant Serenity had chosen, Xander was stunned when he saw her. Tonight, she had let down her wavy brown hair so that it curled on her shoulders. She wore some subtle make-up and was dressed in a long, fitted sleeveless blue dress that sparkled in the light and accentuated her slim figure. He had only ever seen the Android in uniform at work.

She smiled when he gasped. "I said I would surprise you."

"You certainly have. You are beautiful."

Her strange eyes sparkled in the light. "For a robot?"

He lowered his eyes and smiled softly. "I think I could easily forget you are not a human woman. I have never seen one more attractive. Look, I know I am old."

"And I have no age. Sixty-eight is not old. Are you afraid of something? I have all the required functions." She saw the deep blush that spread up from his neck and slipped her hand through his arm. "Shall we go to our table, or are you just going to stand staring at me?"

Xander gave himself a mental shake and nodded. "Sorry, I just did not expect you to look so different." He led her to the table and pressed the pad on the table for the menu. "What would you like to drink?"

She smiled softly and ran her finger over the back of his hand. "Champagne? We are celebrating, are we not? A new step for you—you deserve some happiness."

He looked up. "How much studying did you do before we came out?" He tapped the order-pad to order a bottle.

She laughed. "Enough to know that humans often drink champagne when they are celebrating something."

The champagne arrived and they ordered their meal before settling down to talk. Xander was happy; happier than he had been for a long time. He had not realized how lonely he was until Tiberius had left for space. He had enjoyed his visits, even if Tiberius was trying to find out what had happened in the past.

"You miss him. I can see that."

Xander looked up. "He has been like a son to me. I did not mean to step into that role. It just happened."

"I did not mean Tiberius. Stephen. You miss him."

Xander bit his lip and looked down at the table. "I don't want…"

"If you never talk about him, it will hurt more. You were best friends. You *have* to talk about him."

"It is too soon."

"Thirty years have passed. You need to talk."

"You know I can't; it's not permitted."

She rested her hand over his. "Not about what happened. About him. About your friendship, the hopes and dreams two young officers had. Talk about him as a person—not the man in the photograph. They say if you remember someone, they are never really dead. You broke the glass in the frame, you are still hurting."

He raised his eyes. "I meant it was too soon for me to talk to you; I have only just asked you out."

She nodded. "But you would talk to me anyway. You allow me to notice when you are unwell, and to help you. If you did not trust me, you would not allow me to see you when you are vulnerable. You have asked me out because you need someone, someone who will always be there for you. Someone who is going to be with you at the end. Someone to sit by you when you are afraid. You have offered *me* that trust—that place at your side. If you did not trust me with your heart, you would not have offered it to me. You should not make excuses."

Xander met her eyes. "I don't know what to say; I am sorry. It has hurt for so long, I am terrified of releasing the pain. If you are not afraid, come back to my apartment after dinner. I will feel safer to talk in private. I cannot talk about things here."

"I understand, and I am not afraid. You are right; it is too public here. Forgive me for raising the subject. I should have known better." Serenity pushed the breadbasket towards him. "Have another piece, you have barely touched your soup."

He took a piece and thanked her. "Tell me about yourself. Are you happy in the admiral's office? Or do you feel that with your enhanced programming, you should be allowed to explore the potential the enhancements give you? You have the ability to think and feel, to make decisions. Would you consider a command role? There have been many Androids assigned to deep space missions, why should an Android not command?"

She smiled. "If I were assigned to a command role, I would not have met you. "It is true that no Android has ever had the command of a ship but perhaps it will not always be so. You are right, our enhanced programming fits us for a command role; perhaps they feel that a commanding officer must be a living being, not an artificial intelligence."

"Does that make you sore?"

She shook her head, revealing a diamond and sapphire necklace, sparkling in the light as her hair moved with the movement of her head, displaying her neck. "I am satisfied with my position. There are not many humans who would be satisfied with a job behind a desk in the admiral's office when the whole universe is there to explore. To watch the unknown unfold before your eyes—that is what thrills you. You know, you have been there and done that. You have seen galaxies, planets—all manner of wonders. Do not tell me that it did not thrill you; that it gave you a purpose?"

Xander laughed. "You are right, of course."

"It is understandable for you to miss the work. You spent most of your life in space. It is as though it is in your blood—your DNA—it almost determines your very existence." She met his eyes and saw him lower his for a moment.

"You understand." Xander's voice was quiet. "People who know me do not always seem to get what it means, but an Android does—an artificial intelligence."

"But an intelligence all the same—with a higher IQ than that of a human. You need someone to understand the situation; the pain of being retired from active service before your time—yes, you are still serving, but it was a two-edged sword, was it not? Your long-service award and your long-deserved promotion but being retired to a desk job."

"My resignation was voluntary." Xander sighed, thinking back to the time he began to make that decision. "I made up my mind after that long spell in hospital when I began to get a clearer picture of my illness. I had no choice. To go on would have put my crew in danger as there was no knowing when my death would occur, or in what manner—sudden or prolonged—they did not know. It could jeopardize a mission and endanger lives. I am grateful to have been permitted to remain in uniform and I am in a good position to help those on active duty as I do have the ear of Admiral Kehoe, even if she does not entirely trust me, and I have absolutely no trust in her now. As her chief of staff I am in a great position although I wonder if that is just so she knows where I am."

"You have the will to survive, that is what drives you. You will not allow circumstances to rule you. You are a strong, courageous man, but you need some spoiling. You have been alone for too long."

Xander smiled slightly. "And you believe you are the one to make me happy?"

"You would not have asked me out if *you* did not believe it to be so." Serenity put down her dessert spoon. "You say yourself that humans do not understand you, or what lies before you. I do not have a heart, just a circuit board, but if I had a heart that beats as yours does, it would beat for no-one but you." She reached across and touched his hand. "I am not like the first Androids—I can think *and* feel. My skin feels like your skin. I look and feel like a human woman, I know what a human woman knows. I can flirt like a human woman, but I can love you *more* because I am not human. I am a machine, built not for my own pleasure, but at the command of humans, for their service."

Any doubts Xander still had about this faded. "I need you." That was all he said, and after a moment, he carried on. "Someone who will not hurt me or break my heart. Someone who will be at my side, holding my hand, at the very end. I will not be afraid with you." He took a deep breath and then added, "Serenity is not freedom from the storm, but peace amid the storm."

Serenity looked at him. "Who said that?"

"Someone wise, long ago. I need you, Serenity—my peace amid the storm, my sanctuary. They chose your name well."

She stroked the back of his hand. "You will have that—I promise. Shall we go? We have much to talk about."

Xander nodded. He tapped the order screen on the table, entering his details, and paid for the meal. "We'll get coffee at my place." He held out his hand as they headed to the door.

Serenity slipped her hand into his and tiptoed slightly to kiss him on the cheek as the door of the restaurant swung shut behind them.

15

The Doctor's Observations

Tiberius sat at the table in one of the many conference rooms on the ship. He had a sea of information tablets spread along the length of the table. Each screen was open, showing different files; from log entries to photographs, reports from the hearing to Xander's testimony and various media articles. The loss of a prototype vessel on her maiden voyage had been reported universe-wide and there was one article what would have made him laugh, but for the subject. *Space Titanic* they called it, debating whether the ship lost on her maiden voyage had run into an iceberg of outer space—an asteroid. The writer reminded their audience of the ancient Earth tragedy of the ship *Titanic* who too was lost on her maiden voyage, centuries before. Some of the articles made him angry. There was one which offered the theory that Stephen MacAlpin had been like the old pirate captains who reputedly scuppered their own ships to get their crew to fight with everything they had to take another ship and even commented on him leaving his first officer marooned on some lonely planet like Defoe's *Robinson Crusoe*. Another suggested that the *Wryneck* was floating around space like the *Marie Celeste*: "A celestial ghost ship. Doomed to float among the stars forever." Only one or two were sympathetic; old companies whose business was science and exploration. *National Geographic* called it a tragedy and placed it on a scale along with the 1986 *Challenger* and the 2003 *Columbia* disasters early in humanity's space history.

He experienced mixed emotions, as he pored over everything. He was still searching for answers and the lack of clues, or any information, was getting him down. The silence of officials scared him and the fact that they seemed to have somehow bought Xander's silence made him angry. He angrily thumped the table with his fist; it still puzzled him why the case file was marked CLOSED when, at the hearing, it had been left as PENDING FURTHER EVIDENCE. "*Why?*" he demanded of the empty room. He pulled another tablet towards him and began to read the transcript of the hearing. It was obvious Xander had been manoeuvred into saying certain things—the look on his face at the end of the visual recording said it all. "It has to be here! They can't hide it!" he muttered, almost despairing.

The door opened suddenly, startling him, and he turned to see Doctor Malachi standing in the doorway, her thick black hair tied loosely back from her face.

"You have been here a long time. You look tired. Have you not even stopped for a coffee?"

Tiberius shook his head. "I was only reading."

"And getting yourself wound up."

"Stop profiling me!"

"You really have a bee in your bonnet about that. I am not creating any form of psychological profile. I only know what I observe. You are stressed—let me fetch coffee for both of us and then why not talk things over? You will find me a good listener; sometimes it helps to talk to someone who does not know your situation—other than what everyone in the service already knows of the story and everything we have read."

Tiberius sighed. "Maybe you are right, Doctor. Look, I am sorry that I have not been that friendly to you."

The doctor shook her head. "It's fine. You might not believe it, but I understand—you were disappointed that a new CMO was appointed. I get that you would have been pleased if the doctor you knew had been transferred along with you but High Command did have their reasons."

"Psychological study? To make a report that I am a chronic obsessive, who imagines he is receiving a picture of the past through dreams?!" Tiberius sounded bitter. "I have read your file—you are a renowned psychologist as well as a surgeon."

"I have to make reports, it is part of my job. Although when you put it like that, a study would be amazing." She paused, thinking carefully before she went on. "I was transferred, because of the work I have done with parasitology and pathology. I am well known as a medical microbiologist. I have made extensive studies on germ warfare."

Tiberius stared at her for a moment. "Then they believe…?"

"That the Tamorans are involved in biological or germ warfare? Yes, perhaps."

"Does everyone in my crew know more than me? I am the captain—I should have been included in information like this."

She touched his arm. "They did not want to tell you at the outset, because of what it might mean to you to leave at that time."

He met her eyes. "Tell me that is *not* what you mean!"

She nodded. "There is every likelihood that Rear Admiral Galen's illness was caused by some form of parasite." She knew that would be a shock and she excused herself for a moment, saying something about coffee.

Tiberius buried his face in his hands as the horrible truth dawned on him—this must be why Xander had been so reluctant to talk about his illness, accepting his impending death with such calm. It was most likely he had been told there was no cure.

The doctor returned after a few moments with two mugs of coffee. She put one mug down in front of Tiberius. "Drink it." She sat at the opposite side of the table and took a sip from her mug before pushing an information disc across to him. "Tell no-one you have seen this. It gives only a little information, but I know you should see it now." Her dark eyes were compassionate as she saw his expression. "If what they say is true and that it is some form of parasite, perhaps the cure can be found on Tamora. There must be some kind of medical facility where it was developed and tested. If I can get my hands on the information about the parasite or pathogen, I could perhaps develop a cure if there is not one already." She glanced at Tiberius, whose face was set in a stunned expression. "What is it?" she asked.

"They used him in tests and experiments, didn't they? That's why he was held a prisoner."

"We don't know that."

"They *must* know. When they brought him home, he would have been examined by doctors, and he would have attended a de-briefing. Where are the results? Where is the report from that briefing? He would have made a statement; to tell them what he went through." He shook his head. "They can't say my father abandoned him to that kind of torture—he wouldn't, they were best friends."

"What if something happened? Something that made your father act out of character? He may not have been responsible for his actions."

"They might have done something to him?"

She nodded. "If they did something to Galen, then the chances are they did something to your father. He may have had no knowledge of what he was doing. You say it is as though your dreams are trying to tell you what happened, can you tell me anything?"

"How do I know they haven't asked you to find out stuff to try and make the case against my father worse?"

"You have to believe me. If I were on their side, I would not have given you the information. You need to trust me."

Tiberius took a deep breath. "I think he knew something and was trying to escape when the Tamorans came after them. It was something of grave importance, something which he did transmit to base before he destroyed the ship. I think he destroyed the *Wryneck*, and killed everyone, to save them from what the Tamorans were going to do, what they had done—or were doing to Xander. I need to get hold of that last transmission, and his debriefing and medical reports. I believe that will tell us the truth."

"You believe in a conspiracy to cover traces of this?"

He nodded. "Why else would so many files be restricted and segments of documentation and reports missing?"

"It does sound like there was some form of cover-up," the doctor agreed. "Read the information I have given you. It will give you some idea of what we could be facing." She finished her coffee and stood up. "I must say, I am inclined to believe as you do." She left the room and returned to sickbay. She sat at her computer and opened the file containing the psychological report she had been ordered to make on the captain. She looked at the screen for a while and then began to dictate. "After a long talk with Captain MacAlpin; having encouraged him to speak about his father, the mission, and his wild conspiracy theories, I conclude that he does not suffer from any obsessive or delusional behaviour; showing none of the signs I would expect to see. I observe only a man who seeks answers as all humanity does when faced with a mystery and I see no reason to go on studying him in this manner. This is the final report and there will be no more other than the reports I am duty-bound to make on this voyage." She appended her name to the file and sent it to the medical chief of staff back at HQ. *No more!* The more she had heard and read, the more she was inclined to agree with Tiberius' conclusions. She switched off her terminal and wondered how her refusal to follow those orders would go down with Admiral Kehoe. She would not lie to the captain again.

•

Tiberius leaned back in his seat and exhaled slowly after the door closed. His talk with Doctor Malachi had shocked him. The idea that Xander had been used in experiments sickened him and he wished his older friend would talk about his ordeal, even just a little. He wanted to understand what had happened to him—to understand what happened all those years ago. They must know something to have assigned a doctor skilled in that kind of research, the specialist areas she had trained in—they must be fairly sure that the aliens were performing those experiments. He picked up the disc she had given him and stood up. He went to his quarters and placed the disc in his safe. He would look at it later but just now, he had to return to the bridge.

Kirbie Ross looked up as there was a knock on his door. "Come in!"

Tiberius poked his head into the cabin. "I'm just on my way to the bridge, but I wanted to run something by you."

"Come on in then. Sit down." Ross stood up to let the captain sit in the desk chair. "What's on your mind? Have you been fishing again?" The first officer was beginning to recognize a particular look in the captain's eyes when he had been engaged in research on the one subject that concerned him above all others.

Tiberius nodded. "Yes, but I keep on hitting the same obstacles—there is no real evidence. The files and documents I need to see are not there. I need to see Xander's medical report. He must have been examined when he was released, it would have been regulation but there is no record of it." He paused and then told Ross the doctor's visit and what she had said about pathogens and experiments.

Ross was silent for a while and then said, "You believe he was experimented on by the Tamorans? And that High Command knew about it and hid the evidence?"

Tiberius nodded. "The doctor hinted as much. She is an expert and that is why she was assigned to the *Invincible.* I think we are being sent to investigate this, but for some reason, Kehoe does not want us to know why. She was responsible for the loss of the *Wryneck*; she covered it up and now that we are being sent to the same place, she does not want her part in the events of thirty years ago to be discovered. I believe that she is the one who has falsified and concealed records. She demanded Xander's silence, perhaps by telling him that speaking out would condemn his friend—even though he was long dead by the time Xander was released from prison."

Ross folded his arms. "It sounds incredible that one of the most senior officers would be a party to a conspiracy but say for argument's sake, that you are right, what are you going to do about it?"

Tiberius sighed. "At the moment, I am going to just keep on looking, to keep on trying to break the encryption on the files— I need to find the reports, the evidence. Perhaps this new information will help." He ran a hand through his hair. "I won't lie to you—not knowing is getting me down."

"I have noticed. Why not go and take a break? I'll go to the bridge. You look tired and I don't mind swapping a shift with you."

Tiberius looked up and smiled. "I think I will. I should call Lashinda, I haven't this week." He stood up. "Thanks for letting me talk to you."

Ross smiled. "Any time." They walked to the door together and headed down the passage, only parting company when Ross turned to go to the bridge.

•

Tiberius' face lit up when Lashinda answered his call. "How are you, Lash? I miss you. I am sorry I haven't called."

Lashinda smiled. "You are busy—it is understandable. I miss you too. Do you have any better idea of what your mission is?"

Tiberius knew that he could not talk about the latest developments since his talk with the doctor. "All we know is that something happened—something that was devastating. Something that caused the loss of the ship. How is Xander? Do you see him?"

"Of course, I see him around the base. He has recently been in hospital again for tests."

"More?"

"You knew that would be the case, Tibby. He told you himself that he would deteriorate—they are trying to find a cure."

Tiberius said nothing for a moment. If what he now thought had happened, they were unlikely to find a cure back on the base.

The answer to Xander's illness lay on Tamora—he could feel it deep inside. "I will call him later."

They talked for a while of their plans for the future, and Tiberius promised that as soon as they returned, he would marry her. "I have to go now—Ross told me to get some sleep. I love you, Lash."

She lifted her hand slightly and kissed her engagement ring. "Sleep well, Tibby. I can't wait until you come home. It is a long time."

"Don't—I will just get depressed." Tiberius had not tried to imagine how hard being parted would be. "I have to concentrate on what is ahead of me, and not think of the length of time." He smiled. "End call." He shut off the computer and went to lie on the bed. He let his eyes close. Although tired, his mind would probably not let him sleep. He took a deep breath and lay back on the pillow. Seconds later, he was asleep.

"Keep her steady!"

"Captain, I can't! The power's gone—the helm isn't answering!"

Tiberius tossed his head on the pillow. The dream was back. He did not want to see it. He knew how it ended. That blinding flash and the awful sight of the debris floating slowly in the darkness of space—turning, floating, slowly in the black vacuum.

"Captain! The alien ship is signalling us!"

"Answer them—put them on the screen." Captain MacAlpin turned to the view-screen, face to face with their attackers. *"My name is Captain Stephen MacAlpin, of the Starship Wryneck. We are on a peaceful mission."*

"We know who you are—only too well, Stephen. You do not think that we would not have come after you?" The tone changed. *"You are out of time, in a moment you will be boarded. I am waiting—give me your unconditional surrender and I will not destroy you."*

Captain MacAlpin's voice was quiet when he replied, but everyone on the bridge heard every word. *"I will never give you that! You have already taken more than I am prepared to give you."*

"You will all die! You have but one of your earth minutes left. What do you say, Captain? Will you save your crew by surrendering yourself to us? Your crew will not be harmed if you come of your own free will."

Keeping his eyes on the screen, the captain spoke clearly. *"Computer, begin Auto-Destruct sequence. Everyone, this is the Captain speaking—for the last time. In one minute, this vessel will self-destruct. I am sorry, but you all know our orders."*

Tiberius buried his face in the pillow as the *Wryneck* exploded. "No, Dad! Please! You didn't give Xander to them. You can't have left him to that." He clenched his fists. "Tell me you didn't!"

Just as the time before, his father's face swam before his eyes, in close up as it were, and he saw the resignation in his grey-green eyes as he raised them—seeming to look right at him. *"I had no alternative—no choice. Forgive me."* That was the last message Headquarters should have received, but it had never been sent. Tiberius could see his father's finger on the transmission icon on the screen set in the arm of the command chair—it would have turned green if the message had been sent—it was still not green and seconds later the ship exploded.

No! That was not the case. It was green and he heard words that he had not heard the last time. Right before he said he had no alternative, Stephen MacAlpin said *"Things are not what they seem, they gave me no alternative. I had no alternative—no choice. Forgive me. Help us. Somehow—help us!"*

Tiberius closed his eyes. "You asked for help! You sent the message, but they never came. But they knew—they knew! You did send that last message. They said they never got it. That you killed them all without asking for help. They lied—you did ask." It was a shock. His father had asked for help, too late for him and his crew but he *had* sent the message, seconds before the explosion. He clung to one sentence, *things are not what they seem, they gave me no alternative.* "What are you trying to tell me? What things are not what they seem?" He rolled over and wiped his eyes and leaned back on the pillows. "Things are not what they seem—what did you mean by that?" He sighed. "I wonder if it was to do with what I believe now—that something was going on down on the planet. Did he mean that, whatever it looked like, he did not abandon Xander? Or was there something about the aliens?" It was supposed to be a peaceful meeting. Tamora was in a strategic position for trade and the Tamorans had agreed to meet. Something must have happened at the meeting to change the mood—or had they been set up? He thought back over the many documents and files he had read and the more he thought about it, the more convinced he was that his father and Xander had been set up and, for whatever reason, Xander had been imprisoned and his father compelled to destroy himself, along with his ship and his crew.

He began to doze off again, but his sleep was plagued by the dream; parts of it playing over and over in his mind, his father's face swimming before his closed eyes.

"Things are not what they seem. Help us!"

"Help us!"

He woke with a yell and sat up. "Not what they seem. No, it cannot be!" He pressed the intercom. "MacAlpin to bridge. Commander Ross, please." His voice was shaking as he fought to pull himself together. No-one must ever see him weak. "Come to my quarters. I need to see you."

Ross detected the strain in Tiberius' voice. "I'll come right away," he said. He stood up and handed command over to one of the other officers and called the infirmary before he left the bridge.

Tiberius was sitting up in bed, the lights dim, when the first officer arrived with the doctor. "I only asked for you, Ross."

Ross nodded. "I know, but something is up. You sounded odd. I thought perhaps you were unwell."

Doctor Malachi had pulled out her medi-reader and touched it to the captain's temple. "Heightened brain activity and increased heart rate. Nightmare?"

Tiberius shook his head. "The usual dream. There was more this time though." He began to tell them. "Dad sent a message. He asked for help. In my last dream, it was not clear—it looked like he had not had time to send it. This time I heard the full message and saw him send it. He said things were not what they seemed. Something was wrong and he knew it."

The doctor sat on the edge of the bed, while Ross leaned on the wall, his arms folded.

"He knew it was too late for them. But he hoped his message would help Xander—I am sure of it. Why does no-one believe me?"

"We do," Ross told him. "But I want you to go to sleep now. We will talk about this later—I'll join you for breakfast."

The doctor held out two little white pills and a cup of water. "Take these, they will help you sleep. You have been overworking your brain with all of this. You never rest from your quest; how much use are you going to be if you get sick now?"

Tiberius looked at her in the dim light and reached out to take the tablets. "You are on my side? You don't think I am insane?"

She watched him slip the pills into his mouth and swallow them with the water. "We are all on your side, which is why you need to sleep. This mission needs a strong captain."

Tiberius lay down obediently and closed his eyes. He was asleep in moments and the doctor leaned over and pulled the covers up. She glanced up at Ross. "He needs answers. Come and see the information I gave him. I think you need to understand what I know of the mission so that we can help him better."

Ross nodded. "We should have come to that agreement sooner." He followed her out into the corridor, turning out the lights as they left.

16
Serenity Intercedes

Tiberius stood at the large bay window on the viewing deck. It was a semi-circular area at the ship's prow with a clear view of the surroundings. He clasped his hands behind his back and looked out into the darkness; a darkness studded with stars. He smiled contentedly when three shooting stars arced across the *Invincible*'s bows. He never tired of sights like that, and instinctively watched for more. They were passing an asteroid field right now, and the ship was moving slowly as the science department was scanning and mapping the asteroids as part of their mission of exploration. No ship from Earth had been this far out in space since the *Wryneck* passed this way. The last two years had been quiet as they ventured deeper into space. Their true tasks would not begin until they had reached their destination, the Tamoran region of space with the planet Tamora and its moons Ajax and Hermia, and Garion, its sister world. Tiberius had not given up his search for proof but had allowed the passing time to ease the stress and permitted himself to enjoy the exploration—finally taking the doctor's advice to take a break from the search. He knew now that there was nothing hidden in the files and documents he had in his possession. If it existed, it had never been given to him. He would leave it for a while and return to it when his mind was fresher. As he stood here now, a wave of peace seemed to wash over him as he watched the stars.

He turned when he heard footsteps and saw his first officer coming to stand beside him. "Is everything okay?"

Commander Ross nodded. "It's all quiet. I just came to see how you were getting on." He stood in silence for a while, his hands behind his back. "You spend a lot of time here."

Tiberius laughed. "Look at it. How could I not spend time here? I can breathe."

"Breathe? Are you okay?"

Tiberius smiled. "You're still worried about me? Everything is fine now. I have accepted that I am not going to find what I was looking for in the notes. I was speaking metaphorically when I said I could breathe. My own desperation was stifling me."

"Don't give up," Ross responded. "No-one expects you to."

Tiberius smiled and turned back to the window. "There are shooting stars. See, even the stars share my restlessness."

•

Xander sat with his shoulders hunched over his desk, working on some reports the admiral had given him. As his health deteriorated, so did the level of work. He noticed now that he got little to do, except these tedious lists and reports. Crew transfers, requisition orders, ship movements—there was little of the exciting stuff now. It must be that this stuff did not matter if he were to drop dead in the middle of it. He had been working on better stuff than this up until recently—that had been his last stay in the hospital. More tests that had left him tired and sore. He wondered how long he could go on like that. He was supposed to be Kehoe's chief of staff, but she had another officer filling some of that role now and it rankled.

He heard the door open and looked up to see Serenity standing in front of the desk. She held out a steaming mug. "Break time. Come and sit over here, away from the computer."

He got up and went to sit on the couch. "Sit beside me, I don't need to lie down." He patted the cushion. "How is it that you are the only one who really cares here? And you're not supposed to feel anything."

Serenity looked up. "You know why that is. I love you. Is the work boring you?" she went on, changing the subject.

"It is work that needs to be done, and I am working in the admiral's office."

"Yes, and we all know that you were supposed to be assigned better duties than that," she responded. "You are supposed to be working alongside her in an advisory capacity—her chief of staff."

"And she has now deemed I am not fit. I wish she had spoken to me about it." Xander sighed. He watched the Android opening a pouch taken from her pocket. "You fuss more than my doctor."

"Of course I do, you would forget to look after yourself if I was not here." She took out a syringe and saw his face whiten. "I know you don't like needles, but you know you have to take this."

He bit his lip and turned his face away as she rolled up his sleeve. She sat for a while, looking at his arm, marked with the scars of many injections, many needles. She stroked it softly and then quickly made the injection and put her finger over the tiny speck of blood.

Xander slowly turned his head and looked at her. "Every needle reminds me. I'm sorry."

"I know. I wish there were another way." She kissed his arm and rolled the sleeve down. "Have a nap and you will feel better." She stood up and let him lift his legs up onto the couch so that he was lying back against the cushions. She pulled the rug off the back and laid it over him, watching as he obediently closed his eyes and then slipped out when she was sure he was asleep. She left the office and headed down the corridor towards the admiral's office. She had the idea of speaking to Kehoe about the change in Xander's workload, or at least the content of that workload.

·

Admiral Kehoe looked up as the buzzer sounded at the door and the Android Serenity came in. Most of her staff were these Androids. They were super-efficient and programmed to work hard. Unlike their human colleagues, they did not need rest and sleep in the same way. She had assigned Android Mark 12 #435, otherwise known as Serenity, to Rear Admiral Galen as a personal assistant in order to alleviate some of the pressure of the work. "Is Galen well?"

Serenity nodded. "He is resting, ma'am." She paused a moment, standing very straight in front of the admiral's desk. "He is a little upset by the reduction in his workload. He insists he is well enough and is saddened to see that you have obviously drawn your own conclusions as to the effect his health has on his ability to work."

"You seem to take it personally," the admiral commented.

"I am programmed to serve the officer to whom I am assigned. You will understand that I would be concerned when he is unhappy. He was promised work that he is not being given and he feels that he is being pushed aside because of his illness. He is still capable. I work closely with him and have the task of monitoring his condition when he is not in the hospital. Please do not take away what is left for him."

Kehoe looked at the Android in silence. "You are a machine and yet you speak with passion. Can it be that you have formed a connection, that you have feelings for the man you serve?"

"My programming allows for feelings. Rear Admiral Galen is a fine officer; I respect and admire him, and I do not want to see him suffering and in pain—more of which is facing him. Working helps him to take his mind off his condition and he is bored by the mundane tasks, although he will never tell you that himself. I do not want him to overwork, but I want him to have something that he will feel is fulfilling. He believes you are giving him tasks that do not matter if he is hospitalized, or indeed dies before it is completed. He is being made to feel worthless after all the years of dedicated service he has given."

Kehoe leaned back in her chair and thought about Xander Galen. While as an officer, she admired his courage and his brave fight to go on, despite his rapidly declining health, this courage was a threat. If he insisted on working on, there were things he would be likely to discover. She would monitor the situation and might have to intervene—it would be a shame to end it like that, but there would be no alternative. There was a long silence and then she looked up and met the Android's silvery eyes. "Does he know you have come to speak to me?"

Serenity shook her head. "Oh no, ma'am! He would be embarrassed. I do not wish to shame him, but I do not want to see him used." She stood to attention and said nothing else, hoping she had not gone too far and presumed too much.

Kehoe turned to the computer for a while and then looked up at Serenity. She handed an information disc to her with a faint smile. "There is a research project on this disc. A lot of detail is involved in the compilation of this paper, so I hope he is suitably grateful. Rear Admiral Galen is a brave man and I admire his determination and courage—his will to go on. Tell him his workload will not change but I insist on being lenient with deadlines; I will not pressure him with work that needs instant results. He needs a lot of rest and you have the responsibility of administering his medication; you are best placed to monitor his condition."

Serenity saluted. "Thank you, ma'am. I will not permit him to tire himself. Thank you for your understanding, and for giving him something by which he will feel of use." She tucked the disc into her tunic pocket, saluted again, and left the room. In the corridor, she paused and permitted herself a smile. "I will not let a man like Xander to be robbed of what he holds dear; he has served too long to have it snatched away from him. That time will come, but not yet!" She hurried back to the office and sat at her desk for a while. She popped the information disc into a case and wrote a digital memo to go with it, supposedly from the admiral—it would activate when the case lid opened. She tiptoed into the inner office and put it on the desk where Xander would find it later. She saw he was still sound asleep on the couch and left him to sleep undisturbed; taking a few of the lists and reports with her to work on. Kehoe thought her protective. She was. She loved Xander and was not prepared to see him treated like his life was already over. There would be time enough for that at the end. She sat at her computer and began to type up the notes and figures Xander had been working on. She would do all of his work, if necessary, to keep the admiral off his back. She hoped he would not be too upset with her when he found out that she had spoken to the admiral on his behalf. She knew he did not want anyone knowing his health was declining more rapidly now. It upset her to see him desperately clinging to what now remained; those times, now growing far apart, where there was no pain. She was glad she was there for him. It would be heartbreaking to see him suffer like this alone. And she would not leave him alone as his life drew to a close. She knew he hoped that he would live until Tiberius came home, but it seemed less likely that he would live much longer without help.

She went back to the doorway and saw that Xander was still sleeping peacefully, his head pillowed on a cushion. She pulled the blanket up around him more and bent to kiss his forehead. "It's going to be okay, you don't have to worry any longer."

He stirred a little but did not wake. He murmured something which sounded like her name and then was quiet again. Eventually, Xander stirred, feeling cramped. He stretched and it took him a while to realize that he was not in his bed. He blinked a moment or two and saw Serenity in the doorway. "Have I slept long?"

"A couple of hours," she replied. "Feel better?"

He sat up and swung his legs over the edge of the couch. "Yes, much better." He pushed himself up and went over to the desk.

Serenity waited, knowing he would find the work he had been given. She hoped he would not guess that the admiral's seeming change of heart was due to her intervention. She slipped back to her office and smiled to herself, seeing him settle at the desk and open the case. His sigh of relief pleased her. It would not be long before he could not go on like this but, for now, he could.

Xander listened to the note left with the information disc and then opened up his computer to check for messages. There was one from Kehoe, explaining that she would not reduce the workload, or pass off mundane tasks on him. *You have a fine advocate—she was very persuasive,* she wrote. He realized what she meant. Serenity had gone to the admiral and complained on his behalf. He reached for the buzzer and was going to call her in and reprimand her for interfering. His hand hovered for a moment and then he changed his mind. He was grateful and, therefore, he would not censure her. He turned back to his work and got stuck in with renewed vigour. He felt he could face what was coming a little more now, he had adequate proof that Serenity was going to defend him and care for him.

17

The Mystery Unfolds

Tiberius glanced up from a report he was working on when the buzzer sounded at his door and he turned to see Kirbie Ross coming in when he activated access. "Is it time?"

"We're about to begin gathering so I thought I should summon the host." Ross smiled. "Can I say that we always look forward to joining you for your Independence Day dinner? Your introduction of events like this has had a great impact on morale and the crew look forward to them."

Tiberius grinned. "I have always found that food is a great way to bring people together. I also believe it is important to commemorate the past in order that we can understand the impact it has on the future, and for us to appreciate where we came from to get to where we are now." He paused to laugh and then continued, "I don't like constantly eating the recommended healthy dishes, so the opportunity for a traditional feast is great."

Ross laughed. "Don't tell the doctor—you know how it is, we're away from base for so long that these food regulations are for maximum effect on our health."

"She didn't turn down the invitation, however," Tiberius responded with a chuckle. "She just asked if there would be Kosher options for vegetarians." He stood up and went to the cupboard where his uniforms hung and changed his tunic. These dinners were important to the crew and he knew that wearing his dress uniform was important at a dinner he was hosting in comparison to if the senior officers accepted an invitation to dine with the junior officers. Those invitations were usually accompanied by a sporting challenge—often a game of tennis which Tiberius enjoyed—so casual dress was common.

Many crew members had commented, when asked, that their commanding officer was one of them while also knowing when to separate himself and he was highly respected for that. He could bring himself down from his position of authority and join in with games and social events designed to strengthen comradeship and boost morale. A cynical few said he was trying to curry favour with the crew because of the stigma attached to the name he bore, but it was a tiny minority and was always quickly shouted down.

Tiberius glanced in the mirror, pulled his tunic straight, combed his thick auburn hair and grinned at Ross. "Okay, I'm ready. I fancy a good old-fashioned burger and fries."

Ross laughed as they walked together. He had known Tiberius since he had been assigned to the *Victorious* as a young sub-lieutenant on his first posting. Tiberius Alexander MacAlpin had been twenty-one then, just a few years younger than Ross, and they had become friends. Ross had been assigned to train him and now, seeing him in command of his own ship, he was proud of him and vindicated for any training issues; Tiberius had been quite an independent young man and liked his own way very much although he had accepted the training, but it had been a while before he and Ross had finally become friends. Ross had worked hard to break through the barrier of resentment which had dominated the young MacAlpin's attitude early on; Tiberius had been constantly on the defensive and had got into a lot of ugly situations through his reactions to anyone who appeared to say or imply anything against his father. He felt justified for believing, along with Xander, that Tiberius could forge his own career despite his name and the cloud of doubt and suspicion surrounding his father.

The doors slid open and Tiberius and Ross stepped into the senior officers' mess-hall to be greeted by the assembled officers and crew all rising to their feet and saluting smartly before raising a glass to their commanding officer. Tiberius acknowledged the salute with a smile. "Sorry I am late. I had intended to be here to welcome you." He turned as one of the youngest crew members came forward and saluted. "We want to congratulate you on three years in command and wish to present you with a small token of our respect." She held out a large flattish package.

Tiberius took it with a smile. "Thank you, but I do not need such tokens. I am happy to serve as your captain on a ship such as this. You are a crew of which I am highly proud. But I do appreciate the gesture." He began to unwrap the parcel and his eyes lit up at the hand-crafted, perfectly detailed diorama of the Battle of Lexington. Everyone knew the captain collected military history and the expression on his face showed he was delighted. "Thank you. It is perfect." He set it to one side on an empty table and spent some moments looking over the details with pleasure. It warmed his heart to know that some of the crew had worked on this in their recreation time in order to present it as a gift. He looked up and saw the galley crew were beginning to set out trays and dishes of food and he straightened up. "Help yourselves and enjoy!" He started off the proceedings by beginning to fill a plate.

•

Later, Tiberius returned to the viewing deck and stood looking out at the stars. They were three years into the voyage now and everything was running smoothly; it was all going according to plan. For a while that evening, he had almost forgotten about his anger at High Command and their refusal to let him know exactly what had happened to his father. Of late though, it had not been so important. It was enough to know he had a better understanding of what had happened and, if he could prove it, the extent of the cover-up. He had gained access recently to some of the encrypted files, thanks to the code-breaking skills of the communications officer. He had been hard at it for several months but had finally succeeded and reported his success to the captain. Tiberius had been delighted and was beginning to study the long-hidden logs and reports.

He turned away from the stars after a while and headed for his cabin to spend time reading, with a big mug of coffee. He sincerely believed that this time, he would be closer to learning the truth than ever before. He changed into casual off-duty clothes and made coffee. He was happy; the evening had gone well, and everyone had enjoyed the dinner and it had been nice to take time out of their busy schedules to eat together and celebrate historic events that had impacted significantly on the future of Earth and the universe. He sat at the desk, woke up the computer, called up the files and began to read. He was interested to find that one of the encrypted files was a diary log, recorded by his father, of the days leading up to the meeting with the Tamoran Council and he settled down to listen to it closely, beginning to make a transcript so he could read over it. This meant he had to listen to it more than once, so every grain of detail was picked up on. Stephen MacAlpin had recorded details, however small, and any reports Tiberius had heard, or read, had always been clear and concise. This particular report had been encrypted for so many years that it had to contain something which had caused it to be included in the suppression of data and Tiberius attended very closely, listening for anything, however insignificant, that would give an idea of what had occurred; anything that would point towards the Tamorans having hostile intentions towards the officers from the *Wryneck*.

The first section of the report was clear and well-documented, recorded in the days leading up to the meeting and set out MacAlpin's plans for the meeting. It also said for the first time what the meeting was about and what they hoped to gain:

Tamora is in a very strategic position in the furthest reaches of our galaxy, basically in the pivotal position of a gateway to the galaxies and space beyond. They guard a wormhole, to which they have sole access; a wormhole, through which we would have access to deeper exploration in space. This is exciting! We would have opportunities our ships do not give us. It all depends on the Tamorans—do they want a treaty? Will they understand our motives are peaceful? That we do not want access to the wormhole to bring war? I have been given the responsibility of meeting with the Tamoran Council; it is now my job to present ourselves, a people unknown to Tamora, as peaceful people, and to show that our intentions are peaceful. It is an important task and an amazing opportunity for first contact with this unknown planet. We know nothing of them, other than that they are wary of contact. They are so far out in space that we do not even know if they are aware of the existence of life outside their own planet. None of our ships have ever reached this far; the Wryneck has been designed especially for deep-space missions of this kind. I hope we can be used in the setting up of trade agreements and treaties with other worlds. This is the kind of task to which I have looked forward. There is no data to assist us in understanding them before we meet; we go into these meetings blind. We do not know what form these people take; do they look like us? Will they understand what we have come for?

Tiberius turned to the report recorded on the day after the first meeting had gone ahead.

We were welcomed politely enough; they are a wary people, which is only to be expected from a people who has reportedly had no contact with life outside of their world, but I am not sure I entirely believe this. The officials who welcomed us into the council chamber greeted us in our own language with as much as ease as though it was their own tongue. They certainly were better prepared than I was with the odd words and phrases I had attempted to master from the one document I had received before the meeting. I believe that my effort to thank them for their welcome, in their own language, was well received. That they spoke English was appreciated by me and the first officer. I had hoped that the meeting would go off without hitch, and it appeared to do so. I was uneasy at the beginning because I did not know what we were going into at that meeting. We were together for most of the proceedings, and it worried me when we were separated. For only about half an hour, Commander Galen was escorted from the room with two of the officials, leaving me alone with the leader of the council and a number of others. I demanded that Galen be brought back in, saying that I would not discuss anything further without my colleague at my side. When he was returned, I noted that he was a little pale and he held his left arm close to his side. What worried me more was that he did not speak, contributing nothing else to the meeting. I asked him as soon as he sat beside me if he was okay, and he nodded and that was all. I had a feeling that something was wrong and knew the Council Chamber was not the place for finding out. When we left the chamber, we went to the rooms we had been given for the duration of our stay. I asked Galen what had happened, and he said little. He told me that he did not feel very well and asked me not to bother him with questions and he lay down to sleep not long after that. I could see he was still very pale and appeared to be sweating. I remembered that he had been holding his arm when he returned to the chamber and I waited until he was asleep and then I leaned over and rolled up his sleeve. Clearly visible on his arm were needle-marks, the kind consistent with blood having been taken. His arm was bruised around the marks, but especially around the wrist, appearing that he was held against his will while blood was taken, or he was given an injection of some kind. I checked his other wrist and saw the bruising was the same—he had been held by force. I felt sick and worried. What else would face us? Were we in danger? Or was this merely inquisitiveness and Galen, not understanding their language, had struggled, forcing them to hold him down so he would not hurt himself? I do not believe so—everything in me tells me that we are in danger and I worry about him. I did what I could to make him comfortable as he slept, as he was obviously in some discomfort. I did not question him further when he woke, seeing he was reluctant to offer any information. I kept an eye on him and could see he was grateful for my not pressing him. We returned to the meeting that afternoon after we had eaten something, and I insisted that we not be separated, and they seemed to accept this. When we returned to our rooms in the evening, I found that I had finally received orders and was told that we had to negotiate for access to the wormhole.

We were invited to the home of the leader of the planet's government and were treated to a pleasant meal of local delicacies which were delicious and not as alien as I thought they might be. They eat a lot of vegetables and seem to favour them grilled, along with a white fish. I was still worried about Galen. He was noticeably quiet and ate little, toying with his food, and I worried our hosts would be offended, but he was offered something like a soup with noodles which he seemed to manage a lot better. He deteriorated over the meal and I begged forgiveness from our host and got him back to our rooms and put him to bed. His skin was hot to the touch and he was sweating although shivering as though cold. I wrapped him in the sheets and blankets from both beds and persuaded him to sleep, staying at his side the whole night, helping him to sip at some water when he woke through the night, which was often. He seemed much better in the morning, and the fever, or whatever it was, seemed to have been broken. I got him to nibble at some fruit for breakfast and a sweet hot drink that was a little like tea. He joined me at the meeting, and I was pleased to see that he appeared to be himself again. I am looking forward to getting back to the ship and getting the doctor to examine him and reassure me that everything is well. I have every intention of making a recommendation to have more security in place for first-contact situations; we were unprepared in all aspects of this meeting, knowing nothing much about them—if there was any danger or threat to personal safety, we surely had the right to be warned at the very least. There are protocols for meetings like this and my orders said not to follow them.

Tiberius closed his eyes for a moment. Something had happened to Xander and seeing his father's report of the care he had given warmed him. This was not the report of a man who would abandon his friend to the unknown aliens, who had obviously done something that had distressed and hurt the first officer and caused him to be momentarily unwell. He turned to the next file and frowned as he realized there was not another one to follow. A sudden chill crept over him as he realized that this could have been the last detailed report his father had made. Did they even make it back to the ship for Xander to be examined? Or was he arrested just after this? It was obvious from this report that, for some reason, the Tamorans had targeted

Xander and not his commanding officer. He closed his eyes, wishing he knew what had happened. He listened to the report again and then turned to the other files. He found a short message and realized that it was his father's plea for help in the situation in which they found themselves.

I don't know what to do. I am at a loss; I do not have the knowledge necessary to understand these people and how they will respond to our requests. They have hurt my first officer—my best friend. I do not know if this is because of a language barrier, a misunderstanding, but he is not well and reluctant to tell me what happened. I am worried about him and concerned for our safety. We have come in peace and he is lying in bed, bruised and bearing needle-marks in his arm. He has been restrained by force and has a fever. I am officially requesting advice—I know what my duty is, to negotiate for access to the wormhole, but I cannot do this if my crew are in any danger from these people.

Tiberius scanned the file and, after several attempts, saw that it had never received a reply and it made him angry, realizing his father must have waited in vain for a response. He wondered how he had felt, and if he had sent another plea, and still heard nothing. Had he realized what now was obvious—that they had been betrayed? Tiberius understood now; for some reason, his father and the crew of the *Wryneck* had been sent into this situation and abandoned—betrayed by their senior officers. And for what? That was the biggest question in Tiberius' mind, along with "Why?" What had been so important about this mission that it superseded the importance of the safety of personnel; a full complement of crew on a new and expensive prototype ship—the first of its kind. What could have outweighed all of this? What had been worth so many deaths, the destruction of a ship, and a single survivor now dying from an unknown illness? An illness that Tiberius finally understood was not the cancer they had been led to believe, but an illness that must be related to that injection or blood sample taken by the Tamorans. The years Xander had spent in prison, and the torture he had hinted at, was the cause of his illness. What could possibly have meant more than the protection of men and women who had put their lives on the line daily in service? Each and every one of them knew they could die any day, but not at the hands of their own High Command. He bit his lip and punched the desk in anger. They had been sacrificed but he knew that did not explain why his father had destroyed the ship; why he had been the one to kill his crew. If that had been part of his orders, surely, he would not have carried them out? It was growing more obvious that he had received no further communication since his plea for help. Had there been something in his original orders? He seemed to remember hearing his father's voice in one of the dreams saying that they knew their orders—right after giving the order to auto-destruct.

18
Broken Vows

Tiberius stirred and sat up with a start and realized he had fallen asleep in front of his computer, which had switched itself off. He rubbed his eyes and glanced at his watch. He had not meant to spend so much time on the files that he would fall asleep and actually miss the start of his shift. Running to the shower, he had a quick wash and changed into a fresh uniform. As he pulled on his boots, he called the bridge and said he was on his way. On his way, he bumped into Ross.

The first officer stopped. "I was just coming to see if everything was okay; you are never late for duty."

"I know. I am sorry, but I fell asleep at the computer and overslept."

"Just so long as you are all right," Ross replied. "I was worried. I know you were going to try and look over some files and I wondered if you had found something that made you forget the time."

"I did."

Ross looked at him. "Want to talk?"

Tiberius shook his head. "Not yet. Some of it I kind of expected but I was shocked, and it was hard listening to my father relating the events as they happened."

"A verbal report?"

Tiberius nodded. "Yes. It is hard to hear his voice, knowing I never had the chance to know him." He made a move to walk on.

Ross stood aside and let him pass before falling into step beside him. He knew the captain would tell him when he could.

Tiberius strode onto the bridge and took his seat. He had hardly been sat for more than a moment before the communications officer looked up. "Message for you, sir. It's marked 'personal and urgent', will I put it through to your quarters? It's from your fiancée."

Tiberius nodded. "Thank you, Zee-Zee."

Lieutenant Zeal looked up with a grin. No-one ever called him by his real name of Zelotes Zeal, except officially of course. "Transfer to your personal terminal complete, sir."

"Take over, Ross. I'll deal with this and then come right back." Tiberius stepped down from the command chair and Ross took his place.

"Hope everything is okay, Captain." Ross was worried, urgent personal messages were rarely ever good news.

Tiberius hurried to his quarters and sat his desk. "Computer, open message from Lashinda Davis." He was excited to hear from her. He missed her; talking every day was not the same. They both knew eight years was a long time but when they exchanged promises before he left, they knew their love was strong enough to transcend time and distance. They talked every day and often discussed their wedding plans. Plans they made for two weeks following his return to Earth in another four years' time. He was excited but those years would seem like millennia. Hearing her voice, seeing her face every day was good, and even touching fingers together against the screen—but he missed the physical touching.

The screen flickered and the message opened. The picture on the screen that met his eyes was of Lashinda's beautiful engagement ring. He smiled; remembering how he had borrowed one of her rings to be sure of getting the size right. The screen changed and he went white. A wedding photo filled the screen. A photo of Lashinda—marrying someone else. He felt as though his heart just stopped beating. He caught his breath, feeling like he was choking. The screen changed again, and this time it was her. His Lashinda. He reached out to touch the screen but saw she did not react and knew it was a recorded message.

I am sorry, Tibby. I did love you, so very much, and I would have waited. Eight years is a long time, but I would have waited for you. Then Fletcher came along. He is nothing you are, but at the same time more. He was never going to be leaving me for eight years at a time, and me left never knowing if you would come home. I don't want to be like your mother, maybe never to see you again—never to have a body to bury. I can't do that. I fell in love with him even though I did not mean to.

He saw her turn aside and, when she straightened up, she held a child in her arms. *We married two weeks ago. I meant to tell you. Emily was born two years ago—just a year after I met Fletcher. I lied to you all this time. You do not deserve to be treated like this—I am no good for you. I know I do not deserve your forgiveness, but I know you to be a generous and kind man and I hope that somehow, you will find that you can forgive me for the hurt I know I have caused.*

The screen went dark, and Tiberius slumped over the desk. Betrayed. Lashinda had lied to him; calling him every day while she nursed another man's child and planned her wedding to the father. They had talked over their plans; they had planned every detail. And she had never once thought of telling him; sooner rather than later would have hurt less. Disbelief hit him like a punch in the face. Part of him was telling him it was a hoax, that someone had set it up to upset him. *Call her,* his mind and heart were saying. *You'll get the truth then.* "No! She lied to me—we were so happy. She loved me! She promised to wait." He felt like someone was cutting his heart up into little pieces. He was not aware of time passing; his world had just collapsed, and he did not hear the door open.

Ross looked in. He had been worried about the fact the message had been urgent and then the captain had not returned to the bridge. He stood stock-still when he saw him in tears. His first thought was that her message had been to inform Tiberius that Xander was dead; he knew the captain dreaded that news above everything else. He stepped forward quickly and put his hand on Tiberius' shoulder. "Tell me it's not Xander."

Tiberius looked up, his face red and blotchy. "Go away! She's gone and married someone else!"

Ross caught his breath. "No! You loved each other—she wouldn't." The wedding photo on the screen. He was horrified and really did not know what to say now.

"I waited! I waited for her!"

"I know." Ross' voice was very soft. He pressed Tiberius' shoulder, not knowing what else to say. *Bitch!* "I'll leave you alone. Don't worry about your shift, I'll take a double one." He felt awkward seeing his commanding officer like this.

"Sorry."

"Don't be. When you feel able to talk you know you can always come to me." Ross left and headed back to the bridge, wondering if there was anything he could do to help.

Tiberius buried his face on his arms again. He was not crying as hard as he had been since Ross had come in. He had not been able to say it, but it had helped a little to feel a friend's hand on his shoulder. He had heard the concern in his voice—worried that it had been the worst news. Somehow, *this* was worse. In the back of his mind, despite how he felt about it, he knew Xander was dying. Four years had passed and Xander was still alive— that was great, and it made him happy—but this, however, had been completely unexpected; a bolt from the blue as devastating as the asteroid that allegedly wiped out the dinosaurs on Earth. He wiped his eyes and blew his nose and listened to her message again. Hearing her voice, the tears trickled down his cheeks afresh. She had been his rock; a strong shoulder to lean on when the dreams came. She had protected him, making sure that no-one would see him devastated by disturbing images; always there for him when he had cried out in distress when the images of his father's ship exploding had flashed before his eyes. She had always helped and now she was gone. She would not be waiting for him when the *Invincible* returned to base, triumphant after a successful mission, filled with tales of what this ship could do, what they had seen and done. She was gone, taking another part of his world away from him. He wanted to call her, to insist on real answers, but something stopped him from making the call in haste, maybe pride. He was shattered by the news, but he did not want her to see him broken. He would not let her see what she had done. He would leave it. He did not leave it though. He reached for the keyboard and returned to the message, watching her face as she spoke. When she had said sorry, she had looked directly at the screen, knowing her eyes would meet his. He thought perhaps that was the most truthful thing she had said. She looked sorry. She had known what this would do to him and she had been sorry. But to forgive her? Never. He gave her call-sign to the computer and sat back to wait for an answer. He was not surprised when the call was refused. He sent a message. *I am willing to talk.*

There is nothing to talk about. The reply was almost instant.

Not even an explanation?

I gave you that.

It is not enough. You owe me a proper explanation.

Yes, but not now. Not while you are angry, as I know you are. It is understandable. Call me tomorrow.

I cannot forgive you. Do not ask me for it. I will not call. If you had answered my call, I would have listened to you. Goodbye, Lash.

Tibby, please call me.

No. Tiberius ran his arm over his face. The computer chirped and he looked at the screen. The incoming call was from Lashinda. He looked at the blinking light for a long time, watching to see how long she held on for—waiting for him to accept her call. "Computer, block contact. I do not wish any communication from this source."

The screen went blank. "Contact deleted. No further contact possible," the computer informed him laconically. "Incoming call suspended."

Tiberius angrily wiped his face on his sleeve and seemed surprised at how wet his sleeve was. "Idiot," he muttered. He went to his bathroom and washed his face with cold water. He intended to return to the bridge to continue his shift and did not want any of the crew to see he had been crying. He wondered if Lashinda had told Xander—if Xander knew at all. He had not said anything at all if he did know. He deserved to know; after all, he had been the first to know they were engaged when they turned up at this door in the middle of the night with champagne. He went back and sat in front of the computer and began to put a message together, including the message from Lashinda and asked Xander to call him later on. *I need to talk. Lash betrayed me.* He remembered Xander telling them they had to be sure, because of the time they would spend apart. He remembered her reassuring him that he had nothing to worry about; she would love him forever. He remembered it clearly. He set his jaw hard to stop himself from crying again.

He turned the computer terminal off and sat for a while, just staring down at the desk. Eventually, he got up and headed back to the bridge. Ross had told him to take time out to collect his thoughts but right now he needed the distraction of work and it was with a deep sense of relief that he took his command seat without Ross saying anything other than the usual response, "I stand relieved" and a passing comment on the ship's status, "All quiet, sir."

•

It was two or three days before Tiberius felt his usual self again. It had been a tough few days for him and he needed time to pull himself together. Xander responded to his message late on the third day and they talked for a long time.

Xander was horrified to hear what had happened and did not know how to console the younger man—it was something he had no words for at first; he had never been in that position himself. He also did not want to say that their engagement had worried him, with Tiberius leaving for a long time. He had been afraid it would not last, and it saddened him to see his young friend going through it like this. "She's not worth your tears, son." He had waited, allowing Tiberius to let off steam. "If she were worth them, she would still be waiting for you. And if she really cared, she would have told you the truth and not lied to you all this time. You have to let her go and move on."

When Xander called him son, it was hard not to listen to the man he looked up to as a father in place of his own. And, although it hurt, Tiberius agreed with him. "I love her—I can't just let go."

"You have to."

Tiberius looked down at his hands. He knew Xander was right. He pulled himself together slowly and looked up. "Are you okay? You didn't respond till today."

"I was in the hospital. I have agreed to undergo more tests—invasive tests. Perhaps they can find something to help me."

"I worry about you. I am too far away."

"Do not regret the life you have chosen." Xander's voice was soft. "Stephen would be proud of you, as I am. You always wanted this, and you have it. Meet the Tamorans; finalize that treaty and find out what happened. You can only do your duty now, son. None of us knows what time we have allotted to us, but we can all make that time count for something. Make your time count, Tiberius. Make it count and leave a legacy for the next generation, such as your father left for you."

Tiberius went quiet for a moment and then nodded, leaving his other questions unasked. He wanted to ask Xander why she would have done this, but he knew it was pointless to ask. He would not know the answer to that. Only she would be able to give him that answer, and he did not want to know—not from her. She had hurt him, and he was not ready to listen or forgive. He sat in front of the computer for a while, in silence, after they signed off. Xander had said a lot of things, and he knew the older man was right. He knew that however much it hurt, however betrayed he felt, he had to put it behind him and concentrate on the mission ahead. Xander had confirmed what he suspected; he and his crew were being sent to Tamora to complete the mission on which his father and *his* crew had been engaged. That had not been included in the original orders. The orders had stated a mission of exploration and discovery. There had been no mention of the wormhole Stephen MacAlpin had spoken of in the report he had found—no mention of the failed treaty negotiations. It was only with constant demands that he had been told about the trade deal. What he did not understand was the secrecy surrounding the mission, and why he had not even been told at first what planet or system for which they were headed. He was angry, justifiably so, he thought. He was the captain, the safety of the ship and her entire crew were his responsibility, and he knew less than other senior officers; it seemed that his chief medical officer had been briefed, and perhaps even his first officer, while he had been given encrypted orders, many of which had denied him access. He decided it was time to change things and he sent a message to Admiral Kehoe, asking her for a call. Not many minutes passed before a call came through from the admiral's office. It was Kehoe herself, answering his request.

"Captain MacAlpin, your message had an aggrieved tone. You are dissatisfied with your mission?"

"No, ma'am. Not with the mission, but with the manner in which I have been kept in the dark over various details, including the actual purpose of the mission. What I do know, I have gleaned for your carefully worded orders, which revealed little, and from the files and documents I have managed to access. I am politely requesting full orders, or I will terminate this mission here and now, citing High Command as culpable for my decision. A commander cannot be left in this position, I must know the destination and orders for the success of this mission." He managed not to sound as angry as he felt. He knew from experience that, when dealing with the admiral, it was best not to let her see anger. He controlled his feelings with difficulty and looked at the screen. "I have become aware of the presence of a wormhole, protected jealously by the Tamorans. It was for access to this anomaly and what lies beyond that my father and his crew were sent. To meet this alien people and negotiate a treaty by which Earth would gain passage to the galaxies beyond our own."

"Where did you find this information? It is not available without my express authorization."

"It should not matter where I found it; it should never have been restricted," Tiberius responded. "All that should matter is that I know, and that you sent us unprepared on a potentially hostile mission, knowing full well I did not have the information I needed. How was I *ever* going to be in a position to successfully negotiate for this treaty if I was not even aware that this was my task? With all due respect, Admiral, I had never thought you a fool, until now." Tiberius kept his voice steady and, somehow, still respectful.

There was a long silence and both Tiberius and Kehoe kept their gaze fixed on each other. Tiberius was wondering if he had overstepped the mark with his comment about thinking the admiral a fool. He was not sorry that he had said it, however. He meant it.

Kehoe broke the silence. "Full details of the mission and your task will be sent to you immediately. The omission should never have occurred."

"Thank you." Tiberius tapped the screen and ended the call. He leaned back in the chair and sighed. He had expected to be reprimanded for calling Kehoe a fool in that way. The fact that he had done so, and received the response he wanted, made him believe even more firmly that the admiral was hiding something. He wondered if her acquiescence to his request—his demand—for the mission details was because he was close to uncovering something she wanted to keep hidden.

When Tiberius cut her off, Kehoe tapped the desk with her fingertips and pursed up her lips. He was getting too close, but he was too far away for her to do anything about it. Time would dictate what she must do, but for now, the safest thing was to let him know the full details of his mission. She called up the files on the computer and sent them on an encrypted frequency. It would be several hours before they reached him, even with their advanced technology.

19

The Queen of Tycho

Tiberius yawned and stretched. He was dreaming someone was shaking him as he slept, and he rolled onto his side and tried to pull the pillow over his head. Then he half-opened his eyes and saw Ross standing by the bed. He closed his eyes then reopened them. No, he was not dreaming. Ross was standing there and had obviously been the one shaking him.

"You sleep very deeply," Ross commented when he saw his commanding officer was finally awake.

"What is it? I've only just dropped off."

Ross looked sympathetic, he knew Tiberius had trouble sleeping at times. "There's an uncharted planet on this course and they challenged us—I thought you would want to be on the bridge. They did not give any reason."

Tiberius swung his legs over the side of the bed. "I'll be right there." The minute the door closed behind Ross, he grabbed his uniform and dressed hurriedly. He was still stamping his feet into his boots as he made for the door. He did not like the sound of an unknown planet challenging them; they certainly had done nothing to provoke anyone and, if they had done so unwittingly, he would be able to explain this. He hurried onto the bridge and Ross relinquished the command chair. "Okay, tell me what happened. Zee-Zee, play me the communication we had from them."

Lieutenant Zeal looked up. "I can do better than that, sir. I have the planetary leader requesting to talk with you. Would you like me to put it on the view-screen?"

Tiberius nodded. "This planet is the gateway to Tamora, we need to get past them. Let's see what they want."

Veritas: The Captain's Redemption

The screen flickered and a blue-skinned woman appeared. Tiberius found himself staring. She was beautiful; even her long wavy hair was blue and shimmered with an almost silvery light. "Greetings, Earth Vessel." Her voice was deep and melodious. "I am Araimeer Eksiiss, queen-ruler of the planet Tycho. Welcome to the Ivaldi system."

"I am Captain Tiberius MacAlpin of the United Earth Ship *Invincible*. You challenged us. Why? We are explorers and have never been in this area of space and I am unaware we have done anything wrong. I apologize if we have done something we ought not."

"You have done no wrong, Captain. The challenge is a mere formality to protect my people. It is easier to offer a challenge as that prompts a response such as yours, explaining why you are here. I would like to offer you the hospitality of my people. You are a long way from home. When was the last time you left your ship?"

Queen Araimeer's voice rippled like music and Tiberius was surprised he understood her. "You speak my language?"

She laughed. "No, Captain. We have excellent translation devices. You will, of course, be offered one when you attend me."

"I would be honoured. Does this invitation extend to my crew?"

"You and your first officer will be my guests at dinner. The rest of your crew will be entertained in the Dome—no harm will come to them. We are a people of peace."

The image flickered as Tycho's queen signed off and Tiberius turned to the science officer. "Tycho? What do we know of it?" He knew he would already have been finding the information as soon as the name of the planet was revealed

The science officer turned from his station and looked up. "It is an Earth-like planet with an unusually large axial-tilt which causes extremes of seasonal change. Both hemispheres experience harsh winters, which can last for weeks or months at a time depending on latitude. There are forests of fungus-like organisms covering much of the land areas. The atmosphere is composed mostly of nitrogen and oxygen but has extremely high levels of carbons dioxide and monoxide."

"Making it lethal to humans?" Tiberius observed.

"Yes, sir, but apparently the centre of the planet is protected from the poisonous atmosphere by a glass dome. If we go outside of the dome, we suffocate."

Tiberius nodded. He glanced up as Commander Ross came up to him. "What is it, Kirbie? You look like you have something on your mind."

Ross nodded. "Yes, sir. You know the rules—we're not supposed to both leave the ship at the same time. I should go alone."

"The queen invited us both."

"I know, but you know the risk. Perhaps we should invite them on board." Ross was clearly worried. "The captain is not supposed to be the one to go down to a planet—that should be my job. I understand she is the ruler of this world and that to refuse her invitation would be deeply offensive." He sighed and looked at Tiberius, knowing it was a difficult situation and he did not enjoy continually having this safety argument with his commanding officer.

Tiberius looked at him. "They are a neutral planet, there should be no risk. I understand your concerns but…"

"Sir, I insist that you consider my concerns as legitimate reasons. I hate to say this, but you know what happened when your father and Commander Galen both went down to the council meeting on Tamora."

There was silence on the bridge. Everyone knew that Ross had stepped close to the mark, if not overstepped, by referring to the captain's father.

Tiberius' eyes never left Ross' face in the few minutes of silence that ensued. "Ouch!"

"Forgive me, I should not have said it." Ross sounded really contrite, knowing what he said had hurt.

Tiberius nodded. "It's okay. I know what you meant by it." He looked down at his hands for a moment. "We're going. We cannot risk causing offence to a people we have just met. It's the captain's responsibility to make first contact."

Ross inclined his head. "Yes, sir." His reserved response told Tiberius just what his first officer thought about the captain running risks from which it was one of his jobs to protect him.

Tiberius turned to the tactical officer. "You will take command while I am off the ship; the rest of the crew will follow a strict rota which Commander Ross will put together for their turn planetside. You will go with the third party and Lieutenant Zeal will take command then."

"Understood, sir." The tactical officer was also the second officer, and she was used to taking a stint in the command chair, taking one of the three scheduled shifts.

Later, Tiberius and Ross were preparing to take their shuttlecraft down to the planet. They would be followed by the first group to accept the planet's hospitality. Tiberius and Ross were in dress uniform as they were to dine with the queen. Tiberius glanced at Ross and saw he was still looking concerned. "It'll be okay and hey, you can't deny she's beautiful—that blue!"

Ross laughed. "A very pretty shade of blue. You are incorrigible," he added, his eyes twinkling. "You have had a rough time lately, forgive me for being tough on you because of rules."

Tiberius smiled. "It's okay. I know it is your job to advise me; I warn you, I can be tough to advise."

Ross said nothing but just smiled.

When the shuttle arrived on the planet, they were met by the queen's guard. Tycho was a neutral planet but, like many neutral nations, kept an army of peacetime soldiers who mostly acted as security for events such as these and also so that the planet would not come under sudden attack by enemies who might take advantage of their neutrality.

The guards led them up some steps into a beautiful building, almost like a palace in a fairy-tale, and they were shown into an ornate room and asked to wait. Tiberius looked around. "Wow, peace does have its virtues. Look at this place."

"I see you are admiring our décor, Captain MacAlpin."

The men turned smartly at the voice and saw their hostess standing before them, her hands clasped in front of her. Tiberius noticed that her silvery tunic and sleeveless robe made her skin seem even brighter blue than on the screen, and he found himself holding his breath.

"Welcome to Tycho, Captain, Commander. Please, come with me." She made a gesture with her hand and the two officers followed her through an arched door at the far end of the room. They were met by a server with drinks on a tray. Araimeer Eksiiss took a glass and indicated the others. "Please, take and enjoy." She sat down and pointed to a long, cushioned seat opposite her chair. "Sit, gentlemen, please."

They sat side by side, looking at the beautiful blue woman in front of them. She saw them looking and smiled. "You are wondering why we stopped you in passing, and that our message was in the form of a challenge. I explained that when we spoke; we protect our planet by challenging passing ships to explain their reason for being within Tycho space. But I did have another reason."

Tiberius took a sip of his drink and tried not to pull a face. It was sour at first but then became a syrupy-sweet explosion on the tongue. He saw the woman's eyes on him and saw her smile. "It is a fruit, native to Tycho. It looks a little like what you would call a pineapple."

"It's nice," Tiberius told her. Ross agreed with him, nodding. "It is very sweet, sweeter than natural juices are on Earth." He took another sip and then turned to their hostess. "You said there was another reason why we were stopped. You have invited us to dine with you, is it just the curiosity of a people far from other planets, or is it that you need our assistance with something?"

Queen Araimeer set down her glass. "I confess to some curiosity. We do not get many passing ships who do stop. It is a long time since an Earth vessel last came this way. In fact, you are only the second one."

Tiberius looked up quickly. "Just the second? Do you remember the name of the first ship?"

"You are the captain's son, I believe? You are just like him."

Ross put his hand on Tiberius' shoulder. This planet must have been the last place the *Wryneck* was seen before they headed for Tamora.

Araimeer stood up and offered her arm to Tiberius. "Take me in to dinner, we will talk further on this."

Tiberius took the alien woman's arm and led her into the dining room, with Ross following behind.

20

A Splash of Oatmeal

Admiral Kehoe stood at the window of her office, looking at the rising moon. It was a full moon and there was something about watching it rise that gave a great sense of peace. It was a long time since she had felt this peaceful. A deep-seated fear was gripping her heart, fearing her involvement being discovered. Thirty years ago they had accused Stephen MacAlpin of treason. But he was not the guilty one—he was not the traitor. Those in High Command who had sent them knowingly into danger for their own ends were the traitors. She had been one of those who plotted on this scheme. No-one was supposed to have survived—there should be no-one to accuse and condemn her and her conspirators. Xander Galen was a danger; he could destroy everything they had worked for. She had been looking at the latest report from Tamora on the project for which they had sacrificed their own people. It pleased her that things were going well, and she had responded, telling them that another shipment was on the way. But she was troubled. Xander's survival had led to Stephen's son questioning and challenging her decisions. She had to get rid of him. She would not kill him; another death on her conscience would not help her mood right now, but she knew what she could do. His illness would help her—no-one would be surprised if he were suddenly hospitalized. She nodded as she looked at the moon.

The silvery light shone serenely, silently witnessing her plotting. She would go and see him in the morning—she just had to work out how she was going to do this. It would be Sunday and Xander always rested at the weekend, conserving his strength for the week ahead. She smiled and turned away and went into her room to put her thoughts together to come up with the best plan of action. At first, a little niggle from her conscience disturbed her. She did actually like Xander. He was a good officer and he had been through hell since the loss of the *Wryneck*. She had seen the state he was in when he was released and returned to Earth. No-one had expected him to live much longer after that and the years of hospital treatment had not been unexpected. But he had fought, and he had survived, surprising everyone by returning to active service—taking a command position and serving for twenty years as one of the best captains in the fleet; fuelled, some said, by the pain and suffering he had been through; that what he had suffered had given him the passion and the determination to succeed. It had only been in the last five years that his health had begun to suffer and quickly declined, and he had more bad days than good of late.

She drew the curtains over the window to shut out the moonlight and lay down on the bed to make her plans.

•

Xander opened his eyes as the sun streamed through his bedroom window. He rolled over and lay on his side for a while, watching the rising sun colouring the sky. He touched a button on the bedside and watched the window slide open, smiling as he listened to the birds singing. It might be the middle of the city, but it never failed to amaze him that the birds continued to sing so beautifully. It made him feel alive; that however he felt, so long as he could draw another breath, there was hope. He knew that today was not one of his best days, so he lay back and just breathed in the fresh air. He was expecting a visit from his doctor later but now he was content just to rest. An hour or two later, he pressed the intercom when the buzzer at the door sounded. "Who is it?"

"Kehoe."

"Come in. I'll be a moment." He pressed the button to unlock the door. He got up, pulled on T-shirt and trousers and tucked his feet into slippers before he went through into the living area. "Admiral, please, sit down. I did not expect a visit from you. Is something wrong?"

"Not at all, Galen. I came to see how you are feeling. You have had a lot of bad days recently." Admiral Kehoe sat down and crossed one leg over the other. "Sit down, let's have a talk."

Xander sat down in the chair opposite the admiral and leaned back against the cushions.

"How are you feeling? You look tired." She was watching him closely.

Xander turned his head. "I will be fine. I am always tired first thing in the morning."

"Have you had your medication?"

Xander shook his head. "No, I was still in bed when you buzzed." He made a move to rise but the admiral stood up.

"Let me fetch it. Is it pills?"

"No, there's a syringe in the fridge. I can get it later." He broke off, realizing she was going anyway.

The admiral went through into the kitchen and opened the fridge. She saw the little box that Xander's medication was kept in and she took out the syringe. She went to the sink, pressed the plunger, and watched the medicine run down the plughole. Once the syringe was empty, she refilled it from a phial she took from her pocket before going to the living room. She had a glass of an oatmeal smoothie with her, as an excuse for taking some time. "I thought you would like your breakfast." She held out the glass.

Xander smiled. "I make it the night before—it is supposed to help my energy levels." He held out his hand for the syringe. "Thank you."

"I'll do it." She took his arm and held it tightly enough that Xander felt a rush of fear.

He did not trust her, why had he been stupid enough to let her get his medication? He sensed something was wrong and tried to pull away.

Kehoe turned his arm over and held it locked against her hip as he tried to free himself. She saw the fresh needle marks around his main vein and quickly pushed the needle in.

Xander closed his eyes as the needle penetrated his skin and he felt the slight pressure as the plunger was pushed in. Years of injections should have made him immune, but he felt each one distinctly. He bit his lip as the needle was removed and then felt her finger on the little speck of blood.

"There—all done." Kehoe went back into the kitchen and washed out the syringe thoroughly and filled it from the correct bottle in the fridge and replaced it in the box and closed the door. She returned to the living room and found Xander lying back against the cushions, sweating. His eyes flickered open and he tried to speak but the words did not come out. The glass with his oatmeal drink slipped from his fingers and splashed all over the floor. He managed to push himself unsteadily to his feet. He took a step, then swayed and crumpled up, landing face down on the floor.

Kehoe sat for a while, watching him on the floor, trying to push himself up before he lay still. She stood up and straightened the cushions so it would seem he had been alone and went to erase the computer call log so that her ring would not be recorded. She opened the door and paused momentarily to look back, before going out and shutting the door behind her. She headed home and changed, getting ready to head to the office. No-one would even know she had been to Xander's apartment. She sent a message to one of those involved with her and planted the suggestion that Xander needed taking care of. A few calls were made, and a medical team was secretly dispatched to the apartment where the unconscious officer was quickly stretchered out and into the waiting ambulance, before being rushed to the hospital. A team of doctors met the ambulance and Xander was borne off to an isolation unit while the admiral's security detail set the locks to activate as soon as they closed the apartment door.

•

When Xander woke a few hours later, he found himself in darkness and unable to move. He could feel straps on his limbs and tubes in his nose and throat. He tried to turn his head, but it was strapped down too. He opened his eyes and realized they were covered as the darkness remained. He could hear low voices and felt needles being inserted into his arm and tried not to panic. He felt tape being wrapped around his arm, covering the needles, and guessed he was being put on some kind of drip. He felt hands taping wires to his chest and could imagine the monitors he was being hooked up to. With this amount of attention, he guessed he was not being left to die as he could breathe easily and that was a relief. He did not try to speak or make a sound, the tubes in his nose and throat told him that would be futile. He felt the bed move and heard the steady hum of machinery and then the muffled sound of a door closing. He could not see where he was and did not know that he was in an isolation tube in the stasis bank—identified only by a number on the door.

Later that afternoon, Serenity went along to Xander's apartment. They had spoken yesterday, and she had promised to come along and check up on him and go for a picnic in the park as it was Sunday. She pressed the buzzer and waited. She pressed it again; then again. She frowned. This was not like Xander, he always answered the buzzer. She entered the code he had given her—he had told her she could come in whenever she liked but she always rang. She pushed open the door and went through to the living-room. She saw the smashed glass and the smoothie splashed across the wooden floor. She called his name a couple of times and then hurried to the bathroom and tried the door, wondering if he was feeling sick. It opened to her touch and the room was empty. Looking into the bedroom, she saw the bed was not made but had been slept in. She went through to the kitchen and looked in the fridge. That was worrying, he had not taken his medication. She went back to the bedroom and looked around. His coat and outdoor shoes were still in the closet. He would not have gone out without his coat; he felt the cold too much these days and she knew he was not at the office. For one thing, he would not go out of uniform and it hung there beside his coat, and it was Sunday—he never worked on Sundays. She raised her wrist to her mouth and called his call-sign. There was silence. She tried again. Nothing. She did not imagine that he heard her calling but was unable to respond. She went back to the living-room and knelt on the floor to clean up the spilt drink and then sat on the sofa on the opposite side to where Xander always sat. She looked at the cushion and knew he had sat there as he always squashed the cushion. What had happened? What had made him drop his glass? He was a tidy man and would never leave a spill—he would clean it up. Something had happened here, and it was not good. She got up after a while, went to the computer and called up the buzzer log, wondering if there was anything to explain what was going on. There was nothing since the previous evening when Xander had been visited by a friend, and the next log entry was her three rings at the buzzer. She sat down and called up his schedule and looked to see if he had any appointments that she did not know about. She kept his work schedule up to date, but not always his personal one. The only entry was for his friend Doctor Tierney to visit that afternoon. "Computer, can you call Doctor Tierney for me?" She wondered if he had been already or if something had happened and he had taken Xander with him.

"Calling," the computer responded.

"Xander?" Doctor Tierney answered.

"It's Serenity. Xander is not here, I am afraid something is wrong. His schedule said you were going to visit."

"I have not been yet. What do you mean by wrong? Is he all right?"

"I cannot find him." Serenity told the doctor what she had found when she arrived at the apartment. "I am worried. It looks like he might have had a fall. He might have taken himself off to the hospital, but I don't know if he took his medication. It's not marked up in his little book and he is always careful about spacing the doses."

"Don't worry, Serenity. I'll check with the hospital. You keep on trying to call him; maybe he can't respond just now. If he is having tests or treatment, he will not be able to take your call." Tierney's voice was matter of fact.

Serenity nodded. "Thank you. Please let me know what you find out." She ended the call and sat back. She loved Xander and worried about him very much—she looked out for him almost like a mother over an ailing child. Her main concern was that he had not taken his medication. Going without the drug could be disastrous as he could pass out from the pain—at best he would get very tired and would need sleep. She tried calling him again and then decided to go for a walk and see if he was wandering around the base anywhere. He might even have gone out for something to eat if he did not feel up to getting it himself, and she knew that he did like to walk in the central park, or around the fountains. She went back to the computer and left Xander a message. *If you come home, call me. I am worried about you. S.*

She went to the kitchen and took a spare syringe of Xander's medication and slipped it into her pocket. If he had not taken a dose that morning and had gone for a walk he could be sitting somewhere, too tired to go on. He would need a shot before he could get his strength back to get home. She let herself out of the apartment and locked the door behind her. She knew his favourite walks, and she headed that way. As she walked, she called the admiral's office and spoke to Kehoe's aide, asking if Xander had come in.

"It's Sunday," the aide replied. "Rear Admiral Galen never comes in on a Sunday—he told me that one day should always be set aside from work. Admiral Kehoe is in, did you want to speak to her?"

"No, that's not necessary. I am just looking for him. I was supposed to meet him, but I was late. He did not leave word where he was going." She knew that was a lie, but she was not going to tell the truth. "Let me know if he does come in."

•

Admiral Kehoe stopped at the desk. "Who was that?"

"Galen's aide was looking for him. He never comes into work on a Sunday. I thought the android would know that."

The admiral nodded. "Strange." She went through to her office and called her contact at the hospital. "Questions are being asked. Remember, for now, he is in isolation; needs to be kept free from the risk of picking up something from others. You know the kind of thing. Multiple tests and trying a new treatment. If his doctor asks, you have the record we prepared." She leaned back in her chair and smiled satisfactorily. Xander should not have begun to probe into what happened. If he had just concentrated on his own work, then these measures would not have been necessary.

Shut away in the dark confines of the isolation tube, Xander tried to keep calm. He was scared. He could not move or call out; he had to rely on the medical staff whose job it was to monitor his condition on the computer—his life literally in their hands. He felt his heart rate getting rapid and fought desperately to calm himself down.

The nurse glanced at the computer screen in front of her and saw the readings had changed and her patient's heart rate was up, indicating he was in distress. She tapped the screen to bring up his notes and then stood up and pressed the button. The tube slid out and she opened a little hatch in the side and put her hand in and took a reading of his pulse. She felt his arm quiver at her touch, and she took his hand for a moment, knowing he was strapped down and unable to reach for hers. He seemed reassured by the touch as she felt the shaking hand relax slightly. She felt for the cannula in the back of his hand and prepared the drug she had been ordered to administer if he got distressed. It was a mild tranquillizer and would keep him in a semi-conscious state. She attached the drip to the needle and then withdrew her hands and checked all the tubes running to the machine administering the drugs. Satisfied that all was okay, she tapped the button again and watched the tube slide back into its chamber and resealed the door before returning to her seat. She flicked on the monitor and watched him for a while, seeing that everything was stable.

Xander fought against the drug he could feel beginning to work. He knew they were going to keep him drugged and every fibre of his being struggled against it although knowing it to be futile. The only thing he was able to take as positive was that if they wanted him dead they would not be going to this trouble. He could breathe easily, and he was not in any pain which meant they were administering his prescribed medication.

He stopped fighting and let the drug take effect.

21

"The only danger was the atmosphere!"

As they took their seats at the table, Tiberius took a good look around. The surroundings were ornate—the people of this planet seemed to be very wealthy. Araimeer had told them that all houses were decorated and fitted out in exactly the same, almost extravagant fashion.

Araimeer and her three aides, who joined them via the door at the other end of the dining room, all wore elaborate costumes in bright colours that suited their blue skin. Everyone seemed to benefit from the peace and prosperity of their world and Tiberius smiled ruefully. If only Earth had been so blessed. It was a miracle humans had survived beyond the twenty-first century. It seemed that the more they strove for peace and equality, the more wars and inequality there was, and it had taken many people centuries to be finally treated with the respect that everyone wanted for themselves.

There had been many warnings and finally, it had seemed to dawn on the humans that destroying themselves and their world was not the way. It had taken centuries of misunderstanding, prejudice, and hatred to finally show them they were in danger. But these people, blessed with a world that appeared as abundant as Earth, had developed in harmony. One people, one colour—maybe they had never known prejudice because there was no-one different to them on their planet. Humans were not so—many peoples, many colours; the prejudices of centuries being inherent to each new generation although there were many who did not feel this way, the few had dictated history for so long.

Tiberius turned to Araimeer. "Was there always peace here?"

Araimeer smiled. "Yes. Do you struggle to understand that idea? No war, no fighting."

"No, I do not struggle to understand—I envy it." Tiberius watched as plates were set before them, and Araimeer waved her hand at the table. "Help yourselves. You will find that much here is not entirely alien to you. There is fish, which comes from the river, and fruits and vegetables which are grown here under the dome. There is nothing to harm the human system and the flavours will not be too unpleasant for you. Our native fish is a relative of the salmon on your planet." She leaned across and took a steak of the fish and placed it on Tiberius' plate. "The colour of the meat is different, but the flavour is not dissimilar."

Tiberius thanked her. "Forgive me; I am looking forward to trying the food. Please do not mistake my silence for anything other than wonder—I am intrigued by the similarities in our foods and yet the vivid and obvious differences. I hope you do not think us rude."

She shook her head. "I would be much the same aboard your ship."

Tiberius returned her smile and began to select the food for his plate from the many dishes on the sideboard. Ross followed suit, followed by Araimeer and her officials. When they returned to their places, Araimeer took a taper and lit a candle in the centre of the table. Tiberius watched with interest as the flame flickered and then grew into a steady, strong flame. Araimeer put some black crystals around the wick and, moments later, the flame turned green. She looked up and saw the humans watching her. "A light at dinner commemorates our peace and unity and gives thanks for the plenty we have, just as some of your cultures would have offered a blessing before a meal." She picked up her fork and began to eat.

Tiberius and Ross tucked in and found, to their surprise, that the rather off-putting solid black colour of the fish was not indicative of its flavour. Araimeer had been right, it was like salmon.

They talked as the meal progressed and the subject of the visit of the *Wryneck* came up. Araimeer nodded as Tiberius asked his questions. "Yes, they stopped here a few days and went on their way refreshed. They were heading for the planet Tamora. If we had known then what we know now of the Tamoran people, we would have warned them to be on their guard. I hope they were as cautious as possible."

Tiberius took a deep breath. "They all died. Whatever happened—they all died; except for Commander Galen—the first officer. We do not know why. What do you know of these people? Our mission is taking us to Tamora, and I need to learn everything possible about this world. There seems little recorded."

Araimeer looked compassionate. "Your father perished? I am truly sorry. He was a nice man, and you are his image—even your voice and mannerisms are his. He would be proud of you, I am sure."

Tiberius lowered his eyes for a moment and Ross looked at their hostess. "He never met his father," he told her. "This mission is as much part of our official orders, as it is the chance for my commanding officer to finally find peace over the past—when he knows why his father died, only then will he have peace."

Araimeer nodded. "I understand." She signalled the servers to clear the table and then hot drinks were brought in. "This is *plaki'r*—it is like your coffee." She stood up and poured the drinks and handed them to her guests and took one herself. "Come, let us return to the lounge. We can talk freely in there." She nodded to the officials who had dined with them and led her guests out of the room. She took a seat and waited for Tiberius and Ross to sit. "The Tamorans are a civilized people, but a violent one. They experiment with genetics—they have a breeding programme and take many different species to use in their experiments."

Tiberius glanced up quickly. "A breeding programme? Do you know what kind?" He felt a chill settle over him. What had they done to his father and the crew? Was it because of this programme that Xander was now so ill? All these thoughts were running through his mind and Ross knew exactly what he was thinking.

"We don't know exactly. All we know is that there are rumours and that some of our people have been taken. Ships have come at night, and in the morning, we find we are missing some people; sometimes just a few, the last time it was fifty. We do not have a large population, only two thousand people. And we do not have a strong defence system."

Tiberius forced himself to turn his mind from thinking of his father and to listen to Araimeer. "Perhaps you could install security alarms. They would not break your neutrality and would give you a warning. It might also be a good idea if all your people come inside the dome at night. There is plenty of room for them all and they would be safe there."

Queen Araimeer nodded. "Thank you, I will see that this is done."

"Do not worry; my personal mission will be to put an end to their programme. If possible, I *will* return your people to you. If this cannot be, I will still return to tell you it is over." Tiberius looked her full in the eyes and the queen saw the sincerity and knew that he meant every word he said.

She smiled. "Thank you. If there is anything we can do to help, we will do so." She finished her drink and stood up. "Must you return to your ship? Or can you spend some more time on the planet?"

Tiberius glanced at Ross for only a moment and then shook his head. "I will return to the ship—Ross can stay for a while. I have a lot to think about, and he deserves some relaxation." He stood up and held out his hand. "Thank you for your hospitality. Ross, they have a real pool here. Go and have a swim."

Ross smiled. "Sure you won't?"

Tiberius shook his head. "I will see you later. There is a lot I need to do now."

•

Tiberius walked onto the bridge and took his seat. He pressed the intercom and called for the first officer.

Lieutenant Zeal looked up. "Sir, Commander Ross did not come back to the ship last night. In fact, none of us saw him after you headed back to the ship. The last time we saw him he was heading for the swimming pool."

Tiberius frowned. "I told him he could stay behind but he was to return with the last of the crew returning to the ship. Get the queen for me."

"Yes, sir." A few moments later, Zeal turned back. "Putting her through now, Captain."

"Captain MacAlpin, you are preparing to depart?" Araimeer Eksiiss asked as her face appeared on the screen.

"We were, but I have just discovered that Commander Ross is missing. He was due to return with the last of my crew who returned last night. Have you seen him at all this morning? I wonder if he missed the shuttle and has slept somewhere."

She shook her head. "I have not seen him. I will send a party to search for him. Would you like to join the search?"

Tiberius nodded. "I will, and our doctor will accompany me just in case he has met with an accident. I am fully aware of the toxicity of your atmosphere if he stepped outside the dome." He was worried about Ross and hoped he had not met with any misfortune. In the back of his mind was the conversation they had at dinner about the disappearance of people from the planet. A sudden deep worry settled over him that Ross had fallen victim to the raiding Tamorans and was now a prisoner. No, he must not think like that.

Tiberius and Doctor Malachi joined the search party on the planet and searched the city shielded by the dome and then they regrouped and discussed their next move as they had found no sign of him within the city. The decision was made to search outside of the dome; if Ross had been out, then he was in danger from the poisonous atmosphere. The surface of the planet was covered in a forest of tree-like fungal organisms and there was a lot of undergrowth that they had to get through, and it took a long time. Tiberius and the doctor were given breathing apparatus so that they would not be in danger from the atmosphere. Several hours passed and they had to hack their way through the dense undergrowth which, although fungus-like, was as tough as trees. They broke through into a clearing and that was when Tiberius saw him.

Commander Ross stood with his back against the trunk of the tree, his arms raised above his head. An arrow had been shot through his hands which had been placed together, pinning him to the tree. He was covered in blood and his legs hung limply, looking as though the hamstrings had been cut. He was hanging by his hands, as his legs could not hold him up.

Tiberius felt his heart almost stop; he could not tell if Ross was alive or not until his eyes opened.

Ross' face was grey, with a blue tinge to the skin, he could barely breathe from the pain and the toxic atmosphere. He saw Tiberius, tried to say something, and then passed out.

Tiberius yanked off his breathing mask so he could speak. "Rivkah!" he yelled, calling the doctor by her first name in his urgency. "Help me! I have to get him down!" He ran to the tree and, with the doctor supporting Ross' weight, he managed to break the arrow shaft and they lifted him down and laid him on the ground. Tiberius slid his arms under him and lifted him up. "Can we get back to the Dome?"

Araimeer shook her head. "Not in time to help him—there's a cave nearby and you will be able to breathe in there. Follow me."

Tiberius laid Ross on the floor of the cave and knelt anxiously at his side as Doctor Malachi opened her medi-kit. Her first move was to apply pressure bandages tightly to his hands and the backs of his legs which were bleeding the worst—a very sharp blade had been used to cut the tendons. When these wounds were strapped up, she gave an injection to stabilize him and strapped an oxygen mask over his face and handed the canister to Tiberius. "Use bandages to strap this to his side then we will be able to move him. I need to get him into the infirmary as soon as possible."

The doctor did not need to tell Tiberius that Ross was in a bad way and he worked quickly to get the oxygen cylinder stable. He did not need it to be pointed out that if they had been any later, Ross would have suffocated—if he had not bled to death before that. He rested his hand on Ross' shoulder; he knew he would not know he was there, but it felt like he was doing something to help. He looked up at the queen. "You said we were safe here—no ship came here last night; we were watching for that. He was attacked by someone already on the planet and I demand answers. You said you have no weapons; if you are a people of peace, how can such brutality have been perpetrated?"

Araimeer Eksiiss sighed. "I do not know; I am as shocked as you. Had he remained inside the Dome, this would not have happened—I will look into it."

"You assured us the only danger was the atmosphere!"

The doctor turned to the captain. "Send for security and try and get the answers we need. I will take Ross aboard and you can come and see him later." She needed space to work in. She knew that if Tiberius came into the infirmary, then he would get under her feet as he worried about his friend and colleague. If he stayed on Tycho he would feel like he was doing something.

Tiberius nodded. "I will do that. Look after him—he should not have been injured like this. I should never have let him stay behind." He was racked with guilt. He should have ordered Ross to return to the ship with him—he would have been safe if he had.

The doctor looked up and saw his face. "Do not be angry at yourself; you could not have foreseen this."

"I could have prevented it! They had told us that people were being taken mysteriously." Tiberius pulled a face.

"But no ship came—we watched for that. That means danger was already on the planet."

Tiberius looked at the doctor in silence for a moment and then said, "You think these people are not what they seem?"

She shrugged slightly. "I don't know; all I know right now is that I need to get Ross back on board, and you need to try and find out what happened." She looked up as a shuttle landed and a medical team hurried out with a stretcher.

Two security guards joined the captain, who nodded to them but was watching as Ross was lifted onto the stretcher, wrapped in special blankets to keep him warm. The medical team hurried into the shuttle which left moments later.

Tiberius turned to the queen. "You are the leader of these people and claim to be a neutral planet. You offered us hospitality last night. How can this have happened? How can my first officer now be on his way to the infirmary crippled like that? You saw what happened to him. You saw him pinned to that tree—his legs cut." He was trying not to raise his voice. He needed Ross at his side when they reached Tamora. With hands and legs damaged like that, he would not be of much use to his commanding officer—he would have to face the Tamorans alone unless Doctor Malachi could work a miracle. She was very skilled, and he had some hope for her reputation was very high in the service.

Araimeer Eksiiss had told them the Tamorans were a violent people with an illicit and controversial experimental genetics programme. He could not face them without the support of his friend and first officer. He turned back to Araimeer. "Let's go back to the clearing. I want to see if there are any clues around the tree that will tell us what happened to Ross." He pulled his breathing apparatus back into place and stepped out of the cave with Araimeer and the security guards behind him. Back at the tree in the clearing, he looked around and found the grass to one side of the clearing was crushed and looked as though a struggle had taken place and Tiberius knew Ross must have fought frantically for his freedom. He could not even begin to imagine the pain he must have felt when the blade cut deep into the back of his legs. The crushed grass was soaked with blood in one place and Tiberius knew the maiming of his first officer had taken place here. He wondered if he had been conscious when he was dragged to the tree and held there as an arrow was shot through his hands, leaving him helpless. He stood and looked around and realized the answers would only really come from Ross; he would know what happened.

He returned to the ship after telling the queen he might return for answers. He went along to the *Invincible*'s infirmary and asked if he was able to see the Ross.

Doctor Malachi nodded. "Come in, he is awake." She led him along to the far end of the ward where a screen was drawn around one of the cubicles.

Ross lay propped up on the pillows; the bed had been raised so he was sitting a little and the sheets were pulled up and tucked around his shoulders. He smiled when he saw Tiberius and asked the nurse to switch off the screen on the bedside terminal. He had been reading to pass the time but was glad to see the captain.

Tiberius smiled. "You look pretty chirpy. How are you feeling?"

"I can't feel my arms and legs, and I'm a bit light-headed from painkillers, but I guess I'm okay," Ross replied. His voice was quite bright, but Tiberius had known him long enough to know that he was trying to make light of things.

"Do you feel up to questions? I need to know what happened."

"It's okay," Ross responded. "Doc told me you would need to question me. Help me to lie back a bit and I'll be ready."

Tiberius pressed the button and let Ross lie back. He straightened the pillows and made sure he was comfortable and then pulled a seat across and sat down. Doctor Malachi sat beside him and had a tablet computer on her knee so there would be an official record of the conversation. The ship's psychiatrist joined them; his job to verify there was no coercion and that Ross was comfortable to answer the questions without any impact on his condition.

Ross lay back and closed his eyes as a nurse came over, made some quick scans, and offered him a painkiller. Ross shook his head. "Maybe later. I need to be able to concentrate—the pain will help."

The nurse nodded. "Just stop them if you need a rest."

Ross nodded. "I will." He opened his eyes and turned his head on the pillow. "I'm ready."

The nurse turned to Tiberius. "You're good to go, sir."

Tiberius nodded to the doctor, who tapped "record". "Ready, Captain."

"This is Captain Tiberius MacAlpin, commanding the UES *Invincible*. This interview is convened in the infirmary and is to enquire into the attack on Commander Kirbie Ross on the planet Tycho which has left the first officer crippled. I will be appending a medical report with full details of his injuries which are severe. Doctor Rivkah Malachi, Chief Medical Officer, and Doctor Dante Ravello, ship's psychiatrist, are also present. I will be guided by Malachi and Ravello and allow Commander Ross to stop if the questioning tires or distresses him. He has, however, consented to the questioning and has voluntarily foregone pain medication in order to give a lucid account." Tiberius paused and then continued. "Ross, can you tell us what happened after I granted you permission to join the rest of the crew for the remainder of shore leave on the planet Tycho?"

Ross took a deep breath. "I left the queen's home and joined the remainder of the crew in the Dome where we went to the swimming pool. I had no intention of remaining behind on the planet; I was looking forward to returning to the ship after my swim. As first officer, it is my duty to ensure the safety of the crew, so I ensured that everyone boarded the shuttles to return to the *Invincible*; one shuttle was to return for me." He paused and closed his eyes for a moment. A nurse standing by the bed slipped her hand under his head and helped him to sip some water. He went on, his voice a little stronger. "As I waited for the return of the shuttle, I went to the main doors of the Dome and looked out over the planet where we could not go because of the toxic air. I became aware of a light in the sky and I focused on it, believing it be perhaps a planet or Tycho's own moon. The light grew stronger in intensity and I realized it was getting closer. I heard a sound to my right and turned, in time to see a shadow beside me. My arms were seized, and I was dragged out of the safety of the Dome. I struggled, unable to breathe properly, but the hands holding my arms were too strong for me to succeed in freeing myself." He paused again for more water and leaned back on the pillows in silence and gathered his strength to go on. "My captors dragged me into the forest area outside the city; by now, my head was spinning as the air began to choke me. As I was dragged into the clearing, the light grew stronger, and I became aware that there was a craft sitting there."

"Can you describe the craft?"

Ross nodded. "You know the way people centuries ago talked of flying saucers and UFOs? It looked like that—it was big, like the saucer in the old movie 'Close Encounters of the Third Kind' and it was glowing. The light was white, with a purple and green shimmer to it."

"Thank you. Go on."

"I was choking by now, my lungs felt as though they would explode, and I was on my knees as they dragged me towards the craft."

"Were you taken inside?" Doctor Ravello asked, at a nod from Tiberus.

Ross shook his head. "A figure came down from it and spoke to those dragging me and something was put over my face and I was able to breathe easily. I thought they were just going to take me away."

"When did their manner toward you change? Was there anything that made you feel threatened for your safety?"

Ross shook his head. "There was always a feeling of threat—I was afraid. The figure who came down from the craft appeared to be someone with authority for the people holding me were at attention and they bowed when they finished speaking and I was dragged to the edge of the clearing and pushed to the ground and whatever they put over my face was removed. I felt a sharp pain in the back of my right leg. I tried to scream but the air choked me, and then I felt the same happening to the other leg. They dragged me across to a tree, my legs were throbbing, but I could not feel anything other than the pain; I knew the blood was pumping out and I was getting giddy—being barely able to breathe did not help." He broke off, almost panting.

Doctor Ravello got up and went to the bedside. "Want a break?" As Ross shook his head, he nodded but remained at the bedside, his fingers on Ross' neck, feeling the pulse and it was racing. "Go on, but take it easy."

"I was dragged to the tree and held up against it. The pain intensified as they lifted an arm each and my hands were held together. Another figure appeared from the craft with a weapon which they raised and fired. I felt a wave of agony and the two holding me moved away and I realized that I was pinned to the tree by something which had been shot through my hands. My legs were hanging, and I was unable to support my weight. I don't remember anything else as I must have fainted."

He coughed and Doctor Malachi took Ravello's place beside the bed. "Breathe slowly," she told him. "The toxic air has caused some lung damage, oxygen will help you." She reached for a mask and began to prepare to get her patient onto oxygen. "This interview is at an end for now."

"I have one last question." Tiberius looked at the doctor and then turned back to Ross. "I need to know what they looked like. Were they from Tycho?"

"Shadows, Tiberius. I did not see them clearly. The one who came from the craft—they looked like pure light. I believe they can change form."

Doctor Malachi reached over and replaced the mask as Ross was wheezing. Ross made one last effort as a strong sedative was administered. "Sir, they said Tamora."

Tiberius stood up and put his hand on Ross' shoulder. "Rest now. You did well to get through this, I know the pain is bad. I'll come and see how you are later." He watched Ross' eyes close as the sedative took effect. He turned and looked at the doctors. "Tell me the truth, how is he? Mentally and physically."

"Mentally, he is in shock," Ravello answered. "The shock to his system when the tendons were severed would have been great. His body was fighting for oxygen by that time, and he must have been afraid, although we all know him to be a courageous man. I will work closely with him."

"Will it affect his work?"

The two doctors looked at each other for a moment and then Doctor Malachi spoke. "His mental state is less of a worry at this point than that of his physical condition. You will understand of course that the nerve and muscle damage is very severe. He has already had a number of blood transfusions and will require more when I take him in for surgery."

Tiberius nodded. "We are all aware of the dangers we face out here. But a neutral planet? I do not believe the Tychonians are entirely blameless in this matter. I must speak with the queen again."

"Commander Ross mentioned the Tamorans and you were told that there have been Tamoran raids. Perhaps they have technology that means they were able to slip past the *Invincible* undetected," Doctor Ravello said. "I do not believe Queen Araimeer to have been lying when she told you her people had nothing to do with it. What would a neutral planet gain by doing this? They rely on the power we, and other planets, have to defend them against enemies. You are, understandably, angry and upset. I suggest you take a break before returning to your duties."

Tiberius sighed and nodded. "I'll do that. Do everything necessary—I need him when we reach Tamora." He turned and walked out of the room. He went straight to his quarters and lay on the bed with his hands behind his head. He was worried about Ross and knew it was selfish of him to worry that he was not going to be at his side when they reached Tamora—he should be worried solely for the pain and suffering Ross was going through, and the post-traumatic issues he would suffer.

The doctors looked at each other and Doctor Malachi sighed a little. "Commanding officers are all the same; they expect we can perform miracles on a daily basis."

"He is not denying the serious nature of Ross' injuries," Ravello replied. "He is trying to hide his fear about losing his right-hand man and his worry for what Ross is going through."

Rivkah Malachi nodded. "I understand. I will prepare him for surgery, your work will start when he comes out of the anaesthetic."

"I will come through later—just let me know when. Good luck."

22

"Something rotten in the state of Rome"

It was the following morning when Doctor Malachi called the bridge and told Tiberius that Ross was out of surgery, after fourteen hours, and was awake.

Tiberius told her he was on his way and almost ran from the bridge. Outside the door of the infirmary, he paused and took a deep breath before he entered and went to Ross' bedside and saw he was awake, although heavily dosed with painkillers. "Hey, Kirbie, you up for a visitor?"

Ross nodded weakly and tried to smile. He was on oxygen still, the tubes in his nose easing the discomfort of his burning lungs. Patch-readers were fixed on his bare chest, their wireless technology transferring his vital signs to the screen over the bed. There was a frame over him from the waist down, holding the sheets and blankets off him; he lay flat, a strap across his chest preventing him from moving.

"Do you know what was done?" Tiberius asked.

Ross shook his head slightly. "Not really. I am not long awake." He paused and looked at Tiberius. "I think we both know the answer though. I can't feel them."

Doctor Malachi came over and smiled at Ross. "You look a little more awake. How are you feeling?"

"Numb. My legs…tell me."

The doctor looked at the screen for a while and then turned back. "Your hands were badly damaged by the arrow and made worse by your full weight dragging down on it. Your legs were severed almost right the way through at the back of the knees. I tried to rebuild the damaged tissue—that is why you were in surgery so long. In the end, I had no alternative, there was nothing I could do but amputate. By the time we reach Tamora, you will have been fitted with prosthetic hands and legs and, with the advances made in this area, there is no reason why you cannot continue with your work as first officer. You will have full functionality in the hands." She broke off when she saw Ross' face. "I know and I am sorry. If there had been another way, I would have chosen it."

Ross closed his eyes. He was in shock to hear this news. He felt bad enough already without finding out he was a quadruple amputee—totally dependent on others until his prosthetics were ready.

Tiberius was stunned too but managed to hide it. He did not want to distress Ross any more. He rested his hand lightly on his shoulder. "You'll make it. You always do. You'll go into rehab and you'll be fine."

"Don't go. Stay awhile. I don't think I can face being alone just now," Ross responded. "I wish they had discussed it with me."

"I told her to do whatever was necessary to save you. There was not the time for discussion—you had already lost too much blood and the transfusion wasn't enough. You could have died." Tiberius responded, a little awkwardly. "It was the only way, or they would have found another way—you know that."

Ross nodded. "Oh, I understand, and I think I knew what would be done. I'm not a fool."

Doctor Malachi signalled a nurse who came over and squirted a liquid painkiller into Ross' mouth.

Ross dozed off shortly after and Tiberius sat on the chair by the bed. He was in shock too. His friend—his right-hand man— was unable to walk or feed himself. The simple things they all took for granted, like just being able to scratch your nose. He watched Doctor Malachi go into her office and knew she was immediately getting down to the task of making the prosthetics required. Such advances had been made in medicine that prosthetic limbs were nothing like they used to be, and the wearer had full function—just as they would have had with their own limbs. All controlled by implants integrated into the nerve-endings in the stumps, and fully capable of picking up the brain functions required to move fingers and toes. Tiberius had no doubt that Ross would soon be up and about, quickly learning to use the new limbs; what worried him was the effect the trauma might have. The terrible pain and fear he had experienced might be harder for him to recover from. He had told Ross he would stay for a while and he watched him sleeping before he quietly got up and headed out. He was required to make a report and submit it to Headquarters. He would make a personal log of the events and attach it with the report from the bedside interview and the medical and psychiatric reports—Ross would no doubt be required to answer more questions as he began his rehabilitation. He went to his quarters to record his report and then went to the bridge. He told the bridge crew about Ross and they were shocked. He settled back into his chair and called up the screen in the arm of the chair and sent a message to Tycho's leader and thanked her for her assistance with Ross and apologized for getting a little bit annoyed and accusing her and her people of knowing something about it.

Her reply made him smile. "It was understandable. There are no hard feelings. We wish Commander Ross a swift and complete recovery and hope you find the answers you seek at Tamora."

•

On Earth, Doctor Tierney had drawn a blank with the hospitals in the search for Xander. He and Serenity had concluded that something had happened, and that the "something" was not good. They alerted the police, letting them know of Xander's condition, and that even if he had taken his medication in the morning, he would be in a pretty bad way by now and may be unable to identify where he was to find his way home. He was beginning to suspect something more sinister had happened to his friend and went to find Serenity after she finished with the police.

She looked up as he came over. "I don't even know what he was wearing," she told him. "I know it was not his uniform."

Clark Tierney nodded. "I know, and I think the police won't find him. All efforts to call him have failed. That means he is unable to respond—he cannot fail to hear the call if he is conscious. We all have the receiver and transmitter implants." He paused and then said, "One of the hospitals knows something; when I was asking questions, there was a moment when the name Galen meant something to the person I spoke with."

"They would know him at his hospital."

"That's just the point, it was not his hospital, it was the big one. In a hospital that size with so many departments and experimental laboratories, they even have to look up staff names let alone patients. The receptionist knew the name. It was only momentary, but he knew something he was not telling me. I want to go back and make more enquiries. You stay and work with the police."

"You think he was abducted?"

Tierney looked at her. "Do you think that? If true, we should find out why—it would perhaps explain what happened. Did anyone come to his apartment?"

"There's nothing on the tape."

"If there has been foul play—an abduction—would they not make sure there was nothing on the tape? Are you able to see if the recording was tampered with?"

Serenity nodded. "I could see nothing when I first looked but I will return to the apartment and work on it. Are you going back to the hospital?"

"Not immediately, I will come with you to his apartment. We may discover something important." Tierney paused and then added, "I believe he is alive, do not fear the worst. If he is in the hospital, we have to hope they have given him his medication."

Serenity nodded again and they made their way to the apartment. She went straight to the computer and began to work on the background of the security camera's program. She went back and forward, looking at everything, and then found a line of code that was different from the rest. "Computer, what is this code?" She read out the code. "Evaluate and describe." She sat back and waited while the computer worked.

"This code represents a deletion in the recording," the computer responded a few moments later.

"When was this?"

"At 08:15."

"Can the data be retrieved? Can you tell me who was at the door before that time?"

"Visual cannot be retrieved, but audio can be."

"Retrieve and play."

A moment later they heard Xander's voice asking who the caller was. Serenity was shocked to hear the responding voice. She looked at Tierney. "Kehoe?!"

"I wondered, as I am sure you did," Tierney replied. "We both knew there was something going on and that Kehoe was involved—Xander told me about the tapping of his computer. There is something rotten in the state of Rome, so to speak!"

Serenity nodded. "I want you to go back to the hospital. I am going to see Kehoe."

"Be careful. We know her to be dangerous."

"That is why we have to find out what is going on and put a stop to it. Xander is ill; whatever is happening could kill him. I know his death is inevitable, but not like this. I promised him he would not be alone and afraid when his time came, and I will keep that promise."

Tierney smiled. "I am glad he has you. I always thought it was sad that his experiences in life meant he never had a chance at relationship, family, and love. He needed someone like you who can give him what he needs, and you will not hurt him because it is not in your programming. He always worried that a human woman would leave him when his condition worsened; no-one can understand the ways of the heart. Love is not always ever-lasting like in the stories and movies. It should be, but it isn't. I should know, there have been three Mrs Tierneys. We won't let anything bad happen to Xander." He put his hand on her arm and pressed it, amazed as others were to find she felt just like human flesh.

23
Used as a Warning

All the way to the admiral's office, Serenity was planning what she was going to say. She was almost certain the admiral knew what was going on—either directly involved herself or was a party to the details. She had to tread warily—a wrong move could spell danger for Xander. She spoke to the officer on the desk as she entered and was told that Admiral Kehoe had someone with her at the moment, so Serenity went along to her own office and sat at the desk to do some work. She left the door open so she would have a view of the admiral's door and would see when the visitor left. It also gave her more time to plan what she wanted to say, and how to say it without making things worse.

As she waited, it dawned on her that Tiberius may have been calling Xander and would be worried at not hearing anything; she knew he worried enough about him with his illness and himself being so far away. She opened up the computer and went to send a signal to the *Invincible* but, before she could do so, an orange light flashed showing that she was receiving a call. She tapped the button to accept it and smiled as Tiberius appeared on the screen. "I was just about to call you."

"Is everything all right? I have been calling Xander and getting no response. Is he…?" Tiberius could not bring himself to finish the sentence.

Serenity shook her head. "He's not dead; he's just gone missing. We have not been able to find him yet. I was going to call and let you know—I knew you would worry." She briefly let him know what she knew, from going to the apartment and finding the spilt drink.

Tiberius looked worried. "He *fell?*"

"I thought that at first, but I am inclined to think that something made him fall—that he was not alone at the time."

"It was her, wasn't it? She wants him to die because of what he knows. She will kill him to prevent herself from being disgraced. Find him, Serenity. You love him—don't fail him."

Serenity smiled. "I love him." Her voice rang with sincerity. "I will find him—I will not fail him." She told Tiberius that Doctor Tierney was helping her with the search. She glanced up and saw the door of the admiral's office open and a man came out. "I have to go. Admiral Kehoe is free now and I want to catch her—I have no appointment; I do not want her to be prepared." She ended the call, hurried to the end of the passage, and pressed the buzzer at the door. She heard Kehoe instruct her to enter and she did so when the door opened.

.

Xander had heard Tiberius calling. He had been in one of his waking periods between doses of the drug which kept him comatose. He could hear the worry and fear in Tiberius' voice when he did not respond, and a tear slid silently down his cheek. He was scared and did not know where he was or what was happening to him, but he realized no-one knew where he was. His heart rate shot up, and he felt whatever he was lying on moving, and then a cool hand on his arm, a sharp prick of pain and then blackness again. As he faded out, he knew they did not want him to be found.

.

Tiberius sat in silence for a while after speaking with Serenity. He was shocked by what she had told him; that Xander was missing. He decided to try and take his mind off it by going along to the infirmary and seeing how Ross was doing. He approached the bedside quietly in case Ross was sleeping—he had been when he last looked in.

Ross turned his head as the footsteps approached. He was propped up on the pillows and was still covered by the frame which kept the bedclothes raised. He smiled sleepily. "Hey, Tiberius."

"Sorry, I disturbed you."

"It's okay, I've been sleeping but it will be nice to have a visitor."

"Has Ravello been working with you yet?"

Ross nodded. "Yes, we've been working on the pain; he's pleased with me, says I have conquered the hardest part—accepting the situation."

Tiberius smiled. "I'm glad. It's horrible, but accepting it means that you will get better."

"I know. I'm not afraid any more. Tiberius, it *was* the Tamorans. They were going to take me, I know that. I was going to end up in their genetics programme, but something made them stop. Something prevented them from taking me—something that compelled them to leave me the way they did. I think it was a warning. They hung me on that tree to warn you what kind of people we are dealing with." He moved an arm a little and managed to get it out from under the covers. He held it up, the stump bandaged. "I lost my hands and my legs for this mission."

Tiberius gently rested his hand on his friend's bandaged arm. "It's my fault. This mission—my desperation to know the truth about my father, has led to this."

Ross laughed softly. "It's not your fault. This mission was going to happen anyway—they were always going to send us. It was planned this way. Well, maybe not this bit, but Kehoe was always going to choose you for this role; it was never going to be my command. Don't blame yourself again. When they fit the prosthetics, I will be back on the bridge in no time." He smiled. "I'm thirsty. There's some fruit on the bedside, only I can't help myself."

Tiberius reached over and picked up an orange, peeled it, and helped Ross to eat the juicy segments. "Better?" he asked, tucking Ross' arm back under the covers. He glanced up as footsteps approached and saw Doctor Ravello. "Time for me to go, I think. Here's the shrink."

"Don't call him that." Ross smiled. "He's very good and does help."

Tiberius grinned. "I'll come and see you later." He turned to the psychiatrist. "If there's anything new he can remember, let me know."

Ravello nodded. "He already did, I believe. He told you it was the Tamorans and that something stopped them from taking him. He was left as a warning to you, and I believe you may know who gave that order." He sat beside the bed and looked at the monitor. "Someone who will stop at nothing to guard the truth for as long as possible. Commander Ross believes that, as his captors dragged him toward the craft, the aliens received a message which changed what they were going to do."

"Kehoe." Tiberius slammed his right fist into the palm of his left hand. "I have always believed she is somehow connected with the Tamorans, that my father's disappearance and the loss of *Wryneck* was caused by Kehoe. Directly or indirectly, she did it."

Ravello looked at the screen and then turned back to Tiberius. "I want him to have peace and quiet now—he needs rest. Although he is in a better frame of mind and is healing considerably well, his body is still in a state of shock. Doctor Malachi has given me full sanction to act as I see fit where his mental state is concerned."

Tiberius nodded. "I understand." He patted Ross' shoulder. "If they let me, I'll come back later." He turned away and walked out of sickbay. He hated to see Ross helpless like that and it made him angry, still believing he was to blame. That, somehow, he could have prevented it. But more than that, he was angry with Admiral Kehoe—so angry that it was a good thing he was far away in space and could not get his hands on her. She had destroyed his father and tried to destroy the image he had of him, caused Xander's illness and now had crippled his first officer. It had to be her—in his mind there was no doubt about it. He returned to the bridge and glanced around. He smiled when he saw the bridge officers were looking at him. "I've seen him. He's doing fine; he'll soon be back on his feet. We'll have him back on the bridge before we even know it." He leaned back and sighed, shooting a quick glance to the empty chair beside his. *Ross should be sitting there now.*

•

Doctor Tierney arrived at the hospital where his suspicions had first been aroused and he approached the reception desk again. He saw a different receptionist was on duty this time and he smiled at her as he came up. "I'm looking for a friend, I believe him to be a patient here. Alexander Galen?" *Alexander? No-one called Xander that.*

"Do you know the zone he might be in, sir?" she asked, turning to the computer. "It would make the search easier."

Tierney shook his head. "I don't know, but I believe he is in a critical condition; he has been unwell for a long time. He may have been rushed in, although this is not the hospital where he is normally treated." He watched as she worked with the computer.

After a few moments, she looked up. "I am sorry, Doctor, your friend's name is not on the list of patients."

"Can you see if anyone was rushed in? Maybe an emergency—he might have been unable to give his name. He can get confused when he is sick."

She looked again and shook her head. "I can see nothing." She paused over an entry that had no name on it and then looked up. "Was his illness genetic?" As her finger hovered over the entry, she touched the alert symbol beside it, set up to be used if anyone asked questions about the secret patient.

The word genetics made Tierney look up quickly. "Yes, I believe so. Is that where he will be?"

The computer chirped and the receptionist excused herself to take the call. She put on her headset, listened for a moment and then reached out and pressed a button, calling a doctor to the reception. Tierney did not know the call had come from Admiral Kehoe, in response to alert being triggered, telling them that Tierney was to see Xander.

A doctor appeared; he had left the nursing team to get their patient into a proper bed and hooked up to the required machines. He told Tierney that Xander was in an intensive care unit, isolated because of his condition.

Tierney went with the doctor and was shown into a room where Xander lay. He noticed the machinery and the tubes in Xander's mouth and nose, and he could see that he was either asleep or drugged. He looked at the screen over the bed and saw the vital signs were steady and felt slightly relieved. He took the tablet from its place at the foot of the bed where once it would have been a clipboard and paper and looked at the list of treatments. He saw nothing untoward; Xander was being properly dosed with the right medication, but he was worried by the fact that he appeared to be being kept under full sedation. He put down the tablet and went to stand beside the bed and looked down at his friend. "What are they doing to you, Xander? They shouldn't be keeping you sedated, it is natural sleep you need."

Xander's eyes flickered and he moved his hand weakly. Tierney reached down and took Xander's hand and gripped it. "I'm here. I know you can't speak to me but I'm here." He had an idea and took his personal tablet from his pocket and put it under Xander's hand. "Use your finger. Try and write what has happened. Take your time." He slipped a syringe from the case he always carried when he was going to see Xander and slipped the needle into the cannula in the back of Xander's hand. It was a shot of the medication he should be on, and he hoped it would give him enough strength to try and write.

Xander closed his eyes for a moment and then began to move his finger slowly. It was slow-going and the words ill-formed, but enough made sense to Tierney. *Drugged. Stasis. Scared. She.*

Tierney read the words aloud as Xander wrote them. "Is that what they are doing? Keeping you shut in the stasis bank? Drugged so you don't know what is going on? Why? Who is she?" He looked down and saw Xander's eyes were closed again. He could see Xander was exhausted, and he was angry at whoever was responsible for this. He guessed—he and Serenity had guessed who it was, and it did not take much to work out that Xander had been removed from stasis and placed in a bed to permit him to see him, to stop the questions. He could see Xander was ill; more so than when he had last seen him. The isolation and the drugs were making Xander's condition worse, and he knew he had to get him out of here as soon as he could. He took a medi-reader out of his pocket and rested it on Xander's hand, watching it take some readings. He did not want to rely solely on the equipment here in case it had been set up to give false readings. He rooted around in a cupboard and found what he needed to take a blood sample and test it—a toxicology test. He gently pricked the end of Xander's finger and took the small speck of blood and dropped it into the tester. He watched for a moment and his brows came together in a deep frown. Leaving Xander here would be fatal. If they did not intend to kill him, then it would be accidental—the drugs they were using to keep him comatose were reacting badly with his prescribed medication. He pressed the buzzer and called a nurse in. "This medication—he has to take it. The drugs that are being used here are not helping. I want to see the doctors in charge."

He waited until the nurse left and stooped over Xander and slid another needle into the cannula. "Come on, Xander, I need you to wake up—just a little. I know you don't want to, you just want to sleep. But I need to get you out of here." He slid his arm under Xander's head and raised him a little. "Come on."

Xander's eyes flickered again and he tried to focus on Tierney's face. He closed his eyes again and his head turned to the side. He wanted to tell Clark that he just wanted to sleep but was unable to.

Tierney's heart went out to him. Poor Xander was in a drugged, confused state and must be in pain and frightened—

not knowing where he was. "No, you can't sleep yet. I need to know you are alive—I am going to remove the breathing tubes, but I don't know if you are able to breathe on your own. That's why I need you awake. Can you try?" He lowered Xander back against the pillows and gently began to remove the tubes and wires. He talked quietly as he worked, telling Xander to keep looking at him. When the breathing tube was removed from his throat, Xander coughed and gasped as his body was shocked into acting on its own.

Tierney wrapped the sheets around him and lifted him off the bed and onto a wheeled stretcher. He took another syringe from his pocket case and steadied Xander's hand as he slipped the needle into the tube. "This is going to make you feel sleepy now—everything is going to be okay." He watched as Xander's eyes closed and he drew the sheet up and covered Xander's face. He was banking on being able to slip out without any attention being drawn to them by wheeling out a covered stretcher. He knew they would not get far like this, he was only aiming to make it to the room around the corner of the corridor where he had arranged for a pilot to bring a shuttlecraft in at his signal. He made it to the room without being seen, and he opened the window, leaned out and waved, flashing a signal light as arranged. Moments later, a shuttle landed, and the pilot ran across and helped Tierney to lift Xander out of the window and they carried him carefully to the shuttle and lay him down on a stretcher and covered him in blankets. Once they had him safe inside, Tierney looked up at the pilot. "Get us out of here—before they find he's gone." He rolled up another blanket and slipped it under Xander's head. He raised his wrist to his mouth and gave Serenity's call signal. "I have him, Serenity. He is very sick—I smuggled him out. I don't think they will say anything—they went to enough trouble to hide that he was ever there. I am taking him to my hospital; meet me there. He needs you."

Serenity's voice responded, sounding relieved. "I'll go to the apartment and get some of his things. I'll be as quick as I can." She smiled when she signed off. Xander was alive and would now have his friend treating him. That had to mean he would get better, as much as he could. She hurried to Xander's apartment and sent a signal to Tiberius to let him know—she did it this way to save time. She knew he would not mind that she did not speak to him. She said in the message that she would call later to tell him how he was doing, but right now she had to be with him.

.

When Tiberius got the message a few hours later, he leaned back in his chair on the bridge and closed his eyes in relief. He had been more worried than he would have owned up to if he had been asked. He cared deeply for his father's old friend, the man he called 'pappi'—the man who, when he was able, had tried to be a father to him and to teach him things his own father had taught him, and what Tiberius' father would have taught him. To hear he was safe and would receive care and treatment caused relief to flood through him and made him realize how much he had been worrying, but it also brought back the distance between them and he wished he could be there to help him through this time. He knew it was silly to think this way as it could not be helped, but he could not help it. Xander was the last link with his father—he could not lose him.

.

Doctor Tierney was right when he surmised no-one would come after them, that no-one would raise the alarm at the hospital. It would be as though Xander had never been there, and they would remove all traces he had been. Before they had left the hospital, Tierney had located the stasis chamber in which Xander had been kept and he had seen the restraints and the wires. Poor Xander, he would not have known where he was, and to be unable to move too. It made him angry that a sick man would be treated so—by medical staff! It was this point that angered him the most, more than Kehoe being involved. Medical staff swore an oath to do no harm. It made him sick—the betrayal of all he believed in.

The shuttle reached Tierney's own hospital and he had Xander rushed to the ICU and ordered that he be monitored constantly. He went to his office and slipped a tablet computer into a drawer. He had taken the tablet from the hospital and was going to take the notes and integrate them with his own and write a report on Xander's condition, including an updated diagnosis and prognosis. It would not be hard to determine; Xander was dying. The disease that ravished him would have been kept at bay with the medication he had been taking but the drugs that had been pumped into him had accelerated the progress of the disease. It was going to be so hard—watching him suffer in silence had been tough; seeing him much worse would be heart-breaking.

24

Intensified Dreams

Tiberius closed his eyes and lay back on the pillow. His shift had finished, and he had never been so ready for a break. Normally, he was more than happy to prolong his shift— he loved his work. He was not just the *Invincible*'s captain, he was part of her, just as much as she was a part of him. Xander had told him once that those who were true commanders were as attuned to their ship, with every inch of her, as the old sailing ship captains had been—the wind in the sails as the breath of life to them. In space, there was no wind in full-rigged sails, but the same passion and love was there. If the salty scent of sea air could be in his nostrils here in the far distant reaches of the galaxy, then that would be what drove him. As they had once steered by the stars, just as he did, the *Invincible* silently slipping past planets and stars as the old frigates and galleons had slipped past land under cover of darkness; both they and he shrouded by darkness and stars. It was no different here in space as it had been at sea.

There was a lot on his mind. The mission, Ross' injuries, the news he had received from Serenity about Xander, and the dreams which plagued him still. He hated closing his eyes; it was when he rested that the dreams came. He had noticed something else too; the closer they got to Tamora, the more frequent the dreams became. He forced himself to drift off. He was not long asleep when the moment the *Wryneck* exploded played itself over and over in quick succession. He tossed and turned, disturbed and then he sat bolt upright, punched the intercom and asked Doctor Malachi and Doctor Ravello to attend. He had got better of late about speaking about the dreams and found that, by talking, they were not so detrimental on him as they had been. But he suffered still, and the doctors had told him to call them.

He sat hugging his knees, holding the sheets close around him. He felt cold although it was warm in the room, and he shivered.

When the doctors arrived, they got the captain to lie down and Tiberius curled up on his side, as Doctor Malachi pulled the sheets straight and tucked him in. "Let's get you calmed down." She took out a syringe and gently injected him in the shoulder.

Tiberius stopped shivering and lay quiet. "It was worse this time."

Doctor Ravello sat on the edge of the bed. "Worse? You told us last time that it was worse than before. Does it intensify every time you have the dream?"

Tiberius nodded. "It starts with the explosion—over and over. Between each explosion, I saw my father's face. He was screaming." He felt Doctor Malachi's fingers on his pulse and the touch of her medi-reader on his temple. She would stop him talking if he got distressed.

Ravello began to question Tiberius, getting him to describe everything he could remember, every detail—even the colours— and how he felt each time the scene played out.

"Can you do anything?" Tiberius asked after a while, and after Doctor Malachi had called a halt to the questions. "I don't want this dream anymore."

Ravello shook his head. "I can't take it away; I can just help you talk about it. I believe though that the dreams will end when you have the truth and understanding of what happened to your father and his ship and crew. Until then, they will plague your sleep."

Tiberius shut his eyes and nodded. "I'm afraid to sleep. He was screaming—that worries me. The explosion—death would have been instant. He would not have had time to scream. It bothers me. There's something wrong with the dream."

"What do you think is wrong?" Ravello asked. "Could it just be that it is a dream and nothing more? It is only yourself who believes it to be the past replaying itself to you so you will begin to unravel events—it could just be a bad, vivid dream—details are often weird in dreams."

Tiberius nodded. "Part of me wants so badly to believe that— my brain tells me that it cannot be my father's spirit calling to me because of an injustice that needs to be laid open, so he and his crew can rest. I don't believe in rubbish like that. But my heart wants it to be true and that, somehow, my reaching Tamora will lay tormented souls to rest." He laughed slightly. "I know it sounds stupid and you must think I am a loony."

Doctor Malachi shook her head. "It's not stupid, and there is nothing wrong with your mind. When there is tragedy in our lives, a part of us will always feel that way—that there is some part we can play in easing the pain of the past. Some things are not meant to be, but if you have that hope to cling to then you never know if it is meant to be or not. Hope and faith are strong. So do not stop believing—you need that strength right now." She placed her hand on his arm. "I am going to give you something so you can sleep. You need rest and you're not getting it without help."

Tiberius lay back and felt another sharp jab in his shoulder and closed his eye—he was asleep before the doctors even reached the door.

Doctor Malachi looked at the psychiatrist as they walked down the corridor on their way back to the infirmary. "What's your diagnosis, Dante? You know we should make an official report if the dreams persist. He is not sleeping, and it will affect his ability to command." She stopped and shook her head. "I don't know I could do that to him."

Dante Ravello nodded, his dark Mediterranean eyes smiling. "He has had a lot to contend with since childhood. Neither of us wants to be responsible for breaking his heart so close to the end. I do not believe they will affect him too much if I monitor him daily. Now that we are close to Tamora, and the dreams seem to be intensifying, I must confess to some professional curiosity. He does not believe the dreams to be anything but a dream—I could see that in his eyes the moment I suggested it. But I hesitate to suggest that they are caused by ghosts or some form of spiritual activity. That would take some believing and would be hard to report on convincingly or sincerely enough. Everyone's mind works differently, beyond the fundamental similarities of function—I will work closely with him. Something about these dreams seems real and it is my job to ensure his fitness."

Malachi nodded. Both doctors would back the captain as far as they could go, and they knew that being relieved of command over something like these dreams would devastate him. Tiberius had his heart and mind set on finding the truth and nothing was going to stop him; whatever life and circumstances threw at him. Ross being injured had shaken him, she knew that. But both men were strong, and they were working through the setback. Ross

179

certainly was. He did not complain about his position or get frustrated that he had to rely on the nursing staff to do everything for him. She was pleased with his progress and once the wounds were healed there would be nothing, bar learning to use his prosthetics, to prevent him from returning to work. Knowing that helped Ross and he was reasonably cheerful as he lay in his bed.

Ross asked after Tiberius when the doctor came to the bedside to see how he was. She had been with him when they were called away and he had lain worrying about his friend and commanding officer. He was concerned that these dreams would be bad for Tiberius' record; to have a starship captain plagued by dreams that disturbed and upset him so was not something High Command would tolerate readily. There would have to be a good reason.

Doctor Malachi smiled. "He is sleeping. The dreams come stronger now and he is still convinced his father tries to tell him what happened."

Ross sighed. "And I am of no use to him here. I should be on the bridge to help him. I know—it can't be helped. You don't need to look at me like that." He leaned back on the pillow and let her examine his stumps.

She smiled. "You're healing nicely. That is very good, considering the nature of the trauma. We can try the prosthetics soon and get you learning to use them. It will not be long before you are on your feet again."

Ross laughed. He was being very brave, the doctor thought. The injuries and blood loss had been severe and that, coupled with the pain, had almost killed him. "My legs and hands will outlive me," he said with a smile. "And they won't get old like the rest of me, nice to know that my knees aren't going to betray me—no need for knee replacements when I'm old and arthritic. Don't laugh, doctor. If I did not think like that I would probably cry."

She put her hand on his shoulder. "I understand. Rest now, you will not find the time when you return to work. The captain has great need of you and will keep you busy. For now, *shalom*." She turned off the light over the bed and watched him settle back on the pillows to try and obey her and get some sleep. He was sleeping a lot; his body using its natural defence and power of self-healing to help him recover.

The doctor returned to her office and began to update her patient's notes, stating that she was pleased with his progress and within the month, most likely, they would begin the use of the prosthetics and the hard work would start getting him back to being fit for duty.

During the next two months, Tiberius really missed the first officer being at his side on the bridge. He hated to look over and see the empty chair beside his; he knew it would not be long now, but that knowledge did not stop the time seeming to pass agonizingly slowly.

Doctor Malachi and her medical team worked tirelessly with Commander Ross, putting him through exercises and intense physiotherapy as they helped him learn to walk again, and to regain the use of hands which were so skilfully made that no-one would know they were prosthetic unless he said so. He was astounded at the way they worked—unlike old prosthetic limbs that could be removed, these were the latest in medical technology and used the nerve-endings, skilfully attached to the wiring inside, to allow movement. It was not long before he was able to pick things up, use a knife and fork, write, and care for himself. Walking amazed him too. He had expected his gait to have an irregularity about it but, after the first few efforts which often found him on his face and being helped up by nurses, he found he was able to move as easily as before. Days of intense physio and exercise followed. They worked out in the special gymnasium which was a part of the *Invincible*'s excellent medical facilities and the doctor had him swimming, catching small rubber balls, climbing ropes, and going over an assault course. At first, he was allowed to take it easy and then she ramped things up. At the end of the second week of this training, Doctor Malachi, her physio team, and Doctor Ravello stood watching as he beat his personal best over the assault course and flopped on the mat at the end, taking a long drink of water.

Doctor Malachi came over and helped him up, nodding with a smile. "Excellent. Let's test balance and eye-hand coordination." She caught two racquets that were thrown over to her and slipped off her white coat, revealing a tennis dress. "I think you're ready for a game." She held out one of the racquets and a ball. "Your serve. After this, we will leave you to rest—a swim and an intense massage will ease the aching muscles. After a good night's sleep, I can authorize your return to duty." She smiled, her dark eyes twinkling. "I am very pleased with your progress. You are one of the first to successfully go through quadruple prosthetic limb transplant surgery using this technique."

Later when Ross was discharged to his own quarters, he lay on the bed and pulled the sheets around him. He kicked his legs under the sheets, just because he could now, and laughed for sheer happiness at being whole again. He raised his arms and looked at his new hands and wriggled the fingers. He laughed at himself for being silly, but he knew he was not really—he had almost died and had faced the rest of his life crippled. A little "silly" reaction was totally justified.

25

"Little flame of life"

Doctor Tierney looked in on Xander as he made his rounds in the hospital that night. Xander was still in intensive care, and he would be there for a while yet. He was on a strong course of medication to try and flush out the drugs which had been pumped into his system, causing many issues with his proper medicine. Tierney stood by the bed, noted down the vital signs, and checked the oxygen was at a comfortable level. He had tried to remove the breathing tubes again, but Xander's condition had left him unable to breathe without help for long and it would be cruel to keep making him try.

He went to his computer and began to compose a letter to the admiral, informing her that Xander was to be granted indefinite sick leave while he remained in hospital. He clearly stated that his condition meant he was unable to return to work for a considerable time would likely only be fit to return in a part-time capacity when he was recovered. As he had expected, the response from the admiral agreed to grant the extended sick leave for Xander and she wished him well. Tierney would have been surprised in the circumstances if she had done otherwise. He did not know whether she knew that he had found Xander, in which case he knew some of the shocking story. He had seen the stasis chamber in the genetics hospital and made a general reference to it in his message, showing that he understood some of what had happened.

Serenity arrived while he was at the computer and was sitting by the bed, her hands resting on Xander's arm as he lay there. She worried about him, although a little less so now she knew his old friend was tending him. She talked softly about the many topics which were of interest to them both and told him things they should plan to do when he was better and out of the hospital. She knew he was very ill, but also that there was a chance of recovery if he responded well to the treatment which was being fed directly into his bloodstream through a needle in his main vein. Tierney had told her that there was no point in giving him the correct medication yet, not until the bad drugs had been pumped out of him. Going on with the treatment would be futile right now. She accepted the doctor's statements and remained at the bedside, watching over the man she had come to love. As a cadet, not long after her creation, she had watched her classmates going through relationships, knowing her kind would never know the feelings of love as humans and other beings did. But, after graduation, she volunteered to undergo a trial of new programming that would enhance her abilities and give her more human characteristics. She was a machine; a computer, a humanoid robot—she had no right to even assume she could love a human. But she did. She loved the man lying on the bed, and he was dying. In that moment of realization of what she had, and what she would lose with his death, pain washed over her. She took his hand in hers, held it up to her face and rested it on her cheek. A machine cannot cry, but she would if she could. "Stay with me," she whispered. "You have to stay. Try and breathe—I know it hurts but you have to try. Please, I do not want to tell Tiberius of your death—not yet." She had promised that he would not be alone when the end came, and she would not leave his side until he either breathed his last or opened his eyes and lived. She had wished once that he would be conscious at the end, aware of what was happening, but now she was glad he was not awake to suffer the pain he was no doubt in. She held his hand in both hers and rested her head down on the bed beside him and waited, watching over him.

The doctor looked in from time to time to take scans and make notes. He put his hand on Serenity's shoulder and smiled sadly. "I will do my best, I promise. The drugs they used were designed to sap his mind and energy—they have done that, and the reaction of them with his medication has been almost fatal and may still prove to be. I will not rest until I know I have tried everything I can to bring him back."

Serenity glanced up over her shoulder and nodded. "I know you will try your hardest. I know he too would wish nothing more—only to know you had tried. I thank you for him, as he cannot."

Tierney smiled and took a syringe and carefully drew yet another blood sample for tests. "Sorry, Xander. I know how much you hate needles."

•

At Headquarters, Admiral Kehoe looked at the report she received from the nurse working with Doctor Tierney. She was more than satisfied to know that Xander had not been able to speak or to have regained consciousness. If he slipped quietly away without ever speaking, she would be happy and if he could pass on without regaining consciousness and feeling the pain he was in, she would be satisfied. What she had done had been borne out of necessity and fear. He was an officer she had always respected and honoured for his long service and his loyalty, but he was dangerous to her and those whose hearts were full of guilt. She had not ordered his death but would be happy to hear he was dead. She would be safe and would see he had the funeral worthy of a hero of such long-service which would please those who knew him and of his long illness. One of her greatest fears was that he would speak; telling them who had come to his apartment and injected him with the drug to knock him out. She did not know Serenity had already discovered the truth by successfully retrieving the deleted data on the security log at the apartment. Or that Xander had roused enough to write on the doctor's tablet; he had not named her, but Doctor Tierney had understood who 'she' was—he had not needed to ask.

•

Doctor Tierney sat in his office and looked at the blood he had taken from his friend. He put the test tubes into the testing equipment and carefully made notes. He noted with satisfaction that the toxicology tests were more positive. The drug levels were reducing rapidly with careful use of medication. He ran some more tests and, as he waited for the results, he turned to the computer. The light was flashing, showing he had received a new message. He opened it and saw it came from the admiral's office, from her aide. It was a request for him to come in for a meeting with the admiral and he wondered why she wanted to see him. It would have something to do with his patient, he guessed. He read on and saw a request for a copy of Xander's medical record and up-to-date notes. He responded, saying he would come, but the notes were confidential. He could offer a brief overview of his condition and included this. He turned away from the computer and finished the tests before returning to the bedside.

"His blood tests are looking better," he told Serenity. "The drug levels are dropping. I will come by and check in on him later. I have a meeting to attend right now."

Serenity smiled. "Thank you for what you are doing. I know it was you who developed the medication when you realized the disease was genetically engineered and implanted during his captivity."

Tierney nodded. "I have known him for a long time, and I would do anything for him. Remember that, whatever happens." He gave Xander another injection and tucked his arm back under the sheet. "Keep him warm—he is chilly. His body is enering a mild state of shock and withdrawal as the drug level reduces." He took some blankets from a cupboard and spread them over the bed, tucking them tightly down the edges and the foot of the bed. "There, that will help."

Serenity thanked him again and smiled. "I will watch the screen for any drop in temperature. He is safe with me."

The doctor looked at her. "He is not safe anywhere. Something is brewing and his life is in danger; more than it has ever been now that he cannot defend himself. In his condition, it will not take much to snuff out what little flame of life there is." He stopped as though he had said more than he meant to and turned to the door, slipping off his white coat as he went.

Serenity watched the doctor leave and sat quietly for a while, thinking. She was worried. The doctor seemed sincere, but he had seemed distracted, and his warning had sounded urgent; almost as though he was afraid to warn her. She raised her wrist and called one of her trusted fellow androids and asked her to come and help. "Bring another with you, with weapons. I need to know the room is secure."

Androids did not have family units as humans did, but Serenity and the three other Androids of her batch called themselves brothers and sisters and their loyalty for each other was as though they were flesh and blood. Of the four, Serenity was the only one who had volunteered for the enhanced programming to be integrated with her program. Her siblings had watched her fall in love, and now knew the one she loved lay close to death and they had been called to defend him. They came at once; one was a nursing technician—trained to deal with the mechanical side of nursing—and no-one stopped them from entering the room. The other two stood, weapons drawn, at either side of the door and would not allow anyone to pass them.

They were robots—advanced, yes, with many characteristics that made them hard to separate from humans on first meeting but not like Serenity. One of the attributes with was loyalty and one of their own kind needed help. When Androids had first been accepted into service, centuries before, and acknowledged as artificial intelligence—recognized as sentient beings—their primary function was to serve humans. Over the years, they had become more than robot aides and worked alongside as colleagues. Some even developed friendships.

Serenity looked up as the android nurse came up beside her. "They want him dead, Ayda, and I don't want to lose him. He cannot breathe by himself, he is in shock and has not woken up. I feel so helpless, I can do nothing for him."

Ayda looked at her in silence. "You are at his side as you promised him. You told him he would not be alone. If this is the end for him, he is not alone—he has a loved one with him, even if he does not know it." A quick tap of the computer screen to access the notes and then, "You said Doctor Tierney is treating him?"

"Yes, he said his blood is getting clearer, that the drug level is reducing. Is something wrong?" Fear leapt into her eyes. "Is he making him worse?"

Ayda shook her head. "I am not sure—give me a little while to check everything over."

Serenity held onto Xander's arm and watched Ayda working. She suddenly feared that Clark Tierney, one of Xander's oldest friends, and the man who had discovered and developed the medication to combat his illness, was in the pay of those who wanted Xander dead.

.

Two hours later, one of the android guards opened the door. A junior doctor stood beside them. "He's asking to speak to you, Serenity. You said no-one was to come in."

Serenity stood up, Xander's hand still in hers. "Let him come in. What is it, doctor? I have requested no further medical attention for Rear Admiral Galen."

"I am not here to in the capacity of a doctor, but as a messenger," the young man replied. "I was sent to tell you that Doctor Tierney is dead. His body was found in the fountain in the plaza."

"Dead?! How?" Serenity was shocked. "He was only here a few hours ago and left for a meeting. Was there an accident?"

The doctor shook his head. "Law enforcement doesn't think so; they believe he was restrained and held under until he drowned."

"*Murder*?!" She had feared Tierney was involved in treachery and conspiring to murder Xander and now she felt bad for having doubted him. Now he was dead—murdered. Poor Xander would be upset to lose an old friend. She would not say anything to the young doctor, but she knew of no-one who would wish Tierney's death—and Xander's too—but for one person. Only one person seemed determined that Xander's life should end, someone who had gone to great pains to have him hidden away in a hospital and filled with drugs. And anyone who stood in his defence was also in danger. One person. It had to be her. It had to be Kehoe.

•

Two hours earlier, when Doctor Tierney left Xander's hospital room, he went to his office first and amended Xander's notes with recommendations for further treatment. He recorded a personal message for Xander and sent it to one of his junior doctors with a request to pass it on in an emergency. He sat back for a few more minutes and then left the office and took a shuttle-cab to HQ. He was worried. The admiral was too interested in Galen's condition, and should not be recommending treatments. He had seen the state Xander had been in at the genetics hospital. He had barely even been able to write a few words. He knew the word 'she' Xander had managed to scrawl before his strength failed had meant the admiral. He could think of no other woman who would harm Xander Galen—women generally liked him. Even now, with the illness ravaging his body, Xander was a still handsome man for his age, and his life experience and kindness meant people looked to him for advice when in trouble. Only the admiral feared him because he had lived through his ordeal thirty years ago.

The latest message he had received had confirmed that—an order to ensure Rear Admiral Galen remained in a coma. There was no direct order for his death, but it was implied. As a doctor, who had taken the Hippocratic oath and vowed to do no harm to any living being but to do everything to help and save life, this was something he could not bear. He would mention it and refuse to comply. He would not be the tool to hasten the death of an old friend. He arrived at HQ and was quickly ushered to the admiral's office as soon as he announced himself. There were two of the admiral's personal security detachment outside the door, one on either side. Hands clasped behind their backs, their dark uniforms making them appear even bigger than they were. They were something new; she had never kept a personal guard before now. Was she so afraid of a man lying, unable to speak, in a hospital bed that she had brought in men to guard her?

Admiral Kehoe looked up from her computer as Doctor Tierney came into the room. "Sit down. I have your reply here, refusing to send me the report I requested."

Tierney nodded. "That is correct, ma'am. I refuse to give you access to his notes. There is such a thing as patient confidentiality, and I will not break that. I have given you all the information you require to see. You have asked more than enough of me and have asked me to do what I *cannot* do. Galen is my patient, and my friend, and I cannot do what you ask. It goes against every fibre of my being; everything I live to uphold for my profession. I will *not* be the cause of his death."

She tapped her fingertips on the desk and looked at him. "I suppose your sentiments and ethics do you credit but he can do too much damage. He must die."

"Admiral, he is in a coma, unable to speak. He can do you no harm—you have seen to that. It is unlikely that he will ever recover. Even if he lives, he will never be the man he was." Clark Tierney's voice shook ever so slightly. Part of him would have been pleased to say that Xander was dead, but only because it would mean that he was no longer suffering, that he would not have to go on living in a semi-comatose state, relying on the people around him to keep him alive—people he would no longer know were there. Unable to tell them how he felt—if he was in pain or to say goodbye when the end came. But there was that in him that wanted him to go on living, despite this. To defy all odds and live despite those ordered his death. He looked her right in the eyes and realized he was holding his breath.

There was a long silence and then Admiral Kehoe stood up and looked out of the window. "You're dismissed." As Doctor Tierney left, Kehoe tapped a button on the desk and her security guards entered, and stood just inside the door, their hands clasped behind their backs. The admiral looked up. "*Maak hom dood.*" These two of her personal guard were, like the others, genetically modified for strength, and their capability for brutality. They were trained to take orders from her, which is why she had used Afrikaans. They would obey her, and her alone, when they heard this language, and this without question. The order to kill the doctor would be carried out immediately and she watched them leave with a smile on her face.

•

Tierney headed for the plaza, with the intention of getting some lunch before heading back to the hospital. The plaza was full of people at this time and there was a buzz of activity. He headed towards the fountain, making his way towards his favourite café. As he reached the fountain, his arms were seized, and he was halted. His arms were pulled behind him and he felt his wrists locked together with the plastic handcuffs used by the security forces. He looked over his shoulder and saw the guards. "What is the meaning of this?!" he demanded. He did not struggle, knowing it to be futile. He felt a weapon in the small of his back and did not call out, knowing he would endanger the people going about their business.

They did not answer his question but dragged him to the fountain and heaved him over the edge, holding him down under the water. He struggled now, frantically; his legs kicking until they were pinned down and held in a grip like iron. He wrenched at the cable-ties on his wrists, desperately trying to hold his breath and break free so he could sit up and get some air. Bubbles began to stream from his nose, and he could no longer keep his mouth closed. His eyes were wide open as his struggles began to grow weaker as water flooded into his mouth. He was a fit man for his age and a good swimmer, able to hold his breath for three minutes underwater, but after that time his lungs burned, straining for air, and his chest felt close to bursting. He tried to scream for help but that just made the water flood in faster, more bubbles streamed from his mouth and nose and his movements became jerky and he went limp, and the bubbles came spasmodically as his lungs filled with water. He closed his eyes and let go; there was no fight left in him as he drowned. His last conscious thought was of relief that he had left a message in case of emergency.

The assassins held him down for a few more minutes, to be absolutely certain he was dead, then they released their hold and cut the ties off his wrists and rolled the body over and left him floating face down so it would appear to be an accident. They disappeared in the crowd, as unnoticed as the murder—the execution—had been. They had held his thrashing legs down so there would be no splashing and they had given him no chance to cry out.

The alarm was raised by a little girl and her brother who had run to look in the fountain as they always did when at the plaza. They ran to their mother and tugged on her dress. "Mama! Mama! There's a man in the fountain!"

She ran with them and called Law Enforcement—different from the admiral's security detachment. She drew the children away but remained near the fountain as she had been told. Although they had seen nothing, there would be questions.

Police officers and paramedics arrived with a resuscitation team who worked hard, but he was declared dead moments later. They called it a tragic accident until a police officer lifted one of the limp arms and looked at the wrist. It was bruised, cut and raw, bearing signs of a frantic, terrified struggle, and the officer shook his head. "This was no accident, he died fighting." That changed faces, knowing the man at their feet had died a long, agonized death, fighting to breathe and unable to get free to save himself. Bruises were found on his neck, shoulders, and legs adding more proof that strong hands had held him down as he struggled. At least two had held him under and watched his frantic fight for life as he drowned.

•

Serenity looked up as another doctor came in. By now, Doctor Tierney's staff had heard the news and were in shock at the death of their colleague. This new doctor came to the bedside and looked at Xander's readings and then looked at the android sitting by the bed. "He seems to be doing better tonight. The readings are more normal than they have been." She paused and then held out a data-chip. "He left this to be given to Galen if anything happened to him. In the circumstances, I think you should see it. He may explain what happened and may have left instructions."

Serenity nodded. "Thank you." She tucked the chip into her pocket and turned back to her vigil.

"You can use the computer in his office."

Serenity shook her head. "I do not want to leave him. I will use my tablet later." She did not want to do anything about it while the doctor was in the room. Instead, she watched her with her unblinking gaze as the doctor took some scans and ran another blood test at the bedside. After writing up some notes, she left, and Serenity took out her tablet computer, inserted the data chip, and set the recorded message to play.

Xander, my old friend, or Serenity who, in these circumstances, I believe will be the one to hear this—if you are listening to this message, I will be dead. It will not have been an accident; I believe that I will have been executed because I chose to defy authority and try to save your life, Xander. I was ordered to kill you and it was tempting to obey this order because you are so ill and watching you suffer is painful. It would have been so easy to give you a fatal injection and you would never have known. But I could not. The order was never made clear until today when I was sent for. You were right that she wanted you dead. She has done everything to ensure that whatever she hides does not come to light and I believe that I will not be allowed to live once she knows I will stand firm for my oath, and for friendship. Admiral Kehoe is a traitor and, through fear of this becoming known, she is a murderer. Live, Xander. Live to hear the truth of what caused you so much suffering. Live to bring her down. Please do not let my loyalty to you, my friend, have been in vain. I will die because I believe that I should never harm another living being. I will die because I stand in her way and could reveal what I know about her. That is why I have recorded this message. I pray that you will live to hear these words. Serenity is your guardian angel. Don't let him go, Serenity. Forgive me for not having been able to bring him through this myself. I know you did not trust me, but you had nothing to fear. In my safe you will find a stronger medicine that I was working on—do not let anyone else know of it but use it to bring Xander back to you. The code is the year the Wryneck was destroyed. Clark Tierney out.

Serenity sat silent as Tierney's voice ended, hardly able to believe it. The doctor had feared something like this—the drowning had been an execution and Xander's life was still in danger. She stood up and went to the door and asked the androids on guard at the door not to let anyone in, whoever they were, unless she were with them herself. She hurried down the corridor to Tierney's office and quickly opened the safe. She scooped everything out and tipped it into the doctor's old black bag. She smiled slightly at this little sign of his character. A very skilled surgeon who had worked on many projects to enhance medical science and had developed the medication that had helped Xander previously, despite not knowing fully what had caused his illness, or the effect it would have on him, Clark Tierney had always used an old stethoscope and carried his instruments in an ancient black bag. He had said it was to remind him of how far they had come since the first big advances in medicine around the time of the British Queen Victoria. She closed up the safe, locked it and, as an afterthought, went back and changed the code. Even though she had left nothing inside, she liked the idea of someone being baffled by being unable to open it if they had learned of the code. She hurried back to Xander's room and pulled a trolley over and began to look at what she had removed from the safe. She found a medicine bottle and a box of pills. The box was wrapped in hand-written notes explaining their use. The bottle, Tierney had written, was to be used now to clear his bloodstream of the drugs that were killing him. The pills were then for him to take for the rest of his life. Taped to the box was a data-chip which carried the formula necessary to make more of the pills and medicine if needed.

Serenity looked at the bottle. Her trust in Tierney had wavered momentarily but he had said he could be trusted and now he was dead because of what he was doing. She turned and looked at the man lying in the bed, utterly helpless and reliant on those around him and on the life-support machines to keep him alive. She had to trust Tierney and the very fact that he had been assassinated, seemed to prove without any doubt that he had always been worthy of her trust. She opened a sterile packet and took out a new syringe, filling it from the bottle. She slid the needle gently into the cannula in the back of Xander's hand and pressed the plunger. She could do nothing else now but hope and trust that she had not been the last pawn in the execution game—Xander's execution. She hoped the message Tierney had left had not been merely a ruse to have her administer the final dose that would silence Xander for good and allow Kehoe to get off with whatever it was she had done. She thought back to the wording of the message. Could Tierney really have been that clever? To cover up murderous intentions in a message that showed nothing but sincerity.

She put the syringe to one side and sat down beside Xander's bed and watched him closely.

26

Destructive Electricity

The bridge door opened, and Tiberius glanced over his shoulder. He sprang up, almost giving a yell when he saw the first officer coming in. His face broke into a smile—it was not the same without Ross on the bridge.

Ross smiled, raised a hand, and saluted. "May I resume my duties, sir?"

"Welcome back." Tiberius watched as Ross made his way down the few steps to the centre of the bridge and took his seat in his chair at the captain's side. He held out his hand with a broad smile. "I missed you."

Ross shook Tiberius' hand. "Look at them. Just like real hands. I'm still a bit slow sometimes, but I'm getting there. It beats lying in bed without them and, at first glance, no-one can tell." He pushed his uniform sleeve up. The skin tone was perfectly matched. "I am very pleased with them and I am sorry to have been absent so long."

Tiberius shook his head. "You needed that time." He settled back in his seat. "But it's good to have you back."

Ross nodded. "It's good to be back." He leaned back in his chair and stretched out his legs, looking at his feet. "I still can hardly believe how good they are. I was scared, I must admit. I thought it was the end for me."

Tiberius smiled. "You'll get used to it." He tapped the arm of his chair and nodded to Ross. "You've got the latest of my reports, you've got some catching up to do." And he laughed.

Ross pulled himself upright and tapped his access code into the panel on the arm of his chair and began to read through the reports the captain had made. "These are extra detailed. You made them especially for me?" He grinned, teasing the captain.

Tiberius looked up. "Neither of us can afford for you to be behind on events," he responded. But he smiled. "As I said, I need you."

Ross smiled. "How have you been? What about the dreams?"

Tiberius nodded. "I am getting them under control, but they are worse. Ravello is worried that if I don't work well with him to get through each night the dreams come, I could end up making mistakes because I believe the dreams are a message." He briefly told Ross about the last time it came. "He's good and he has helped to some extent, but I can't let go in case I miss something."

"He is good. I worked closely with him while I was in recovery—I did get pretty low for a while. Naturally, I suppose, due to the pain and the amputations." Ross laughed slightly. "We're lucky with the medical team we have."

Tiberius nodded. "We're the best in the fleet, they made sure of that. Kirbie, do you regret sticking up for me? You didn't want me as captain at the first."

Ross reddened. "I was a jealous, selfish fool—thinking only of myself and my career and not what an achievement it was for you. You are an excellent CO and a good friend. I regret nothing but my rudeness to you."

"You're not still bothered, are you? I forgave you a long time ago and we're friends now." Tiberius' voice trailed off and he suddenly put his hand to his forehead before gripping the arms of his seat and slumping forward, a look of agony on his features.

Ross was worried. "Captain? Captain MacAlpin!" He gave him a shake. "Tiberius!" He quickly touched the intercom. "Doctor to the bridge!" He turned back and shook the captain again. "'Help is coming—it's going to be okay."

By the time the doctor arrived, Tiberius had recovered himself and was sitting up. "I'm fine," he insisted.

"You're not," Ross responded. He described what he had witnessed to the doctor and she nodded.

"Do you remember anything?" she asked, turning to Tiberius. "You held your head, is that where it hurts?"

Tiberius shook his head. "No. Yes. Not really. There was a lot of light, and screaming in my ears and my head began to ache. I thought I was going to pass out."

Doctor Malachi put her fingers to the captain's wrist and took his pulse. "Your heart rate is very fast."

Tiberius suddenly writhed in his chair, his expression one of anguish and great distress. He gritted his teeth. "Get me off the bridge," he hissed. "Ross, take over."

The doctor helped Tiberius to his feet. "Can you manage?"

He shook his head. "Everything is fuzzy. I can't really see." He put his hand on her arm and let her guide him from the bridge.

Ross looked concerned as he watched them leave. He could not help but wonder if this was connected with the dreams. If so, it was very worrying. Before now, the dreams had only come at night or when he slept between shifts but, this time, he had been wide awake. The mental strain had been evident in his face, and seeing him guided out by the doctor was great cause for concern. At least the medical and psychiatric teams on the *Invincible* were excellent. Ross had no doubt that Doctor Ravello would be able to help Tiberius control the effect the dreams had on him. If they were now violent, mental attacks during waking hours then were they ever really dreams and had the captain been right all along? It worried him deeply, and he wondered if it had been the first such attack or if there had been others.

Doctor Malachi helped Tiberius along to the infirmary and got him to lie down on one of the beds. "Just lie quietly for a while and try and rest. I will go and speak to Ravello."

Tiberius obediently lay back and closed his eyes. His head was pounding, and he wanted to curl up into a ball and just stop feeling. He was tired of the pain every time the images came. At first, it had been emotional pain, but now it hurt physically. His brain ached and his eyes felt sore. He was worried too, afraid the doctors would declare him unfit for service and relieve him of duty while they worked with him.

The doctor returned shortly with the psychiatrist and they stood quietly for a moment, taking note of the pain written on Tiberius' face as he tried to rest. To them, it looked like a severe migraine but they both knew it was more than that.

Ravello went to the bedside. "Captain, can you open your eyes for me?"

Tiberius shook his head. "They hurt. I can't look—I don't want to see them."

"Do you see anything when you close your eyes?"

Another shake of the head. "Only when I dream. This is different."

"Is what you see different from the dreams?"

"No, it is the same. Only more intense. Can you stop them? I can't function like this."

"Perhaps you need a rest. Now that Commander Ross is back…"

"No! Don't do that—don't take me off the bridge." Tiberius opened his eyes and looked agitated. Being relieved of duty was what he feared the most.

"Calm down, Captain." Ravello's voice was soft. "I will not recommend that, but if you go on this way you will make it the only alternative. You are under severe mental strain. You need my help, but I can only help if you allow me to. I suggest you voluntarily relieve yourself of command for a fortnight. Ross can take command until we are ready. We are six months away from Tamora; you will be back in command long before then. You have a position to maintain, your officers cannot see you helpless with agony on the bridge. You will make errors of judgement if your mind is suffering. You will put your ship and crew at risk. Is that what you want?"

Tiberius shook his head. He weakly raised his wrist to his mouth and spoke into the transmitter. "Ross, I am relieving myself of duty for a short while in order to get this issue under control. You will assume command from this moment until relieved. Have Popovych assume the role of first officer. His assistant chief will take the science department under her command until then."

Ross took a breath and then responded. "Aye aye, sir. Get well. I'll look after things until then." He moved to the captain's seat and looked up, turning towards the chief science officer. "Popovych, orders from the captain. You're acting first officer until the captain returns to duty." He was worried but knew Tiberius had made the right decision to stand down until he was well again.

Anton Pavlovych Popovych immediately left his station and took his place in the first officer's seat.

•

Tiberius lay back against the pillow. "Satisfied?" He was trying to sound as though it had been against his will, but he knew it was the right thing to do. Doctor Ravello had been right—he could not put his ship and crew in danger, and he was barely able to even think just now. He thought it would have hurt more, perhaps it would have hurt more if he had been compelled to leave the ship. At least he could feel her around him; he hadn't left her.

"We do not need to be satisfied," Ravello replied. "You made a wise decision; we did not want to have to force you. Doctor Malachi is going to run some brain scans for me and then we'll see. You can close your eyes and try to relax while we do this."

Tiberius obediently closed his eyes and felt the doctor's hands on his head, taping to his forehead wires which were linked to her state-of-the-art neural-scanning equipment. He was tired and his eyes and head hurt. He felt his head raised, and it went dark as a soft eye-mask was placed over his eyes to protect him from the scan, he supposed. It was not—it was to make him better able to relax. The sheets were tucked snugly around him, and the scanner settled over his head. Just as Doctor Malachi had hoped, he relaxed and began to fall asleep. He had said the images came when he opened his eyes so she had wondered if covering his eyes would work, giving him a chance to rest.

•

Lieutenant Mikailah Klein, the enthusiastic assistant to Lieutenant Commander Popovych, and now acting chief science officer, looked up from her station. "Chief, could you take a look at this? I am reading unusually high electrical impulses from outside the ship. But there is nothing in the vicinity from where it could be coming."

The Ukrainian science officer went over, and his fingers tapped over the screens for a moment before he told her to run some long-distance scans of the area to see if they could pick it up. He took note of the frequency of the electric charges and passed them on to communications. "Track this—see if it is a signal of some kind. Report to me as soon as you have something." He went back to the first officer's position and reported to Ross. "I recommend caution, sir. It is a strong beam and appears to be coming from nowhere. I was wondering…"

Ross looked at him. "Wondering what? That this electricity is affecting the captain? Is that what you are thinking?"

Popovych nodded. "I was only wondering—there are strange things in space. What if the Tamorans have something to do with this? What if the dreams and images he sees are caused by his mind being attacked by something from outside the ship?"

Ross caught his breath. "Thought suggestion?"

"Not quite, but somehow making him see what they want to show. What if all he has seen is generated like an old projector with a movie." Popovych looked up. "He may never have dreamed—they may have forced him to see the images."

Ross thought for a moment. "Then that calls everything into question. If we do not know what he has seen is true, or if it has been generated—all of that could be a lie. We don't know what to believe."

"Do we report it?"

"No. We will both record it in our official logs but not send it to HQ. We know now that something is wrong at the heart of command—at least with certain people with influence." Ross smiled. "We'll get to the bottom of it. While it's quiet, do you want to work on it with your team? I know you've been moved at a time when you would be working hard with them."

Popovych nodded. "Yes, there are some things I can check." He got up and joined his deputy and two technicians at the science station; they were soon involved in a deep discussion, stooped over the computer screens.

Ross looked across to where the science team were busy conferring over various things. "Should we tell the doctors? It may help."

Popovych looked over his shoulder. "Yes, it might. But we don't know if it is the cause. We are still tracing the location."

Ross nodded and tapped the intercom. "Doctor Ravello, could I see you on the bridge for a moment?"

Doctor Malachi nodded as the message came through. "I'll run the scans and wait for you. Your work begins after I have the evidence."

The psychiatrist nodded and hurried to the door and swiftly made his way to the bridge. He wondered what was up; calling the 'shrink' to the bridge was unusual. If there was an emergency, they would call the doctor. He was met by Ross and Popovych, both looking serious.

Ross leaned on the back of the captain's chair. "We may have found something significant—it could be what is afflicting the captain."

"What is it?" Ravello's interest was piqued.

The science officer explained the pulses his team had discovered. "We have been testing it. We move the ship further away, and the pulse intensifies. It is aimed directly at the ship. I would like to witness readings of what happens to the captain when the pulse intensifies. I would stake my reputation that there is a significant spike in the electrical activity being recorded in his brain."

Ravello looked at him in silence for a moment, knowing it was a big thing for an officer like Popovych to stake their reputation on something of which there was no actual proof—it was a guarantee that it was as he said. "Show me what you have, and I'll take you to the CMO. She will want to hear what you have to say, and she will show you the readings you want to see. We may have found answers here."

•

Back in the infirmary, Doctor Malachi was being puzzled by the rapid spiking and dipping of the readings and the pain caused by the spikes. Every time the readings went up, Tiberius writhed in his sleep and tossed his head from time to time, regardless of the scanner resting on his forehead. She was baffled; the activity was mostly in the limbic system of his brain, the area believed to control emotions and motivation; it was also supposed to have been affecting the area predominately used in the processing of dreams. The activity itself, however, seemed to be caused by artificial means; it was hard to believe these readings were natural. They were stronger than even the most vivid of dreams would be. She did not know what to do and could not figure out how to help him without knowing what was causing this rapid, painful activity. She looked up when Ravello came in with Popovych. She could tell something had happened by their faces. Ravello called her aside, and she left a nurse monitoring the captain. "What is it?"

Popovych began to explain what had been discovered and she looked shocked, but also that understanding was dawning on her. She went to fetch the scans that had been made and the three looked at them together. She nodded after a while. "Can you find where it is located? We need to find who is doing this and if there is a way to destroy it?"

Popovych flicked between the scans on the screen with his fingertip, looking at the differences in activity levels and knew the captain must be in excruciating agony. He looked up and nodded. "I will locate it and I will put a stop to it."

He was interrupted by a cry from the captain and the nurse hurried into the office. "Doctor, you need to come at once—his nose is beginning to bleed. There is too much pressure."

27

"Part of their damned experiments"

Doctor Malachi got up immediately and went after the nurse. At the door, she turned back. "Find it now and destroy it. It will kill him."

Popovych looked at her and was shocked to hear this. "It is that bad?"

The doctor nodded. "It is. He cannot withstand much more of this pressure in his brain; I do not want him haemorrhaging. If he does, there is little I can do—even with this technology—to stop it." She turned and left the room.

Ravello looked at the science officer. "I know this does not make it any easier, but his life is in your hands."

"No, that does not make it any easier, but I will succeed." Popovych stood up and walked out of the office and went to where his commanding officer lay writhing in his bed. He looked down at him for a moment, then turned on his heel and strode out of the infirmary. He had taken the image of the captain with him so that when it felt like he was failing he would close his eyes and see Tiberius' pain and it would renew his vigour in the search. He had an idea that whatever was projecting the electrical pulse was not far away from the *Invincible*. Scans had only detected the beam, but he had a sudden flash of inspiration and he almost ran back to the bridge. He hurried to the science station and began an animated discussion with his team. He pointed to an area on the screen. "Here, this little asteroid field. Have we looked here?"

"Not a thorough search, sir. It is too small to be hiding anything significant."

"It does not need to be large," Popovych replied. "I believe the beam may be coming from a small craft or device, concealed in an area such as this asteroid field—somewhere we may not think of looking. Set the scans to read through rock if necessary. I want to know what is behind each asteroid."

Lieutenant Klein nodded. "Yes, sir." Her fingers began to tap coordinates and range onto the screen pad in front of her. She sat back and looked up at Popovych who nodded. "Computer, begin a scan of the asteroid field." She looked back up at the Ukrainian as she gave the order. They had scanned here several times, but she knew him well enough to know that if he had a hunch, it was usually right. After ten minutes, she turned again to Popovych. "All it shows is the fact that the electrical pulses are emanating from the asteroid field, but it does not show the presence of any device or craft."

Popovych scratched his chin, momentarily puzzled. "There's only one more thing we can do—take a shuttle over and search the area that way. You will go yourself and take two technicians with you. Keep close radio contact."

"What do you expect us to find, sir?" Klein knew, without having to ask, that he believed without a doubt that there was something, the source of these pulses, out there.

"I expect, as I said, a small device or craft, possibly unmanned." Popovych ran his hand through his brown hair, thinking. "I believe it has the ability to conceal itself. That could explain the failure of our scans to locate and identify."

She stood up. "We'll get right to it, sir." She called the main science lab and asked for two technicians to meet her on the hanger deck. The technician beside her was taking control of the bridge station while she was away.

Ross looked up. "Keep me informed, and I need a full report when you return. Whatever it is out there, find it—do not destroy it if at all possible. Try to deactivate it so we can examine it. If it offers resistance or threat, then use whatever force necessary. Keep safe." He watched them leave; Popovych going too, to see them off from the hanger deck. He fell to wondering what they would find, and if this would be an end to Tiberius' suffering. Over the years they had worked together, these last few had been the worst—for the dreams at least. Ross could not remember him complaining of them when they had served together on the *Victorious*. If he had dreamed, Tiberius had never complained of pain caused by them—but now, to end up in the infirmary with crippling headaches—he must have been in so much pain but never spoken of it until it was so bad it had caused his collapse on the bridge. He touched the intercom and asked the CMO for an update.

Doctor Malachi looked at her patient; two nurses were supporting him, holding his head, and trying to stop the flow of blood from his nose as the captain moaned in pain. "It needs to be stopped. I can do nothing more except try to keep him calm. The pressure in his brain is too great—I worry about any lasting effect this may have. He cannot withstand very much more without critical damage. Every time the pulse intensifies, his nose bleed worsens, and he is only semi-conscious through the pain. Painkillers and sedatives are useless against this. Ravello is with him right now, trying to focus his mind on something other than the pain."

Her voice showed how she hated to be at a loss and Ross told her that even deep scans had revealed nothing and that a manned shuttle had been launched. "They will deactivate it so we can examine whatever device they find. It may give answers. Keep me informed—if the captain's condition deteriorates, tell me at once and I will have it destroyed rather than risk his life." He signed off and looked up as Popovych returned to the bridge and resumed his seat in the first officer's position.

•

At the helm of the shuttle, Klein looked at the screen in front of her as they drew closer to the asteroid field. She looked across at the technician to her right. "Scan, please—pinpoint its exact position and guide us in." She was more inclined now to believe, as Popovych did, that there was something here. Something that was cleverly concealed, somehow able to defy intense deep scans from state-of-the-art equipment. That in itself was sinister. If it was doing no harm, why was it hiding from them and why was it attacking the captain? They measured its frequency again and made another attempt at contact.

As they ran the scan, the pulse intensified—this time to such a high level that Tiberius screamed and thrashed in his bed and had to be held down by four of the nursing staff and Doctor Malachi tried again to use sedatives to calm him. The doctor shook her head and had him restrained so he would not hurt himself. They were just in time, as another pulse went through Tiberius' brain and he screamed again, blood pouring from his nose and onto the sheets. The pulses had escalated, and he was left thrashing and screaming in agony as wave after wave of electrical energy bombarded his mind.

Doctor Malachi grabbed another, stronger sedative, and injected directly into Tiberius' main vein, hoping to get it flowing through his blood more quickly. Tiberius was screaming and moaning as he tossed his head on the pillow, his whole body jerking and straining against the restraints. Then she spotted it—what she had hoped and prayed would not happen. Blood was beginning to seep out of the captain's ears, a sign of a brain bleed, and she was worried even more now. She had told Ross if the captain's brain haemorrhaged, there was little she could do to stop it. She bit her lip and carried on working, trying everything she could. A sign to a nurse got the life support computer started up. Just in case it was needed. She prayed hard that it would not be needed.

•

The shuttle made its way into the asteroid field and more scans were made. At first, it seemed as though nothing was there except for the intense, relentless pulsing, then Klein saw it. A small capsule-like device, right in the shadow of an asteroid; it was of the same colour as the asteroid and had been, obviously, cleverly disguised. She, and her team of two, prepared the device they had devised to mute, and hopefully stop, the beam by turning its pulses on itself. They jettisoned the device and guided it into position by remote control and activated it. She ran her finger lightly over the screen and began another scan. Within moments, it showed the pulse had been stopped and she turned on the tractor beam to take the offender back to the *Invincible*. She called the ship and told them it had been successful.

Ross, who had just heard from the infirmary, was in no mood for tolerance just then. "Do not bring it back here. Make your examination on the shuttle and then destroy it. Whatever happened just before you stopped it almost killed the captain."

"Yes, sir."

Ross leaned back and closed his eyes and then handed the bridge over to Popovych and headed down for the doctor's report. He was shocked by the sight that met his eyes as he walked into the ship's infirmary.

The captain lay very still, his head slumped to one side and two nurses were cleaning up a lot of blood. The blood-soaked pillow was on the floor and another nurse was getting a clean one. Doctor Malachi was taking off the restraints and then a nurse was rubbing warm oil onto the skin on Tiberius' wrists where his struggles had rubbed the skin raw. Ross saw the dark, dried blood around his nose and ears and over the front of the hospital gown he wore. "How is he, Doctor?" His voice was shocked. He had not expected it to look that bad.

Doctor Malachi nodded to the nurse and turned to the acting captain who was looking on with such a horrified expression. She saw him watching as the nurses changed the bloodstained gown and sponged Tiberius' face and then settled him back against the clean white pillow and pulled the sheets up, tucking him in. His face was very pale, and his eyes closed.

Ross had a sudden sinking feeling and swallowed hard. "He's sleeping, right?"

Doctor Malachi shook her head. "He passed out. He is in a coma, but the electrical pulses have ceased to bombard him. We are preparing to use gentle stimulation to rouse him. My recommendation will be that he does not return to work for a while. He needs rest."

Ross nodded. "Of course. We have plenty of time. We could even stop on another planet to get some rest ashore."

"That's an excellent idea. He will not refuse—he is going to feel out of it for a while."

Ross agreed with her. "Keep me posted. I will do likewise when we discover what the device was—where it is from, although I have an idea."

"Tamora? But, if so, why? What could be gained by such torment? Could he have been right, that the dreams held a message? Why would they try to kill him? Do you think this message was supposed to stop him coming to Tamora?"

Ross shook his head. "All the information we have seems to point to it being necessary that we go to Tamora, I don't understand why they would do this. Unless it is part of their damned experiments!"

•

Klein and the technicians brought the device aboard the shuttle and made scans, taking readings and images on their tablet computers. It was not a large device by any means and Klein opened up the hatch on the side and took out a transmitter device. "The capsule appears alien in composition." She began to record her report. "I have located transmission and receiving apparatus concealed behind a hatch, but it is not of the same design or workmanship." There was a pause and then she added, "The communication equipment is of Earth design and construction. For some reason, an alien device is being controlled by Earth technology. Is this because the planets are allies? Or is this technology stolen? I am searching to see if there are any clues to the origin of the alien technology, but it appears to have been constructed in such a way as to conceal its identity."

One of the technicians called to her at that moment. "Look, there is some writing here." He took a photograph of it so they could examine it more closely back on the *Invincible*.

The final examinations were made, the capsule was jettisoned, and a quick burst of fire from the shuttle's laser-cannons destroyed the device in a bright flash and a little shower of sparks and debris. They turned the shuttlecraft and made their way back to re-join the *Invincible*.

Ross and Popovych were waiting for them on the hanger deck. Ross, especially, wanted answers. Seeing the captain lying in a coma in a bloodstained bed had made him realize just how much pain he must have been in and he wanted to be able to tell him it was all over.

They went together into one of the science labs and began to pour over the report and various images and scans. Ross was intrigued by the writing. "Let's see if we can try and find out where this is from." He was shocked to find out that they had discovered Earth technology inside the capsule. He looked at Klein as she made her report. "That is unbelievable. If I were not faced with the evidence, I would have said you were mistaken."

The technician, searching the library for the identity of the writing, looked up suddenly. "Sir, this writing is an ancient, barely used script, now only used by the political and religious sects of the planet Tamora."

Ross looked up sharply. "Are you certain? There is no doubt?" He looked at the screen, showing the sample retrieved from the device, and with the picture in the library database. "How do they know? Why are they hounding him like this?"

Popovych shook his head. "If we knew the answers, we would know what we are facing."

Ross laughed slightly at the science officer's matter of fact response. "Well, find me some answers. I am going back to the infirmary to see if there is any change." Doctor Malachi had not said it in so many words, but there was the possibility of brain damage from the severe mental attack. He would be a fool if he did not realize that. He had seen the state he had been in and knew that bleeding like that was really not good at all. Tiberius did not deserve such a horrible fate. He needed to be able to find the answers he was seeking, not to spend the rest of the voyage incapacitated in the ship's infirmary.

28

"I will hold on to hope"

Leandri Kehoe sat at her desk and read through the message she had received from her contact on the *Invincible*. She was a little surprised to hear that Tiberius was incapacitated and then smiled as she read on to find out how. It had worked. MacAlpin and his crew were completely ignorant that the Tamorans were aware of their pending arrival at the planet. She had long been in communication with the political leaders of Tamora, for far longer than anyone would guess. Her connection with Tamora went back to before the *Wryneck* set off on her fateful voyage of discovery, only for whatever it was they had discovered to be the death of them.

The planet Tamora was in a position of strategic importance to Earth in their voyages through space, seeking always to go further than before. Just beyond Tamora lay a wormhole that would open up chances and possibilities for further exploration of which some could only dream. If they could gain access to that wormhole and what lay beyond, it could change everything. It could lead to galaxies full of strange worlds and riches to discover. Trade deals between worlds could be set up, and likely planets could be set aside for colonization as the population of Earth peaked. Kehoe had been heavily involved in the negotiations for trade and passage beyond Tamora; right from the very beginning, long before she finally made admiral. Only she knew what she had done; she knew her involvement—and what the extent of that involvement had been—would lose her everything if it came to light. Rank, reputation, career—she would lose it all. She had to make sure no-one would ever find out the extent of what she had done. She had traded with many lives over the years. Her hands, like Lady MacBeth's, were stained with blood. It had begun small, but more had been demanded and it had become impossible to refuse. It had come down to the voyage of the *Wryneck*—she was guilty of the blood of every soul on board. And now the *Invincible*, and she could not have stopped it even if she had wanted to. Safe conduct for merchant ships and ships carrying colonists would be guaranteed safe passage after this time. They had assured her their experiments had been almost successfully concluded and the new species ready to relocate on the regenerating planet.

She had known of the genetic experiments right from the start; how the Tamorans were experimenting with selective genetic breeding of their own people with those of many different species. They had needed a lot of subjects and she had been able to provide hundreds at a time. Not only had humans not been safe, but she had also condemned the people of other worlds by the shipload. It had all worked according to plan for her and the three others who were involved with her until Xander Galen was discovered to be alive and the Tamorans offered him as a trade—a political bargain as a step in the negotiations. She remembered the meeting well; seeing Galen dragged in by two Tamorans, barely even able to remain upright on his knees. He was naked, arms bound, and eyes covered. She had wanted his death then but had been sent to accept his release—to do otherwise would have meant her exposure. She had seen how ill he looked and assumed he would not survive long. She had been wrong. Every day, she had waited for news from the hospital to say there was no hope. Instead, he had begun to recover, albeit slowly, and she had to silence him in other ways. The hearing where he had been pushed into saying certain things and his apparent condemnation of his commanding officer had been enough for them to condemn the *Wryneck*'s captain. That, and the fact he was reluctant to speak of what had happened to him—the needle marks and scars were proof enough. He had said experiments had been performed but had never said any more and she counted on his shame at being tortured and experimented upon, and his guilt at being the only survivor of the *Wryneck*. She wondered why he had not been killed along with the others who had not been selected for the program. Her determination to keep him silent had led to more guilt. She had ordered his murder at the hands of his doctor, and when Doctor Tierney had refused to obey this order, holding steadfastly to his oath to never cause harm, she had ordered his death. There was another reason too. Revenge.

Years ago, when they were both still cadets, she and Xander had dated but she had left him for someone else not long after they graduated. She had blamed Xander, saying he had chosen his career over her. She blamed him that her marriage had ended in less than two years. She blamed him that all her relationships ended in angry outbursts and she could not see that she was to blame in any way. She was so full of anger that all she wanted was his death. She saw him happy with the android—a robot— when he could have had her! She slammed her fists on the desk. Years of hatred and bitterness had eaten away at her until it consumed her and all she should uphold as an officer, a high-ranking officer, was almost forgotten. Oh, she could act. Outwardly she remained cool and professional when others were around, but inside she had lost control.

She bit her lip hard until it bled, forcing her to focus on the sudden pain. She turned back to the computer and continued to read the message she had received. It gave her details of Commander Ross' injuries, his convalescence, and gradual return to duty. It then informed her that Captain MacAlpin lay in the infirmary in a coma, brought on by the dreams he had which suddenly had seemed to take over every moment he was awake. It told her the doctor had not ruled out the possibility of brain damage. She frowned. This was not in her plan. Tiberius MacAlpin was necessary to her plan—a central player. She read on and saw the device described and that it had been identified as Tamoran. She sent a quick message in return, acknowledging receipt and asking to be kept updated about the captain's condition. After that, she contacted the Tamoran authorities to ask about the device that appeared to have attacked Captain MacAlpin, pointing out that she had given no such orders. After she had spoken with Tamora, she contacted the hospital to enquire about Xander's progress. She was told there was no change, Rear Admiral Galen was still in a comatose state and there had been no signs that this was going to change any time soon. *Good,* she thought. *If he can just pass quietly without waking up.*

•

Serenity remained watchful at Xander's bedside. She looked at the clock on the wall and saw it was time for another dose of the medicine Doctor Tierney had left. As before, she gently slipped the needle into the cannula and injected the dose. So far, it had made no visible difference. Again she looked at her fellow android, the only one of the nursing staff she could trust. "Take another blood test. There must be some change—we have been treating him with this for a month now."

The android nurse nodded and took a syringe. They took blood every time they dosed him and examined it closely looking for even the slightest sign that the bad drugs were being pushed out of his system. Serenity watched as the syringe filled with the dark blood. She always felt bad they were using needles when his poor arm was so scarred with the marks of numerous needles. She clasped his hand in hers as she put a finger over the little spot of blood on his scarred skin. "It will be over soon, dearest, one way or the other," she whispered, stroking the back of his hand with her thumb. She watched the nurse busy with the microscope and just sat, watching Xander's face. It had not changed once, not even a flicker and his chest rose and fell ever so slightly as the machinery breathed for him. It was as though he was already gone. She shook herself. It did not help to think like that. His heart was still beating, that was what mattered. She started as a voice spoke beside her and she looked up and saw the nurse.

"The blood results." The nurse held out the tablet.

Serenity took it and looked at the figures. She had to read everything several times, just to be sure she understood what it said. She looked up. "He's clear? This medicine worked? That means we can begin using the pills Doctor Tierney left and he will wake up soon?"

"We don't know that; we have to take it one step at a time. It is enough just now that the drugs have been purged from his system—the long and sustained administration may have done the damage."

Serenity nodded. "Yes, of course. I understand. But you will go on treating him with this?"

"Of course. I believe Doctor Tierney meant it to replace the medication he was taking previously." She went across to the machine that was functioning as the sick man's organs and tapped the screen for a moment.

The gentle hum of the machinery ceased suddenly, and Serenity looked up. "What is it?" The nurse's fingers flew over the screen again and the hum began again. The gentle hiss of the oxygen flowing through the tubes in his nostrils reassured

Serenity and she looked up at the nurse. "He is still unable to breathe on his own?"

The nurse nodded. "I am sorry, I should have told you I was going to test that. For now, it is enough that we know his system is clear of the drugs. We can work from that."

Serenity nodded and squeezed the hand she still held. "I wish he knew I was here, I told him I would be. Do you think he knows?"

"Do not torment yourself. You know he has not been able to think or know anything for himself, probably since he was abducted and drugged—if he knew anything at all, it would have just been confusion and fear as he would not know where he was or what was happening. When he wakes, then you can tell him that you were there. He will probably say he knew you would be—that has to be enough. You must not punish yourself for not being there when he was taken." She had guessed that was part of the problem. Serenity was angry she had not been at his apartment that morning; he had been alone when they both knew he was in danger.

She was right. Serenity could not forgive herself for having left him alone when he was unwell and vulnerable. He would have said he was fine; in fact, he had the night before when they had walked back to his apartment after dinner. He had just been tired and asked if it was okay that she did not come in for a drink as usual, he wanted to go straight to bed. She had kissed him, saying she understood and told him to take his medicine and go to bed, saying she would see him in the morning. She should not have left it that late to go over—she should have gone early to make sure he was all right. But she had delayed, knowing he needed sleep. She knew he would have told her she was fussing, but if she had gone, she would have been there and he would not now be lying in a hospital bed, in a coma, wired up to a machine which was performing all his bodily functions for him.

The android nurse looked at Serenity. "You know he should be under the care of a doctor."

"Look where that got him," Serenity retorted. "I cannot trust anyone with him. I did not even completely trust Tierney and he was one of Xander's oldest friends—now he is dead. I disbelieved his intentions were just and my faith in him wavered, and yet he developed that medicine in secret and it has cleaned Xander's blood. I am afraid to trust anyone else."

"I understand." The nurse lifted Xander's hand and felt the pulse in his wrist. "It is a little stronger. That is a good sign, perhaps he will wake soon."

Serenity looked at him, so still and white against the pillows and nodded sadly. "I wish he would. Every day he remains in this coma makes it harder for him to revive."

"You have the ability to feel, to hope—you must hold on to that hope. You chose the enhanced programming. You wanted to think and feel—humans are not always happy. They have pain, they grieve, they hold on to hope when it seems futile. You chose to join their weak struggles when you could have remained superior to them."

Serenity nodded. "I chose the path I wanted. I will hold on to hope; however small and hopeless."

The next few weeks passed painfully slowly for Serenity. In the end, she capitulated and permitted a doctor to be brought in. But she had her brought in without the knowledge of the admiral, and after checks had been made to ensure she had not been in any contact with Kehoe. She had also asked the chaplain to attend, knowing Xander was religious. She had wondered over this many times at his refusal to work on a Sunday, and that he chose to spend time in a small church close to the base. It had surprised her, but somehow it was fitting for him so she had asked the minister of that church—incidentally, the hospital's chaplain—to come and anoint him, knowing that he would request this himself if he could and she knew the significant importance it had to him that he be prepared should death claim him—and even more so now as he was still unconscious. When he finished, she smiled. "Thank you. I know it would mean so much to Xander. I should have called you sooner."

The chaplain shook his head. "You did not want to believe the end could be close. I understand that. I know you are without a faith—you are an android, but the fact you did call me shows me you understand the beliefs of another. He is a very fortunate man to have the love of such a woman. I will keep him in my prayers."

Serenity smiled as he left. He had spoken to her as he would a human woman. He had not called her a computer, or a robot, or a machine. He had acknowledged her capability to love as a human and thanked her for acknowledging Xander's faith by having him prepared for death. She reached out and took Xander's hand and held it up to her cheek. "I am not going to let you go," she whispered.

The doctor carried out more tests and scans while Serenity held Xander's hand. She had set up a drip of the medication Doctor Tierney had left, and this was now attached to the cannula in Xander's hand along with drips to hydrate and nourish his unconscious body.

Serenity watched her all the time, nothing would escape her. Everything the doctor did, she checked. No-one was going to take his life; there was little left for him to cling onto and she was going to fight for him.

Another long week passed, and the doctor came to the bedside and held out a tablet. "His will—he does not want to be kept alive artificially once everything has been tried. He has suffered long enough now." Her voice was serious, and she knew the time had come to think of the future.

Serenity took the tablet computer in her hand and stared at the document on the screen and read the clear instructions Xander had left in case of this very situation.

I, Alexander Zachary Galen, being of sound mind, make this request. I have suffered much since my captivity and I have no wish to be kept alive by artificial means and ask, if I am incapacitated, that life support is switched off.

She put the tablet down and took his free hand in hers and kissed the palm. "I don't want to let you go, but I will always do what you want." She buried her face on his arm.

The doctor stood silently, waiting. She looked at the main screen of the life-support machines and saw his vital signs were slowly dropping. "He named you his next of kin, that you are to make the decisions he can not. I need your consent."

Serenity looked up and nodded. "We must do as he wishes." She wished more than anything right now that she could cry. It was unfair that there was no-one here to shed a tear for him. "You can switch it off." She stood by the bed and stroked Xander's greying hair. "I love you, Xander." She bent to kiss him softly on the cheek. She would have kissed his lips but for the tube in his mouth, taped into place. "You can be at peace now— no more suffering." She felt empty as the hum of the machines suddenly stopped and the room was silent.

In silence, the doctor leaned over and began to remove the breathing tubes, the cannula and the wires taped to his chest. The nurse came over and pulled the sheet up to his shoulders and tucked him in securely. The doctor put her hand on

Serenity's shoulder. "It will not be long now. We will leave you alone until you call us."

Serenity nodded and watched them leave. She turned and looked at Xander. He lay so still, his eyes closed—she had never really noticed how thick his lashes were, they were so dark against his pale cheeks. He looked peaceful, as though sleeping. She held his hand and rested her head down on the bed beside him. She would not leave him—she had promised he would not be alone when the end came, and she was going to keep that promise. Her fingers rested lightly on his wrist, feeling the faint pulse. The doctor had been unable to tell her how long he would last once support was withdrawn. Just feeling that faint beat of life still there, still hanging on, made her feel sad and she stroked the cold hand; gently caressing the knuckles. The day dragged on, evening slowly turning into night and she stayed there, her head still resting beside him. With every moment that passed, she knew she was closer to losing him, but she clung fiercely to the last shred of hope with the weak flutter of his pulse.

Midnight passed and the sun of the next day began to lighten the sky and Serenity stirred. Androids did not need to sleep, but she had closed her eyes and allowed her mind to close down a little in rest. She felt something and lay still, wondering what it was. Then she realized she was not holding Xander's hand, and that the 'something' she felt was his hand stroking her hair. She turned her head slightly and looked up.

Xander's eyes were open and he smiled weakly when he saw Serenity looking at him. "Hey."

His voice was only a whisper, but it was the best sound she had heard for a long time. "Xander?" She reached up and took his hand which still rested on her hair. "You're awake! You're alive—they switched off support." She stroked his hand. "I thought I had lost you."

His fingers moved slightly in hers and he gave a faint smile. "Never."

His voice was weak and husky but to her, he sounded wonderful. She had thought she would never hear his voice again, and it was a miracle to her. He should be dead, his body had ceased to function on its own—probably while he had been imprisoned in the stasis tube at the genetics hospital. He had only been alive because of the support machines. When the doctor had switched it off and removed all the apparatus and drips, he had basically been given a few hours before he just slipped away.

Serenity kept hold of his hand and told him to rest. "Go to sleep. Your body needs to rest."

He smiled again. "How long?"

"Four months."

"You?"

"Every moment of every day since we found you. Just like I promised."

"I remember—I was afraid. I couldn't see, or hear, where I was."

"Ssshhh! I'll tell you about it later. Sleep now." She held his hand up to her cheek and kissed his palm.

She watched for a while as Xander closed his eyes. When he was asleep, she called the doctor in.

29

Sick Leave Layover

Kirbie Ross turned to his computer as it informed him of an incoming transmission. He had left the acting first officer in command on the bridge while he rested. He saw the message was not addressed to him, but to Tiberius—he had all messages for the captain diverted to his terminal in case there was anything important that needed to be dealt with while the commanding officer was incapacitated. The message was marked urgent and he saw it was from Serenity. He was worried suddenly and glad that Tiberius was unable to receive messages just now, especially if they contained bad news. Knowing how much Tiberius had been dreading receiving news of Xander death. He opened the message and scanned it quickly. He read that life-support had been switched off and Xander was being permitted to die peacefully and with dignity as he had requested. A glance at the time it was sent told him it would all be over by now; due to the distance, messages took some time to reach the *Invincible* and he saddened by the news. He knew Tiberius had been hoping for a cure to be found in time or, if not, that he would at least have been at Xander's bedside. This news would devastate him, and he was glad that he did not have to go and tell him right away—it would give him time to find the best way of breaking the news. He sat back and thought about the man he had served beside as first officer on the *Victorious* and would grieve for him just as Tiberius would, and the rest of the crew who had transferred to the *Invincible*. Xander did not deserve this—he should have learned the truth of what had happened to his crewmates, and what had really happened to him during the torture and experiments, he had deserved to live long enough to have answers. He shed a few tears for the man who had been a good friend and comrade to them all. Xander had mentored him and trusted him with training Tiberius, his own protégé. It made him realize how quickly life could end and thought that was something everyone tried not to think about, as though that would somehow prolong life. He rested his head down on his arm on the desk and closed his eyes to think over the news he had received and how it reminded him uncomfortably of how close he had himself come so close to losing his own life.

An hour later, the computer laconically informed him of the arrival of another message. He sat up and rubbed his eyes; he had been almost dozing off. He saw the new message was from Serenity and he held his breath for a moment, wondering what further news was coming. An official confirmation of Xander's death, he supposed. He bit his lip and then told the computer to open the message. He read it quickly and closed his eyes, shaking his head as though he did not believe what he read. Xander had defied all odds and was alive. It appeared that at the very moment he should have been breathing his last, he had rallied and had come out of the coma in which he had been for months. "Thank God," he whispered. And he was thinking of Xander then, not that he no longer had bad news to take to his commanding officer, especially when he did not know how long it would be before he would be able to pass it on or what effect it would have on him. He dictated a return message, expressing his delight at the news and, so as not to alarm her, told Serenity that Tiberius had been injured and was in the infirmary. *I will inform him of the good news as soon as I am allowed to speak with him—I know without asking, however, that he will be more than delighted to hear that Xander is alive.*

He received another message a couple of hours later, explaining in further detail what had happened that had brought Xander closer to death than he would have been otherwise. He was shocked. He would not have imagined the situation could have reached this point. Tiberius had been right—something was up, and lives—loyal, dedicated lives—were at stake. It made him wonder if they were in danger. The *Wryneck* had been sent off and its destruction covered up—what if...? Although he did not want to believe that some of High Command were corrupt, he knew it to be true. He wished Tiberius was up and about—he knew how the captain must have felt when he was injured and laid up. He would have needed his first officer—just as now he wanted the captain at his side.

He stood up and headed for the infirmary. He saw Doctor Malachi sitting at the desk in her office, looking at some scans which he could see were of a brain—the captain's brain, he assumed. He poked his head around the door and looked in. "Is there any change?"

She looked up with a smile. "Sit down."

That was a good sign, surely? She would not be smiling if she were about to tell him the captain was suffering irreparable brain damage from the bleeding. He sat down and Doctor Ravello came in and sat in the other chair. He assumed the doctor had summoned him from the screen pad on the desk in front of her. "What is it? Please tell me."

Ravello cleared his throat, a habit of his before speaking. "Captain MacAlpin suffered a serious brain haemorrhage under the strain caused by these dreams. However, we have been able to reduce the bleeding and the pressure this has caused on the brain. There is no permanent damage, but he must not return to work for several months. If we were on Earth, I would recommend that he be placed on indefinite sick leave. But I also know the captain would resent that."

Doctor Malachi nodded, smiling—they knew Tiberius well. "It is my recommendation that you search for a planet where the air is good, and we can layover for a rest. The crew has worked hard and deserves a break and Captain MacAlpin must rest if he is to be any use when we reach our journey's end. I understand he is to act as a negotiator for Earth with the Tamoran Council. He will need his wits about him. Ravello will inform the captain of our diagnosis and recommendation when he wakes. You will wish to be here when that happens, I am sure."

Ross nodded, his face was full of utter relief. He had been horrified to see the state Tiberius had been in and would not have been surprised by bad news. The relief at hearing that rest ashore would be enough to set him back on his feet was very welcome. "I am sure he will be sensible and accept your prescription. A dose of planet-side fresh air will be a tonic for all of us." He thought about the last planet they had landed on and how he had ended up but shook the memories aside. That was an exception—something had been amiss there, even though they had never found out what had really happened, other than that it was an attack by Tamora, just as this savage attack on the captain's mind had been. "Call me when he wakes; I do want to be there."

Ravello stood up. "You might as well stay. Doctor Malachi is going attempt to rouse him now; we have been subjecting him to gentle stimulation."

"Mild electrical pulses," Doctor Malachi continued, "Especially developed for traumatic brain injury or a situation as we have here where the alternative is brain damage. The electrical pulses, unlike the ones that caused the damage, connect with brain activity, however little that may be an attempt to re-activate the brain." She put down the scans she had in her hand and stood up. "Let us begin." She led the way to Tiberius' bedside.

Ross saw with a shock that Tiberius' wavy red hair had been shaved off completely and his bald head was covered in patches with wires attached which ran to the computer beside the bed. "An old-fashioned method? I thought you said this was specially developed."

Doctor Malachi smiled slightly. "Some of the old methods are faultless but this is up-to-date, it is just the delivery that appears old fashioned. But it is completely necessary that nothing, such as hair, blocks the way of the stimuli." She called a nurse over and nodded. "It is time."

The nurse busied herself for a few minutes and then looked up. "Ready, doctor."

Ravello touched Ross' arm. "Stand here, with me—we do not know how he will respond when he rouses."

Ross nodded and stepped aside, allowing the doctor to access the computer monitor the nurse had brought to the bedside. "I'm worried," he confessed. "He's been through a lot already."

Ravello nodded. "Shore leave is paramount. He must rest—regardless of how he thinks he feels. He is an excellent, dedicated commanding officer, and he will want to return to the bridge. You must help him to understand that it is for his own good and that he will soon be back in command. One of your duties as first officer is to safeguard the captain."

Ross laughed. "They're hard to convince. I was Galen's first officer too—they are every bit as stubborn as the other when it comes to issues of their own safety and well-being and yet they worry over everyone else. I've been faced with impossible tasks before. This one is only a new challenge."

The procedure seemed to take a long time and Ross was on tenterhooks, worrying about what was going on. After what seemed ages, Ross saw Doctor Malachi put her hand on

Tiberius' chest. "Lie still, Captain." She placed a small scanner to his temple and closely watched the readings it gave.

Tiberius closed his eyes and then opened them again. "Ross?"

"He is here. Don't speak, you must lie quietly until I have finished my examination." The doctor pressed a button, and a larger scanner came down from the ceiling and rested against Tiberius' forehead for a moment. She watched the small screen intently and then sent it back to its position. "Very good. The procedure was successful."

"Good," Tiberius said weakly. "I will return to the bridge."

The doctor pushed him back down against the pillows. "You *will* not. You have been in a critical condition." She listed the symptoms and the effect they had on him.

Tiberius was shocked. "I remember the pain. Was it that bad?" He lay back obediently and closed his eyes. There was a dull ache and he felt tired.

Ross stepped forward. "Do what the doctor says, the ship is safe with me—you know that." He put his hand on Tiberius' shoulder. "You need a rest. When you are fit, then you can return to duty. I am arranging shore leave."

"No! We don't have time."

"Yes, we do!" Ross responded firmly. "You nearly died—you need to be strong for what is ahead of us and a short detour will not make much difference to what we face. We are already en-route to a planet nearby that is recorded as a place of peace and tranquillity with an earth-like atmosphere—perfect for us. The people offer hospitality for travellers and there is a spa where you can rest and get your strength back." Their eyes met.

Tiberius was the first to lower his. He knew what Ross was saying was necessary. He had tried to raise his head from the pillow, and it felt as though the whole universe was spinning around before his eyes. He was a sensible man and knew the last place he should be in this state was on the bridge. "I understand of course." He smiled slightly. "What happened?"

Doctor Malachi came over. "No more talking." She signalled a nurse and had the captain quickly and skilfully tucked in and he was given a mild sedative to ease the ache in his head and to get him off to sleep more quickly. The doctor turned back to Ross. "Thank you—he needed firmness then. He will do what is required."

Ross smiled. "I did not think it would be too hard. He knows he needs to be strong and well—he would have been a fool to fight us. I will return to the bridge and make a course for Xylanthia."

"Xylanthia?" Doctor Malachi queried. "Is that the agricultural planet?"

"Yes; but they have big beaches on one side of the planet," Ross replied. "The people are known for their hospitality towards visitors. The records show there are hot springs and health spas which is what the captain needs."

She nodded. "I agree, and not just the captain could do with that!"

Ross laughed. "I know. We have plenty of facilities on board, but it is not the same as being planet-side and breathing fresh air. I know I am looking forward to it, even if I will be spending most of my time with the captain."

"It is good of you to volunteer; friendship will play an important role."

"It always does," Ross replied. "Friendship is often overlooked as a healer. Time is all very well, but the importance of the company of a friend cannot be denied. Tiberius' company was important during my recovery, I can repay my debt." He turned and headed for the door and left the infirmary.

As the *Invincible* was only six hours away from Xylanthia, it was not long before she was in orbit around the planet and Popovych, still acting first officer, requested clearance to dock. They had already informed the planet's space-dock officials that they were coming and that one of the crew was injured although now in recovery. Permission was granted, and the *Invincible* made her docking run and Narelle Forsyth, the navigator, positioned them perfectly for Helm to make an easy docking. This was her first posting in deep space and as a new ensign she was still slightly in awe of the experience on the bridge, but she was a skilful officer and completely able in her position.

Ross leaned back in his seat and watched Popovych directing the docking procedure and was proud of the way the crew worked well together. The chief science officer made an excellent first officer and it was no surprise that Tiberius was fiercely proud of his crew.

The crew had been warned of their commanding officer's condition, so that none of them were shocked to see him carried off the ship on a stretcher, under the personal charge of the CMO. They were shocked though to see the pain in his face. Although beginning to recover, it would be a while before the headaches would leave him and the risk of further bleeding ruled out.

Tiberius had been ordered to spend the first few days of their stay in bed and he was actually pleased to submit to the doctor's orders—he was exhausted. The medical team took him to the hotel in the city which was in the beach area of the planet. It was a very large resort which catered for all, similar to holiday resorts on Earth. His room was a large suite with a balcony overlooking the beach. It was hot, but not badly so. His bed was set up on the balcony so he could rest in the warm air; there was a gentle breeze and it reminded him of a mild day in California. Doctor Malachi and a male nurse lifted him into bed and tucked him in with a light sheet and propped him up on pillows so that, although reclining, he would still be able to see what was going on. He thanked them with a smile and asked if he was allowed visitors.

The doctor smiled. "Of course. Ross is waiting to see you. I'll allow three if they don't stop you from resting."

"They won't," Tiberius promised. "I'll make sure of that; I want to be back on the bridge sooner rather than later."

The doctor nodded. "That is why we ordered this leave. There was no other way for you to get the required rest—there is no way you would rest on the ship. We know you too well."

Tiberius pulled a face, knowing this to be true.

The doctor left and a short while later, Ross arrived with Popovych, and Kiana Yoshizaki—the Japanese tactical officer. She was a good friend of Popovych's, and Tiberius liked to hope a little more than *just* friends. As professional serving officers, relationships were kept off the bridge, but Tiberius did not discourage his crew from forming relationships—as they were so far from home, and for so long, it would not be fair to demand they not have relationships. He just made it clear that nothing was to get in the way of their work. And it worked well enough—and he had had the pleasure of performing the marriage ceremony for several couples over the years they had been away. He had grown to be good friends with the science officer, and he hoped that he would perform the ceremony for him. He turned his head on the pillow when he saw his friends come in and he smiled. "Hey, guys."

Ross came to the bedside and looked at him closely for a short while, and then smiled. "You were a mess when I saw you last. You almost frightened the life out of me!"

Tiberius smiled faintly. "Doc told me there was a lot of blood. The dream did it?"

Ross nodded. "Kind of." He looked at Popovych and the Ukrainian briefly told the captain what had happened and how they had found and destroyed the device which had been scrambling his mind.

Tiberius leaned back on the pillow and closed his eyes for a moment. "Were the dreams even real?"

Ross nodded. "I think so, but this machine was used to make them worse—to make you see things that were not true; things that were not there."

"I don't know what is real anymore." Tiberius gave a sad sigh. "They had been with me all my life. Who did it?"

"Tamora."

Tiberius' eyes flew wide open, and he made as though to sit up. "Ugh!" he grunted as his head swam.

Kiana and Popovych helped him back down and propped him back up on the pillows. "Lie down, sir!" Kiana said. "The doctor will kill us if we get you excited or stressed. You are here to rest— I don't think we should have told you!"

Tiberius raised a hand weakly in surrender. "We won't let her beat us."

Ross realized he was not referring to Doctor Malachi and knew who he meant. "We won't. When you feel better, we will talk about everything. But I won't risk the doctor's wrath. Plus, I want you back on the bridge and fit for work. The first stage is bed rest, then gradual getting up for some of the day—we're laying over here until you're fit again. The ship could do with some minor repairs and the crew won't say no to a bit of recreation time."

Tiberius smiled. "Thank you, and I'm sorry I frightened you. I was scared myself, very scared. Anyway, sit down—don't just stand around. It means I have to look up at you."

They pulled chairs over and sat down, talking softly for a while, until they saw Tiberius was drifting off to sleep. They crept out; sleep was the best thing for him right now.

Ross closed the door quietly and looked at the others. "It's going to be tough for him, but he'll get there. He's too determined not to."

They walked down to the beach and sat in the sand. Ross pulled his boots off and dug his toes into the warm sand. "This is perfect, I've almost forgotten what going to the beach is like! I can forget that I can't feel the sand."

Popovych had begun to laugh but stopped, remembering the first officer's prosthetics. He sat beside him and pulled off his boots. "I'm going for a swim. Coming?"

"Later on," Ross replied. "Don't look like that—I can go in the water." He had glanced up and saw Popovych looking shocked, as though realizing what he had said. "I'll lie here a while. You go, I'm happy to just watch you enjoying yourselves."

"With your eyes shut?" Kiana asked, teasing.

Ross grinned lazily. "I'm sleepy." He closed his eyes again and lay back in the sun as his companions headed for the sea. He would enjoy a swim later, but for now, he was content to just bask in the hot sun. Like the others, he had spent many years in space and, although their ships were equipped with everything they could possibly need, nothing could compare with being planet-side—however much they loved their work. He was more tired than he realized, probably from the stress of the last few weeks. He leaned back, let his breathing relax and he was asleep in moments.

30

"Good surfing waves"

Tiberius stirred a few hours later. The sun was beating onto on his face and he slowly opened his eyes. It was warmer now than it had been earlier, and he rolled onto his side a little and curled up, enjoying the quiet and the fresh air. He dozed off for a while and then stirred when he heard a footstep. He looked up and smiled.

Doctor Malachi returned the smile. "I looked in a couple of times, but you were fast asleep. How are you feeling?"

Tiberius gave a sleepy smile. "I'm okay. If I could get rid of the headaches, I would feel a lot better, but I understand that will take a while."

"Is it bad?"

He nodded. "I'm sorry."

"Don't be, it's not your fault." The doctor held out a pill and a glass of water. "Take this, it will ease the pain. It won't make you sleepy but will dull the pain. If you're careful you could read for a little while. But you must not tire yourself."

Tiberius took the painkiller and nodded. "Could I have a tablet computer? I'd like to read Ross' logs if that's okay? I promise I won't do any work."

She laughed. "I'll come back in half an hour to take it off you; that is all I can allow for now." She held out the slim tablet. "I brought it with me as I knew you would ask. If the pain comes back, press this to call me." She tucked a little device into his hand and raised his pillows slightly.

"Thank you. I'll be okay, but I will call if I need help." He watched her leave and lay back for a while, looking down at the beach and could pick out some of his crew and smiled to see that they were getting the chance to enjoy a time of relaxation, even though it was at the expense of his own health. The attack could even have cost him his sanity—he did not fool himself on that score; he knew he could have died or been left seriously incapacitated. After a few moments, he touched the screen of the tablet to wake it up. "Open messages."

"Do you wish to view all messages or just the latest ones you have not read?" the computer responded. "You have many messages since you last signed in."

"Any personal messages? I do not wish to see anything official—Commander Ross is handling them," Tiberius told the computer.

"You have two personal messages, they are not recent and have been responded to by Commander Ross, stating your illness as the reason for responding for you."

"Let me see them." He leaned back and began to read the message that had been sent by Serenity. His face grew paler as he read, and he dropped the tablet onto the sheets. "*Pappi!*" He could not believe it—life-support had been switched off. A tear slid down his cheek and he did not read on to see the second message. His fingers closed convulsively and pressed the button on the pager the doctor had left with him.

Doctor Malachi rushed in and was shocked to see Tiberius crying. "What is it? The pain should not have returned so soon." She scanned him quickly. "You do not appear to be suffering pain."

Tiberius pointed at the screen. "Xander is dead."

The doctor took the tablet and scanned the message quickly, catching her breath as she read, understanding why he was so affected; it was no secret Xander had been like a father to him. "I am so sorry. I know you wanted to be there with him." She looked at the screen again. "Ross replied, stating that he would tell you when you were well again." She scrolled down the screen and looked up. "There is another message you should read."

Tiberius held out his hand and took the tablet. He wiped his eyes and then read the message; originally sent an hour or so after the first one.

It's a miracle. The doctor gave him no longer than an hour to live once life-support was switched off. I was prepared to watch him slip away, but he defied them. At the very moment that he should have died; he came out of the coma and spoke to me. He is going to live.

Doctor Malachi watched his face. "Good news?"

Tiberius nodded and passed her the tablet. "He's alive but they don't know how."

The doctor smiled. "Doctors don't have all the answers—if we did, there would be no more suffering. Some things are just meant to be, and we can't explain why." She held out the tablet again. "Do you want to send them a message right now?"

Tiberius shook his head. "I need to let it sink in." He looked down at his hands and saw they were shaking. Xander dying before they returned from space was his greatest fear. Eight years was a long time to ask a dying man to hold on for and he knew if his time came then it was cruel to wish him to continue—especially if it was artificial. They had talked about it once before; Xander had a horror of being kept alive by a machine—he had said he wanted to die naturally and in peace and Tiberius was glad Serenity had been there to see his wishes were acknowledged; he could see, from the way she wrote, that her love for Xander was genuine and very real and he was glad. He had been surprised when first told but had seen the way both wrote about the other, and he no longer worried about the fact Serenity was not human. She was not even an alien. She was a constructed device, capable of human interaction; created to work alongside and assist humankind and one, out of the hundreds serving, just one had chosen to become as close to being human as possible. Xander deserved happiness, and he deserved to live—to be given time to experience happiness and love, and he had found that in Serenity.

Tiberius understood. Starship captains did not have time to for relationships. With loyalty to the ship and crew, commitment was something so many sacrificed. Xander had sacrificed that and had lost his liberty and was left to rot in an alien prison, tortured and afraid, and very alone. Xander should marry her, he thought. She had stayed at his side through illness, and even to the point of death. She made him happy—he needed to live the rest of his life in comfort, surrounded by the love he must have yearned for all his adult life.

"You should send a quick message," the doctor said after a period of silence in which she had been busy taking notes from the medi-reader she had stuck to his temple. "Ross informed Serenity that you were ill; she will worry about you and has probably not informed Galen, for the same reason Ross did not tell you of the messages—protection."

Tiberius nodded as she removed the reader. "I'll do that, and I'll not get mad at Ross. I was going to ask him when he was going to tell me."

"Don't do that." Doctor Malachi shook her head gently. "He takes his duties very seriously, including protecting his commanding officer. He was very upset and angry to see you in so much pain. He will find facing the Tamorans just as hard as you will. Do not censure him for not holding back news he knew would distress you. Even though you know Galen is alive, you are still upset—upset that you were not there with him."

Tiberius met her eyes in silence. "I thought Ravello was the psychiatrist."

"I'm right though."

Tiberius nodded. "I saw how tired he looked—how ill. He said he was okay. I had to leave, knowing I might never see him again."

"That's life in our work. We all had to leave someone behind. You need to let it go—all that pain and anger will destroy you and put the crew in danger. You must be able to function; this must show you how close you have come to death and to losing your ability to function as commanding officer of this ship." Tiberius lay back on the pillow and went very quiet, and the doctor knew she had touched a nerve; every captain would dread losing the ability to command. She lowered the head of the bed so he could lie down. "Get some sleep, you can send a message later. I want you to rest; you're showing signs of stress and we don't want another headache—you're already taking pain medication, I cannot give you any more." She took the tablet from his hand and tucked the sheets in.

Tiberius obediently closed his eyes and tried to shut out the pain which was threatening to engulf him.

The week passed slowly for Tiberius as he lay in bed, on the balcony for most of the day. He had steadily improved, although needing assistance with walking as his balance was a little off. He had discovered that when attempting to make it to the bathroom without assistance. He had ended up on the floor and had to call for help with the buzzer the doctor had given him. He was still a bit wobbly and needed an arm to lean on, but the doctor said he could go and join the others on the beach. She took him down herself and saw him settled comfortably on one of the sun loungers available. Tiberius laid back with a sigh and stretched as he felt the sun warming his limbs. "That's so much better."

The doctor smiled. "It will not be long before you are fit to return to work. We just need to work on those dizzy spells." She looked up as a shadow fell across the sand and saw Commander Ross coming over.

The *Invincible*'s first officer was dressed in his swim things and had a towel thrown over his shoulder. His deepening tan showed he was spending most of his time in the water, the only visible places without a tan were his prosthetics and it did not bother him unduly that there was a stark contrast. He smiled. "How's the skipper, Doctor? Is he well enough to come swimming?"

Doctor Malachi shook her head. "Not yet. He still takes dizzy spells, and we don't want that to happen in the sea."

Ross nodded, understanding, and put his towel down on the sand. "I'll keep him company for a bit—you go and take a break." He sat down on the towel and looked up, squinting in the bright sun.

The doctor nodded. She slipped off her boots and walked barefoot to the water's edge and wandered along, letting the waves break gently over her feet.

Tiberius turned his head and looked at Ross. "I know about Xander."

Ross met his eyes. "I was going to tell you. Please don't think I would not have done so, I could not tell you while you were so ill though. It would have made it worse."

"I know. It's okay, Kirbie. I am not mad at you." Tiberius leaned back and closed his eyes. "I have spoken to Serenity, she didn't give me any detail but said he is still in hospital and that it will be some time before he is able to leave. I wasn't able to speak to him, but she said she would tell him I called. I knew he was ill, but it just seems like it was something more than just the expected decline in his health."

"I guess Serenity will tell you as soon as she knows." Ross lay back on the towel and stretched. "I could get used to a planet like this. Good surfing waves. It reminds me of home, just more like Paradise."

"Santa Monica? Paradise?" Tiberius laughed, remembering Ross had an apartment there when he was not in space. "Pretty, but not paradise surely?"

Ross shook his head. "I'm a Gold Coaster—I meant home as in Australia, not where I live for work. I'm lucky California is good for surfing, but nothing beats Straya's east coast for me. That's paradise."

Tiberius noticed Ross' accent strengthened as he spoke, even dropping into the vernacular, and he smiled. "I never learned to surf. Mother wouldn't let me—said it was too dangerous and I was all she had. She didn't even like me playing hockey, but I am Canadian—I couldn't keep off the rink." Tiberius sighed. "I'm a city boy. Mother freaked out when I got a motorcycle when I was sixteen."

Ross grinned. "I guess that was from Xander."

Tiberius nodded. "Yeah, he gave me cool stuff; stuff I think dad would have got me."

"Your dad would have been pleased to know you had someone—even if Xander was away a lot after he recovered." He knew Tiberius still got hung up on the things he had missed.

"You're right; I shouldn't feel too bad—I can't make things change," Tiberius sighed, looking out to sea, and then turned back. "The waves are good, go and catch one. I am content just to lie here and watch you."

Ross smiled and headed off to join some of the crew who had hired surfboards and were gathering at the water's edge.

Tiberius leaned back on the cushions and watched them enjoying their recreation time.

31

On the Road to Recovery

"How is the patient?" Serenity looked up as the doctor approached and smiled, but there was a wariness about it as she felt she could not fully trust the medical staff. She knew she was being silly, this doctor worked hard with Xander and had fought through two relapses. If she had wanted him to die, there had been ample opportunities to let him go but she had not. So she smiled. "He is asleep; I believe it is best that he sleeps as much as possible."

The doctor agreed. "You still will not tell me what drug you used that eradicated the poisons which had been introduced into his bloodstream?"

The android shook her head. "No, I cannot. Doctor Tierney lost his life because he would not take Xander's—I will not surrender his work to anyone. Not until Xander has no need for the medication—I will not risk losing it." She was afraid the remaining medicine would be stolen before he was well enough to do without it.

The doctor sighed. "I wish you could believe that I wish him no harm. While you keep me at arm's length, I cannot be of any more help."

Before Serenity could say anything, Xander stirred slightly and coughed. He was sick and a nurse only just got a bowl there. The drugs were working their way out of his system and it was making him pretty sick from time to time. Serenity stroked his hand as the nurse wiped his face with a wet cloth. "It's okay, Xander, you'll feel better soon."

Xander reached for her hand and held it while the medical team were busy getting him comfortable. What he had been through over the last months had confused him and he was not sure what had happened; in fact, all he knew for certain was that he felt really ill but so long as Serenity's hand held his, and he heard her voice, he felt better. He had heard her voice all the time, even before coming out of the coma, he had heard her talking to him, telling him everything that was happening, or just making up things. He had heard her read from books, and from messages Tiberius sent. He had never been afraid as long he knew she was there; she had allayed his fears of being alone when he died. He had been alone for too long. When he was released from his captivity he had been hospitalized for some time, and it had been a while before he was told about the loss of his ship and, as the realization that his shipmates and his best friend were all dead set in, he had felt an overwhelming emptiness. They had served together for more than ten years and he grieved for a long time. Twenty years of grieving, the mystery surrounding the circumstances of his captivity and the destruction of his crew-mates, and his worsening health had deepened the loneliness. A loneliness that would not leave until he had noticed Serenity. True, she had worked as his aide since he was given his position on Admiral Kehoe's staff, but he had not noticed her in any way other than that of a member of the admiral's staff, and someone who was always pleasant to him. She was an android, he had never even thought of anything other than that she was an excellent creation and was an asset helping with his work. He had first noticed how she had insisted he rest and take his medication. He had been grateful for that—he was never very good at remembering to take it at the exact regular intervals required by the doctors. Her programming meant that she could remember many things without effort, and his medication always seemed to be the most important thing to her. He had noticed the regulated attentions had turned into real care, and he had warmed to this machine—the machine he had come to realize he was in love with. That day he had asked her to have dinner with him was the day he knew; when he saw her at the restaurant, looking like a beautiful woman. He had shied away from human relationships; he had lost his trust in their intentions, and because of this he had missed out on one of the things he yearned for more than anything else—companionship and love.

He knew it was silly to fall in love with an android. But she cared for him and made him feel loved. Yes, he would be told that it could not happen—but it had. To him, she was a real woman; the kind of woman he had always dreamed of. Did it matter that she was a machine? She had told him once that she was programmed to serve him, and she would not hurt him as his own people had. He turned his head on his pillow and opened his eyes slightly and smiled at her. "I want to go home."

Serenity stroked his hand. "You can't go home yet, Xander."

"Please! I am scared." His voice shook. "I couldn't see—there was no sound. I couldn't move." He was remembering little pieces of being shut away in the stasis chamber.

"You're not there now. Look, everything is bright. There are flowers on the bedside, and you are breaking the hold of the drugs." Serenity gripped his hand and reached out with her other hand and stroked his cheek. "You've been very ill, but everything is going to be fine now."

Xander looked around a little and saw the vase of brightly coloured flowers and smiled, knowing she must have brought them in. "Where's Clark? He brought me here." He remembered the few moments of lucidity when Doctor Tierney had rescued him.

Serenity tightened her grip on his hand. "He's dead, Xander. Kehoe had him killed. Your room is under guard—to keep you safe. He was ordered to kill you, but he refused, and she sent assassins after him." She watched his face and saw the sadness. She knew he and Clark Tierney had been friends for a long time and understood he would feel the loss of another friend deeply. She did not know what to say but took both his hands in hers and held them. "I am so sorry." She felt him squeeze her hands and heard him sigh. "He was a true friend." She told him how Tierney must have known his life was in danger and had left instructions and his newly developed experimental medicine. "I thought I was going to lose you and I could not cry. I cannot cry and I felt bad because you needed someone to grieve for you." She told him how she had watched him slipping away and how she had called the chaplain.

Xander looked into her eyes. "You did that for me? You knew that is what I would have wished—that means more to me than any tears." He smiled as he felt her return the grip on her hands. "Will you do something for me? There is a small case on top of the wardrobe in my apartment. Bring it to me, please."

"I do not want to leave you—I have never left you alone. I do not trust them."

"Serenity…Serenity. You must trust them." Xander's voice was soft. "Not everyone wants me to die—you have to relax and trust the doctor." He felt her hands tighten around his fingers. "I am the one who is afraid—I want to go home. I do not want to stay here, but you are here, and that helps me not to be afraid. I have to trust them, and I need you to trust them too."

Serenity nodded. "I will go and fetch what you want." She leaned over and kissed him. "Your chaplain was nice, he didn't talk to me like I was a machine." When she reached the door, she turned and looked over her shoulder. She seemed to be about to say something but then left without a word. She paused in the corridor and spoke to the guards at the door before turning and walking away. She took a shuttle-cab back to the area of the city where Xander's apartment was and let herself in. She looked around, it was just as she had left it months ago when she and Doctor Tierney began their search—even the stain still showed on the floor where Xander had dropped his oatmeal when he passed out. She went to the bookshelf and took down a couple of books she knew he was fond of and then chose some clothes that would be comfortable when he was allowed out of bed. She looked around and found a bag at the bottom of the cupboard, folded the clothes and placed them with the books. She then got a chair and climbed up to look on top of the wardrobe. Right at the very back was a metal box with a lock on it. She lifted it down carefully and blew the dust off the top before putting it into the bag. She was about to pick up the bag and leave when she turned back. Everything had been left as it had been, even the bed unmade. She went and stripped the bed and remade it. She knew she had told Xander he could not leave the hospital yet, but she suddenly wanted his apartment ready for when he could. She ran a duster over the surfaces and then picked up the bag and headed out, locking the door behind her. She headed back to the hospital and hurried to his room, not wanting him to be alone for much longer.

Xander turned his head when she came back into the room and smiled warmly at her. He had been lying flat when she left, but the head end of his bed had been raised and he was propped up on pillows.

"Oh, you're sitting up!" Serenity leaned over to kiss him on the cheek. "I brought you some books and the box you wanted." She took them out of the bag and put them on the bed beside him. She watched him pick up one of the books and turn the pages. In these days of advanced technology, it was nice to see someone with the appreciation for something tangible. She put the clothes in the cupboard and told the nurse they were there.

Xander held out the box to the nurse and asked her to put it in the cupboard by the bed. "I do not need it just now; I will ask for it when I do."

The nurse stowed the box safely and then stuck a medi-reader onto Xander's temple and took readings of his vital signs. "You are doing much better. The doctor is pleased with your progress." She glanced up as the doctor came across and spoke quietly.

"Well, Admiral Galen," the doctor said. "You are doing so much better than you could be and I am very pleased with you. I think we can try and get some solid food into you instead of the drip and perhaps some time outside on the balcony. It is a lovely day, and the fresh air will do you the world of good."

Xander's eyes lit up. "Oh, please! I do not like being cooped up inside, and I am hungry."

•

A couple of weeks later, Xander's bed was wheeled out onto the balcony outside his hospital room, and he sighed with relief— every day he was outside it felt wonderful to feel the fresh air on his face. It had rained earlier in the day and the city had the freshness that comes after the rain. The sun was warm again and Xander was propped on his pillows with blankets to keep him comfortable in the gentle breeze. He asked Serenity to bring out the box he had asked her to fetch from the apartment and thanked her with a smile when she brought it to him. He opened it up and began looking through the contents.

Serenity sat watching him looking at some old photographs and saw him open a flat black box. She saw his face sadden slightly and saw he was looking at a medal. "Is that yours?" she asked softly.

Xander nodded. "Yes—for bravery. As though that would make what I had been through better."

She put her hand on his arm. "You deserved it, Xander—you were brave. It took more courage than you probably ever knew you had in you to survive, and all these years you have kept on fighting. It was not because of what happened—that medal was not part of the cover-up."

He felt her hand on his hair and smiled. "Survivor's guilt. I still do not understand why I was the only one to come home. It is on my mind all the time. They say Stephen betrayed us. If he had, would he not be the one who survived? What it if it was me? What if I betrayed them?"

"Don't, Xander." Serenity took his face between her hands and looked into his eyes. "You are hurting yourself. All these years of grieving, combined with your illness, the not knowing—it hurts, I know. Thirty years have passed; you need to try and heal. It will not dishonour Stephen's memory, or the memory of your crew-mates, to let go and accept their deaths."

Xander met her eyes and she saw pain. She had been right—he had held onto his pain for too long and it was hard to let go. "I will try. I have been too afraid to let go in case I forget them."

"You will never forget them; you could not."

Xander reached up and put his hands over hers. "What would I do without you?" he asked. "You have helped me so much over the years."

"Stop talking," Serenity responded. She leaned forward and kissed him warmly on the lips. "Ssshhhh!" She gently took her hands away from his face and got him comfortable. "Call me if you need anything."

"Don't go." Xander grabbed her hand. "I have been alone too long—please don't leave me alone."

"I will not go if you do not wish it."

He squeezed her hand. "I don't want you to ever leave me. Serenity, I have been through things I do not ever wish to speak of—the torture and the experiments."

She put her finger on his lips. "Then do not speak of it."

"No, but it is because of this that I have been unable to develop relationships or to settle down; I am too late now to have the family I dearly longed for. I never knew what it was to feel truly happy, and to enjoy the company of another until I met you." He slid his free hand under his pillow. "Serenity, I did not believe it possible that I could ever care for anyone—that I could fall in love. But then I realized it was possible and that I had fallen in love with the most perfect woman I could ever have imagined— a woman I can trust with my life. Serenity, my darling, will you marry me?" He flicked open the small blue velvet box he held.

Serenity stared at the slender gold ring with a single diamond sparkling in the pink light of the setting sun. "Xander, it is beautiful. You are asking me to marry you—you have forgotten that I am merely a machine? A robot—an android. There is nothing inside but circuit boards and wires."

"I have not forgotten, but it is *because* you are not human that you have stolen my heart. You have been more to me than any human ever could be." Xander lifted the ring from the box. "I do not need a wife because I desire a family, I am as unable to have that as you are as an android. I need a wife who will be my companion in my old age. Someone with whom I can share my sunset years."

Serenity held out her left hand to him. "Then I would be honoured to be your wife. I loved you from the moment I was assigned to you. I underwent advanced programming shortly before—programming that allowed me to think and feel like a human woman. I did not expect to receive your affections. I was happy for it to be my secret love." She watched him slip the ring onto her finger. "It is so beautiful and looks old."

"It was my mother's," Xander replied simply. "I had dreamed of a more romantic proposal, not lying in a hospital bed."

Serenity leaned forward and slipped her arms around his neck and rested her head on his shoulder. "To me it was perfect."

Xander closed his eyes and smiled, feeling that he was, at long last, on the road to recovery.

32

"I can stop running"

Commander Ross looked up as the bridge doors opened. He smiled and stepped away from the command chair. "Captain on the bridge!"

Tiberius smiled as the crew snapped to attention. He strode to his chair and took his seat almost with a sigh of relief. "Stand easy, you can return to your positions." He leaned back in the chair and closed his eyes for a moment. "This feels so good; I have missed it. Two months is a long time to be away from my post." He stroked the arms of the chair and then turned and looked around and saw the crew watching him with smiles. "I think we have delayed enough. Ross, please take your position." He patted the arm of the chair beside his.

Ross took his place in the first officer's seat next to the captain's. "Helm, set course for Tamora." He turned and looked at Tiberius. "Would you do the honours, sir?"

Tiberius smiled. He was back on the bridge, where he belonged, and he was happy. He loved this life and coming close to losing it had given him a renewed energy. He settled back in the chair. "Let's do it!"

"Aye aye, sir," Dinesh Patel replied. He was one of the crew who had transferred from the *Victorious* and had been serving there even before Xander Galen had been given that command fifteen years ago. He was one of the oldest and most experienced of the crew and an excellent pilot. Tiberius had once said he would trust the Indian to manoeuvre the ship through anything, or around any obstacle, whatever the size. His response to any request, however impossible, was always "Aye, sir," with a smile on his face.

Veritas: The Captain's Redemption

Tiberius watched as Patel's fingers tapped at his screen and then his fingers were spread over the steering screen, each delicate touch of his fingertips controlling every movement of the ship. The captain smiled. It was nice to feel the movement of the ship again—to sit on the bridge and watch the stars seeming to fly past the windows. They had the option of 360-degree clear vision around the bridge, or to screen the windows and look ahead only on a huge viewing screen, on which they could magnify and examine any obstacles in their path. Tiberius loved the windows—the stars had always held him with fascination. Growing up as a boy in Manitoba, he had loved to sit in the yard of his grandparents' home and look up. His grandfather had taught him to look for shooting stars, and how to make a wish on a falling star. Young Tiberius had only made one wish—for his father to come home; a week later, the officers had arrived with the news that he was dead. He had never made another wish after that. He lived in the city; only six years of his life had been spent in Canada as his mother had decided to move to America, to be closer to her husband's work—even though he was gone. Every summer, he had been sent to stay with his father's parents and he had loved growing up on the farm. They had encouraged him to dream too, and to work toward making his dream a reality; they knew he would follow his father's footsteps, despite his mother's protests. He smiled, remembering their encouragement and their insistence that Stephen would be proud of his son. Now both well into their nineties, he kept in touch with them and discussed his search for the truth of what had happened to Stephen. He had found it impossible to discuss it with his mother—she just shut down. He snapped out of his reverie as he heard his first officer speak to him. "Sorry, Kirbie—Ross." He corrected himself quickly, a stickler for keeping familiarity off the bridge. "I was miles away in the stars—remembering they are what drew me to space as a boy—other than my father."

Ross nodded. "None of us had much choice—the influence was always there, but I joined up because I was always running, and space was the furthest place I could run to."

Tiberius looked at him. "I didn't know that. What were you running from?"

"I don't know. Myself, I guess. Or family expectations," Ross responded. "I was the youngest in my family and was running from the shadow of my brother and sister."

"Did you? Escape the shadow, I mean, or are you still running?" Tiberius watched him and smiled. "I need you to be sure."

Ross laughed. "My brother is a neurosurgeon, and my sister is a judge. That's what my family wanted for me, but I just wanted to surf my way through my teenage years. I scraped through school and didn't know what to do with myself. There was a talk in Brisbane with people like us, space explorers. Something about space appealed to me, I would sit out watching the stars. I'd even surfed at night—moonlight and waves made me forget my troubles. I got to speak to some of the speakers and I told them what I was up against. One of them must have believed there was something in me, because she sponsored me through the academy. I had a good time as a cadet, and I worked hard. I guess I made good and I can stop running."

"I'm glad. I'd hate to think you were still trying to prove yourself to them." Tiberius changed the subject. "The last leg of the voyage and we're only two months away from Tamora. What do you think is going to happen?"

Ross looked out of the window in silence for a moment. "Whatever happens, you have to be strong. Do not risk your ship and crew for a personal vendetta."

Tiberius looked up, shocked. "You think my feelings still get in the way?"

The first officer nodded. "If you want me to be honest, then yes, I do think that. Your grief over the condemnation of your father, and the fact that you still do not know what happened to him. You are upset that Xander is ill, and that you do not know why he lived—if you can call slowly dying from an unknown illness living—while your father died. Your nightmares, they consumed you and almost proved fatal. You have been so concerned with all of this that you sometimes forget to be yourself—rather than the avenging angel for your father's honour. You should be happy with the fact that you honour him every day by believing in him, and he would be proud to see you in command as he was."

Tiberius lowered his eyes for a moment before he looked up and met Ross' blue eyes. "Why do you always have to be right?"

Ross' blue eyes twinkled, and he laughed. "It's part of my job to be right. It keeps you safe."

"You're my first officer, not a nursemaid." Tiberius' tone was light and teasing, but his eyes said *thank you*. He appreciated

241

everything Ross had done, and how he continued to help. He remembered how he had been at first when he realized that he did not have the command. There was no sign of that resentment now, and he was glad—he had understood, and was glad he had persevered with requesting his assignment to the *Invincible*.

Ross glanced at him and seemed to know what he was thinking. "You need to forget that. It never was an issue. I was a fool."

"You need to stop doing that," Tiberius retorted. "It's scary—like you read my mind."

"I'm sorry. Your face mirrors your thoughts, sometimes it is not hard to guess. And you were looking at me." Ross laughed slightly and leant back in his seat. "Don't let it worry you—my desire is to serve you. There is no resentment at all."

Tiberius smiled. "I am sorry. I should know better—you have more than proved yourself."

Ross looked pleased that Tiberius acknowledged this. "We are ready. You and I make a good team and that is what we need for whatever we face on Tamora."

The captain nodded. "I agree." He tapped the screen on the arm of his chair and began to read some department reports.

33

Mona

Admiral Kehoe swung her chair around from the computer, stood up slowly and went to the window, hands clasped behind her back. Unbeknown to Tiberius and his crew, the admiral had a spy onboard the *Invincible* and she knew every little thing that went on—every up and every down. She knew how ill Tiberius had been and that this illness was the reason for the long layover at Xylanthia. It had worried her, MacAlpin had to be on the bridge when the *Invincible* arrived in orbit around Tamora. Everything depended on it. She went back to her desk and tapped the computer screen, going back to her messages.

There was a coded one from the president of Tamora, asking how things were going, although they knew there were still two months before the *Invincible* was due to arrive. There was an undercurrent of distrust in the message, as though the Tamorans believed any issues were caused by the admiral. She quickly responded that Captain MacAlpin had been ill and ordered to rest. *He is well now, and on the way. They will be with you in less than two months.* She leaned back when she sent the message. Hopefully, the rest of the voyage would go according to plan. She was sure MacAlpin and his crew were unaware that there was a traitor in their midst—in fact, she knew they would be shocked. She tapped out a message; normally she would communicate orally as everyone did now, but for the fact that her voice would incriminate her. Her typed messages were sent with secure encryption, and there was nothing to show it even came from her office, let alone her own computer. Her instructions were clear and concise, mainly just to observe and report. She sent a similar message to her second spy, established in the hospital where Xander Galen still lay. She had been notified of his condition, and the way he had been kept under with drugs until Serenity ordered the doctors to stop treating him, and how the doctors had said they could not save him, only for him to revive once life-support was switched off, much to everyone's surprise. The spy had reported he was being treated with an experimental drug and, along with the medication he had been taking, was beginning to make progress. She read the last report and sighed. She hated Xander for being alive; the threat of the damage he could cause if he chose to open his mouth and tell the truth was great but she, although a cruel and unscrupulous woman, knew better than to have him killed at this point. It would cause too much of a stir now, as he had been so close to death and now seemed to be making great progress. She would have to find another way of silencing him; if he died in a suspicious way now, people would talk, and some might even begin to put two and two together. Many of them would remember the death of Xander's doctor, and that some believed it was no accident—that he had been murdered, perhaps for nothing more than being the friend and physician of a man she wanted dead. As she read, she wondered if Xander knew what had happened to Doctor Tierney, or if his death was being kept from him in order not to distress the sick man. He would be shocked and upset if he did know—would he be afraid, always wondering if he was next? He would realize how easy it had been for them to keep him sedated with the cocktail of drugs and medicines he had been given. She shook her head. No, he was not likely to know, or to understand fully yet. She should go and visit him in the hospital, she told herself. Act as if you are worried. She laughed slightly. *As if he would believe that.* He would remember she was the last one he saw. She knew he had been kept in a drug-induced coma and hidden away in a stasis chamber for close on two months. He had been hidden there, unbeknownst to many of the staff, who had only been aware that some 'experiment' was being made in the genetics laboratory. They were not aware an officer had been abducted and was being held in secret. There were many who would have been shocked if they did know—something like that could bring the facility into disrepute but there was a team she trusted, some of whom were as involved as she was in the events of the past. She would bide her time; it did not seem likely that Xander would be leaving the hospital in the near future; her informant had said he was still far from well, and that the experimental drug—the origin of which they did not know—was not making an obvious impact on his illness, despite it having been a contributing factor in cleaning up his blood from the drugs.

•

Xander turned his head on his pillow as footsteps approached the bed. He had been dozing; he slept a lot as his body worked hard to recover, and the medication he was on made him very sleepy too. He smiled sleepily as he saw it was Serenity. "You weren't here earlier," he said, as she kissed his forehead.

"I'm sorry, I thought you were asleep. Did you need me?"

He shook his head. "It's okay. The nurse helped me, I only wanted a drink. It's their job, not yours. Where did you go?" He knew it would not be to rest; she did not get tired. Serenity smiled softly and he laughed. "I love seeing you smile. I'm glad you enhanced your programming."

She sat down beside the bed and held the hand that did not have the cannula in the back of it. "I went to do something very special; something I never thought I would do. I went to try on wedding dresses."

Xander squeezed her hand. "Did you find one? What is it like?"

Serenity gently stroked the back of his hand. "I did, but I am not going to tell you what it is like; I want it to be a surprise. But it is the most beautiful dress I have ever seen, and I cannot wait for you to see me in it."

Xander sighed softly. "I wish I could get better quicker. I know," he added quickly. "I could have died. I should not be impatient." He felt her fingers stroking his hand. "I don't feel safe, Serenity. I know she will try to kill me. I am not strong enough to fight them."

Serenity turned and looked into his eyes. "You are worried? Has anything happened to make you think that? You must tell me."

"I want to go home. Please, take me home—she has spies here." Xander gripped her hand tighter.

"You feel like that because you woke up and found me gone. You are always woozy when you first wake."

"No, you know that doesn't worry me—Kehoe does. There is one nurse—I don't trust him. He watches me."

Serenity was worried now. "Xander, they need to watch you; that is how they can help you." But she knew he was not being paranoid because he was unwell. She too had her suspicions. "I will request the doctor dismisses that nurse." She stopped as the door slid open and the nurse they had been discussing came in and approached the bedside. He had a syringe with him as it was time for Xander's next dose of medicine. He slipped the needle into the cannula in the back of the patient's hand.

Xander tried to draw back, but his hand was strapped down so that he would not move and hurt himself because of the needles and wires attached to so many places on his arm.

Serenity reached over and stopped the nurse from pressing the plunger.

"What are you doing?" the nurse demanded. "You know he must have his medicine regularly."

"I want it tested—right here, so I can be certain nothing bad is being done."

The nurse looked her full in the eyes for a long moment and then withdrew the needle and held out the syringe. "You know how serious withholding his medication could be?"

"Yes, just as dangerous as if he was given the wrong medicine," Serenity responded. "Bring me a lab kit. I want it tested here, where I can see the results are not tampered with."

The nurse looked at her and then glanced at the man in the bed, sighed, and let her take the syringe. "You know how difficult it is for us to treat him when you constantly insist on a change of nursing staff, new doctors, and tests of medication."

"She is doing right," Xander said quietly. "Numerous attempts have been made on my life since I was brought into this hospital—attempts that should make you agree with her. One of the nursing staff is trying to kill me. Until they are discovered, this will continue."

The nurse met Xander's eyes almost without blinking. "I will fetch what she requires." He left, to return a few moments later with the testing kit and one of the doctors.

The doctor came to the bedside while the nurse helped Serenity to set up the testing. She laid her hand on Xander's forehead, checking for fever. "I am Doctor Jessup, I have been attending you while you were very sick, but you've not officially met me yet. You can call me Mona, everyone does." She smiled softly. "You are safe with me, Serenity has allowed no other doctor near you. So, I hear you have accused yet another member of staff of unethical behaviour." She looked at the monitors by the bed and then looked back at her patient. "However, on this occasion, there are higher levels of drugs in your system than you should have with your medication." She tapped the screen for a moment or two and then nodded. "Your medication has been administered along with a sedative—no doubt that is the reason you have been sleeping a lot." She took a small device from the pocket of her white coat. "You'll feel a small scratch." She lifted one of his fingers a little and touched it with the device. "It's just a drop of blood to test."

Xander nodded. There was something about this doctor—he trusted her. It was that nurse he did not trust. He looked at her badge. Dr Mona T. Jessup, it said. There was something familiar about her, but he did not know what it was. She said she had attended him, but he must have been too sick to know. He didn't recognize her.

The doctor took the device over to the bench where Serenity was working and began some testing of her own. She looked up after a moment and told the nurse he could leave, and asked Serenity to come to the bedside. She pulled up a chair up to the other side of the bed and sat down. "You were right, Serenity, it was another attempt on Admiral Galen's life," she began. "Along with every dose of your medication, a sedative was being administered. Eventually, you would not be able to wake up. I want to withdraw treatment temporarily so I can see the actual state of the disease and its progress. It will highlight if the medication you insisted on is actually making an impact. I have accessed Doctor Tierney's original notes and am aware of the studies he made on your condition, and how it was caused by the experimentation you went through during your captivity." She paused and looked at Serenity and then back at Xander. "This is what I would like to do, but I need your consent because you will suffer until treatment is reinstated."

Serenity reached for Xander's hand and squeezed it. She was worried because she had seen him when the pain was so bad that he could hardly breathe; the medication he had been on was the only relief he got. "It's your choice, Xander."

"You have Tierney's notes? You worked with him?" Xander asked.

"I did my training under him too. Doctor Tierney was my father; I qualified a few years after I married—that's why my name is different." She smiled. "I know you are afraid, but you have me for an ally. I will ensure your treatment is overseen and administered by myself and we will find the ones responsible. Withdrawing life support brought you out of a coma; perhaps withdrawing treatment will kick start your natural ability to fight the disease."

"Now I know why you seemed familiar—you have your father's features. Be careful—they killed him for refusing to end my life." Xander leaned back on the pillows and then nodded. "I can face it. Withdraw treatment until you are satisfied."

Mona Tierney Jessup smiled as she stood up. "He left behind a drug he was convinced could help you, I can honour his memory best by getting you well again." She glanced at Serenity's hand which rested on Xander's arm and noted the beautiful diamond ring she wore. "I'll get you on your feet again; let's see if we can have you dance at your wedding." She watched as Xander looked into the android's strange eyes and she smiled. He must have been through hell for him to give his heart to an artificial intelligence rather than a living woman. But she also saw the way Serenity held his hands and spent every moment of her time at his bedside. Who was she to say that a love like that could not be as fulfilling as if he was to marry a human? Perhaps he was luckier because she was not human—humans were not always so loyal and loving in their own relationships. She glanced at her own hand where her wedding ring had once been. That was one of the problems with a job like this; sacrifices were made—and not all of them good.

34

Security Breach

Tiberius MacAlpin frowned and tapped his computer screen. "Run security scan on my personal logs," he told the computer. "State number of times my log entries have been accessed and the date and time for each access." He waited as the computer worked and then was shocked as a long list appeared on the screen. He frowned again and spoke into the transmitter chip in his wrist. "Commander Ross, come to my quarters, please."

Ross appeared a few moments later. "You wanted to see me, sir?" He saw the captain was frowning and was concerned. "Is everything all right?"

Tiberius looked up. "You wouldn't access my private logs, would you?" He saw Ross' face. "I'm not accusing you. I just need to ask, before I go through everyone else."

Ross leaned on the desk. "No-one would and I most certainly would not."

"Look." Tiberius pointed at the screen. "All the dates and times match with periods where I was on duty."

Ross was frowning now. "Computer, were these logs accessed from Captain MacAlpin's terminal, or remotely?"

The computer responded in moments. "Access was made via the captain's terminal."

"What about security? Was there a breach?"

"There has been no security breach on Captain MacAlpin's personal logs. Security codes were all verified."

Tiberius looked at Ross and shook his head. "No-one knows my security codes! And only you have the emergency code."

"Was the first officer's emergency code used to access the logs?" Ross asked, turning back to the computer.

"Affirmative. The logs were accessed by Commander Ross on all occasions."

Their eyes met and Tiberius stood up, and at that moment he completely lost his temper, raising his hand and striking Ross across the face. "You lied to me! Never *ever* lie to me! You told me you had not done this. I have thought for some time that there was a spy on board—I did not expect it to be you. Go to your quarters and remain there until I decide what to do."

Ross was reeling from the slap across his face. "*Captain!*" In the shock he could not find the words to remonstrate—not even to defend himself against a gross misjudgement. He knew he had done nothing wrong.

"Get out! Do you want me to call security and have them escort you to the brig? That is where the spy belongs—I am trying to leave you your dignity while I get to the bottom of this. You are my right hand, why would you do this?!" Tiberius looked hurt and angry—too angry to let Ross speak. "Leave! *Now!*"

Ross turned away and left, Tiberius following him out. He went into his quarters, next door to the captain's, and stood facing the door until it slid shut. He heard the sound of the security lock being set and knew that he was basically under arrest. He sank down on the edge of his bed and rested his face in his hands. He understood his commanding officer's anger, but it rankled to be locked in his quarters when he had done nothing wrong. His face smarted from the slap—he had expected that least of all.

Tiberius turned away from Ross' cabin door—his heart heavy. Ross had assured him that he had not been the one who accessed the logs, but the computer said he had—using the emergency code that only the first officer had. He felt bad for striking him, he had not lost his temper like that before. Could Ross possibly be spying for Kehoe? He could not believe it—he did not want to believe it; but for security and his own peace of mind, he had to restrict Ross' movement. He was painfully aware that this would mean, if Ross *was* innocent, the spy was still free to carry on their espionage. All this time—with everything they had been through including Ross' own traumatic injuries could he, despite all that, betray his commanding officer and crew? He gave a shudder and felt as though his blood was running cold. Was this how it had happened thirty years ago? Had something Xander had done been the catalyst? He shook his head. He had to stop thinking like that. He called Commander Jackson Rae, his chief of security and ordered a guard posted on Ross' door; and then had the chief go over the security breach with him.

Every breach carried the first officer's emergency clearance, and Tiberius' heart sank even further. Rae saw his face. "Ross couldn't have done it, sir. He's loyal to you. I believe, but it will take some hard work to prove it, that Commander Ross' security codes were hacked and that there is another at work." He spoke quietly for a few minutes, giving a couple of options to the captain.

Tiberius nodded. "Good idea. If they think I believe Ross to be the spy, it might make them bold."

•

Ross sat on the edge of his bed, wondering what was going to happen now. He knew he had done nothing wrong. He looked up hopefully as the door opened, expecting to see Tiberius. His face fell a moment later when two security officers entered.

"Please, come with us, sir." As Ross stood up, they cuffed his wrists which was standard procedure to prevent security being attacked.

Ross knew, for some reason, that he was being transferred to the ship's brig and he was worried and confused. "What is happening?" he asked as the cuffs locked over his wrists, holding his arms awkwardly behind his back.

"Sorry, sir. Captain's orders."

He was marched down to the brig and was ushered into one of the cells. The handcuffs were removed, and the guards retreated, turning on the energy field to keep the prisoner from approaching the door, which was locked behind them.

Ross stood for a few moments, looking at the locked door as though he could not believe it, before going and sitting on the edge of the narrow bed. After a while, he lay back on the mattress and tried to work out what was going on. Tiberius must really believe it—he must have found something to make him really think he had done it; there was no other reason he would have his first officer locked up. He would normally rely on him in an investigation.

In the brig, the ship-wide intercom was not audible, in order that a prisoner would not know what was going on, so Ross did not hear the captain's announcement to the crew. The crew all stopped what they were doing and listened as the captain's voice came through to them. "There has been a security breach—we

251

have had a spy on board. Commander Ross has been arrested and is in the brig. I am satisfied the spy has been caught."

Tiberius switched off and leaned back. "Forgive me," he whispered, looking at the empty seat beside him. "I have used you as a decoy. I am sorry. But I need to catch them—I will make it up to you."

•

Three days passed and Ross was panicking a little. He had not seen Tiberius and had no contact with any of the crew except for the guard who brought him meals. He tried to find out what was going on, but it was obvious the guard was under orders not to tell him anything. He felt isolated and began to even doubt the truth. What if he had done it? What if something weird was going on and he had been made to do it by forces of which he was unaware? He took the plate and mug of coffee from the guard. "I want to see Captain MacAlpin," he demanded, as he asked every day.

"I am sorry, the captain has said he won't see you." The same response every day.

Ross snapped this time and flung his plate of food onto the floor and kicked the tray, almost hitting the guard with it. "I will go on hunger strike until he does see me," he almost yelled. "Tell him that not another morsel of food or drink will pass my lips until he sees me." He took a pace forward and the guard quickly reactivated the energy field. It was invisible to the naked eye and Ross stepped into it and was flung almost right across the cell by its power. He picked himself painfully up off the floor. "I have to see the captain! Fetch him for me now!" He leaned on the wall, feeling giddy. The energy field was more powerful than he had thought it would be.

The guard left the cell and locked the door. He went to his station and spoke into his wrist transmitter. The cell was sound-proofed, and Ross could not hear what was said.

A few hours later, Ross was lying on the bed, still shaken from the force of the energy field which had been strong enough to throw him right across the cell. He glanced up when he saw a shadow pass by. The glass was obscured so that anyone outside could see in, but the prisoner's view was restricted. He watched the shadow outside the cell and then rolled onto his side so he couldn't see it—he could not make out who it was or hear anything that was said, and it only frustrated him trying. He did not even move when the door slid open, and the energy field crackled as it was turned off. Footsteps approached and then stopped.

"Ross, look at me." It was Tiberius.

Ross sat up slowly and looked at his commanding officer. "Why?! I told you..."

Tiberius interrupted him. "Don't say anything. Let me explain."

"What is there to explain?! You had me arrested and locked up here—with no contact for three days. What do you expect me to think?!" Ross tried not to raise his voice, knowing he should let the captain explain.

Tiberius put his hand on his shoulder. "I am sorry. I had to do it—every log, official and personal, has been compromised. Every log carries your emergency code. To the computer, it seems as though you have done it. I do not want to think that you did it—I trust you. I am so sorry, Kirbie—I needed a lure; I needed a way to make the spy strike again. If it was you, and your access to the computer was restricted, then it would not occur again—if it was someone else, then they were free to carry on and we would see the proof. I needed it to look as though I believed I had caught the spy, and that I would have stopped looking. You had to be unaware of what was going on—I needed it to look real, which is why I had you arrested." He paused. "When the guard came and told me you were refusing to eat because I would not come and see you." He paused again and looked down. "I had to come and speak to you then. I did not think you would take it so badly."

There was silence for a while and then Ross pulled away from the hand that rested on his shoulder. He swung his legs over the edge of the bed and stood up. "I was upset that you seemed to have no trust in me when I have shown you over the years how much loyalty I have for you and this ship and crew. I told you that I had not touched the logs and you slapped me, and you had me marched to the brig in handcuffs—it hurt that you thought I would lie to you. But I understand, and I trust you still. Now you have explained to me what is going on, I can forgive you. I will accept what is going on and cease to make a fuss about my imprisonment. I can endure the solitude as long as I know that the spy will be caught."

"I was wrong to treat you like that, but I must confess that I was scared—I suddenly felt like everything was going wrong, that it must be how everything began thirty years ago—that

Xander must have done something. He won't tell me what happened, and I just couldn't deal with it. I'm so sorry that I hit you. I should not have lost my cool like that."

Tiberius broke off and Ross shook his head. "I don't believe Xander did anything wrong," he said. "But he does know what happened, I am convinced of that. And, one day, he will tell you." He sat back down on the edge of the bed and looked up at the captain. "I understand how you feel, but you must try not to let the past rule you. I have said it before, and I will say it again. You cannot afford to let not knowing to get in the way of what is ahead of you. It could mean the difference between success and failure."

Tiberius smiled slightly and then nodded. "I know, and I do try. You have helped with that. I wish this spy nonsense had not happened. I don't even know how long a spy has been on board, perhaps since we left home. Everything we have done, all my logs—does this mean that someone knows everything?" He sighed. "I really need you on the bridge."

"But you need to catch the spy," Ross replied quietly. He lay back on the narrow bed. "I am prepared to be sacrificed—my apparent guilt will be necessary, as you said. Does anyone else know that you know I am innocent?"

"Only Rae; he went over the logs with me. He suggested this plan of action. I value his advice—he is security chief, and it is a serious breach."

Ross shook his head. "You do not need to justify yourself any more. You should go back to the bridge." He watched as Tiberius left and he heard the energy field crackle back into life and the door was locked. He had said he did not mind being a sacrifice in order to catch the real spy but, if he had known how long it would be, perhaps he would have minded. The days seemed to drag by, and he began to lose track of time as he was unable to see out of the cell. Even just seeing a change of guard would have given him some idea of time. Meals arriving were the only real sense he got of time passing and he counted them to work out the days. Another five days had passed, and he was trying hard not to get anxious. He had not seen the captain again in that time and he began to fret about not knowing what was happening.

Tiberius was getting a bit anxious too. So far, since having Ross confined to the brig, there had been no activity on the logs and the fear was niggling that it was the first officer all the time. He looked at the empty seat beside him and sighed. Had he been

254

wrong to trust him—had Ross still been lying? He had not looked as though he was when he had spoken to him in the brig; but was he just a good actor? Could he possibly be hiding something behind the assurances of loyalty? Or was he telling the truth? "Why are you even questioning his loyalty?" he asked himself. "If you always question him, how can you ever trust him when he sits there beside you? His role is to give you advice; to help and guide you—you have to believe him." He ran his hand through his hair and sighed. "What can I do? Ross is right—I must get rid of the insecurity." He reached for the screen on the arm of his chair and tapped it. "Run a security scan on my official and private logs."

He leaned back and waited for the scan to be completed. The screen flickered and he looked down at the screen. "Access being made to your private logs at this moment," the computer told him.

"Where?"

"Access is being made via the computer terminal in your quarters, captain."

Tiberius looked over to the security station where Commander Rae was busy going over some reports. "Rae, secure the door to my quarters and meet me there—we've got our spy."

Rae rapped out a command to the computer and then spoke quickly into his wrist transmitter. "Door secured, sir, and two of the duty security detachment are on their way there." He stood up and came over to the captain. "Do you have any idea who it is?"

Tiberius shook his head. "I was hoping you might have. You have gone over the crew roster?"

The security chief nodded. "Everyone checks out, sir. Unless someone had something to hide during selection, and they have all been on board since we left—bar two that we picked up when we laid over six months ago. I have requested full access to their records."

Tiberius nodded. "It must be one of them."

"Perhaps, but I would not recommend speculations, captain. You know, of course, that Admiral Kehoe was fully involved in the crew assignments—it could be anyone. Well, other than those on the bridge right now, and Ross as he is in the brig." Rae smiled. "You worry so much, captain—we can easily put an end to this by going down to your quarters and catching them in the act. They will be unaware they are a prisoner in your quarters until we unfasten the door, and they also believe themselves to be safe. They know you believe Ross to be the spy, and they will not think that you will have continued with your investigations. There would be no need with Ross imprisoned."

Tiberius stood up. "Let's go." He was worried; it hurt knowing that one of his crew was a spy. Someone who had been passing information back to the admiral he supposed, and this was disconcerting in the least. He knew that somehow, in the very middle of all this, sat Admiral Kehoe. She was, without a doubt, the key to what happened to his father and the *Wryneck* all those years ago, she was the reason Xander lay in hospital terminally ill; and the reason behind Ross' traumatic injuries and his own brush with death due to the dangerous turn the dreams had taken. He knew that she was behind it all, but she was safe because it could not be proven—at least not yet. He turned to where Dinesh Patel sat at the helm. "You're in charge until I get back."

"Yes, sir." Patel immediately called for a replacement on the helm and took the captain's chair as Tiberius left the bridge with his security chief.

Tiberius and Rae headed down to the deck where the officers' quarters were and saw the security detail outside the captain's cabin. Rae told them to close in and block the exit once he and the captain had entered, in order to prevent anyone inside from leaving. He glanced at the captain who gave a nod, and then entered his security code on the keypad, removing the lock. The door slid open, allowing the officers to enter quickly, the door closing behind them.

A figure in uniform was sitting at the captain's desk, their back to the door of the room. They were so engrossed in their task that they did not hear the door open or footsteps crossing the floor. By the time they realized there was someone behind them, it was too late. They gasped as a hand fell on their should and looked round in shock.

Tiberius gasped too. "*You? Why*?!" He had expected it to be one of the two who had joined the ship later and was shocked to discover that it was not. It was one of the crew who had transferred from the *Victorious*.

Athina Neller had been Xander's personal assistant when they served on the *Victorious* and had continued to fill that role for Tiberius. As the captain's personal assistant, she had access to his logs, although not his private log, and there was no reason for her to be accessing these logs with the first officer's emergency codes—unless there was a reason for covering her tracks.

"Why?" Tiberius demanded again. "You have been in a position of trust—you have been my personal assistant all this time—you have had access to my logs. And yet, all this time, you have been spying—you have done my admin; you did the same for Admiral Galen on the *Victorious,* and all the time you have been sending information back to Admiral Kehoe." She began to speak but Tiberius shook his head. "No, save it for the courtroom." He paused and then added, "Tell me one thing— how long has this been going on? Since we left?"

She shook her head. "Oh no, a lot longer than that. I carried out the same role on the *Victorious.* Don't look at me like that, Captain MacAlpin, we all have our orders."

Tiberius looked disgusted. "Don't speak to me of orders and obedience. How can you obey an order to betray your commanding officer, your ship, and your crew? You put everyone in danger when you undertake a role as a spy—you have seen everything that happened. You saw Ross when we brought him back on board after he was attacked and injured—you saw me in the infirmary when the dreams went bad and you even saw how ill Admiral Galen became."

"You do not understand, do you? I do not care. My loyalty lies with Admiral Kehoe. It always has done."

Tiberius nodded to Commander Rae and the security chief stepped forward and pulled her up from the chair. "You are under arrest." Handcuffs snapped shut on her wrists.

She did not resist, knowing that she had no choice now. She had succeeded for many years and had always known that one day, she might be caught.

Rae led her to the door and handed her over to the security guards. "Take her to the brig."

Neller turned her head to look at Tiberius. "It is at least another four years before we are due to return to Earth. You will have me confined all that time? I have rights."

"Don't try and appeal to me. You knew the risks and consequences of your actions. You have no right to even ask me for clemency," Tiberius replied. "I have had the first officer confined for too long because of you—you made my trust in him waver because you used his access. You have done enough damage and I will not permit any more. You deserve much more than being locked up, but I have no authority to make that decision. There is only one thing you are entitled to, and that is a fair trial, and you will get that within the next few days." He turned his back. "Take her away—I don't want to see her any more. I'll follow in a bit and release Ross myself." He stood in the door of his quarters and waited until he heard the footsteps reach the end of the corridor and then headed towards the brig. He spoke quickly to the duty guard and the door to Ross' cell was unlocked and the energy field was turned off. Tiberius stood in the doorway and looked at Ross who was sitting on the edge of the bed. "You're free—we got the spy. It worked. I am sorry."

Ross stood up and shook his head. "You don't need to apologize again." He smiled and saluted. "Permission to return to the bridge, Captain?"

Tiberius returned the smile. "Permission granted." He let Ross walk past him out of the cell and then fell into step beside him.

"Who was it?" Ross asked.

"Neller."

Ross stared at him. He had not expected that. "Your PA? No, she was Xander's assistant too—she has a long service record." He was shocked.

Tiberius nodded. "I can't believe it either. I cannot understand anyone throwing away a career like that. She would be eligible for a long service award soon—in fact, I was in the process of drafting a nomination. That is out of the question now. She will be lucky if she escapes a prison sentence—which I hope she does not. She told me her loyalty lies with Kehoe. I am going to have Rae make some deeper enquiries into her background etc. There has to be a reason why she would risk everything to play spy."

As the bridge doors slid open, Tiberius stepped aside slightly. "You go ahead of me," he said, breaking protocol where the captain would always be at least a pace in front.

Ross stepped onto the bridge and there was a cheer from the officers as they looked up from their various stations. He was well-liked and everyone had been shocked to hear that he was confined to the brig, seemingly suspected of espionage. Ross smiled as he took his seat, Tiberius taking his place a moment later.

The captain looked across and grinned. "Welcome back—I did miss your presence on the bridge. It always feels wrong when you're not there."

Ross smiled. "I missed it too, it's not nice to be locked up like that. I hope you never have to experience that, especially the not knowing why. It made me think about Xander."

Tiberius looked up quickly. "Please don't make me feel any worse about it. I was thinking of him too, but I knew I had to do this—you know that. Don't make me feel more guilty."

Ross saw the cloud in Tiberius' eyes, and he smiled again. "It's okay. Now, pass over some of your reports to me; let me get back to helping you."

"Glad to," Tiberius replied, laughing. "You know how I feel about reports!" The captain hated admin. "I'm going to be stuck with a lot of it now that Neller is in the brig."

"I'll sort it out for you," Ross responded. "Staffing issues come under my remit. Don't worry—I know you're too busy to have time for the non-essential workload." He tapped the screen on the arm of his chair and saw that Tiberius had transferred a long list. He glanced up. "I said some!"

"Believe me, that is just some. You should see the rest." Tiberius chuckled. "I've been worried the last few days and didn't keep up." He watched Ross settle down to some work and knew his first officer was glad to have something to do. He turned his attention to some reports of his own. They were not that far away from their destination now. Only about a month and he turned his attention again to the orders they had received four years ago.

•

The next couple of days were taken up with the hearing convened in order to pass judgement on Neller for her spying role—on her own admission, it had been going on for a long time, for years, and she had been a direct report to Admiral Kehoe. On questioning, she admitted under oath that Kehoe had been maintaining surveillance on Xander Galen, and now on Tiberius himself, and that every detail, however mundane, was passed back to the admiral.

Tiberius looked at her, his hands resting on the table. "Why? What did you gain from breaking the trust of your commanding officers?"

Neller said nothing.

Ross leaned across to Tiberius, pushing a tablet over. "Read this section."

Tiberius looked at the screen and scrolled in silence for a few moments and then looked up slowly. "Commander Ross requested your service record—it seems this is not the first incident leaving you with a criminal record. You received a short sentence at that time but were released early and there have been significant sums of money transferred to an encrypted account. "Blood money, Midshipman?"

Neller pursed her lips and declined to answer any further questioned, speaking only to state "no comment."

Tiberius was supported by the first officer, and Kiana Yoshizaki, the second officer, and a representative from the Judge Advocate General's office—all ships in the fleet carried one in their crew compliment—going so far into space they did not have the luxury of waiting until they reached home so a representative was assigned to each ship. Any hearing or court martial could be held as soon as the occasion arose and in accordance with regulations.

The JAG officer, Commander Nicola Villegas, was accompanied by her assistant, Chief Petty Officer Zara Fenton, who would fulfil the role of court recorder. After another round of questioning that proved futile, Villegas stood up and the officers left with her to discuss and make some decisions. She looked around at the captain, Ross and Yoshizaki. "I know what my recommendation will be, Captain. A four-year sentence of confinement to the brig, and a full court martial on our return.

Tiberius nodded. "And the outcome of a court martial?"

"She has a previous conviction which carried a short prison sentence and a reduction in rank from Lieutenant to Midshipman. It will be prison again and dishonourable discharge; no pension."

Tiberius nodded again. "That sounds acceptable. She has put lives at risk for too long, who knows what her next move would have been." He stood up. "Thank you, Commander. Let's get this over with." He led them back in and sat back at the centre of the table with Villegas at his right hand. He leaned forward and rang the old ship's bell which sat in front of them. Another old naval tradition that was still adhered to.

Commander Villegas took a deep breath. "Midshipman Athina Neller, please stand to receive your sentence." A moment's pause as Neller obeyed and then she continued. Her voice was serious as she pronounced sentence and explained what the final outcome would be.

Tiberius nodded to the security detail waiting behind Neller and they took her out, taking her straight to the brig where she would be held until their return to Earth. All that remained was for the captain to sign the paperwork that would be submitted to HQ. He could not help wondering how that news would go down with Admiral Kehoe.

35

Arriving at Tamora

Tiberius stood at the window on the observation deck, looking out at the stars as they passed. He often came here, finding a sense of peace as the inner tension mounted as, with every passing moment, they drew closer to Tamora. They were just days away now and he was trying not to get stressed over the unknown. It felt more than a little strange to be here and wondered if, thirty years ago, his father had stood here, in this same position, watching space pass by, wondering too what lay before them.

There was stress for another reason too. He had called the hospital and had been told of the changes in Xander's condition and that another attempt had been made on his life, and that all treatment had been withdrawn in an attempt to finally purge his bloodstream of drugs so that his normal medication would begin to work again. That upset Tiberius more than he let on. Xander was terminally ill, he had finally accepted that. This new medication was a glimmer of hope for him, or at least a pain release, allowing him to come peacefully to his death. To have that medication withdrawn, forcing the sick man to go through chronic withdrawal and pain as the disease gripped him—well, he hardly dared to think about it. Xander did not deserve to suffer, not after everything he had been through. But he knew Xander had given his permission to try anything possible. He sighed. Soon he would have no time to think about him. He had hoped to speak to Xander himself but had been told it was out of the question. He had left a message with the doctor to be passed on and that had to satisfy him.

He heard a footfall behind him, and he turned slightly. "I want to be alone."

"I know—I'll leave if you want me to," came a soft voice. It was Laura Harsant, his new aide.

He turned and smiled. "I really would prefer to be alone." He sighed a moment later when he felt her hand slip into his. "You know this isn't meant to happen?"

"It rarely ever is meant to, but it just happens," she replied. "But you do not want to be alone, it is one of the things you fear the most. Just as you now fear a relationship, because of what happened with your fiancée."

Tiberius sighed again. "I should stop thinking that everyone wants to hurt me. Is there anything I can do to prove that I don't think you will?"

"You already did—you told me about Lashinda." She squeezed his hand. "It is hard being a ship's captain. You always have to present a particular appearance, and your personal life is always the first to suffer. Now you can tell me to go away," she added.

Tiberius responded by bending and kissing her, cupping her face in his hand. She rested his hands on his chest and smiled, as he ran the other hand through her long red hair. "I should not distract you from the mission."

"I need a distraction," Tiberius replied, and she felt his breath on her face. "I have read the orders until I can recite it word for word. We'll be there tomorrow. Ross is on duty this evening. Will you have dinner with me?"

Her hazel eyes lit up and her freckled nose wrinkled as she smiled. "Only if you have some of the old wine you enjoy."

Tiberius smiled again, feeling his heart lighten as he did. "Of course, no meal is complete without it."

She looked up again and smiled. "It is not forbidden for the captain to fall in love you know."

"Am I in love?" There was a lightness to his voice that showed he was teasing. He touched her cheek. "I believe I am." He reached for her hand and they left the room together. Later that afternoon, Tiberius was lying on his bed for a nap before his shift began. He stirred as something disturbed him. He opened his eyes and listened. As the sound did not come again, he rolled over and closed his eyes. He had just closed them when the sound came again, and he realized it was his call sign in his ear receiver implant. He tapped his wrist to activate the transmitter. "Hmmm?" he murmured, still half asleep.

It was Ross. "Captain, there is a message coming in from Tamora."

He sat up quickly, rubbing the sleep from his eyes. "I'm on my way—hold them as long as you can, I have to dress." He was already clambering out of bed as he spoke and grabbing his uniform from the back of the chair where he had hung it before collapsing into bed earlier. He hurried to the bridge as fast as he could and took his seat. "Okay, put it through." He tapped the arm of the chair. "This is Captain Tiberius MacAlpin. Greetings."

There was a pause and then they heard a Tamoran for the first time. "Captain MacAlpin, we bear greetings from the planet's council." The screen flickered and the bridge crew were face to face with a representative of the people of Tamora.

Tiberius took a deep breath. He had been dreading this moment, all kinds of ideas running through his mind, including the thought that this could be the one who had ordered the torture of Xander—the one responsible for the destruction of the *Wryneck*. He was convinced now that his father's death was caused by the planet's people rather than something his father had done. He knew he had to swallow the anger and hatred he felt. They had come in peace—he was the leader; he had to represent that peace. They were there under orders, partly to find what had happened all those years ago; and Tiberius was determined to find out.

The figure on the screen looked similar to a human, in form and appearance. He was obviously a person of importance by his bearing, and his English was good, speaking with little trace of an accent. A diplomat, perhaps. Tiberius met the Tamoran's eyes, and the alien bowed his head. "Please do us the honour of dining with the council this evening." His voice even but raspy.

Tiberius glanced swiftly at his first officer who flashed him a quick look. He turned back to the screen. "We would be honoured but allow me to extend the invitation to you and the council to dine on board the *Invincible*." He knew a refusal would mean something was up. They had come in peace, the ship was safe territory. If he left the ship to go down to the unknown planet, he would be putting himself at risk; a risk his officers would not allow him to take.

"That is agreeable," the Tamoran replied. "We dined aboard your father's ship on the night the *Wryneck* arrived at our planet."

He was watching Tiberius closely, Ross thought; almost as though he was trying to get a reaction from him. Perhaps he was mistaken. He hoped so.

Tiberius nibbled his bottom lip slightly. Any mention of his father and the *Wryneck* was still pretty raw. But he had to let go. Could he let go of the anger and pain? He had to—Ross was right, he used the feelings of hurt and anger to fuel his desire for revenge and his search for the truth, to the extent where he took risks and had put his ship and crew in danger a couple of times. He took a deep breath and looked up, glancing at his first officer.

Ross' finger hovered over the touchpad on the arm of his chair. "You can't keep him waiting for an answer to that. What you will say next will have a big impact on the future of…"

"The mission," Tiberius interrupted. "I know. You don't need to tell me." He nodded. "Okay, I'm ready." He stood up and faced the screen as the image of the Tamoran reappeared. "I apologize for keeping you waiting. It will be as great an honour for us to host the Tamoran council as it was for my father and his crew. I look forward to meeting you in person."

"Likewise." The Tamoran bowed and the image vanished.

Ross cut the connection. "Well done. That was hard for you, I know."

Tiberius nodded. "It's okay—it was not too bad once I began."

•

As the connection shut down, the Tamoran president turned to the rest of the chamber who had not been visible on the screen as they were positioned in front of him.

A bright blue light shimmered around him, like the light of static electricity on a ship's mast—St. Elmo's fire, as it was known, supposedly a sign to sailors during an electrical storm that their patron saint was there to protect them. The light framed the tall, lean figure and as he nodded to his colleagues. "The stage, once again, ladies and gentlemen, is set." He laughed. "They have no idea."

A female Tamoran turned to him. "Do not underestimate the captain, Dayelh. He did not sound entirely convinced—there was something in his voice. And he cut the call for a long time. I think he knows, or is suspicious, that there is something going on. If he is as intelligent as we think him to be, as intelligent as we knew his father to be, then it will not be easy. I sensed it—his distrust of you, his distrust of his orders. He is not happy with the orders he has been given. We know that a lot has happened during their voyage, he has suffered. He is a strong man. He will not allow setbacks and pain to interfere—he has come here for one thing, and not what he has been sent here for. He has come to find the truth, and he will not give up until he finds it." She stood up and her folded wings extended. They were beautiful wings, with a span of four meters. The layers of feathers went from deep violet to a soft pink-lilac which contrasted with her dark muscular body.

The Tamorans were shapeshifters and could appear in full human form. They were humanoid, but in their winged form they were closer to eight-foot taller than the average human; they had more upper body muscles, but their lower body was slender and trim. Long, sturdy legs ended in eagle-like talons which were a glossy black, as was the rest of their feathered body. Their faces were almost human in appearance but had the sharp, watchful eyes of a bird of prey. Tiberius and his crew would not see them in this form. In the presence of their visitors, the Tamorans would take human form, and not allow them to know they could change. They also had the ability to become invisible when necessary and this was one of their most-used abilities as this was how they had been able to appear and disappear so suddenly during their abduction raids on other planets in the system, such as the planet Tycho where Ross had been left so horribly injured.

The president turned towards her, fully reverted to his usual form. He inclined his head. "You are wise and quite correct. His eyes showed just how much distrust he carries within. He must not be allowed to discover what he has come for. He believes he has come for one thing; we know otherwise." The chamber echoed with laughter as they all thought of the innocence of the *Invincible*'s captain, believing him still unaware they had been sold out by a woman afraid of the consequences of her actions ever being laid at her door.

•

Admiral Kehoe had the blood of hundreds on her hands, and the last thing she wanted was for anyone to discover that she alone had orchestrated the events which had lead up to the destruction of the *Wryneck* and the death of her captain and crew. No-one must know that she had been asked which crew member she would offer to the aliens for their experiments, or how much she had accepted to betray them like this. She had chosen Xander Galen, choosing to save him from death aboard the *Wryneck*, but condemning him instead to ten years of fear, torture and terrible, painful experiments and humiliation. Even her one-time relationship with him had not stayed her hand in condemning him to his suffering. She had lived in fear every year since Xander's release, afraid he would say something that would cast suspicion in her direction. She wondered if he had no idea it had been her doing or was he keeping silent to protect her, not wanting her to suffer the consequences of her actions? She would lose her rank and position and almost certainly go to prison for the rest of her life. Perhaps he was so much better than her, that his own pain and suffering were enough, and he did not want to lay blame on a superior officer; a woman he had once dated. If that were so, he was much better to her than he should be. She deserved to be in prison for what she had done, if not worse. She had to hope he meant never to tell—she did not know that he had already voiced his suspicions, even naming her as the visitor to his apartment. The last thing Xander remembered about that day was the admiral offering to get his medication and bringing him a drink. It had not been hard for him to understand that she was the one who had drugged him.

Xander lay in his hospital bed now, thinking about Kehoe—knowing he should tell the authorities what part she had played. But he felt too sick—all medication had been withdrawn after he had given his permission and it had not been too bad at first. He had just felt sleepy and had been in some pain. But, with every day that passed, the pain got worse and he began to go into withdrawal. He closed his eyes, as though it would shut out the pain as he began to sweat. His body, reliant for so long on his medicine, began to tremble and shake and he went from hot to cold. He clenched his fists as he felt his palms getting clammy. A cool hand slipped into his and held it tightly, stroking the back of it as he tossed and turned fitfully as the disease which had been ravishing him began to take over his body again as it was racked with the withdrawal from the drugs which had riddled his system. He heard voices from far away and could feel hands on him from time to time, helping him sip water and taking his pulse or laying cold cloths over his burning forehead. He dozed off, only to wake a short while later, feeling straps being tightened on his limbs and across his body. He knew somewhere in the back of his mind that they were to stop him from hurting himself as the fits grew worse. But his muddled mind freaked out, remembering being restrained by the aliens as they experimented on him. He began to fight and didn't realize that he was screaming.

Veritas: The Captain's Redemption

He was naked, his arms gripped by strong hands, being dragged towards a table. His legs were dragging as fear took over and he could not walk. His eyes were covered, adding to the terror. When able to look danger or something that is feared in the face, the terror is somewhat diminished. But, unable to see, he heard himself whimpering. At first, he had been strong. It had taken months to break him. The table was cold under his bare back and he fought to throw off the restraining hands. Shackles were fastened around his wrists and ankles and he was jerked into a star-like position and rendered helpless. Hands touching all over, probing—he felt them around his private area and was unable to stop them. He yelled at them, his body desperately trying to fight its bonds. He yelled and cursed at them until they gagged him, laughing as his shouts died away to muffled sounds. He went through this every day—the probing, the touching and the psychological torture of his senses being stopped from functioning. The needles again and his senses swam.

He was back in his cell, chained up. Sometimes he was allowed his freedom. Freedom?! That just meant he was not bound, and able to lie down and sleep. Mostly he was chained to the wall and kneeling awkwardly, his arms locked above his head. Always naked, he had forgotten what clothes felt like. It was always dark—his eyes covered constantly. He never heard his captors coming. A soft sound and then their hands on him. He heard screams again from somewhere close by. Another captive being tortured. It was not just torture, it was the experiments. The probing and needles going places they should not. The experiments did not stop, even when he got sick. They carried on, but he was not always taken from his cell now, he was kept chained up in the tiny dark room. He passed out again, his body hanging by the wrists. But he was not allowed the release of unconsciousness. An injection brought him around and he was woken up every time he fainted from the pain, and the illness. He was sick and was kicked in the stomach. He vomited again and was slapped across the face. Tears rolled down his dirty face and he wished he could just die.

Serenity reached out and stroked his cheek as he cried. She was upset to hear him screaming and knew he must be having flashbacks. He screamed the name Stephen a few times, almost desperately. She guessed he must have called out to his friend, perhaps begging him for help; perhaps hoping to just hear his voice—maybe hoping he would not. If he did not reply it could mean he was safe. She held his hand and stroked it gently, wishing she could remove the restraints but knew he was going to get worse before he began to get better.

He fell silent after a time and opened his eyes and saw Serenity at his side. "I'm so tired."

She smiled and stroked his cheek again. "Try and get some sleep before the pain gets bad again."

Xander's eyes closed obediently. He was not a young man, and this was exhausting. Serenity's hands were gentle as she sorted out the pillow, turning it to find a cool spot, pulling the sheets straight and tucking him in, smoothing the sheets with a caress like a mother tucking in a child. He was asleep, his breathing soft and gentle. She sat down beside the bed and sat, her hand resting on his chest, over his heart. It was beating rhythmically under her hand. It was not just her love for him that made her do this. The doctor had informed them both of the risks as Xander was an older man—the strain could be too much for him. She knew he was not strong—the drugs had taken their toll and she worried. Feeling his heart beating was a comfort to her.

He stirred fitfully after a while. His dreams, or memories, troubling him. It was the day he was arrested. Stephen was walking away from him, leaving him behind. His wrists were being locked behind his back. He was shouting for his friend, his commanding officer, to help him as his captors were dragging him away. Stephen turned when he shouted. *I can't help*, he had replied.

Xander woke with a cry. Serenity's hand went immediately to his cheek. "What's wrong? You were shouting for help."

"Stephen didn't abandon me—he was arrested too. They told me he left me. I saw it this time—his arms were chained like mine. He was walking away from me, but he was a prisoner too. He said he couldn't help me—it was true because he was unable to." Xander broke down. "All these years, they made me believe he betrayed me. I should have known better—I should have known him better."

Serenity wiped his face with a tissue. "Did you ever truly believe he betrayed you?" she asked. "I don't think you did. You were confused and worried about it all, but you *did* know him better. You were never truly angry with him."

Xander shook his head. "No, I was angry that I wasn't dead too." He sniffed and let her wipe his cheeks again. "I was angry I was the only one left and that I had been kept alive all that time when I wanted to die. Serenity, I will never tell you what they did to me. I cannot bear to even remember it, but it keeps coming back—I can't shut it out." He paused and then turned his head to look right into her eyes. "Does it change how you feel?"

She shook her head. "Nothing can change the way I feel about you. I know you went through things you do not ever want to talk about. Do not hate yourself—it is not your fault. I know you feel bad that they all died except for you, but you did nothing wrong. You did not hide from the ship and lived because of cowardice—you would have died with them willingly, I know that. But it was not to be that way. For some reason, you had to suffer, but you are alive." Serenity smiled. "When you feel better, you can let all that guilt and pain go."

Xander nodded, leaning back on the pillow. "Did Stephen die in prison? I wish I knew—I wish I knew if he went through the same as I did." He sighed. "Can I have a drink? I feel sick."

Serenity reached for the glass of water and slid her arm under his head and helped him to drink. "You will feel sick until the drugs completely work out of your system."

Xander closed his eyes and managed to doze off. That night was the worst he had been through since this treatment had begun and Doctor Jessup was called to his bedside during the small hours and he was closely monitored.

Serenity paced up and down as the doctor and her team worked at the bedside. She looked around the room and noticed as if for the first time, how white everything was. The walls, the bed and its linen, the doctor's coat, Xander's face against the pillow—all white like milk. She could hear the medical team talking from time to time but did not hear the words. All she could hear was him moaning and crying and it hurt. This must be the pain her sister android had referred to when she said she had chosen to feel what humans feel. Yes, she had chosen this. She loved Xander just as truly as any human woman would— she had chosen that when she elected to have her programming advanced. She looked towards the bed and saw his tormented body writhing in the restraints as he screamed and sobbed. She closed her eyes for a moment and wished she could cry. He needed someone to cry for him. She clenched her fists tightly and knew that she would not change this—this pain, and the love she felt for the sick man, she would not change it for anything. Without this, she was just a robot. With this pain, she was what she wanted to be—a woman.

36

White Fish, Trifle, and No Alcohol

Tiberius glanced at Ross as they sat on the bridge. He was still thinking over the conversation with the Tamorans. "Was I wise to invite them?" he asked.

Ross looked up and nodded. "Wiser than accepting their offer to go down to the planet. Here, they come on our terms. It is not neutral ground, but we are in control here. I will not allow you to go down to the planet. It is against all regulations."

Tiberius stopped him with a look. "For diplomacy, you know there are times when only the direct presence of the captain is required. Regulations do *not* state that the captain may not leave the ship and go down to the planet—it is only specified that *all* command officers may not go together. If I go, you should remain with the ship. And vice versa. Don't look at me like that— you know the rule book as well as I do." He grinned. "You do a good job, Kirbie, but you can't take all the fun for yourself."

"I don't know what to do with you," Ross responded. He ran his fingers over the arm of his chair, a contemplative expression on his face. "Funny, I used to take feeling something under my hand for granted; I only know what something is made of now from looking at it." He paused. "I lost these, so you did not have to. Don't look at me like that. I did not know it was going to happen, but it could easily have been you had you stayed. Now, do you see what I mean? It is not safe for the captain to put himself into danger when there are others who are expendable."

Tiberius looked around the bridge, noting where every crew member sat at their station, each engrossed in their work. "No-one is expendable, Kirbie. This ship needs each and every man and woman and I won't allow anyone to be lost. I am only the captain, the rest of the crew are more important because, without them, I cannot run this ship."

Ross smiled. "I do my duty as I see fit. I know you would not have me do otherwise. Now, one of my duties will be preparing for our visitors. What do we know about them?"

"Nothing," Tiberius replied. "No, hold on—I remember something in one of the few log entries of my father's that I was able to read. He said they eat a lot of cooked vegetables, and something like a white fish."

Ross nodded and stood up. "I'll go and get preparations under way." He stopped when he was halfway off the bridge and leaned on the railing around the back of where the command seats were situated. "Full dress, I presume? After all, it is the planet's president and council." He watched a cloud pass across Tiberius' face and knew he was wondering what had happened when the Tamorans had first set foot on the *Wryneck*. The captain's next words showed him how right he was.

Tiberius nodded. "Of course! We're pulling out all the stops. I wish there were follow up logs available—I would love to know what happened at this meal, what preparations my father ordered." He sighed and shook his head. "I know, it is no use thinking about what cannot be." He saw Ross about to speak and nodded. "I'll send it to your terminal. I thought you might want to read that log entry. I hope there is something you can use there to help." His fingers tapped across his screen as Ross left the bridge.

•

The Tamoran president took his seat in the council chamber and looked around at the others. The oval chamber was very bright as the light streamed through the arched windows, set high in the stone walls. The table was set in a horseshoe shape and the council members sat around it in high backed chairs. The chairs were ornately carved and were large enough to accommodate their immense wings. The wings folded neatly along the length of their backs, in the same manner as a bird's, the tips overlapping to protect the delicate feathers. The chair was perfectly designed to accommodate the length of the wings in a slit between the back and the seat. It gave them a very regal look; they were immensely tall anyway, but held their posture very straight, even when seated, and that made them appear to be even taller.

The president stood up and rested his hands on the table. "We have been invited aboard the *Invincible*, to dine with the captain and his command team. What do you think he knows, if anything, about what transpired after our visit to the *Wryneck*? Do you believe that Admiral Kehoe kept her vow and remained silent?"

"She promised when we released the commander. To buy silence and protection from her—we made that gesture, releasing a dying man who was no longer of any use to us," one of the females replied. "She was afraid her role would be revealed; that her superiors and government would discover what she was. She will not betray us, as she does her colleagues. She risked so much with his release; had he spoken she would be ruined. It was fortuitous for her that he was so close to death and that he too did not know everything. It was enough to release him as we did, knowing his comrades were long gone."

The president watched her face. "You got too close; I warned you about getting romantically involved with the experiments."

She dropped her lashes. "Male humans are always so interesting. So strong, so handsome, and they fight long and hard—such resistance is compelling. You should not have chosen handsome men."

"It is well documented that the better-looking the human, the more pride they will take in their appearance," the leader responded. "And that kind will always fight."

The others nodded in agreement. "He was not compatible with our needs in the end—the experiments proved this. He was not genetically strong enough for our purposes. We risked a lot releasing him, but it was a risk worth taking—he was not going to live long." They would have been surprised to know that, rather than dying, Xander was still living and was slowly making progress towards getting well again. This was a detail that Admiral Kehoe had deliberately omitted to tell the Tamorans.

•

Tiberius glanced up as his personal assistant, Laura Harsant, came onto the bridge. She stopped by the captain's chair and leaned down to whisper something in his ear. He sat upright when she straightened up and stood up. "Our guests have arrived. Ross, Popovych, you're with me. Narelle, you're in command until I return."

Narelle Forsyth, the navigator, looked as pleased as punch to be put in temporary command while the captain was performing his diplomatic duties, supported by the first and second officers. "Yes, sir," she said, brightly. This was the first time she had been asked to take charge on the bridge—every member of the crew looked up to their captain and being singled out by him for an important task was highly prized. She moved from her position, her place being instantly taken by a crewman summoned to relieve her, and she almost shyly sat in the seat the captain had just vacated. She sternly told the butterflies in her stomach to settle down and she watched the three senior officers leave the bridge with Tiberius' aide.

Tiberius glanced back and saw the young navigator settled in his seat and smiled. He always knew the right choices to make; he had made it a point to get to know his crew, the bridge officers in particular. He made only one error as they left, and Ross noticed it at once. Protocol dictated that the captain left the bridge first, the others at pace or two behind. Instead, he let his aide go first, and Ross noticed that they allowed their hands to brush together, and he wondered. He was a little surprised too, although pleased, Tiberius had made it pretty clear that all he cared about was finding what happened to his father. He had also been adamant that he was done with relationships after he was dumped by Lashinda not long into their voyage. *Perhaps time really did heal some things.*

The captain and his companions walked into the shuttle bay where the Tamoran craft had landed. It was a strange-looking vessel and like nothing they had encountered before. It appeared lightweight, formed from some material unknown to the explorers from Earth. It had immense wings which folded back along its tapered fuselage when not in flight. It was coloured like a night sky when the sun has gone down, leaving the last strains a purple glow just before the darkness finally falls. The wings had scalloped edges, like the feathers of a bird's wings and there was a strange beauty about it.

Tiberius stepped forward, at the same time as the Tamoran he recognized as the president. His palms felt clammy as nerves kicked in; it had been easier to hide his nerves when they had met on screen. But to stand face-to-face with the alien leader— he had been dreading this moment, not knowing what either of them would say or do. He knew how he felt about these people, whether it was right or not. He had hated them passionately for years, even when he had not yet learned their name and knowing it had just deepened his hatred. He had no idea if the Tamorans knew of his feelings and did not really care if they did—except for right now, standing facing them. He knew how much he did not want them to know how he was feeling. He was an ambassador for his people; he was the commanding officer of this ship and had to set an example to his crew. Diplomacy was one of his mandates. He had to swallow his hatred and act as if he knew nothing about what had happened on this planet, even though he knew the Tamorans knew he knew. They knew nothing of these people: only Xander had met them, and he never spoke of it. If he had made an official statement as to their nature and appearance, it had never been released. Tiberius took another pace forward and held out his hand. "Welcome aboard the *Invincible*, President Dayelh. It is an honour to host you and members of the Tamoran council for dinner." He realized that none of them even knew if these beings were able to shake hands in the way they did, what if offering his hand caused offence because they were unable to reciprocate the gesture? It was a relief when Dayelh extended his long arm and took the captain's hand in his strong claw-like grip.

"The honour is ours," President Dayelh replied. "We do not often receive visitors this deep into the galaxy. The visit of a ship from another world is a welcome diversion." The clasp of the alien's hand was strong; the long, thin fingers curling around Tiberius' hand, applying enough pressure that the nails dug in slightly.

Tiberius glanced down. The nails were more like talons than fingernails, but he dared not try to draw his hand away. Dayelh was clearly testing him. After a moment, Dayelh released the captain's hand. "We are pleased to accept your hospitality."

Each of the party wore a floor-length cloak, with a high collar, effectively concealing that they were winged beings. Dayelh introduced the female who stood a pace behind him as his wife and consort.

Tiberius extended his hand again. "Welcome, High Lady Delmaa." He gritted his teeth inwardly as her fingers touched his, almost caressing them. Where Dayelh had been apparently testing his strength and his reactions, Delmaa seemed to be testing him in another way and it freaked him out.

Delmaa released Tiberius' hand and said something to Dayelh and laughed. At least, Tiberius assumed it was laughter as her mouth opened slightly, showing an array of sharply pointed teeth. The sound was harsh and grated on the ears. He dared not snatch his hand back but forced himself to smile in return as she bowed her head to him. It was at this moment that Tiberius wished even more that his father's logs were complete. In situations like this, with visiting dignitaries, it was a customary practice for a tour of the ship to be made, at least of the areas with permitted access. What if his father had done the same and the aliens had been able to use that to blow up the *Wryneck* or to compel his father to do it? He was leaning more towards the idea that his father had been forced to destroy his ship, either because he was unable to resist, or it was the only way to save his crew from whatever the aliens were going to do. It was another moment for a split-second decision and Tiberius smiled again. "My first officer, Commander Ross. I have to return to the Bridge for now. I will leave you in Ross' capable hands for a brief tour of the ship before dinner." Tiberius turned to Ross who nodded in silent reply to what he knew the captain meant—enough of a tour to satisfy their diplomatic duty, but not enough to fuel the captain's fears. Tiberius returned to the bridge and sat down, collecting his thoughts. He tapped the computer screen and scanned the folder which held what remained of his father's logs. "Computer, scan for all references to the Tamorans coming aboard the *Wryneck*." He leaned back and waited, watching the screen flickering as the computer scanned the logs. "There must be something I've missed."

"There is one entry. An audio recording and transcript. You have listened to the first few minutes but have not completed it."

"Play audio." He mentally psyched himself to hear his father's voice again.

I should stop worrying. Commander Galen is the best in diplomatic situations, and I can always rely on him to be at my side when it counts. My main concern was any language barrier. We have never met these aliens before. We have no knowledge of them, and they know nothing of us. It appears that their president has some knowledge of English and we managed some conversation, even if some of it was pointing at things and miming their use. We gave them a tour of the ship and then entertained them to dinner, and it was a success. They were willing to try all our dishes and ate plenty, especially of fish and cooked vegetables. They also seemed very partial to the dessert we call trifle and the galley had to prepare a fresh supply six times! What concerns me now is our visit to the planet. Regulations dictate that the two most senior officers must not leave the ship at the same time, to safeguard the chain of command in the event of a problem, but the

Tamorans are insisting that both of us come down. I do not feel that we can refuse. They have been reasonably pleasant, but there is an aura of threat radiating from them.

Tiberius tapped the screen and his father's voice stopped. He gave the computer a reference and, a moment later, his father's voice began again, giving his account of what had happened on the planet when the first signs that things were going wrong had made themselves evident. He had listened to this many times, it was the only complete remaining log—all others had been lost or erased. As he listened, he realized this was the first time that he fully noticed the fear in his father's voice. Whatever had happened had terrified him. Tiberius understood. The Tamorans had managed to give him the creeps—especially the female and the way she had touched him. He glanced up as a footstep sounded and he saw Laura Hansart, his aide, step up to stand beside the chair. He smiled. "Waiting for orders? Tell the galley to prepare plenty of trifle in addition to the fish dishes I've ordered."

"*Trifle?*"

He nodded, grinning. "Yes, trifle. Lots of it. I believe the Tamorans enjoyed it before."

She shot him a quick look, thinking he was joking. She knew him well enough, however, to catch the serious undertone and nodded. "Yes, sir. I will see to that now." She turned to leave the bridge but turned back as she heard him move in the chair. "Yes, sir?"

Tiberius' cheeks turned a little pink. He had turned to watch her walk away but now he had to quickly think of a reason as he could not tell her that—at least not in front of the others. "No alcohol."

"Understood, sir."

37
The Mines

At the entrance to the mine, one of the prisoners looked up at the sky as the crimson sun began to set. "I heard there is a ship up there," she said. "Do you think it's come for us?" She turned and looked at some of the others sitting on the ground close by. Some of them formed a chain gang, being forced to mine for fuel, and the precious stones the planet used for currency. They were a mixed bunch, with many planets represented. The Tamorans abducted people from all worlds and set many to work the mines, as well as using them in their genetic breeding experiments. They were dirty and exhausted. Hard labour showed clearly in their faces and dull eyes. Pain, suffering, and humiliation took it right out of them, even the strongest among them.

The woman walked back, the chains on her ankles clanking and sat on a rock by the men. "No hope again?"

"What do you think? The last time we heard a ship was coming we welcomed some more in the mines soon after. For the sake of the universe, I want no more ships to come here," one of the men replied. "You can tell him though—one day, he will find a way out for us. He promised years ago."

She slid off the rock and made her way to an area, deeper inside the mine. She stopped, watching one man using a short-handled pick to break chunks out of the wall.

He was a tall man, chained and barefoot as were the others. His legs were scarred, and there was fresh blood running down his shins as chips of stone flew out from the wall and struck him. His feet were caked in the clay-like mud he stood in. He must have heard something for he turned his head and saw her watching. "Come," he said, in the woman's own tongue, although he was not of the same world. He laid the pick aside, after checking there were no guards close by. His bare back bore the marks of many beatings—for anything from being slow to stopping work, or just for being there. He was older than the others, and had become respected by his fellow prisoners, and was treated as an elder. He had been a prisoner a long time, and the others marvelled that he had survived. A trickle of water ran down the rock face at which he had been chipping. He cupped his chained hands under the ledge from which the water trickled. He turned to the woman and held his hands out awkwardly for her to drink the water. They got no food or water while they worked and made the best they could from the little they could gather, even from the wet mud underfoot. He drank the few sips she had left and leaned on the wall and stretched his chained arms and legs as best as he could.

"There's a ship in orbit around Tamora. I heard it is from your world."

"Earth?" His thin face softened slightly under the sweat and grime. "You should not be working still."

She put her hand on her stomach. "You noticed? They will come for me soon enough—we are treated better when we carry one of their precious experiments." She watched his face. "On your world, does grey hair mean you are wise? Is that why we call you father?"

"It means I am old," he replied. "I think you call me father because I have been here so long. I have been here since before most of you were born—I have seen many born, grow up and die before their time. I watched you grow up."

"I was born here? I knew no other world?"

He shook his head and stooped to lift his pick. "Go now, the guards are coming. You do not want to be caught talking to me—you know that. Not while we work. Go, child." She was no child, but he had known her since she was born.

•

That night, locked in his cell, the old man lay staring up at the ceiling in the dark. He imagined decorating the cell again. Bright colours, not the constant darkness. His eyes had adapted to the darkness, to such an extent that the Tamorans covered his eyes when he was brought up from the mine every night. Even moonlight caused pain. He rolled off the straw that formed his bed and paced around the cell as best as he could when the long chain attached to the cuffs on his ankles was fastened to the wall.

As usual, he could hear the screams and cries of those the Tamorans chose to torture that night, and every moment he expected the door to open and bright light would be shone in his face, sending him to his knees in pain. He had given up the hope that anyone would ever come for him. Some of the newer prisoners talked of how their governments would negotiate for their release. He had thought so at first but with every day that passed it had grown less likely, and then the Tamorans had told him the truth. That he had been sold to them—he and his crew. He might have given up hope, but he had not forgotten who he was and repeated his name over and over to himself, clinging to the last vestiges of his identity after the Tamorans had robbed him of almost everything else—his pride, his strength, his self-esteem.

Many of the young prisoners were his offspring, genetically modified it was true, but formed from the seed the Tamorans stole from him. That was why he was still alive, he knew that. He was fertile—all the males were used that way. Farmed for their sperm and the women artificially impregnated with the modified foetuses. It still made him sick when they called him father, well, it could be true. He lay back on the straw and curled up, trying to keep himself warm. As he tried to get to sleep, he wondered again if his friend was still alive; they had been held together for a short time before being separated. He had heard his screams as he was tortured every night. He had never seen him again, either in the cells or in the mine. The Tamorans never answered his questions when the screaming stopped. He assumed he was dead, and he certainly never guessed he had been released years ago, as part of a trade negotiation. If he was dead, he was glad. Poor Xander did not deserve to suffer. He blamed himself—he should never have let the situation arise, he should have stopped them from being separated. Then he remembered—he *had* tried to prevent it. He had fought back when they came to drag Xander out of the cell. He had been pinned to the floor and beaten as they dragged his friend out and he had lain on the floor, Xander's cries echoing in his ears. He had wanted to die—some of the things that they had done to him had made him long for death.

But Stephen MacAlpin was not dead. Somehow, he had survived.

38

"I promised I would be here"

Xander Galen stirred in his hospital bed and his eyes flickered open as his head moved on the pillow. The bed creaked a little and the quiet sound was enough to bring Doctor Jessup to the bedside. She leaned over and smiled. "How are you feeling? You've been sleeping for a long time—which is for the best." She took a pen-torch from the pocket of her white coat and gently shone it in his eyes, checking his responses. She smiled again and gently released the restraints now that he was no longer in danger of injuring himself as the withdrawal, from what had become high drug dependence, had tormented his already weakened body. He had been very sick and twice the resuscitation team had been rushed in as the immense strain stopped his heart from beating. He was out of danger now and could get the rest he so desperately needed.

As soon as the straps were removed, Xander rolled onto his side and curled up with a deep sigh. He was exhausted and had no strength to even speak, he just cuddled down as Doctor Jessup tucked another blanket over him to keep him warm as his body began its natural healing process, beginning with deep sleep. Jessup watched him fall asleep and then went to tell Serenity.

The android had stayed with him every moment of his withdrawal, she had been there for every scream, every ranting of a tormented, delirious mind. She had held his hand as his heart was restarted. She had been afraid when he finally fell silent, immediately fearing the worst. It was a relief to be told that he was merely sleeping at long last. She had stepped out for a while, at the doctor's insistence, sending her to fetch some more things he would need to help his recovery. Books and some more clothes—the doctor had the idea of getting him to begin spending a little time out of bed each day, and he would feel a bit more comfortable in pyjamas and a dressing gown, rather than a thin hospital gown.

The doctor knew that, although an android, Serenity needed something to take her mind off her concern for Xander and had persuaded her to spend more time on her wedding plans.

It meant even more to Serenity now—their marriage would symbolize new life for Xander and, after all he had endured, he deserved a new life and someone with which to share it. She did not make too many plans, she wanted Xander's input for some—not wanting to leave him out. She returned to the hospital to be met by the doctor, smiling.

"He is sleeping," Doctor Jessup told Serenity. "He is still far from well but is no longer dependent on the drugs that were killing him. When he wakes, we will begin administering the medication needed for his condition. Rest and some proper nourishment will complete the treatment."

"Will he recover? He has been through a lot and he is not strong. This will have been a strain on his heart, won't it? You will tell me the truth?"

Doctor Jessup nodded. "I know I cannot hide the truth from you. It will be a long hard slog; his body has been through a terrible amount of strain over the years, but we know the medication my father developed *did* work as Xander's notes show. He was making progress until the other drugs were administered."

"I don't want to lose him, not now," Serenity replied. "He has fought so hard, so valiantly."

"It is not in his nature to give up," Doctor Jessup replied. "Although a fatalist, accepting whatever the outcome would be, he was never going to let go for as long as he could hold on." She put her hand on the android's arm. "Come on, if he could hold onto hope when there appeared to be none, then you can hold on to the bright hope there is. Come and look at him. He is completely free." She led Serenity into the room, and they stood beside the bed.

Serenity saw him curled up on his side, his head pillowed on his arm against the pillow, no longer held down by restraints. She leaned over and gently stroked his cheek and stooped to kiss him. "I love you," she whispered. "Thank you for coming back to me."

Xander stirred slightly and a smile flickered on his lips, but he did not wake up. It was enough, Serenity thought, to know he knew she was there. She stroked his grey hair for a few minutes and then turned to sort out the things she had brought with her before sitting by the bed. She looked down and gently rubbed the solitaire diamond in her engagement ring. It was simple, but beautiful, and was very old. Xander had told her it had belonged to his mother, but it looked even older than that and had perhaps belonged to his grandmother too. She hoped so. To have something that had been in Xander's family for generations, and was now bringing her into the family meant much more than she would ever know how to put into words.

When Xander woke a few hours later, his eyes fell on her first and his thin, pale face, lit up. "You're here?" he whispered, reaching out a hand.

"Of course I am. I promised I would be here when you woke." She took his hand and caressed it between hers. She glanced up and, catching the eye of one of the nurses, nodded.

The nurse hurried over and, between her and Serenity, they raised the head end of Xander's bed a little, so he was propped up on the pillows. It was obvious he had little or no strength left after the fight for his life, but they could start now on his treatment and recovery.

"The doctor will be back shortly," the nurse said. "She left orders that he was to take a little nourishment if he can once he woke." She turned to her patient. "Would a little tea and toast be nice?"

"I could eat you," Xander replied, laughing slightly which made Serenity happy. "Sorry, nurse. Yes, please. I am starving."

•

Mona Jessup sat in her office, reading over every detail in Xander's notes—going right back to the medical examination made after his release and every subsequent check-up since. She wanted to understand him every step of the way, and to not miss anything that might be vital. She looked at the reports alongside the reports made by her father and compared them. Her father had left detailed notes, including his belief that Xander's disease was of alien origin, and that it was to be treated as such, stating that this was why he had developed the medication. He pointed out that Xander, in the first couple of years after his return, had been hospitalized on many occasions and had even endured intense cancer treatment for a condition that was not cancer. It was documented in his notes, that this treatment had almost killed him. She locked the notes away and picked up the syringe she had filled from the hidden supply of the medicine her father had been developing. There was enough to treat him, a couple of months' supply—that was all she anticipated. After those months, she would release him, with the pills developed alongside the liquid medicine. The information sheet said Xander was to take those for as long as necessary once the initial treatment had been successful.

The office door locked behind her as she came along the corridor and into Xander's private room. A glance told her the nurse had prepared him for injections and she slipped the needle inside the cannula and pressed the plunger. She smiled as she glanced up, sensing she was being watched.

Xander hated needles and had to psych himself up to any injection. Every prick of the needle made him want to cry out although the use of the cannula meant there was no pricking of the skin at every injection. The pain was not so bad now, not through the hand this way. His arm was covered in white scars where needles had penetrated the skin and he wanted to scream as he watched the needle. It was the sight of the needles—he remembered the sharp pain regularly in his arm as he was injected with whatever they had given him.

Doctor Jessup smiled and patted Xander's arm. "Well done. I know you hate injections. Everything will be okay now. This time you will get well." She nodded to the nurse and Xander was tucked in warmly and his bed returned to its usual position so he could sleep again. The first month was like that. Injections every day and sleep and gradual nourishment for the first time now he was off a drip. He had not been able to eat in what was quite a long time, and she made no secret of the fact that no cure was to be had on earth for the disease that raged through his body.

It was close to the end of the second month and Xander was sitting up in bed, propped up on the pillows and was back at the position health-wise he had been in so many months ago when he was drugged and abducted from his apartment. He accepted the doctor's word, knowing the medicine was only ever going to keep it under control and give him the best quality of life as possible. The doctor had been right to call him a fatalist. He was resigned to this but was not giving up the fight. Two of the male nurses had helped him up earlier and got him his first real shower in ages and then assisted him into pyjamas and dressing gown. He felt much better now and was hoping to be released from the hospital soon. He would be glad never to see the inside of a hospital again, although he could not deny the exceptional care he had received over the last few months. But he wanted his life back. He knew he was still ill and would remain so unless Tiberius was able to discover whatever it was the Tamorans had done to give him this terrible condition. He turned his head and smiled when Serenity and Doctor Jessup came to the bedside. "Well, doctor, can I go home?"

Doctor Jessup smiled and nodded. "Yes, your condition is under control and you know how to administer your own medication. I think it is safe for you to be released. You are a little stronger and your strength will return to a point where you will be able to return to work. I will inform the admiral that you are fit to return to work within the next three months, and you can be discharged next week—I want to monitor you for a few more days." She stood up and put her hand on his shoulder. "I am glad I have been able to fulfil my father's desire to help you. I feel I have honoured his memory."

Xander looked at her. "He would be very proud of you. Thank you for everything you have done." He leaned back and closed his eyes.

39

An Awkward Dinner

The meal was drawing to a close and Tiberius checked again to see that everyone had all they wanted. He took a sip of his drink, and slowly set down the glass. "So, President Dayelh, tell me about your work in genetics. Is this just a scientific interest, or do you have plans to use your experiments?"

Dayelh's eyes quickly met Delmaa's and there was a tangible change of atmosphere. They all felt it, and it was not a nice change. Ross looked at Tiberius and, although he said nothing, his eyes did, and they were saying "What are you thinking of?!" They had agreed not to mention this subject.

Dayelh turned to face his host. "We have a sister world which lost most of the population almost forty years ago in the worst drought and famine this part of the galaxy has ever experienced. We are repopulating with genetically modified beings—modified to withstand the planet's conditions. Each one is carefully modified, and created, adapted to suit that planet."

"Testing?"

Dayelh laughed. "Of course, no-one brings anything into being who does not also test that it works. Strength, fertility, resilience to disease. Nothing is omitted. We must ensure that those we will send have every chance of survival." He was watching the captain's face.

Doctor Malachi leaned forward. "I assume the victims, I mean subjects, consent to the experiments and testing?" She had not intended to say anything, but she remembered the fight to save Ross' life, and the struggle he had gone through as he learned how to walk and use his hands again. She remembered the captain himself lying in bed, blood streaming from his nose and ears as the intense pressure caused his brain to haemorrhage and it had been touch-and-go whether he would live or retain his senses. She knew Xander's story and that his illness was likely caused by these people. As a doctor, she could not be silent and listen to that raspy voice talking about their experiments as though there was nothing wrong with torturing living beings for the sake of science.

Dayelh turned his head. "You are a scientist, Doctor. I would like you to see for yourself what we do—I am sure you will find it interesting."

Rivkah Malachi looked at the alien and knew she had to say something. The science of genetics itself was fascinating, but not the torture of countless people; forcing them to undergo genetic modifications and to be used in cruel and barbaric testing. Lab rats for a cold and barbaric people filled only with thoughts of their own world—other people had no worth or meaning to them. She would not find it interesting. It would be beyond heart-breaking.

"A visit to the laboratories can be arranged, Doctor."

She knew Tiberius was watching her. This topic had been taboo, and she had broken it. Yes, the captain had started the topic, but she had asked the loaded question. Only she could get out of this mess. "My work on the *Invincible* keeps me very busy, but if Captain MacAlpin permits, then I would accept your invitation."

Dayelh inclined his head, almost as though acknowledging the manner in which she had extricated herself from the sticky situation. "Then it shall be discussed with your commanding officer."

Tiberius shot the CMO a look, begging her not to say anything else.

The Tamoran party left the ship after the meal and the captain and crew heaved sighs of relief—it had been quite an intense visit.

Tiberius sat in the officer's mess, enjoying a cold beer. As he had forbidden alcohol at the table, it was a welcome treat. He fingered the bottle as he held it in his hands, feeling the cold glass begin to relax him. His face ached from the smiling, he had dared not let the mask slip, even when the doctor had made things awkward. She had only asked the question on all their minds. But it had scared him—what if it put any captives in danger? A people as merciless as this would surely have no compunction with executing them if they chose. He hoped they would do no such thing and thought perhaps they were safe, as Dayelh had invited them for a visit. The Tamoran President would surely not do anything to create an incident at this moment. He glanced up as footsteps approached and he nodded in greeting. It was Ross with Rivkah Malachi.

"May we join you?" Ross asked.

"Sure. I think we could all do with a drink. It got a little tense."

"That is entirely my fault, and I must apologize for that," Rivkah said. "It was just the idea of them torturing people and making them ill for their own ends—to see if they can create people who can survive natural disasters. As a doctor, it offended my principles."

"Instead, you got an invitation to inspect their work? They're sick," Ross said.

"Perhaps they don't think they are wrong—we know nothing about them," Tiberius said. "I'm trying to work out how they could justify it—so many must die. What do they do with those who do not mutate the way they want and what about those who resist? Do they just kill them? It hardly bears thinking about." He paused and took a long drink. "I am trying so hard not to just hate them for the sake of it, but I know they killed my father, and they made Xander so sick. Did they do the same to dad?" He broke off and looked down at his beer. "I hate them so much. How can I be objective when I know what they have done?"

"Because, if you don't, you risk your life and the life of everyone on board this ship," Rivkah replied. She smiled as Tiberius looked at her.

He spotted dimples in her olive-skinned cheeks which he had never noticed before. Her long dark hair, which was normally kept tied back to be practical, was still loose and falling below her shoulders as she had worn it at dinner. He found it impossible not to return the smile. She was a very attractive woman, and he could hardly believe that he had been determined to distrust her because she had been assigned to the *Invincible* by Admiral Kehoe, replacing the *Victorious*'s old doctor whom he knew and trusted. He had known Doctor Linus Todd since he had first been assigned to the *Victorious*, not long after finishing his studies and graduating as an Ensign. He knew that at that time he had still been rebelling against change, although delighted with his new command, he had not wanted to let Xander go, knowing how he would feel if he had to resign his command through ill health. Any good captain had the intention of dying in service—remaining standing alone on the bridge as inevitable death approached. Maybe a romanticized ideal, but true of any in command. Like sailors of old, the captain would go down with his ship. He shook his head. Thinking like that would do no good. He rested his elbows on the bar as the others got their drinks and sat with him. "We need to decide what we do next," he said. "Do we go down as we have been intending, or do we offend them by refusing, making us look suspicious of them?"

"They already know we are suspicious," Ross replied. "They were testing you all the time they were on board—it was obvious. We need to not be so obvious—but equally, we must be careful. I am not prepared to let you go into danger. No, not even in diplomatic situations. Not without a lot of thought. I should go first—you know that, and I will keep on reminding you."

Tiberius looked up and frowned slightly and then smiled. "I suppose you are right." He paused as his call sign sounded in his ear. He raised his wrist. "Yes?"

It was his PA. "Captain, you have a private call. Will you take it in your quarters?"

Tiberius drained his glass and stood up. "Thanks. I'll go right away. Patch it through." He nodded to the others. "Have a drink on me," he added as he left the room.

Tiberius headed straight to his quarters and sat at his desk, wondering who the call was from. He rarely got personal calls, excepting his mother who called once a month. "Connect call," he told the computer, leaning back in his chair. It was not his mother's call sign on the screen, and he sat upright when the screen flickered, and he saw Xander. "*Pappi!*" In private there was no need to be formal. His eyes flickered over the background. "You're out of bed? Are you home?"

Xander smiled, pleased Tiberius was so happy to see him. "I am still in the hospital, but I have been out of bed for the last two days. It feels so good." He sounded tired. He was sitting on the balcony of his room, enjoying the sun shining on his face, getting a bit of colour into his pale face. "I managed to dress myself today, for the first time," he went on. "I get help in the shower still in case I fall, but I am getting there."

"Take it easy, you've been really sick for a long time—you mustn't overdo it."

Xander smiled again. "I have news for you. I asked Serenity to marry me, not long after I came out of the coma; before I got sick again. She has been everything I would ever imagine a wife could be. She never left my side the whole time I was out of it and even when I was raving as I was weaned off the drugs."

Tiberius' eyes softened. "Did she say yes? Isn't that the most important bit?" and he laughed.

"She said yes. I don't want to waste any more time, Tiberius. I am still a sick man although the treatment works to an extent. I do not know how long I have left. We were thinking of waiting until you came home, but anything could happen in four more years." He paused. "I wanted you to be there, to stand up with me. Like I would have asked your father." He paused, knowing this was a big thing.

Tiberius held his breath a moment and then smiled. "I wish you every happiness. Why don't you have a small private wedding, and then a big one when we return? You could get married 'live' in front of the crew. That would mean just as much to me—I can still be your best man even if not physically beside you."

"Do you really mean that?"

Tiberius nodded. "Of course I do. You could arrange to use the hospital's chapel—that way you can go ahead without having to wait until you are completely well enough to leave the hospital." He smiled to see the expression in the older man's eyes. He understood—he had lost so much time, first a prisoner for ten years and now a sick man and had been in a critical condition for more than six months. He knew Xander did not want to wait. "Go ahead. I'll let the crew know and we'll share this time with you although we are parted. Can you get things sorted for this time tomorrow evening?"

"I think so," Xander said. "Serenity has already got my chaplain on standby. She tells me I had the last rites more than once over the last few months. She knew I would want that. I don't want anyone else to marry us—just him. He always attended immediately when things were bad."

Tiberius smiled. "I am truly happy for you, Xander. I can't wait to meet Serenity. She sounds like the best thing that could have happened to you right now. Go and tell her the plan and call me later with the details. I'll have the crew ready, in full dress. It will be just the thing before we get stuck into what is ahead of us."

There was a moment's pause and then Xander said, "You've met them? The Tamorans?"

Tiberius nodded. "They're as creepy as hell. What are they like, Xander? I mean really like—the people behind those cloaks. What are they hiding?"

"I don't know, Tiberius, I truly do not know. Anything I heard was hearsay—my face was always covered, or I was being blinded with bright lights. I never saw their true image, but I heard enough to know that they are not what they seem at first appearance. I never heard them coming and never heard them leaving. There was just a soft sound. I know this is going to sound silly, but it was like the sound of wings. Not like on a little bird, but on something bigger—maybe an eagle. I can't explain it better than that. I was asked to describe them at the hearing, but I couldn't. All I could say then was what I have told you now." Xander stopped and looked away from the screen. "I know you always wanted me to tell you what happened to me. The truth is that I do not know. I never saw them; they were just there, and I could only feel pain. Every day, I never knew when they would come and take me to the room where they tortured me. I wish I could help you, Tiberius. I wish I could have seen or heard something that I could tell you. They made me sign a document to say I would never reveal details of what happened to me. I signed it because I was forced to but also there is nothing I can reveal."

"Xander, can I ask you one thing? Do you know what started all this—how the *Wryneck* ended up in that position, and why you ended up in prison?"

Xander raised his head slowly and met Tiberius' eyes. "You know I must break my oath to tell you? They made me promise."

Tiberius nodded. "I understand, but I think too much time has passed; too much has happened for that oath to have any meaning—plus being forced to make that promise is dubious. You were imprisoned and tortured, you lost your commanding officer and crew, and were forced into a silence you should *never* have been made to keep. I think you need to tell me. You know I already have an idea. I know you probably don't know the reasons, but you know who betrayed you." He took a deep breath before he continued. "I think it would be putting us at risk to withhold anything further." He saw Xander's face change and knew he was close to crossing the line. He knew the older man still suffered from the trauma he had been through, and that often when he closed his eyes he was transported back to the prison and relived the fear and torture. "I'm sorry."

Xander looked up again and smiled slightly. "It's okay. I believe you are right. I have let a long time pass and have buried the truth. Perhaps finally letting it go will help me heal." He almost managed to disguise the sudden change in his voice, but Tiberius heard it and knew this was going to be hard for both of them. Xander took a deep breath and then said, "I think you know that Admiral Kehoe is involved, and that is why she has been trying to have me killed. I do not know the reasons behind why she had us betrayed, but I had managed to find enough proof that she has been well paid. It is not only her, there were others too—I believe all officers in high command, and maybe someone in politics. It is something to do with experimental genetics."

Tiberius nodded and told Xander of the discussion at the meal with the Tamorans.

Xander nodded. "It was not just genetic experiments—they were not just taking people to modify them. They ran fertility tests and chose females who seemed strong enough to carry their modified embryos. The ones they chose for breeding were treated marginally better than the rest, I believe. The males were picked for their virility."

"Is that what happened to you?"

There was a pause and then Xander shook his head. "No. I never understood what they were saying, but I do know they left me unable to have children, because of how the testing damaged me. Death was not even an option, they made sure of that—not releasing me even though I begged them to let me go. They would not kill me, and my hands were always chained so I could not even take my own life."

Tiberius could not imagine it. To be so frightened, and in so much pain that all you wanted was to die, and that release being denied. "I'm sorry, it is upsetting you."

Xander gnawed his bottom lip for a short while and then pulled himself together. "When my release finally came, it was a complete surprise. I had expected every day that passed would be my last. Somehow, my release had been organized as part of a trade agreement, from what I later learned. She was there—smiling, welcoming me as though she had not condemned me to that hell, or the hell she was going to put me through later. The hearing, the determination to have me condemn Stephen. She was the one who wrapped a blanket around me and helped

292

me to a waiting craft. When we reached Earth, I was treated to a 'hero's welcome'—the press and universal media were there. I was carried ashore on a stretcher and I didn't want to speak to anyone. I was too weak to hide my face from them. Tiberius, don't let it happen again. Don't let your crew be harmed."

Tiberius wished he could reach out and touch him; he wanted to pat him on the arm and say everything would be okay. "Just one thing more, what happened to make father destroy the *Wryneck*?"

Xander smiled slightly, as though he knew that was going to be the next question. "Your father never destroyed the ship. He never got the chance. It had been planned, to save the ship from these people, but we were taken prisoner before we ever got back to the ship. They are capable of creating illusions, trust nothing."

"Then my father did not die on the *Wryneck*? He was a prisoner on the planet?"

"Yes, the second officer must have followed the emergency plans. And that was to save the ship and crew at all costs."

"Then he wasn't a traitor?"

"No, but they made me believe it at first. I believed it for a long time even though I did not want to believe. Serenity found the missing records—somehow, she was able to hack into the encrypted areas and remove those files. The Tamoran President made a detailed record of what happened to the *Wryneck*." Xander paused a moment and turned away from the screen. "I have a translation here." He cleared his throat and then read, "Once the captain and his first officer were secured below on Tamora, we sent a ship to board the Earth vessel *Wryneck*. A warning shot was fired across her bows, and they were told to prepare for boarding. Instead of surrendering, the *Wryneck* chose to get underway and attempted to evade our fighters. We sent more craft to intercept and succeeded in forcing the *Wryneck* to stop. Their acceptance of the call to surrender was relayed to me, and we did not expect their next move, which was to self-destruct, taking four of our fighter-craft with them."

"The second officer?"

Xander nodded. "She was an excellent officer, and it is such a shame that was the biggest command decision she had to make. I often think about her."

"Was she special to you?"

Xander's laugh was very soft. "You could say that. Cat—Lieutenant Catherine Larsgaard was my baby sister."

Tiberius' eyes softened with sadness. "I didn't know."

"Not many remember, she was on the roster under her married name. I am glad the Tamorans did not get her. For all of them, death was a blessing in disguise."

"There is one more thing. If father did not die on the *Wryneck*, did he die on the planet? Did they kill him?"

"I don't know, Tiberius," Xander replied. "I just don't know. I never saw him again after that day we were arrested—that last time I looked back and saw him being dragged away too, that was the last I saw of him. I do not know if he lived or died. In a way, I hope they killed him—quickly and painlessly. I could not bear to think of him suffering what I went through."

Tiberius was very quiet for a moment, so quiet that Xander said, "Hello? Tiberius, are you still there?"

"Sorry, yes. I was just thinking. I will find out what happened, I swear it. And I will find a cure for what they did to you."

"I know you will try." Xander's eyes crinkled up at the corners as he smiled. "I do feel better for having told you what I know."

"I've made you talk too long, you need to rest."

Xander leaned back in his seat. "It's warm here, and peaceful. It has been restful enough and I needed to talk about it. I have not talked about it for a long time, as if ignoring it would make it go away. I owe Stephen more than that." He turned his head, obviously to look at someone as Tiberius heard footsteps, and saw Xander reach for a hand and squeeze it. "Tiberius, say hello to Serenity."

A woman's face appeared as she squatted by Xander's chair. "Tiberius, we have spoken before but have never met."

Tiberius found himself staring for the android was beautiful. With her dark hair tied back softly from her face, she looked human—even the intonation in her voice was perfectly human when she spoke. She smiled just like a human woman, but her silvery eyes shone strangely, the only thing to show she was essentially nothing more than artificial intelligence. He saw Xander stroking her hand with his thumb and the skin moved just as it would on a human hand. "Xander tells me you are getting married," he said. "I am very happy for you. I'll leave him to tell you what we discussed. Look after him, Serenity. He needs someone special and I can tell by the way he looks at you, and the way he talks about you tells me he is confident that he has found that special person."

Serenity took Xander's hand in both hers and smiled. "Do not worry, Tiberius, all I want is to look after him. It is time now for him to get some sleep."

Tiberius nodded. "Of course. Sleep well, Xander. I'll look forward to tomorrow."

"Me too."

Tiberius sat back when Serenity ended the call, thinking over everything the Xander had said. He was so happy for Xander and glad they had talked, pleased the older man had finally broken his silence. It had been good for him—the heaviness lifting from his face had been evident. Later, he would speak to Ross and tell him what he had learned, but for now, there was happier news. "Open a ship-wide channel, authorization T. A. MacAlpin Zero Epsilon One," he instructed the computer. "Good evening, crew. I have some news and an invitation for you. Many of you served alongside me on the *Victorious* under Xander Galen. All of you know his story or at least the parts which have been made known. It is my pleasure to announce that after all the lonely years of suffering, he has fallen in love and is getting married. We have been invited to the wedding, but this wedding will not take place when we return to Earth. Oh no, it takes place, hopefully, tomorrow in the hospital chapel, transmitted live to our recreation room. I want everyone there at 19:30, in full dress. There will be a celebration when we return, but he wants to share the private ceremony with us. I am delighted that we can share this special time in the life of a beloved comrade." He signed out and sat back with a smile; that announcement would have caused a stir.

The next evening, the crew of the *Invincible* gathered in the recreation room, all looking very smart in full dress uniform. They waited, chatting amongst themselves.

40

"As I place this ring on your finger"

Xander looked up from the chair he was leaning back in, waiting for the nurses to attend to him. He had asked two of the male nurses to help him get ready; the job he would have asked Stephen or Tiberius to perform, or even his old doctor Clark Tierney, but all those close to him were dead or far away. The nurses came and helped him to shower and put on his dress uniform—the first time he had worn it in such a long time. He looked at himself in the full-length mirror as the tunic buttons were fastened by one of the nurses as the other supported him. He was still quite weak and struggled to stand very well without assistance, and he had asked both, personally chosen by Doctor Jessup to attend him, to flank him so he could stand up for his wedding. "I don't want to be in a wheelchair, although it was kindly offered," he told them.

His cap was handed to him. "You put it on, sir. You can manage that," the nurse told him with a smile. They all liked Xander and it was nice to see him getting a day of happiness after what he had been through—a day they hoped would lead to a much happier future for him.

Xander took the cap and held it for a moment, looking at it and then, after what seemed ages, he raised his hands and settled it onto his silver-threaded hair. He smiled at the reflection, seeing a still handsome, if rather tired-faced, overly thin man looking back at him.

The nurses looked at each other and smiled. They had both witnessed the suffering as Xander was weaned off the drugs that were killing him. They both cleaned him up on numerous occasions when he was sick or too weak to get to the bathroom. It was obvious today meant so much to him.

•

Serenity had asked Doctor Jessup to be her matron of honour and was almost ready now, dressed in the bridal gown she had loved the most when she saw it. Elegant and classic—she knew Xander would love it. She tucked her feet into peep-toe shoes with a low heel. They were ivory, like the dress, with a lace panel and sequins across the top. She was tall enough, so needed no more than the 81mm heel. The dress would cover them most of the time anyway, she thought as the doctor brushed her hair. She knew she could manage herself, but she had been reading about being a bride and having a matron of honour. No android had ever experienced this, and she was going to enjoy every moment of being as human as she ever could be. She looked into the mirror and kept her head still, looking at the subtle make-up Mona had helped her with. She watched as her long wavy hair was pulled back and run through curling tongs before being lightly twisted at the nape of her neck and allowed to cascade over her left shoulder. A lace Juliette cap was set on her head, holding her long veil in place to fall straight around her shoulders and down her back, a wispy cloud of *voile*. A bouquet of orange and yellow roses lay on the dressing table, their stems wrapped in ivory silk.

Her dress was just as simple. A vintage dress from the 2016 collection by the designer Jennifer Packham, she had fallen head over heels for the gown when she saw it in the shop window. It was a slim-fitting ivory silk sheath dress, which hugged her figure, the thin straps holding it on her shoulders. Over the top of the simple dress, there was an over-dress of tulle, embellished with zigzag patterns of sequins, pearl beads and silver thread flowers decorating the bodice. Soft tulle fell over the shoulders in capped sleeves. A beaded belt emphasized her slim waist, and the sequinned skirt fell straight to the floor with a little train behind. The V-neck lengthened her neck and shoulders and she almost gasped at her reflection. This was something she had never dared to imagine but had read about; how so many human women wanted to feel like this—how they wanted an emotional connection with their wedding dress. She felt exactly as she wanted to feel. A bride, ready to be married to a man who needed her at his side for the rest of his life.

Mona Jessup reached for a slender black case and opened it. "Xander sent you this; it's a wedding gift."

Serenity looked inside. She had no jewellery, besides the engagement ring, and the sapphire necklace she had worn the night she knew Xander was in love with her. A simple gold chain with a single pearl drop. There was a short note inside. *This was my mother's. X.* She smiled as the necklace was fastened around her slender neck. It was beautiful.

Mona handed her the bouquet and smiled. "No-one would ever guess you are not human."

Serenity smiled. "That is a great compliment. I know I can never be human, but I can get close." She stood up and turned sideways, looking in the mirror. "Do you know why I have chosen not to get married in uniform? I am always in uniform and I wanted to look different and to be a symbol of what we are committing to. For him. He never had the chance when he was younger, he likes traditions. I know looking like a bride and not a serving officer will make it special for him." She tilted her head slightly and looked at her image reflected in the glass. "Will I take his breath away?"

Mona Jessup laughed. "Do you want to?" She smiled as Serenity nodded. "You make a perfect bride and of course you will take his breath away. Come on, dear—let's go and stun him." She squeezed the android's hand. "I am so happy for you."

They left the room and headed the short distance to the hospital's chapel and Serenity stopped for a moment in the doorway. She saw Xander waiting, leaning on the arm of one of the nurses for support. She knew how much he had wanted to be strong and able to stand for the wedding and she knew he was far from ready and that he was relying on the young man's strength to get him through the short ceremony. She saw the nurse turn his head and then say something softly to Xander.

Xander turned and saw her standing framed in the doorway and his jaw dropped. He knew she was beautiful, but he had not imagined that she could look even more stunning. At that moment, he forgot everything except for the vision of beauty smiling at him from the door.

Everyone watching from the *Invincible* saw her too and saw Xander's reaction and Tiberius watched with a smile on his face as the android began to walk towards Xander. No, today she was not that—she could not be labelled—today she was simply a bride.

Xander watched her walk all the way towards him and reached out a hand when she was close. She looked him right in the eyes and smiled as she took his hand and squeezed it. "You look mesmerizing," he said. "Beautiful."

Serenity smiled. She had done what she hoped; she had taken his breath away. "Do you like the dress?"

Xander nodded. "It is lovely. All of it—the veil, the hair—charming and absolute perfection. Uniform would have done, but this is more than I imagined." He returned the pressure on his hand and they turned together to face the chaplain.

Tiberius saw, as they turned, that Xander slipped his arm from the nurse's supporting hand and leaned on Serenity's arm and he smiled sadly. The android's strength would be more than enough to support the frail man beside her. It saddened him that Xander was not strong enough to stand alone.

Xander turned to the screen and the camera that was projecting the scene to the *Invincible*, happy to see them there on the screen. Many of them had served with him before and he was pleased to have them share this time with him although many light-years separated them.

The chaplain smiled as the two turned toward him. He had known Xander a long time and knew his faith had helped him through some very rough times; a faith he had clung to, even when there were few who shared his beliefs. "We meet again in happier circumstances," he said. "The last time I saw you, I had been called yet again to administer the last rites—once again you have defied the odds and lived."

Xander smiled. "Should I ask forgiveness for wasting your time? Thank you for coming when Serenity called—she knew I would have wished it."

"You have an excellent companion in her. I know her love was as equal as your faith in bringing you through the darkness to being able to stand here beside her, to marry at last." The chaplain looked at Serenity. "You have shown as much love, if not more, than many human women. This man is blessed to have earned your love."

Serenity smiled. "You need not be afraid, I love Xander." She patted the arm she supported. "I do not want to rush anything, but Xander will need to rest soon."

The chaplain nodded and, opening his book, began the ceremony.

Tiberius listened to them making their vows to each other and watched Xander force himself to stand unsupported as he placed a simple circlet of gold on his bride's finger.

Serenity never took her eyes off Xander's face. She smiled as the metal touched her finger and imagined it being warm from his pocket. She listened as he spoke, gazing into her eyes. It was not the traditional words of the marriage ceremony, but his own rehearsed words.

"Serenity, as I place this ring on your finger, may it always remind you of my never-ending love, and may it always remind me of the precious treasure I have in you. Wear this ring with joy, for your love has made me complete."

Serenity opted for the traditional words when she placed her ring on Xander's finger, promising to love, cherish, and obey him "until death us do part," she finished softly, knowing what that meant for both of them. She held both his hands tightly.

The chaplain declared them married and then smiled. "Your old crew-mates are watching. Do you want to do it?"

Xander laughed and cupped Serenity's face in his hands and kissed her, accompanied by a cheer from the video screen as the crew of the *Invincible* rejoiced.

Tiberius ran his hand across his cheek and was shocked to find it damp. He was glad they had been able to share this moment with a man they all cared about. He had been a well-loved captain and his story and constant struggle to overcome the terrible ordeal he had been through in the time before he captained the *Victorious* was well known. Everyone who had watched this simple ceremony had been moved, knowing how much this love meant to Xander. He stood up, clearing his throat. "Rear Admiral Alexander Zachary Galen—Xander, the man I called Pappi as a child—and Android Mark 12 #435—Serenity, thank you, from myself and the crew of the *Invincible*, for allowing us to share this happy time with you. We wish you every happiness. Thank you, Serenity, for saving Xander—your love was what he needed to break the curse of the past."

Serenity looked into Xander's eyes and then up at the screen. "It has been my honour to serve him as I was programmed to do; it is now my honour to serve him as his wife as I have chosen to do."

Xander tucked his hand back in Serenity's arm. He looked suddenly exhausted and Serenity knew he needed to rest. She glanced at the screen and saw that Tiberius had noticed too for he nodded to someone across the room. A crewman stood up, a traditional bo'sun's whistle in his lips which he blew and every member of the *Invincible*'s crew stood up and snapped to attention, saluting, and then formed ranks, every fourth pair holding ceremonial swords, forming a guard of honour as though they were in the room.

The older man's tired face relaxed for a moment as he smiled his thanks. He pulled himself upright, waving the hovering nurse aside, and walked down the short aisle, appearing only to lean lightly on Serenity's arm as they went through the double doors.

The nurses followed closely behind and caught Xander who collapsed as soon as the doors had swung shut behind them. They got him back to his room, helped him undress and got him tucked up in bed.

Serenity came and sat on the edge of the bed and stroked his hands. "Go to sleep," she said. "You have had more excitement than your body can take. It's okay; I don't mind you sleeping." She knew he would fight sleep, wanting to stay awake, not wanting to leave her alone so soon. She knew the risk they ran; that Xander could still die from the disease that ravished him. That was why they had not waited any longer. Every day, he grew a little stronger, but every so often he had a relapse and the medication seemed useless. Then he would rally and get stronger, only to experience setbacks again and again. She hoped desperately that Tiberius would find the antidote to whatever this disease was and bring it back before it was too late. Xander had courage and determination on his side. The will to live was a critical factor; enabling some to survive situations where others would crumble and surrender to the inevitable without a fight. Surrender was not Xander's way. He had survived ten terrible years of pain and torment; he had been in his thirties when imprisoned, and in his forties when he was released. He had lost a decade of his life and had lost friends and comrades under such tragic circumstances. He had survived against all odds, in the prison, and then in hospital once home. He had recovered to an extent where he was able to return to active service and was given command of the *Victorious*, only for the disease to return with a vengeance; forcing him to undergo regular hospital treatment, until the day he was abducted from his apartment and his existence became as hell-like as when he was a prisoner on Tamora.

•

Tiberius turned to his comrades and was not ashamed for them to see the tears on his cheeks. "Getting soft in my old age." He laughed slightly.

Ross shook his head. "No, you're not. It meant a lot to all of us. It was moving—a few shed tears are a tribute to what it means for Xander to have finally been able to move on. For him to be finding peace at last, after everything he has been through, he can spend the remainder of his life happy."

Tiberius nodded. "I know, he deserves this." He blew his nose. "Drinks all round, I think. We need to toast the bride and groom."

41

"I swear by Apollo the Healer"

Tiberius glanced around the table at his command team and paused before speaking. "Well, now we have the wedding out of the way, we need to decide what to do with the Tamoran situation. Do we run the risk of offending them by refusing their invitation to visit the planet; or do we put ourselves at risk by going down to the surface?"

"We run that risk, with either decision," Ross said. He shook his head as Tiberius opened his mouth to speak again. "No, with all due respect, Captain, you *need* to hear me out. You insisted that I come aboard as your first officer because of my experience. You have to listen."

Tiberius looked at him and nodded. "Go ahead." He knew Ross was right and he knew the whole team did too.

"We know what the Tamorans are; you told me what Xander finally told you. They are evil. They are doing things that should never be done—torturing people for experiments. They destroyed Xander, caused your father's death and the death of every single member of the crew of the *Wryneck*. We *cannot* take those risks. I know what we are here for, to negotiate that trade treaty; just as your father was. We must ask ourselves whether the Tamorans want to negotiate? Is this *truly* the reason? Or are we here, yet again, as a sacrifice—sent by the evil designs of Admiral Kehoe? She withheld so much from you; your 'official' orders were a farce, worded in such a way that you were not sure what was being asked of us. We had no alternative but to obey— but it was wrong! We have been sent to the ends of the galaxy, to be used by the Tamorans for the same purposes as the crew of the *Wryneck* before us."

Tiberius sat in silence, watching Ross' face. It was as though the first officer was his own inner thoughts being spoken aloud. Everything he knew and believed himself about the voyage and their mission—Ross was saying it out loud. "Kirbie, if that is so, does it not behove us to put a stop to this evil? The atrocities they commit against any people who cross their paths cannot be permitted to continue. We have been sent here for a purpose. It is our duty to change that purpose. There are people here, suffering as Xander did. We should do everything we can to save them." He looked around and saw the same expression on the faces of every member of his command team. He could see they knew he was right. That if there was *any* way they could rescue the tormented prisoners on the planet, then they had to do it. There was no alternative. They had been given that chance. It was their duty, a risk they had to take. He looked around and nodded. "You agree?" He looked at Ross and smiled, seeing his right-hand man biting his lip. "I know this goes against every rule—every protocol, but we have come too far to abide by *every* rule and regulation. Many more could die because we argue about which rules we should keep. Are rules and orders worth more than saving the lives of helpless people suffering torment at the hands of evil?"

Ross shook his head. "Not when you put it like that. No, there is nothing further to argue. We have to do everything we can."

Tiberius nodded. "Your concerns are duly noted." He turned and looked down the table to where Doctor Malachi sat. "Doctor, I suggest that you accept the offer to go and see their laboratories and experiments. I don't know what you will find, but we must face it sooner or later and…"

"And it is my fault," Rivkah Malachi replied. "If I had not spoken out of turn at dinner, we would have the element of surprise—they would still think us innocent of the knowledge of what they do."

"I wasn't going to say that," Tiberius responded. "You said what we were all thinking, and you took an oath—it must be so painful to see the suffering caused by medical methods."

"I swear by Apollo the Healer, by Asclepius, I will use treatment to help the sick according to my ability and judgement. I will abstain from all intentional wrong-doing and harm, especially from abusing bodies. If I carry out this oath, and break it not, may I gain for ever for my life and art; but if I transgress, may the opposite befall me." She looked up. "I paraphrase, but

Hippocrates wrote that so long ago. It has been modernized so many times, but the original has so much more meaning to me. I chose to take that oath, in the original form and language when I qualified. I will not and cannot allow the torture of living beings when I can prevent it."

There was silence around the table as the doctor finished speaking and Tiberius smiled. "I guess there's nothing we can say in response to that—it makes your decision very clear, and we will back you up." He smiled again, remembering how he had doubted her at the start, unsure because Admiral Kehoe had appointed her to the crew in place of the original CMO of the *Victorious*. He had thought she was there to report on them; he had thought so for a long time—right up until the time when he watched her fight to save Ross' life when he was so horribly injured in the unknown attack on Tycho, and then her fight on his own behalf when the energy pulses were tearing his mind apart. "We'll need to put a plan together; decide what we will say and what we will do. And we must work out a safety plan in case everything goes wrong."

Lieutenant Commander Popovych, the chief science officer, looked up. "Would you order the destruction of the *Invincible*? As your father did?"

Everyone looked around at the Ukrainian. It was an understood taboo to speak of what Captain MacAlpin's father had done—only Ross knew the absolute truth; that Stephen MacAlpin had put the plans in place, with the understanding they would be carried out if no other alternative remained, but that he had not given the final orders himself.

The silence that hung in the room was almost tangible, but then Tiberius laughed. "Don't all look at him like that, he has said nothing wrong. His question was a legitimate one, and one I have been refusing to think about. But it is a question we must discuss. Would I go that far to save my crew from whatever the Tamorans are doing? The answer is simple—yes, I would. Without hesitation." He looked around the table again and saw the serious faces. He knew, without having to ask, that they all agreed with him. That he did not have to ask for their support— he already had it. He smiled slightly. "Let's make that a priority for discussion. I'll see you all back here tomorrow morning. If you could all come up with some ideas, we can see what we can put together." He tapped the screen set in the desk in front of him and it flickered and went dark. "Dismissed." He watched the others stand up and file out of the room. He sighed when the door slid shut and he let his head drop down onto the backs of his hands. A chair creaked and he looked up. "I thought you had left."

Ross shook his head. "I thought you could do with some moral support. It was a courageous thing you said then. I know you well enough to know what you said to be true, and that you will keep your word to protect and defend your ship and crew."

"Are you shocked?"

"Shocked?"

"That I said I would destroy the ship if I had no choice."

Ross shook his head. "I think any commanding officer knows they may face such a decision."

"Do you think the crew will think that is my intention?"

Another shake of the head. "No, they will not. With all due respect, you're being silly."

Tiberius burst into a laugh. "You know what is coming when someone says that."

"It is true, Tiberius. We have become good friends and I feel that you expect this frankness on my part. You have to stop thinking the crew will assume you will do the things your father was supposed to have done." Ross stood beside the captain's chair and smiled. "You are a good commanding officer. You have brought us this far and you know that getting us home depends on what you choose to do; how you choose to act could get us all killed." He heard Tiberius catch his breath and knew his words had hit their mark. "If you keep your head, everything will be fine; you'll carry out your orders to negotiate for access to the wormhole, discover what happened to your father and get the precious antidote for Xander. You can't save him if we all die." He stopped there and turned, walking out of the room quickly before Tiberius could call him back. He did not look back, not wanting to see the captain's expression just then. He knew his words had been close to crossing the line, but he also knew that the captain trusted his first officer to tell him the truth, even if it hurt. To say what was on his mind, without fear of being reprimanded. It was part of the job, but he hated to hurt the younger man. He had been through enough from childhood— he did not need his friends and colleagues to hurt him. But he knew that he had had to say it. They had come too far to make mistakes now.

Tiberius did not look up as the door slid shut behind the one man on his command team that could say things like that, and not be reprimanded. He was right—he could lose everything by making one error. He had to pull himself together and to somehow find the strength he did not feel right now to make this mission a success. He tapped the screen in front of him and then paused, his finger hovering over the call icon. Then he stood up and shook his head. Then he sat down again and touched the icon, calling Laura Harsant to come to join him. "Bring coffee," he said. "I need you to go over the Admiral's orders with me." He leaned back in his chair. That was what he would do. He would put together a plan, and then go through it with Ross and the others. They had strict orders, but he had to decide what came first, the treaty negotiations, or the rescue of prisoners on the planet below. He could not shake off the idea that the treaty was a ruse. Words from an ancient poem came to him.

> *Beyond this place of wrath and tears*
> *Looms but the Horror of the shade,*
> *And yet the menace of the years*
> *Finds and shall find me unafraid.*

> *It matters not how strait the gate,*
> *How charged with punishments the scroll,*
> *I am the master of my fate:*
> *I am the captain of my soul.*

He smiled ruefully. He was the master of his fate, the captain of the soul of everyone on board. A slip from him could condemn them all. He stood up and went to the window, looking out into the blackness beyond. There seemed to be no stars here, in the horror of the shade—the darkness. The past, the not knowing, that had been his menace of the years. But he had been afraid. Until now. Any fear he had felt had gone—he knew he was no longer afraid of whatever they might face, whatever the danger. The need to know what had happened, the desperate need to save whatever prisoners there were on the planet below, outweighed any other feeling. He was not afraid any more.

42

"Beauty is not reserved for the gentle"

Doctor Malachi tapped her wrist and gave the captain's call sign. "Captain, may I see you?" The reply came at once, as clear in her ear receiver as if he spoke in the room. "Yes, I'm where you left me." She went at once to the conference room and found him sitting at the table with his aide.

Tiberius looked up from his screen and smiled. "What's up?"

"I had a message, the official invitation, from the Tamorans—they are sending a shuttle for me."

"You accepted?"

She nodded. "I thought I should. We need to know, I need to see what they do."

"Are you afraid?"

She felt his eyes on her face and looked down to see him leaning back in his chair, looking up at her. She smiled. "Of course I am. I know I am going into danger, but we need to learn, to understand, what is going on. I do not believe they will harm me—they know we will expect it." She shook her head as though able to read Tiberius' thoughts. "No, I will not take a guard. I must show them the same respect we showed them on their visit. If I come with an armed guard, they will see we do not trust them, and they will not trust me and will not show me what they do."

"You are a brave and wise woman," Tiberius said.

Doctor Malachi laughed. "Or a foolish one. The shuttle from Tamora will be here shortly. Will you come and see me off?"

Tiberius stood up. "Of course. That will be expected too." He turned back to the table. "Thank you, Laura. Will you send a copy of the orders we have deciphered to Ross and Popovych? Tell them we will discuss later."

Laura Hansart stood up and saluted. "Yes, sir. I will do that at once." She began to gather up what they had been working on, along with the tablet computer. She watched them leave out the corner of her eye and blew Tiberius a kiss when he glanced back. When anyone else was around they had to keep up the appearance and formality expected between the captain and his aide, even though they were secretly in a relationship.

•

When Tiberius and Doctor Malachi reached the hanger deck the Tamoran shuttle had already docked at the external docking bay, and the airlock had just opened to allow one of the shuttle's occupants to come aboard.

The Tamoran had to stoop very low to come through the airlock as he was immensely tall. He straightened up and inclined his head to the captain, giving a form of salute, peculiar to their world. The thumb tips overlapped, and the palms faced down, fingers together, creating a shape almost like a butterfly, and he bowed his head low over his hands. Quick to realize what it was, Tiberius quickly copied the gesture and bowed.

This seemed to please the Tamoran as he smiled as he straightened up. "President Dayelh greets you," he said, his voice only slightly hesitant on the words, showing he had learned them for the occasion. "I am Colonel Daviir, commander of Tamora's armed forces. The doctor is ready?" He turned to Doctor Malachi and bowed to her. Unlike the Tamorans who had attended the meal, he did not wear the heavy cloak the others had worn. Instead, he wore an almost skin-tight outfit of black with braiding on the shoulders giving it the appearance of being a uniform, which Tiberius thought it must be, as he called himself a soldier.

"I am ready," the doctor replied and turned towards the shuttle as Daviir gestured towards it with a wave of his hand.

"Rivkah!"

She turned back as the captain called her; it was unusual for him to use her given name. She smiled, understanding; he was worried about her going alone. "I'll see you later," she responded, waving as Daviir took her hand, politely helping her to step through the airlock and onboard their shuttle.

Tiberius watched the airlock closing behind them, and he tried not to let the sense of foreboding take hold. He hated letting her go off like that; none of them knew what faced them once they were on the planet. And, true to her ideals as a physician, Rivkah

Veritas: The Captain's Redemption

Malachi was unarmed, not even carrying a concealed weapon. To him, that seemed like the worst decision to make; to not even have the chance to defend yourself if the worst happened, but he remembered watching her go through her daily Krav Maga routine and knew she was well able to take care of herself should the need arise. In fact, being a doctor probably meant she knew more ways than one to put someone out of action without causing them actual harm. He smiled slightly when that thought crossed his mind. *Never mess with a medic.*

•

As the strange-looking shuttle disengaged from the *Invincible*'s docking-port and headed towards the blue planet they were orbiting, Rivkah Malachi settled back in her seat and looked at her escort. It was clear English was not a language that came easily to his tongue, but he managed well enough. His accent was clear and clipped, giving his words an odd formality. She guessed he was one of the few who had learned some of other languages, especially as he would work with the president in diplomatic situations. She glanced at him, trying to size him up as they sat side by side in silence. These people were hard to read, like there was always something hidden. He was reasonably good-looking, she thought. Very pale-skinned though, almost a bluish colour. His hair was dark, with some silver threads running through it— older than he looked perhaps. He seemed muscular too, his uniform left little to the imagination and she tried not to be caught looking as she ran her eye over him. She glanced at his back as he leaned forward to reach for something which lay on the empty seat facing them. Something puzzled her. His back was bulkier than the rest of his body, and his outfit seemed to have two long openings down the length of his back. Curious, she asked him about it and then wished she could bite her tongue and take the words back. That was a personal question, and she did not want to cause offence.

He turned and looked at her. "You have never met our people before," he said. "It is understandable to be curious." He stood up slowly, his movements fluid and almost cat-like. He reminded her of a panther moving through the jungle. The next moment she gasped as he turned side on, and immense purple-pink wings unfolded from the two slits in his back. There was just a soft whisper as the feathers rustled and he looked down at her. "Is that what you expected?"

She shook her head. "Not at all. But they are beautiful. Are all of you winged? Do you fly?"

"We can." He let the wings fold and they disappeared inside his suit and he took his seat beside her. "It is one of our abilities." He paused and then added, "Do not tell Dayelh that you know. It is not supposed to be known—we normally wear cloaks to hide them, but I find it cumbersome as a soldier. But I have broken a strict rule by allowing you to see my wings."

She shook her head. "You have my word." Perhaps he would be an unlikely ally; she could get him into trouble with his leader and that was something that obviously bothered him otherwise he would not have mentioned it. She smiled at him, even though there was something very creepy about these people, and she knew they cared nothing for other people—performing unspeakable experiments on others, to further their own species. She hated them for this but was unable to hate the individual. She found him open and willing to talk, and he was not treating her with the arrogant contempt President Dayelh had dished out when he was a visitor on board the *Invincible*. Perhaps there were some Tamorans who were not evil. There was something different about Daviir, he did not seem quite like the others. She could not put her finger on it but there was something. She stood up and went to the window to look out as they came closer to the planet. She was the first of the *Invincible*'s crew to see it for real; the others could only look down on it from orbit.

From a distance, it was a large ice-blue planet, dwarfed by the ringed planet Garion, its sister world, and orbited by its twin moons, Ajax and Hermia. One of the few things that had not been hidden over the years had been the stellar cartography the *Wryneck* had worked on and sent back; this area of space had never been mapped by humans before and the names of planets and moons unknown until these first maps had been drawn up and names given to the celestial objects they came across during the voyage.

Tamora was shrouded by wisps of purple strands of cloud and looked tranquil as the Tamoran shuttle came into land on the landing pad down on the planet. Doctor Malachi was interested to note how it landed differently from their own shuttles, which landed vertically with the use of thrusters. The Tamoran shuttle landed on a short runway, like an old-time aeroplane. She watched another shuttle across the runway and saw how it employed wings, which slid out from the length of its body to land and take off smoothly. Even the shuttle's wings were delicately formed, the edges almost feathered, like the people's wings. She guessed they did not use these light craft for deep space flights and assumed they had more substantial ships.

Daviir saw her looking. "You find them beautiful." It was not a question, but a statement.

She nodded. "I do not understand how the creator of something so beautiful as these wings could be capable of such barbaric tortures as we have heard."

"Beauty, its creation and appreciation, is not reserved for the gentle, and the peaceful. In Earth's history, were not some of the most cultured and creative peoples also those who practiced barbaric punishments, or those whose actions are deemed among the evilest, also were collectors of fine artworks?" Daviir remarked. "Is it not wrong to make assumptions on the basis of those perceptions?"

She smiled. "You are right." She looked at Daviir and smiled again. "Are you trying to change the perceptions we have of your people even though you work closely with the president? You do not like what happens, do you? You are a rebel. Are there others like you?"

"Shhhhh! No-one must ever know. I would be killed if it were discovered." Daviir looked out of the window as the shuttle came to a standstill. "There is a small group of Tamorans who do not want Garion to be re-populated, and certainly not in this way. We are working to try and stop these experiments, but it is not easy—I have lost many of my comrades, and then your ship arrived. This could be the end of this regime and it will not end a moment too soon."

She looked at him. "You are one of the experiments?"

"I am a hybrid, and I have been experimented on as a child. My biological father is one of the prisoners—he was given to my mother for a time. I want to stop what they do and let them go. I have never been able to help him, and I can clear my conscience by getting the prisoners released. I could not do that without a ship coming to the planet. Not many worlds have been right for this—just Earth and one or two others. Most of the experiments are made on humans, they are strong and fight and we—the Tamorans—like that, they make good studies, and are perfect for the hybrid species that will populate our sister world." He paused and then said. "You will be shown the laboratories and I will be there as an armed guard, to make sure that you don't see things not for your eyes—I will look out for you too." He turned his head and met her brown eyes. "I suppose it will be too much to ask if you trust me. We have only just met; I am a member of this barbaric people and I am asking you to trust me."

Rivkah Malachi had always been a good judge of character and knew that she could trust this strange, winged man. She smiled. "You have been honest and open with me, and I do not sense that you are duping me. You are either a very good liar or you are telling me the truth. I believe it to be the latter."

Daviir stood up as the shuttle door slid open. "You will need to keep believing that—I will not be able to show that I am on your side at all. It would mean your death and mine." He stepped out of the shuttle and reached up to take her hand to help her down. "Welcome to Tamora. Please, come with me." His voice had changed subtly as there were soldiers waiting for them, probably the president's guard of which he was commander. He looked at the doctor as he helped her down. "You know you will not be allowed to return to your ship once you have seen this? It never was their intention to let you go."

"Why are you telling me this?"

"My mother is High Lady Delmaa, the president's wife."

"Dayelh is your father? Technically?"

Daviir nodded, tight-lipped. "No more. We must not be seen to have anything between us, it will be fatal for both of us if there is any inkling that I may have spoken."

She nodded. "You can trust me, most definitely." It was enough to know they intended to keep her prisoner and she knew him to be speaking the truth when he said they would not hesitate to kill her. She stood beside him as the soldiers formed ranks behind them and she was escorted off the landing area. A land shuttle awaited them when they left the shuttle dock. Like the air shuttle, it was elegant and streamlined and a dark greyish purple. The party entered the shuttle and took their seats. Daviir spoke to the pilot; their language was spoken rapidly, with a variety of velar sounds, glottal stops, and clicks, and then the Tamoran commander of the guard returned to take his seat beside the doctor.

Rivkah settled back in her seat and looked out of the window, wondering what Tamora's terrain was like. It had been obstructed by the purple clouds shrouding the planet as they came into land. The shuttle took a path to the left of the airbase, skimming three foot above the ground. In moments, trees surrounded them, and the light was almost cut out by the branches and leaves mingling overhead. On emerging from the darkness of the forest, Rivkah blinked as the bright light returned and she saw a huge body of water, almost like a sea. It was surrounded by grassland, but the grass was not green. It reminded her of the savannah lands on Earth, burnt dry by the heat. There were even some animals grazing by the water.

A few minutes further on, the gates the city wall appeared before them. The shuttle stopped as a soldier stepped out of the guardhouse set in the wall by the gates. Daviir stepped out of the shuttle and spoke to the soldier for a few moments and then returned as the gates opened.

Rivkah glanced at him and saw his face was serious. He felt her eyes on his face and glanced up slightly and then looked down.

"Do you have many cities?" she asked, attempting to cover up the awkwardness caused by his trying not to be aware of her scrutiny. "This is your capital?"

"This is the heart of Tamora," Daviir replied. "There are no other cities, only villages where some of our people live, depending on their work. Most live here in Tamora City. The villages are mostly for those who work for the mines."

"It is a beautiful city. That building looks like it comes from an Earth fairytale—an enchanted castle." She pointed to a tall building, appearing to be fashioned from blue and white crystal glass.

Daviir followed her pointing finger. "That is the president's palace and the home of the city council."

The shuttle pulled up in front of a large building and Rivkah guessed it was either a hospital or research facility of some kind. She glanced at Daviir. "Is this the laboratory?"

He nodded. "Yes, this is where our tests and research are carried out—experiments too."

They stepped down from the craft and she was escorted through the doors. A team of scientists greeted her. Scientists—that is was Daviir called them. If these people were the ones who performed the atrocities, they were butchers, not scientists, she thought.

Under cover of looking around, she spoke quickly and quietly into the chip implant in her wrist. "Beauty conceals the darkness. We may have an ally inside—his name is Daviir." She stopped as one of the scientists motioned to her to walk with them. She hoped they had not seen her talking. She needed to keep the only way of communicating with the *Invincible*. She looked over her shoulder and saw Daviir and the guards were not following them and that was when the first real alarm bells rang. *Was I a fool to accept this invitation?* she asked herself. She knew they needed to know the truth, but at what cost?

A door opened to the left of them, and they gestured to her to step into the room. Surprised, she did as she was bidden. This did not seem to be the main thoroughfare, and she had expected to be taken straight to the laboratories. The room was dimly lit, and she suddenly realized there were figures behind her. As she moved to turn, she was restrained by hands on her arms and her arm was turned over, palm upwards. She felt a sharp stab of pain in her wrist and then her head was held. A hand clamped over her mouth stopped her from crying out and her eyes filled with tears of pain at the sharp stab of agony. There was a weird sensation, like hot water filling her ear and she realized it must be blood. Almost like in a dream, she watched her wrist being bandaged and then felt the soft wad of something like cotton wool in her ear. If she had not been held, she would have fallen; she felt giddy and a bit sick from the sudden pain.

•

Tiberius turned suddenly to Lieutenant Commander Popovych. "Doctor Malachi's signal has dropped—get her back!"

The science officer nodded and turned to his computer and began to work. After a moment, he called the communications officer over and the two put their heads together.

Tiberius watched them, and the more time that elapsed, the less confident he felt. He had every faith in his officers' abilities, but this worried him.

His fears were realized a moment later when the Ukrainian came over. "Captain, I am sorry. There is no connection. It is like she does not exist."

"Nothing?!"

"Nothing, sir. Not even static. We just have to hope she is all right."

"Do you think they knew about the implants? They may have seen her pass that message on." Tiberius was very concerned. She was his responsibility—even though she had volunteered to go; it was her choice, her decision. He had voiced his concerns but, at the same time, had agreed to her going. Had he been wrong to let her take that risk? "Zeal!"

The communications officer swung round on his chair so fast he almost fell off at the sound of the captain's voice—it had almost been a roar.

"Get me the president!"

Lieutenant Zeal swung back, and his hands raced over his control panel, sending a signal to the planet. "Come in, Tamora. This is the *Invincible*. Captain MacAlpin requests communication with President Dayelh."

Tiberius drummed his fingers on the arm of the command chair as he listened to Zeal repeating the message over and over. "They're not responding?"

Zeal shook his head. "No, sir."

"Threaten them. Tell them we have our weapons locked on and will open fire."

Everyone on the bridge looked round in shock. That was something they would never resort to so soon. The captain always insisted you only fired on an enemy if they fired first. You only ever reacted in self-defence, weaponry was not to be used as a threat. Zeal swallowed hard, looking around at the others. He knew better than to question the order, the look on the captain's face boded ill for anyone who did.

Ross leaned over. "Captain, if they persist in their silence, you will have to follow through. You will have to open fire."

Tiberius looked at him in silence. "Belay that order."

Ross closed his eyes for the fraction of a second in relief. "Zeal, keep trying to raise them."

The Tamoran radio operator looked up at Dayelh. "They are still trying, President."

"How long?"

"Twenty minutes."

"You may respond."

The operator leaned forward and flicked a switch. "Come in, *Invincible*. How can we assist?"

Tiberius almost rocketed out of his seat. "We have lost contact with Doctor Malachi—her signal has dropped completely. You told me there would be no interference. I want to speak to her—now!"

Dayelh's voice, very soft but at the same time still harsh came through. "I am unaware of any interference. Your doctor has been escorted to the laboratories as arranged for a tour of our facilities. There may be signal issues because of the equipment. I can send a message to her escort and ask that she contacts you. Will that suffice?"

Tiberius dug his nails into his palms in an effort to calm his fraying temper. Dayelh's quiet voice had really got to him and he was trying not to lose control. "You have thirty minutes, then we take action." He frowned as the communication was abruptly terminated. "Damn them! Something is wrong, I know it."

•

The hands holding the doctor's arms were removed and she was able to stand alone. She was taken down a maze of corridors, past lots of closed doors. They were not ordinary doors—they had a shutter in them, and a trap-door—like prison doors. The shutter would be slid open, and the prisoner checked on without anyone having to go inside the cell. She wondered who were concealed behind those doors. After what seemed like ages, she was led into a large room filled with light and she looked around. She did not need to be told what this room was, she had seen many of them. It was a hospital operating theatre. And it was in use. There was a figure lying on the operating table and she only needed a quick glance to see it was a woman. A closer look revealed the woman's wrists and ankles were strapped down, and her face wore an expression of abject fear. Her head turned from side to side, almost frantically, as she struggled to free her arms and legs. Rivkah saw she was gagged, a fact which, no doubt, added to the woman's terror.

Rivkah turned back to the Tamorans. "What are you doing to her?" She was not sure she wanted to know the answer. She could feel the woman's pleading eyes on her as clearly as if she were looking at her.

One of the Tamorans pulled her aside and held out a bundle of silvery cloth. She looked around and saw the others were pulling on the cloths, and she saw it was a long robe, a surgeon's gown. She shook her head resolutely. "No! I will not be a part of this."

"You have little choice," one of the Tamorans responded. It was the first time any of the aliens had spoken to her, and she had begun to think that they could not speak English. He held her arm and pulled the gown over her head and fastened it. "You will perform the operation. A test. Will you kill her to save her or not?"

She stared at him, her anger plainly obvious. They were going to force her to perform whatever operation they wanted on this terrified woman and it was clear they meant to do it without the use of any anaesthetic. Almost stunned with shock and anger she saw her hands being forced into gloves of the same colour as the gown and her long hair was pulled inside a cap. She was almost shaking—they must have meant this from the beginning. Right from the first invitation, and she had walked into their trap.

Two young male Tamorans yanked her back to the operating table and covered the lower half of her face with a mask, identical to the ones they wore. She was handed a tray of medical instruments and she took a moment to examine them. They were similar to instruments she would use herself, although many of her procedures were performed with a greater level of technology than presented to her now. She looked up, turning to the Tamoran to her right. "I can't do this."

"You have no choice. If you do not comply, we will kill her and then you." He sounded totally calm, as though he had just made any statement, and not threatened her with death. He held out a clear liquid-filled receptacle which contained, Rivkah realized with horror, a foetus.

With hands that shook slightly, she took the jar and peered closely through the liquid. The foetus seemed to be about 11-weeks old as she could see limbs were developing and ears and eyelids forming. She could also see clearly that it would be male. Then it dawned on her—she was being asked to transplant this foetus into the womb of the woman on the table. It was Tamoran. She could see the buds on its back that would grow into the wings when it was older. The woman on the table was not Tamoran, she was human. Further realization dawned on her. Tamoran babies were being borne by women held captive and she wondered why. Was this part of the experiments they carried out?

The woman on the table was looking at her, eyes wide with fear. She had to do it—this young woman would die if she refused. She knew the Tamorans were not bluffing when they said they would kill her. She looked back at the Tamorans and then picked up the scalpel lying on the tray. "*S'lach li, Avi, s'lach li*," she whispered as she turned back to the table. *Forgive me, Father.* A quick prayer was all she had time for.

43
Losing Contact

Doctor Malachi was dragged into one of the little cell-like rooms after she cleaned up. She did not go quietly but struggled and fought the whole way. "How dare you do this?! I was invited by your president!"

The Tamorans laughed—a harsh grating sound. Then the one who spoke English said, "For an educated woman, you are being incredibly naive and stupid. President Dayelh planned it this way. The invitation—well, it would have been discourteous to abduct you from the ship under the nose of your already suspicious captain!"

She staggered as she was shoved inside and, as the door was slammed, she pounded on it with her fists and continued to do so even after the sound of the door being locked, followed by footsteps leaving, showed her the futility of what she was doing.

"It's no use doing that." A voice spoke from the darkness behind her. "They will not return, and you will only hurt your hands."

Rivkah turned slowly and looked into the direction of the voice. It was too dark to see. That it was a woman's voice was all she could say for sure. She peered into the darkness again, but the blackness was so dense it seemed almost tangible. Even though her eyes grew used to the dark, she still could not see who had spoken.

"They will hurt you if you make a noise. We all used to."

Rivkah slid down the door, her back against the unyielding surface. She looked in the direction of her unseen companion and sighed, beginning the strangest conversation she had ever had—talking to a woman she could hear but not see. "I don't understand. I was invited here."

"We all came under an invitation—I was brought from a neighbouring world. President Dayelh's intimation to my family was for me to be the bride of his son. You were brought here because of your skill as a surgeon, and you're a human doctor. You will try to save lives every time so their experiments will be safe with you."

Rivkah leaned her head back against the door. "How do you know?"

"I heard them talking. They'll use you if it comes to a hostage situation."

•

For what seemed like the millionth time, Tiberius looked up, running his hand through his wavy dark-copper hair. It was short to regulation standards, almost the old military 'short back and sides', but since he had almost been killed by his headaches, he kept it longer on top and the crew were well-used to seeing their skipper run his hand over his forehead and through the wavy lock that fell onto his brow. It was one of his mannerisms that would have been missed if he stopped. It made him seem more like one of them—that he had a habit which always surfaced under stress.

He had been doing it a lot for the past few hours and Ross was watching him covertly, preparing to suggest he take a break. He knew the captain was worried about the silence from the doctor and shared his fears, but it would not be good for him to break under the strain. It was one of his jobs to suggest a course of action to the commanding officer, and to look out for his welfare. He took that role seriously. The captain's well-being—physical, mental, and emotional—was important to the health of the ship and crew, important to the success of the mission. He was aware of the mounting strain in the captain's face and demeanour, and he was concerned. Dayelh had been given half an hour to have the doctor make contact—and that had expired six hours ago.

Ross gnawed his lip when the captain demanded of Commander Popovych again why he had not got the connection with the doctor back. He saw the science chief was looking even more stressed than the captain as he was asked yet again to achieve the impossible. The tension on the bridge was oppressive. He stood up when Tiberius slammed his hand on the arm of his chair and demanded an answer from Popovych.

"Captain, I cannot give you an answer." The Ukrainian's voice was tired and subdued. "I cannot give you the answer you want—there is no connection." His fingers were still working but they were shaking.

Ross made up his mind. "Captain, can I speak to you in private? Now!" he added as Tiberius seemed about to refuse him. He leaned forward slightly. "Your ready room. Now…sir." He added the last as an afterthought. He did not want to sound as though he was giving an order. "It is important."

Tiberius nodded. "Right now?" He stood up and headed across the bridge to the door leading to his ready room. He sat down at the desk and looked at Ross who stood in front of the desk, waiting for the doors to close before he spoke. "Is something wrong, Kirbie? You sounded rather fierce."

"Permission to speak freely, sir?"

Tiberius looked closely at him. "Are you okay? You keep calling me 'sir', that's not like you. What's up?"

"What the *hell* are you playing at?" Ross demanded. "Poor Popovych is trying to do what you ask—he's told you his instruments are fine, but the connection is gone. He can't get it back if it is not there anymore. You are demanding blood from a stone—he's got nothing more to give. He's a science officer, not a wizard! I know you are worried about the doctor but alienating the crew is not going to make things any better. The tension out there is almost tangible, and the crew are noticing. You can't afford to slip up like this."

Tiberius' mouth had dropped open at the word 'hell' and he had continued to sit there in total silence, waiting for Ross to finish. "Leave," he said, his voice hard, as though he was having difficulty in restraining himself.

"Sir… I…"

"Go!" Tiberius rapped. "I need to think!"

Ross swung on his heel and strode out of the room. He went directly to his seat and leaned back, his eyes closed for a moment. It was only momentary, but it did not go unnoticed.

Lieutenant Zeal, the communications officer, turned around. "How did it go?"

"I don't think it went at all, please don't ask any questions," Ross responded. "I think everyone is a little tired—there is a lot of strain just now."

Anton Popovych looked up from his position at the science station. "It is my fault. I could not get him the answers he wants."

Ross looked across. "No, it's not. I know he has a lot of respect for the skills and talents of crew members, but that does not give him the right—even as captain—to treat anyone like dirt because they cannot give an answer. If the connection were there, you would have got it back. The fact that you cannot, means that something serious has happened, and we should be applying our efforts to finding out what that is. I think the captain understands that now."

After the door had closed behind Ross, Tiberius sat for a long while in silence. He had been shocked by Ross' anger, but now he thought about it, it was completely understandable and totally deserved. He was wrong to have spoken like that when he knew the science officer was trying his hardest to reconnect with the doctor's signal. He was quick-tempered but usually had it under control and Ross had made him very ashamed of his outburst. Before he could think any more about it, he raised his wrist to his mouth and gave Popovych's call sign, and then asked him to step into the ready room.

Popovych responded and then turned and looked at Ross. "He's asked to see me."

Ross nodded. "Don't keep him waiting." He smiled, understanding Popovych had been hurt. He watched the Ukrainian stand up and cross the bridge to the door behind which the captain was waiting.

Tiberius looked up and smiled. "Sit down." He paused while the science officer sat opposite him and then said "I owe you an apology—a big one. I know you are unable to reconnect, and I expected you to be able to do the impossible. And I was angry with you." He held up his hand as Popovych went to speak. "No, please let me finish. I have allowed my temper to get between myself and the rest of the crew, allowing my personal feelings to get in the way. My determination to get the answers I want has allowed harm to come to some—such as Commander Ross' injuries, and that we have now lost contact with Doctor Malachi, and I have now injured your feelings when I know you have done everything possible. I ask for your forgiveness."

Popovych's blue eyes twinkled. He was a pleasant-tempered man and forgave easily. He smiled. "You do not need my forgiveness, but I will accept your apology. The fact that you expect the impossible means you think highly of our skills. We do what we are able to do, it is natural for the captain to demand highly." He held out his hand and the captain shook it gladly.

"What is your opinion?" Tiberius asked. "I have not allowed you to tell me."

Popovych looked up. "I do not believe she is dead, but I believe they know of how we communicate, and they have removed the device from her. As soon as that was done, the connection would have been severed."

"Can you be certain she is not dead?"

"No, of course not, but I do not think they want her dead—at least not just now. They have a purpose, just as we have always thought. They will find her skills useful, and I suspect she will be forced into working with them, and that she will be an excellent bargaining tool for the Tamorans." The Ukrainian held the captain's gaze, watching for his reaction. "I am sorry, it would probably be better if she were dead, from what we know of them."

Tiberius stood up. "Then we must plan a way to rescue her and put an end to what these people do. I cannot stand by and know that they are mutilating and torturing people who can no longer defend themselves. It makes me sick."

"You know Ross will not let you go," the science officer responded. "You will not be allowed off the ship when there is every chance you will be captured and killed."

"My life is just as expendable as the next."

Popovych shook his head. "That is not so, the ship needs the captain. You are needed to coordinate the mission and get us home." He stood up and looked down at his commanding officer who was just a little shorter. "We are here to obey your orders, and we look to you to get us home safely. What you say is to be done, will be done. But we will not risk your life. If Admiral Kehoe has planned some catastrophe, then we have the means by which we can confound her."

Tiberius exhaled slowly through his nose. The science officer was right; that was why a commanding officer had a crew. They were the ones to face unknown dangers—that was their role. It did not make him happy though, he hated sending them into dangers he was forbidden to share. Constant reminders of his duty as the commanding officer—to remain in command—that he could not be so easily replaced. His crew were relying on him to get them out of this one and see them safely home. It did not help that every time he was reminded of this, he remembered that his father had left the ship and that something had prevented his return, leaving the second officer in the unenviable position of being the one responsible for making what would have been the hardest decision of her entire life. He nodded. "Of course.

323

We will devise a plan of action. You're dismissed for now." He watched him leave before he stood up and returned to the bridge. Pausing by the communications station, he spoke quietly for a moment and then took his usual seat.

Lieutenant Zeal put the message out that all command team officers were to report to the main briefing room in precisely thirty minutes. "That is at 15:55, Comms out."

Ross glanced at Tiberius. "We're going down?"

A brief nod was the only answer he got.

44

"It won't hurt if you let go"

The tunnels and caves below the planet's surface were dark and dank. A stream ran through the centre of the main one. It was wide and ran fast, showing the ground sloped the deeper into the cave it progressed. The ground, where it was not rocky, was thick with dark slimy clay-like mud that clung to the feet and legs of the prisoners who were forced to work down there. It was dark, the only light coming from lanterns fixed at intervals in little alcoves scraped out in the walls. That morning when the prisoners were marched in, the long line chained together at the ankles as always, there was a noticeable change in the air and not for the better. The guards, who were always cruel, were tense and even harsher than normal. They carried their usual heavy-duty whips and lashed them more often. One of the prisoners slipped and fell, pulling down the two chained in front and behind him. All three were beaten and then dragged back to their feet. No-one else dared to fall, even a stumble was punished with a lash across naked shoulders. It was easy to slip and fall as, with chains on their wrists, they could not save themselves easily and today it seemed that the guards were aching for any chance to brutalize their prisoners.

Stephen MacAlpin, at the head of the chained column, slipped on the slimy ground and almost fell, and would have dragged half the line down with him. He gritted his teeth hard as the whip lashed across the back of his neck, adding to the scars and welts he already bore. He would not give them the satisfaction of hearing him cry out in pain. He felt the hands of the woman behind him on his elbow, awkwardly managing to support him despite her chained wrists. He steadied himself and carried on walking. He wondered if the change in the guards was because of the ship that had been reported as having arrived at Tamora. Could this possibly mean that there could be an end to their suffering? He slipped and fell a couple more times and was roughly dragged up and given five lashes every time he fell. They normally got a few beatings for falling, but this was worse than usual.

After what seemed ages, the prisoners reached the main cave and the linking chains linking were unfastened, leaving them free to move independently of each other although their wrists and ankles were locked in heavy cuffs with enough chain to allow them to walk and to use tools as they were forced to endure hard labour from daybreak to nightfall, every day. There were many fights among the prisoners; they had looked out for each other at the very start, but it was everyone for themselves now. Food was scarce, and less had been provided every day. Stale bread and strips of raw meat did not go a long way to stave off hunger, and the water they were given to drink was thick with mud. They drank it because they had no choice. When the guards brought the food, they kept the prisoners back at gunpoint. A month ago a Tamoran guard had been killed when he omitted to keep the prisoners back and they had rushed him. More guards had rushed to help and there had been executions that night in revenge. Only Stephen MacAlpin never fought and was never attacked by the others. He worked alongside them and refused to eat until others had, and usually was offered a handful by one of the younger prisoners. They had, in their desperate way, a lot of respect for the man many called father due to his age and the length of time he had been held a captive. Some of them marvelled the man was still alive. He often wondered the same. Every day that passed, he expected to be his last and even more so these days.

He picked up the hammer and chisel he used to chip at the rock. He was used to the cold and dark down here too. The passing days had soon been lost in time, and he no longer remembered how long he had been a prisoner, but he knew it was a long time. His red hair had faded into grey and was worn long. They all had long hair, and most of the men had beards, but Stephen managed to maintain a relatively clean-shaven face, using a sharp rock to scrape his face, leaving just stubble behind.

The guard in charge of the work party thrust a short-handled pick into Stephen's hands and shoved him towards the rock face. The old man stumbled as he was pushed; his bare foot struck a rock, but he did not cry out—he was beyond the point where pain bothered him, acclimatized to it over long years but that did not mean it did not hurt any less and he glanced down and saw the blood around the broken nail. He angered the guards by his refusal to be cowed. His strength and courage were how he had quickly been recognized as the leader of the prisoners; the one they all had turned to when things got tough. It was as though the older man's courage in the face of adversity gave them all strength when they needed it most. The rumour was still going around that a ship from Earth was orbiting Tamora, but it had never been confirmed or denied. Stephen wondered, and not for the first time, if this could somehow be the end to their ordeal.

It was dark where he stood, the light from the closest lantern did not penetrate the gloom and he felt with his hands for the cut in the rock face where he had begun working the day before. He swung the pick with the steady rhythm of long practice. For people kept on the barest minimum of food and water for survival, long hard years of constant labour had kept them reasonably fit and muscular. He chipped away at the rock, keeping his mind fixed on the task in hand. He had found, early on, that allowing his mind to dwell on anything else was just distressing. He never forgot; he just had to bury it deep inside his heart.

Suddenly, his pick buried itself deeper in the rock than it should have and he tried to wrench it free. The whole rock face seemed to shift and, with a roaring sound, exploded inwards. Stephen turned and tried to run but the chain linking his ankles hindered him. He stumbled and went down under the rush of rock with a cry. The others working nearby dropped their tools and hurried over, immediately starting to scrabble at the rocks, dragging the huge pieces aside to rescue the man buried underneath. The conditions were made harder by their chains and the water which was now gushing through the cavity and it was steadily rising among the rocks, unable to drain away due to the clay-like mud in which they were kneeling. Hearing the commotion, guards appeared with lanterns. One of the prisoners shouted out who was under the rubble and the guards broke into a run, grabbing for picks and shovels. They were under orders to protect Stephen from harm. He was very important to the Tamorans' experiments and they risked execution if he died on their watch. Lanterns where thrust into the hands of two of the women, with a terse order to stand up and hold them so they could see, and then the guards pitched in to help the prisoners. One of the prisoners uncovered a hand.

As Stephen fell, he had flung out his arms and his hand moved slightly as the weight of the rocks was lifted off. He felt someone take hold of his hand in theirs and squeeze his fingers to reassure him. He tried to move but the weight of the entire section of the rock face pinned him down. It was eerily quiet, and he was struggling to breathe as the fall had knocked the breath out of him and the rocks pressing down on his back made it difficult for his lungs to expand. Then he felt water around his face and almost panicked. He couldn't move his head and felt the water beginning to creep into his mouth and nose and he was choking. His head ached and he knew he must have been unconscious momentarily and remembered something hitting the back of his head. He faintly heard voices—urgent, shouting voices. Someone was saying something about the water rising too fast. It was. It had risen up the side of his head and he could feel it in his ears and his throat. *It won't hurt if you let go*, he told himself. He couldn't hold his breath; there was no breath to hold as there was no room for his lungs to expand. *Just let go and it will all be over.*

Suddenly he felt the air on his face and hands under his face, lifting it out of the water. He gasped, coughing up water and bits of clay that he had breathed in. His lungs fought desperately to draw in oxygen, but he was in obvious pain and having great difficulty breathing. His face twisted with pain and his breathing became more laboured. His skin had a bluish cast, and he made a few frantic efforts to breathe before bloody foam suddenly formed on his lips and the man holding his head up out of the water found he had blood on his fingers.

"Can you breathe?" the man asked anxiously.

The answer was the merest shake of his head and more blood trickling from the corner of his mouth. The pain was so much now that his senses began to swim. His chained hands clawed at the wet clay for a moment before his head slumped in the hands that supported it.

One of the guards rapped something in his own tongue and, turning, ran as fast as he could towards the entrance to the mine.

•

Rivkah Malachi blinked as light suddenly streamed into the cell as the door opened and it took a moment for her eyes to adjust, and she recognized her escort. "Daviir?"

"Hurry, we need you in the hospital," Daviir said. "There has been a bad accident. Our most important prisoner has been critically injured—he is human, and your skill will be better than ours."

She slowly left the cell and was surprised that her arms were not immediately pinioned. Her face was covered with a cloth tied behind her head and she groped for Daviir's arm.

"I'm sorry, they don't want you to know the way. Just keep hold of my arm."

She understood and did not resist however much she wanted to; if she did not know the way from the cell to the hospital block or the laboratories, then she could not try and escape, they knew that. Right now though, her thoughts were occupied with the fact that she was needed as a doctor. She held onto the soldier's arm and shuffled along beside him, the short chain linking her ankles preventing her from moving at her normal pace. That was why it was almost unnecessary for them to bind her arms. She would not get far, even if she tried.

When they stopped, the blindfold was removed, and she looked around as Daviir stooped and removed the ankle shackles. "You will not get far even if you do run," he said. "But I think your vocation would not allow you to do so right now."

He was right. A gravely injured man was more important than her desire to get away from these people. She looked around. It was a different room to the one she had seen before and guessed the main hospital and the labs were kept separate. From what she could see, it was a fully equipped operating theatre, with what seemed to be a couple of private rooms to the side.

Two Tamoran nurses appeared beside her and she was assisted into the same silvery surgical gown she had worn before and hands tied back her long black hair, tucking it inside a cap. She was directed to a sink and she scrubbed her hands ready for whatever procedure with which she would be faced. The injured prisoner must be pretty important, she thought, for them to be making this much of a fuss over him when mostly they seemed to torture and maim them. This was different even special somehow. She heard the sound of running feet and wheels and the doors at the far end swung open and a wheeled stretcher was rushed in by an armed escort.

Rivkah watched as a naked man, covered in mud and blood, was transferred to the table and covered with a sheet of the same silvery material as her gown.

Daviir spoke rapidly to the guards and then turned to the doctor. "A rock face collapsed in the mine, trapping the prisoner underneath for a long time. The rising water has almost drowned him, and there are multiple fractures and crush injuries. They say he has been bleeding from the mouth and has not been breathing at all for the past few minutes. Before that, his breathing caused great distress."

Rivkah nodded and beckoned to the nurses. "Do you understand my language?" she demanded, knowing an inability to communicate would make things difficult.

One of the nurses nodded. "I understand enough English to serve the esteemed surgeon," he said formally.

The other nurse shook her head. "Very little," she said, almost shyly.

Rivkah found herself wondering again if all the Tamorans were cruel or if those trained in medicine were different—trained to ease suffering, not to cause it as the scientists did. She turned again to the table and inspected the prisoner. The injured man's eyes were covered. It seemed mandatory; if the prisoners were not in the cells or the mines then their eyes were covered. She set the female nurse to use a suction device to clean the airways which were likely blocked from the water and clay he had inhaled. She pulled the sheet back a moment and frowned before calling Daviir over. "Take the chains off. He's not going anywhere!" she added when he hesitated.

Daviir blushed slightly at the disdain in her voice and took out a strange-looking device, unfastened the cuffs and removed them.

Rivkah looked at the scars upon scars on the man's wrists and ankles. They told of years of being forced to wear the chains constantly; to work in them. She wondered if he still struggled to break free, or if that futility had abandoned him. The pale skin was scarred with the marks of many serious beatings and there were dozens of marks of old wounds, some of which had not healed well. A glance at his feet showed the broken nails and misshapen toes—he had broken all his toes at one point. Hardly surprising, she thought, if they were forced to work barefoot in the mines. He was, all in all, a thorough mess, made even worse by the new injuries caused by immense falling rocks. A quick examination of his chest and stomach showed broken ribs and internal injuries so she set to work stabilizing him and then reached for a scalpel. She needed to operate. Back on the

330

Invincible, she had equipment by which she could diagnose the condition with a quick scan. Here, he needed to be opened up to give her any clues. And she hated to do that; there was so much that could be done without putting his already battered body through the trauma of being cut open. She showed the other nurse where she wanted to make the incisions and asked him to sterilize those areas. "There's too much mud," she said, "And he is already at risk of infection." She checked the progress of the other nurse and then decided to put her patient on oxygen at this point and hunted through the various drugs and found something to sedate him once they got him breathing.

Later that evening, Doctor Malachi returned to the private room where her patient lay. She stood by the bed in silence for a few minutes and saw his eyes were still covered. She felt a deep wave of sympathy for this poor man who, she had been told, had his eyes covered every time he left the dingy light of the mines. They told her it was to stop the bright daylight damaging his eyes after the darkness he was used to, but she thought it was more likely that it was to keep him from knowing where he was. She stooped over and gently laid her hand on his arm. "Don't be afraid," she said kindly. "You are in hospital, you were in an accident."

The man nodded slightly. "I remember." He moved a hand slightly, as though about to reach for his head.

A gentle hand laid his hand back down and tucked it under the sheets. "Don't touch it," she said. "You have some nasty cuts and bumps on the head—your head is bandaged. I am not one of them. I am a doctor from Earth." She made a quick decision and turned the lights low. "I'm going to take the blindfold off. Can you see without it?" She wondered if years in the dark had damaged his eyesight and she wanted to check. She had been commanded to care for him and she was going to use that to her advantage.

"If it isn't too bright." His voice was quiet and ragged with pain.

She slid her fingers down his arm and felt his pulse. It was racing so she slipped a couple of pills between his lips and helped him sip some water. "That will help with the pain." Getting him comfortable again, she unfastened the blindfold and removed it slowly.

He went to screw his eyes shut and she gently put her hand over them and told him to relax and let the light in slowly. "There, that's not bad, is it?"

He shook his head slightly and let his eyes flicker open.

Rivkah smiled. "Lie still, you're not going back to the mines for a long time—the injuries are severe, and they know you have to rest and recover before you are of any use to them again." She was looking at his face as she spoke. He was an older man, she could see that, but guessed he was younger than he looked—hardship had aged him considerably. His eyes were a grey-green, and there was something oddly familiar about his features, despite the lines.

"Can I see? My face, I mean."

Rivkah hunted around and found a mirror and held it up. She wondered how long it was since he had seen his face. She found some wipes and began to clean his face. "We had to cut your hair very short to get at the wounds." She remembered the argument with the Tamorans—the man was unconscious and still they would not let the blindfold be removed. She had to work around that impediment.

"It's been long for so many years, I had forgotten what short hair was like." He turned his head away slightly, not wanting to look any more.

She held up a razor. "Would you like a proper shave?" She smiled when he nodded, and she sat on the edge of the bed and began to shave him. As she got through to the skin, she saw the scars and knew he had tried to keep the growth down himself, probably with a sharp stone. When she had finished, he slowly reached up with one hand and touched his face and then smiled.

The smile startled her, not because she did not expect him to smile but because years dropped from his face when he smiled, and she was again hit with the belief that she had seen him before; or at least someone who looked like him. "My name is Rivkah, Rivkah Malachi. What should I call you?"

"Stephen," he replied. "Stephen MacAlpin." It had been a long time since he had said his name out loud, and he was pleased to hear the sound of it. Her sudden gasp made him turn his head. "What's wrong?"

"You were the captain of the *Wryneck*?"

He nodded slightly. His head hurt too much to do more. He took a ragged breath and closed his eyes a moment. The painkillers were helping a little by now. "Yes. I have been here a long time, it must be over thirty years now. They won't let me die like they let the others."

She reached over and touched his cheek. "I will get you away from here. I swear it."

"They say there is a ship in orbit. Are you from there?"

She nodded. "I am." She watched his face. "They believed you were killed when your ship was lost."

"I wish I had been. What is her name?"

"The *Invincible*." She watched his face. "Her captain is your son."

"Tiberius is a captain? Can you speak to him? Tell him to get the ship away—they'll do it all over again!"

He began to get agitated, and she put her hand on his shoulder. "Keep calm," she said gently.

He took a few moments and then managed to calm himself although his pulse was racing. "How long have you been here? Have they told you about Xander? How long after we were captured was he killed?"

She saw the grief in his eyes and wondered how he had kept going all these years while grieving for his best friend, and his entire crew. "They didn't kill him. He was held a prisoner for ten years and then released as part of a trade deal. He was very ill— they tortured him and infected him with a serious disease. A new medication has been found that helps with the symptoms and he is beginning to get better. He was promoted to Rear Admiral just before we left on our voyage." She watched his face and saw a tear slide down his cheek and she smiled softly. "He resisted death, just as you did."

"I heard him screaming every night," Stephen replied. He felt her hand on his shoulder and smiled slightly. "You promised to get me away from here. How can you? You are a prisoner too, aren't you?"

She nodded. "I am. They force me to help with their experiments. But I try and do what I can for those poor people. I think I have a way to save everyone that I can, but I will say nothing for now. If you don't know, they cannot force you to betray me. Not that I think you would." She saw him smile again and at that moment, all the trouble and pain left his face until the smile faded.

Stephen closed his eyes, leaned back, and struggled for a few breaths and she watched a while, making mental notes, and then decided to put him back on oxygen so he did not have to fight with his injuries to get the breath into his lungs. She busied herself for a moment with equipment and then asked if he felt more comfortable. He nodded a little and seemed to relax. She took a hypodermic and turned his arm over, preparing to give him a sedative. She examined the scars and saw the marks of many needles.

He saw her looking. "They did a lot of tests and experiments in the first few years before I was chosen."

"Chosen?"

"For their breeding program. I was deemed very fertile. That is why they have kept me in reasonable health, despite the suffering in the mines. Many of the prisoners here are born from what they take from me. They are, essentially, my children."

She said nothing but listened, the syringe unused in her hand.

"Milked like cattle for our sperm. There are a few of the males who are kept fit for this. The females who are chosen for the ability to carry healthy babies are kept like caged hens. Carrying babies of other species, but with the Tamoran strain that mutates them. I have seen them—winged creatures. The poor babies have no chance, they develop their wings about six months after birth. Then they are sent away to the other planet. They don't see their mothers, and the women are immediately impregnated again; giving them no time to adjust to giving birth and having the baby taken away."

"Do you see them? The women?"

He shook his head. "There is no contact once they are visibly pregnant. The ones who do not show so quickly are still working in the mines until it is obvious. Some of them hide it and hope the work will be too hard and heavy for them and they will lose the baby—anything to save the child from what it will become." He closed his eyes and the doctor put her hand on his arm.

"No more, just sleep now. You need a lot of rest." She gently slipped the needle into his arm and soothed him when he flinched. "This will ease the pain and help you sleep." She watched as his eyes closed and she put her fingers on his pulse and counted until it slowed, and she knew he was asleep. She sat beside the bed and recorded the surgery notes the Tamorans requested. She recorded another set, giving an account of what she had learned from him. She recorded this set in Hebrew so they would be concealed as if in code. She had just finished when she heard a soft sound, like a rustle of a large bird's wings, and she turned and Daviir was standing beside her.

"He rests?" the Tamoran asked.

She nodded. "The injuries are serious, but he will recover with rest. He must remain here and not be taken back to the mines."

Daviir nodded. "The orders are that you will do everything you see fit to preserve his health and strength."

She was silent a moment and remembered their conversation on the shuttle. "You said you are not fully Tamoran," she said suddenly. "Are there many of you who are not of full blood?"

Daviir nodded. "I am not fully of my people, as I told you. I am a product of the experiments. An early one—I was born without wings and had them transplanted when I was three years old."

"You said the President is your father."

He laughed slightly, a harsh sound. "In as much as he raised me as his son."

"So one of the prisoners?"

He nodded. "Yes, and one of the women carried me until birth when I was handed to my mother, Delmaa." He looked at her and then pointed at Stephen. "He is the man whose sperm fathered me. We don't usually find out, but Dayelh took pleasure in telling me."

She stared at him, scarcely able to believe it. "How does that feel? To see him an old, broken man—a prisoner of a people who do this, and shut him away in the dark for over thirty years?"

"His spirit is not broken," Daviir replied. "He is a brave, strong man but I would never dare to let him know that he is my father."

She watched his face, searching for any signs that he was lying. She saw none. "I want to save them."

He knew what she meant. "I have a few of the experiments, the ones who did not work out and were cast aside to make way for the more advanced mutations. We are made to serve those who have had more work done on their forming. We are the soldiers and workers—the mine guards. Not deemed fit enough to live on the old world and make it thrive again. Do you want an uprising? You will need a man who can lead an army. I am the commander of the guard. I have a lot of importance at the palace, and I am the president's son—none would question me although he does not acknowledge me publicly because of my imperfections. I think he made me colonel because he had to treat me differently to the others."

"You would do that? You would risk your life and the lives of others like you to save them?" She was still watching his face.

He nodded. "I have never liked what is done. Genetic experiments are one thing but to torture someone—hearing them screaming continually, begging to die, then hearing the screams choked off and knowing they have not been put out of their suffering but gagged so they can no longer scream with the pain. I do not like the torture and I do not like the reason for it. It is to find the strongest ones—they are then modified to withstand the harsh elements of Garion. Only the ones who survive the torture, and the genetic enhancements, get to be selected."

"What about diseases? Do they find a way to stop illnesses?" She was thinking of Xander and the disease he had been returned with. "Did you ever hear of one who was sent back to Earth?"

Daviir nodded. "They do test for disease and try to find a vaccine." He paused and then said, "That was before I was born. But I have heard of him. He was very ill and was not going to live. They returned him to your people as part of a hostage deal. His records are in the laboratory."

"Do you know what the disease was? It was one that was created and mutated, wasn't it?"

He nodded again. "He got sick, and they changed it to see how bad it could be before the vaccine stopped working. It was like cancer but much worse. I hope he died soon after his release," he added. "I have seen the footage—he was in a very bad way."

Rivkah smiled. "He lived despite the odds and is an old man now, but he still serves. He is still ill, but something was found to help him. I want the vaccine to take back and cure him completely. Will you help us? I need to call my ship."

"If we are caught, we will be killed. Are you prepared to take that risk?"

She met his eyes with light-brown eyes that did not falter. "I have always been prepared to put my life on the line for my comrades, and my people. I am a doctor, and I will not bear arms in battle, but I will fight if I have to. If you and your secret army are true, then I will not need to raise a hand against another living being, but to tend to the prisoners."

Daviir smiled. "I believe you," he said. "It takes more courage to face war with peace. I respect you for your determination not to kill, not even an enemy. How can you do that?"

"I swore an oath to protect life," Rivkah replied. "But many thousands of years ago, my people also were commanded not to kill—I have lived by that command all my life." She smiled. "It is very hard not to raise a hand in anger. I see so much suffering here and I do feel a burning desire to wipe out the people who have done this, but I will not."

"You would have others do it for you?"

"Sometimes it is necessary. I know that." She reached out and touched his back right where the ridges around the wing slits were. "Does it hurt?"

"Not anymore, but it did when I was a child. It is normally done as a baby, but I was three years old. I felt it, and it was hard to learn to use them without passing out with the pain. I am only twenty-three now and I am used to it; the pain is only bad when I have to have extra bone removed as my body heals itself."

She stared at him. "Heals?"

He nodded. "Yes, the implants were not successful, and my body heals itself over time; once every three years I have to have some of my back bones removed so that the wings can unfold." He turned his face away.

She tried to imagine what it was like, to have had his genetic makeup interfered with, and for it to have gone wrong. Tentatively, she put her hand on his shoulder. "I can save you too if I can. The wings could be removed."

He turned and looked at her. "Could you?" He stood up and walked up and down and then came back to her side. "If I get you in contact with your ship, will that help to start with?" He paused and held his finger to his lips. "That's the guards." He broke off and turned to the bed and Rivkah hardly had time to notice what he was doing before she saw Stephen's wrists were locked in cuffs attached to the bed, and the dark cloth was tied over his eyes again. By the time the door opened, her own wrists and ankles had been cuffed and her eyes covered and Daviir was leading her to the door. He had told her quickly that if they did anything to arouse suspicion, she would not be allowed to come back every day to nurse her patient.

She protested at first, knowing Stephen needed someone at his side and she was worried as she heard the door closed and locked behind them as she was taken back to her cell. She should have guessed she would not be allowed to remain there, and she hoped that he would not need anything until she was escorted back. Unable to see her guide, she felt a moment of fear, wondering again if all they had discussed had been a trap. A door opened and hands on her arms brought her to a stop. The blindfold was removed, and she was pushed into her cell. She tried to look back to see his face, but it was dark, and she could only hear him as he closed the door and locked it behind her. Putting her chained hands out in front of her, she felt along the wall until she found the edge of the ledge where she slept on the hard stone. In the darkness, she listened for the breathing of her cellmate but there was silence and she realized that she was alone. Having someone to talk to had whiled away the time and had stopped her from being afraid. She lay down and struggled with the rising fear of being alone in the dark and silence. She had one thing to reassure her and that was that the Tamorans kept saying her patient was an important prisoner—they would surely keep on allowing her to tend him. She closed her eyes and allowed herself to drift off into a troubled sleep.

45

The Crisis

Admiral Kehoe looked up as the door opened in answer to her invitation to enter. "Take a seat, Galen," she said as Rear Admiral Xander Galen came in. She gave him a quick once over with her keen gaze. "You look much better."

Xander returned her gaze without faltering. He knew she had tried to have him killed, and he knew she must have guessed that he knew. "Thank you, ma'am."

"You used to call me Leandri."

Xander smiled softly. "That was fifty years ago, ma'am. What relationship we may have had then ended when you left me. I respect you as a senior officer, but there has been no affection, or nostalgic reflection since that day. I would be grateful if you would remember that *you* broke up with me, not the other way around. Do not use that as a means for a grudge against me. I am sure you did not ask me here to remind me that I was once young and foolish enough to believe I was in love with a woman like you."

She was silent and watched his face as he spoke. "I could make you regret that last remark."

"You have tried, more than once," Xander replied, evenly. "Now, Admiral, your message informed me that I was to attend this meeting. I assume others are joining us?"

Before she could answer, the buzzer sounded at the door and three more senior officers entered. Admiral Kehoe stood up and motioned to the officers to follow her through to the inner room. They took their places around the long table where the Admiral held her briefings and waited while some more officers joined them via the door at the other end of the room.

An Android orderly entered and sat at the only space at the table with a table-top monitor. The other places had a screen set

339

into the tabletop. The Android was to take minutes of the meeting and was Kehoe's own personal orderly.

Admiral Kehoe looked around the table and then nodded to the Android who tapped his fingers for a moment across the keypad. "Ladies and gentlemen, if you look at your screens now, you will see the orders that were issued to the *Invincible*; to be acted upon on arrival at the planet Tamora." There was a rustle of movement as everyone leaned forward to look at their screens which had lit up as the information was sent to them. "Their orders are to negotiate a trade deal, one which will provide Earth with rights of access to the wormhole which Tamora guards so jealously." She looked up, her eyes meeting Xander's across the table. "It was with this same order that Captain Stephen MacAlpin and the crew of the *Wryneck* were sent in 2783. Due to the unfortunate loss of this ship and crew, we were unable to obtain the rights we wanted." She smiled as the only signs of any feeling in Xander's face were an involuntary tic in his cheek and a hardening of his jaw.

Xander tapped the screen and enlarged the orders. He steeled himself to read the orders he had first seen more than thirty years ago. He glanced up and saw Kehoe's eyes on him from the head of the table. But it was not just her eyes, he felt others looking and he glanced around. It was as though everyone expected him to be affected. He leaned back in his seat and tried to control his feelings. Every time he saw or heard anything to do with his ship and crewmates, it did affect him. He did not want it not to, he used the deep pain of loss he still felt to remember them. He could see all their faces; hear their voices. He would never forget but he did not want others to see how much it distressed him. He fiddled with the wedding ring on his finger and listened to the admiral talking about the negotiations that the crew of the *Invincible* had been sent for, but something inside him wondered how much of a front it was, that the real mission was the same as before. Had Tiberius and her crew been sent as a sacrifice, just as the crew of the *Wryneck* had been—for whatever reason high command had given? He heard Kehoe talking about the 'humanitarian crisis' the Tamorans faced, and their sister world becoming uninhabitable. She was talking about the genetic work the Tamorans did on their prisoners as though they were great scientific improvements. He felt a wave of anger and sickness; anguish and pain at what he had been through. He looked up and the room spun around at an alarming rate. He pushed his chair back and made to stand up and the room rocked. He felt someone guiding him out of the room, a strong grip on his arm—the officer sitting beside him had seen what was happening.

Outside the room, Xander staggered and leaned on the wall, his palms sweating and his head down between his shoulders. He shook his head, unable to answer his companion's concerned queries, and felt heat rising in his throat; then he was falling. When he came to, he was lying on his side. A warm blanket had been placed over him and concerned faces were looking down at him as he opened his eyes. He tried to sit up, but hands pushed him back down.

"You were taken unwell at the briefing," a woman's voice told him. "There's a medical team on the way."

He was trembling as though with cold and was sick. He opened his eyes. Several of the officers from the briefing were kneeling beside him. More boots sounded on the floor and he heard Kehoe's voice asking questions, concern in her voice.

"Get her away from me!" Xander demanded.

Shocked, one of the officers stood up and went to the admiral. "It's under control, ma'am. A medical team is coming, and I'll stay with him and then update you. I think you should continue with the meeting." He did not know why Xander had fiercely demanded her removal from his presence, but the rear admiral was a sick man and he looked dreadfully ill just now. Anything they could do to help him would be beneficial.

Kehoe looked across at the man on the floor and then nodded, turning to go back to the briefing room. She paused at the door and looked back for a few moments before she went in and the door slid shut.

Xander closed his eyes as he felt someone raise his head a little and help him to sip some water. The medical team arrived a few moments later, and one of the officers helping had called Serenity and she was close behind them. Xander put his hand on the younger officer's arm. "I need your help again. I need you to go back in, don't stay with me. I need to know what happens, what she says. Please?"

The younger man nodded, understanding. "Okay, I'll come and see you later and update you." He moved to allow the medical team to reach Xander and saw Serenity hurrying towards the group.

•

That evening, the officer who had helped Xander arrived at the hospital to see him and found him lying propped up on pillows and warmly tucked in, attached to several monitors and a drip, with Serenity sitting by the bed—concerned to see him back in the hospital although the doctor said they were not worried unduly; saying they thought he was trying too much too soon, but had agreed to give him another course of his treatment to help his system.

Xander smiled when he saw his visitor. "Commodore Franklin. Thank you for your help earlier."

Commodore Troy Franklin, more commonly known to his friends and colleagues as Ben, was a man in his early fifties and was reasonably good friends with Xander despite the age difference. The older man's collapse had worried him, and he smiled to see him looking quite bright. "Are you sure you are okay? You gave us quite a scare. We don't like seeing you in the hospital again."

"I don't like being in again," Xander replied softly. "Sit down and tell me what happened after I collapsed."

Franklin sat down and crossed one leg over the other. "Well, first of all, Kehoe suggested relieving you of duty due to your collapse; she pointed out that you have had too many incidents recently. She called for a vote, but no-one voted against you."

"That will have upset her; she wants to be rid of me," Xander replied.

"She lost that one," Franklin laughed.

"Did she talk about the 'crisis'?"

Franklin nodded. "Yes, she made it clear this time that the Tamorans make demands for 'material' and that she is heavily involved, with three others I think." He held out his personal tablet computer. "I accessed this, without her knowledge. Her orders from that time. The *Wryneck* was never intended to come back. There were to be no survivors—you were all supposed to end up in Tamoran prison cells. Your crew would have been enough to begin the repopulation of Garion." He watched Xander's face. "But you guessed that, didn't you?"

Xander nodded. "I cannot understand *why* though. Why would she betray her own people? Her comrades."

"Money; she invests in genetic engineering," Franklin replied. "Her father owned companies that supplied research equipment and she inherited these on his death. The explosion of the

Wryneck saved a lot of innocent lives, if death can be called saving. I wish we knew what had happened."

"It was planned. If anything happened to Stephen, or myself, Cat—I mean Lieutenant Larsgaard—was to destroy the ship. That was Stephen's order before we left the ship; better that we all die than to allow the Tamorans to take prisoners." Xander leaned back on his pillows and closed his eyes for a moment. "I can hardly believe it. I had always wondered; there was always something bothering me. So, she did betray us?"

"Worse, somehow. I could almost understand a straight betrayal, say, just giving your position. But she *sold* you! She put a price on you all." Franklin watched Xander's face. "That is sick. Can you imagine her fury when she was told the crew were all dead—by their own hand? Her plan foiled?"

"Except they had me and Stephen. Ben, why did they say Stephen destroyed the ship? He's been condemned as a traitor— a murderer—but he was on the planet with me, and never went back to the *Wryneck*."

"I can only imagine that Kehoe realized blaming Stephen would take any scrutiny off her. The investigation and the tribunal focused on Stephen, even when it reopened when you had to go through that inquisition. Everything was focused away from her, even the way she greeted you on your return to Earth, it was all about how good she looked in the situation."

"I need to warn them."

"You need to rest," Serenity interposed softly. She looked at Commodore Franklin. "He does need to rest, he gets so tired."

"I understand, Mrs Galen," Franklin replied and did not fail to see the delight in her face to be called this; as an Android, she was only ever called by her designated name. To be called Mrs Galen showed she was accepted as an equal being as Xander's wife.

Franklin turned back to Xander. "Admiral Kehoe has put me in charge of communicating the final orders to the *Invincible*'s commanding officer. I shall use that as cover to alert Tiberius to the truth and warn him."

Relief crossed Xander's face, and he closed his eyes. "Please God it's not too late," he said, and Serenity squeezed his hand. "Ben, we have to stop her, it mustn't happen again."

Franklin stood up and pulled his tunic straight. "I won't let it happen again, Galen."

46

Tiberius Breaks the Silence

Tiberius stirred as a hand on his shoulder gently brought him out of sleep. He always tried to sleep when not on duty—either that or he would swim or work out in the well-equipped gym. His eyes flickered as he rolled over. "Hmmm?" He opened his eyes and saw Laura Harsant.

"Sorry, Captain, there's a call for you from the Admiral's office." She was smiling softly as he sat up and pushed the lock of red hair back from his forehead. She might officially be his Yeoman—his personal assistant—but he was also the man she loved. They kept their relationship professional in front of the crew—there was a lot of responsibility and potential difficulties surrounding dating the commanding officer.

Tiberius slid off the bed and took the tunic held out to him and then stamped his feet into his boots. "Thanks, I'll take it here." He went to the desk and waited until the door closed before tapping the screen. "Okay, Comms, you can put it through." He pulled his tunic straight and smoothed his hair down as he waited for the screen to change. A moment later, a figure appeared on the screen and Tiberius recognized Commodore Troy Franklin, Admiral Kehoe's deputy chief of staff. He steeled himself for orders he did not want. "Commodore?" He leaned forward to see the screen better.

"Captain MacAlpin, this is an unofficial call—you will be receiving further orders shortly. But this is a warning, to put you all on your guard." Franklin paused and told of the briefing and how Xander had been taken ill, being affected by things that had been said. Then he told of his conversation with Xander and the facts that had come to light.

Tiberius listened in silence, shocked. He had guessed much of this. "How is Xander?" he asked. "Tell him I asked and that I worry about him."

"He is much better. He works a little too hard sometimes and does not always rest when he should. But Mrs Galen keeps her eye on him and, with rest and his treatment, he is slowly pulling through the worst."

Tiberius smiled. "I am glad he has someone to care for him— he needed that and I thought he would never find it because of what he suffered." He took a deep breath and met Troy Franklin's eyes. "She means to sell us too, doesn't she? Everything was carefully planned to be the same. The same model of ship, the *Wryneck*'s captain's son in command that's why I was promoted over Ross—I should have guessed."

Franklin nodded. "Yes, her plans are so good, none of us could have guessed. It is only now that things are coming to light. Oh, and one other thing—your father did not die on the *Wryneck*. He was on the planet with Galen. They were both held captive. Kehoe had to cover her part in the events, so it was better to blame your father and all the investigations were focused then on his part, not on her or the other officers involved."

Tiberius nodded. "Xander told me that it was his sister, the second officer, who gave the order. I found out that my father wasn't there. He died a prisoner, I understand that. I guessed Kehoe had something to do with it, but I wasn't sure. She betrayed every one of them and I will not allow it to happen again."

"Has anything happened yet? Have you met the Tamorans?"

Tiberius nodded. "Yes. Doctor Malachi went down to the planet and we have lost contact." He explained how that had come about.

Franklin frowned. "That is worrying," he said. He paused and then turned back to the screen. "I have to go, someone is at the door. If I am found to have spoken to you in this way I will, no doubt, be the next casualty. I will speak to you again when she gives me the orders for you."

He touched the screen to close the call, but not before Tiberius saw that Admiral Kehoe had entered Franklin's office. Tiberius hoped the screen had gone black before she had seen to whom Franklin was speaking. He leaned back in his chair and sighed, wondering what his next move should be. He raised his wrist and gave Ross' call sign and then when the first officer responded, asked him to come and see him.

When Ross presented himself in the captain's quarters, he found his commanding officer sitting at his desk, appearing to be sunk in thought. "You sent for me, Captain?"

Tiberius looked up. "Come and take a seat, Kirbie. I need to talk to you." His voice was very serious, and he did not speak for quite some minutes. He just sat looking at the desk and then slowly looked up. "We need to do something, Kirbie. I can't sit up here, knowing Rivkah—Doctor Malachi—is down there, perhaps a prisoner. We need to go and find her."

Ross met his eyes. "No, sir. You know the rules. I will not allow you to go into danger, you *must* remain on the ship."

Tiberius laughed. "You sound so fierce when you insist that," he said. "You are very strict about the rules."

"It's my job," Ross responded firmly. "It's more than my job is worth to let you violate protocol and risk your life by going into a dangerous situation when there are others to do that for you. If you are determined to rescue the doctor by going down to the surface, then I will do it." He stood up. "I will put a rescue team together. I am just as worried as you."

Tiberius smiled. "I want to believe the reasons are legitimate. That the Tamorans are interested in the negotiations for the wormhole, and that Rivkah's silence is to do with the planet's atmosphere."

Ross was at the door, but he turned as it slid open. "Do you believe that? Or is that what you are telling yourself because you feel guilty that you did not stop her going?"

Tiberius' cheeks burned. "Why do I let you get under my skin?"

Ross smiled. "Because I am right, and you know it, sir."

"I just want this to be over, and I don't want to lose anyone."

Ross smiled again. "You know that each of us knows the risks our job involves, and you know we are all trained and prepared to die in service if that is what is required. To defend our ship, and our captain, is something each of us would give our lives for."

The door slid shut behind the first officer and Tiberius slumped at the desk, burying his tired head on his arms. Why did knowing the loyalty of his crew not make him feel any better? He gave a harsh laugh into his arms; he knew the answer. Because their loyalty was steadfast, and they would die if they had to. Just as he would for them. Had they come this far for this to be the end? He sat up and ran his hand across his face. No, this would not be the end. They would succeed and clear up the mystery of what had happened when his father and his crew were here. He sprang to his feet, hurriedly combed his hair, and splashed cold water on his face and almost ran to the bridge. "Give me ship-wide transmission," he rapped to Lieutenant Zeal.

The communications officer gave him a swift glance and then tapped the screen. "Ship-wide open, sir," he said, wondering what was up. Tiberius MacAlpin did not often look so stone-faced. Right now, he could have been carved out of marble.

Everyone on the bridge swung around in their seats, turning to watch as Captain MacAlpin sat in his seat, his hands resting on the arms of the chair. His head was down as though sunk in thought. There was silence for a while and then he slowly looked up and looked around at the silent bridge crew. He looked last of all at Ross, sitting quietly in the chair beside him, and he nodded with a hint of a smile. He straightened up, sitting with his back as straight as a board. "Crew of the *Invincible*, this is your captain speaking."

All over the *Invincible*, her crew stopped what they were doing, and all turned facing the sound of their commanding officer's voice, as though they could see him. There was something in his voice that told them this was serious.

"Over thirty years ago, another ship and crew orbited this planet. Every single member of the crew on board died—betrayed by one they should have been able to trust." Tiberius looked around and saw Ross nodded encouragingly. "I do not speak of my father. Captain Stephen MacAlpin never betrayed his crew—he would have died with them if he could have, but I have learned he was on the planet. A prisoner alongside his first officer, and where he died. The one who betrayed him, and the crew of the *Wryneck* is the same one who has betrayed us. What happened to them, is supposed to happen to us. But I will *not* allow it. The Tamorans require fresh material for their genetic experiments, and we are supposed to be that material—sold by one of our most senior officers, Admiral Leandri Kehoe. Doctor Malachi is down on the planet, and we have lost contact with her—I have been trying to convince myself that it means that she is maintaining radio silence, but I believe she is a prisoner. I do not think they will kill her, they are more likely to force her to work for them because of her skill. She has studied parasitology, pathology, and germ warfare. She is not just a medical doctor but is also trained as a microbiologist. She has skills the Tamorans will find more than useful." He paused and took a deep breath. "I will not allow Kehoe to destroy another crew. We were sent here to obtain rights to the wormhole beyond Tamora. Part of me believes that to be a front, an excuse to get us here. I intend to leave here with *everyone* on board, and the rights that would benefit our world, and that of the Tamorans. Commander Ross is taking a team down to the planet's surface to search for the doctor. I know asking you to volunteer for such a mission is a big thing for me to ask, and I would rather not have to order anyone to go. I want that choice to be yours; for it to be entirely voluntary. I know there are dangers, and I make no secret of that to you. Yes, you could be killed. That risk goes with any mission we go into where we do not know the odds against us. In this case, either way, death stares us in the face. We have seen these people, and we know the danger they present. Of an entire crew, Rear Admiral Galen is the only survivor and look at the suffering he still endures. Whatever they did to him while he was a prisoner has left him a very sick man. He may still die, he collapsed again just today. Do we not owe it to the memory of those who went before to clear up the mystery, and bring down those who betrayed them? I know it makes it worse that our betrayer is one of our own—someone we should respect because of their rank and position. We have been sold as though we are worth no more than trinkets. I vow that I will give my life, if required, in defence of my ship and my crew. Captain MacAlpin out."

There was dead silence as he nodded to the communications officer and then he stood up without a word and strode off the bridge.

Tiberius made sure there was no-one around and leaned on the wall, closing his eyes. That speech he had made to the crew seemed to have drained his energy, as though he had been running. He knew it was his emotions all running at full strength and colliding with each other. His anger at betrayal—the betrayal of his father and his crew, and now their own. Grief at the loss of his father, still as strong as ever for the man he had never known. Fear for the danger his crew was in, that Ross and his team would go into; and the leaping mixture of fear and excitement that went before any step into the unknown—the same feelings that had first drawn him into space. He leaned his head back on the wall and took some deep breaths and then turned and walked back onto the bridge. He retook his seat and smiled when he saw Ross looking at him. "Sorry, I just needed a moment."

Ross shook his head. "It's fine. We would follow you anywhere, especially after a speech like that. Stop judging yourself."

Tiberius grinned suddenly. "Thanks. We need to decide what to do—how you will go down and where you will land. Is there somewhere that will give good cover? We don't know anything about Tamora, so we need to do some reconnaissance."

"We don't really have time for that," Ross interrupted. "Once we make a move they will know, and that will be the end of it. They will not rest until they find where we are concealed. Every moment we have is precious."

"Let's do it then." Tiberius watched Ross stand up. "Send me the list of the team you choose—I'll coordinate from here." He could go down to the hanger deck with them, but he wanted so badly to be on the team that it was easier for him to stay here. He had never liked the fact that, as commanding officer, it was expected that he would avoid going into a potentially dangerous situation. He always wanted to be at the forefront of any mission like that, believing that if he asked his crew to go into danger then he should face the same risks, but Ross overruled him and quoted regulations at him, as was his right as second in command. It irked him, even though he understood the reasons. He heard the doors open and then turned. "Ross, in the last communication we had from the doctor, she gave a name. Someone she thinks may help us, perhaps. Someone called Daviir. Find them." He turned back to look at the screen set into the arm of his chair and heard the doors close behind the first officer. "Can we scan Tamora without being spotted?" he asked, looking up and turning to the science officer.

Anton Popovych nodded. "We can, but not a deep one. We would run the risk of them finding out."

"Can you find me somewhere the shuttle could be concealed? Any woodland or something?"

The Ukrainian science chief swung around to his station and his fingers tapped at the screens for a moment and then, "Captain, come and look at this." Popovych swung his chair around. "I have not been able to get anything conclusive, I think the atmosphere blocks the equipment from working effectively. But we have discovered this. Tamora seems to have only one real settlement which must be their city. The rest seems uninhabited;

for what reason, I do not know. I cannot see clearly if this is because it is desolate, or if they are not a populous people and therefore have no need of towns. There seems only to be one other place of activity and that is here, to the north of the city. There are a lot of what seems like huts clustered around a scar-like area of cleared ground. It looks like an old aerial image of a quarry or mine." He pointed to the screen. "These red dots are heat signatures—there are a lot of people here, underground, not in the huts. I would hazard a guess that it is a mine, and the huts are where the miners live." He met Tiberius' eyes. "When I say miners, I believe they will be the Tamorans' prisoners."

"Is there anywhere close by that Ross could land?"

"They will hear the shuttle but there is so much open ground that it would take the Tamorans a while to find where he has landed. Surprise might be our only option right now." Popovych pointed to the screen again. "Here, about ten miles from the mine area, there is dense woodland. If Commander Ross can get the shuttle down there without being intercepted, they can conceal themselves in the woodland for a lot longer than in the open territory. We will not be able to keep radio contact with them; they will be on their own."

Tiberius nodded. "Send those instructions to Ross. Tell him to be careful. I hate not being able to keep radio contact, it scares me." He strode back to his seat and clenched his fists. Radio contact was a comfort—while that could be maintained he knew his people were all right. Without it, anything could happen, and he would not know; would not be able to help. He wondered if this was how Cat Lasgaard had felt when she had been left in charge of the *Wryneck* when Stephen MacAlpin and Xander Galen were on the planet's surface, knowing she had a horrible decision to make, and not knowing what had happened down on Tamora.

•

Ross strode down to the hanger deck where the *Invincible*'s shuttles were housed. As he went, he rapped a brief list of names into his wrist transmitter, ordering them to report to the hanger deck. He was not taking a large team—fewer people meant fewer chances of being discovered for as long as possible. He sent the list to the captain's computer and it was approved in moments— even if the captain did add a comment, asking if there was room for him to come along. Ross smiled. He knew Tiberius was joking, however much he wanted to go. Another quick word had the armoury team bring a supply of sidearms for the team. He looked over the weapons and signed for them. He stood to one side and watched the team he had chosen select their weapons and enter the shuttle. He took a moment to choose his weapon, testing its balance in his hand before nodding approval. His prosthetics were exceptional, but some things could not be replicated, such as feeling something in his hand. He could feel the weight and shape of something, but not things such as the smooth coldness of the weapon's slender butt. He bit his bottom lip and knew he could not allow this to put him off, however much it bothered him deep down. And it did bother him. The psychiatrist had been pleased with his mental progress after the traumatic injuries. He was strong and that had helped him significantly. Likewise, the doctor had been pleased with the physical progress. The work she had done with the prosthetics had been amazing, and Ross was grateful—knowing the alternative was death or being a cripple for the rest of his life. But he did miss being able to feel things when he touched them. He slipped the weapon into the holster which was part of the landing team kit and checked he could draw it easily. He had not had any reason to handle a weapon since being injured and he wanted to be sure he could use it well. He stepped into the shuttle; a tall man, he had to duck his head as he went through the door. He touched the control panel and the door slid shut as he took his seat to the right of the pilot.

The pilot looked up and smiled at him. "Ready, sir?" Her hands were hovering over the controls. "We head straight for the planet? Any particular area?"

Ross leaned across and tapped the navigation screen. "These coordinates, Ensign. There is supposed to be a wooded area that will conceal our presence for a time."

"For a time? You expect us to be discovered?"

"The Tamorans are not stupid. They will know we are there, but just not where we are. The woodland is a long way from any settlement, and there do not seem to be any military outposts anywhere. We must just go ahead and hope for the best." Ross leaned back in his seat and took a deep breath and then spoke into his wrist transmitter. "Permission to take off?"

The hanger doors slid open, accompanied by the warning siren as the pressure changed as it was opened up to meet the vacuum of space outside.

"Permission granted."

Veritas: The Captain's Redemption

The pilot pressed her fingers to the steering control positions on the screen in front of her and deftly steered the shuttle out of the open doors and into the star-studded blackness without.

47

"An experiment gone wrong"

The *Invincible*'s shuttle appeared on the Tamoran radar screens and the duty technician watched for a moment and then called the guardroom.

Daviir turned to his terminal and watched the shuttle. "Thank you. Do nothing for now. Let them think we are not aware of their presence. Locate their position when they land and report to me again. If they are not attempting to land here, then they are attempting to surprise us—let them believe they are undetected for now. I want to see what they are up to." He leaned back to watch the shuttle on his screen. As his back touched the chair, a stab of pain shot through him and he almost cried out. He felt something warm on his back and slumped forward over the desk. His long, clawed fingers pressed an emergency button and moments later two soldiers came in and locked the door. He had devised a signal to call the two of his soldiers he trusted more than anyone else if he needed help. He made an effort to pull himself upright when they approached the desk.

"What is it? You are in pain, Daviir."

He nodded. "I wanted to speak to you both anyway." He made a gesture at the screen and then gasped. "Help me get the top off, I need to know how bad it is."

One of the soldiers gingerly touched a dark patch on the skin-tight black material of Daviir's uniform. His hand came away with sticky purple blood on the fingertips. "You are bleeding." They eased his uniform top off, leaving his back and shoulders exposed as he leaned on the desk.

"Can you open your wings? The blood comes from their openings."

Daviir nodded painfully and leaned all his weight on his hands on the desk. Normally he could open his wings without trouble, and certainly without pain, but agony washed over him as he made the effort. As the wings emerged and opened, their normally soft, beautiful pale purple feathers dripped with blood. The pain brought on waves of sickness and the colour drained from his face. "No-one can know," he whispered, panting. "If our doctors knew they would tell President Dayelh, and I would be relieved. You know I could not bear that."

"What about the Earth woman?" one of the soldiers said. "She is a doctor and she will not tell them."

"Fetch her, I cannot go out like this. Don't let anyone see you bring her."

The soldiers left, locking the door behind them to protect their captain from being discovered in this condition. They hurried to the cells and dragged Doctor Malachi out of her cell. In the few moments before her face was covered, she had seen they were soldiers and she struggled and kicked. Some of the female prisoners had told her the soldiers took them to the guardhouse sometimes and she wasn't going to go without a fight.

One of the soldiers struggled to muster up the little English he could manage and said. "We will not hurt you. Daviir is bleeding."

She stopped struggling at once, and let them lead her, stumbling a little, as they hurried. Once they got into the guardhouse, she felt the cuffs being removed and then the blindfold came off and one of the soldiers handed her a bag. She looked inside quickly and saw medical supplies. She looked up at the soldiers and her eyes asked the question as she realized they would not understand her questions.

"In here." The soldier by the door unlocked it and pointed. "Help him." She was pushed inside.

Rivkah looked around as the door shut behind her and heard the lock click. Daviir was standing at his desk, his hands bracing his weight, his head down. The first thing Rivkah noticed was his open wings. They never opened them unless they had to; Daviir had told her that. She had only seen them once but still marvelled at their beauty. The soft purple-pink feathers reminded her of the colour of a dolls' house her sister had when they were children. Taking a step behind Daviir, she looked at the blood-stained feathers and the dark purple blood trickling from the slits in the Tamoran's back which housed the wings. "What happened?"

Daviir raised his head and she saw he was very pale. He raised a hand and pointed shakily at the screen. "A shuttle from your ship is landing on the planet. I said I would help you. I need this pain to go."

Rivkah looked around. There was not much in the room except for the desk and chair so she ducked under the wings and put her arm around his waist and helped him down onto his knees on the floor and then got him to lie down as comfortably as possible.

He clenched his fists, his breathing short, pained gasps. He closed his eyes and breathed through his nose as the doctor knelt beside him and gently touched his back.

"It's okay. This will help the pain while I try to fix you up." A needle slid into his arm and he flinched slightly but lay still. "What caused it, do you know?"

He gingerly shook his head. "The pain gets bad and then I need bones removed to free up the wing movement. I said I was an experiment that went wrong, do you remember?" He ended on a muffled cry as he clamped his lips tight shut.

Rivkah ran her finger around the edges of the wing sockets. "I can remove them. They are still bleeding badly and, if I managed to get the wings back inside, they could get infected. How would you feel? They have been part of you since you were a child."

"They are nothing but a curse to me," Daviir replied. He was almost in tears and she understood that this was not the first time he had been in pain like this.

"I cannot do it here, I will need something to cut the wings. Your soldiers do not speak English, they will not understand." She pulled out some antiseptic wipes and ripped the packet open with her teeth and gently began to wipe up the blood. She paused when the breath hissed through his clenched teeth. "It is dark. If they help you to your quarters, it will be easier there and we will not be disturbed."

He nodded. "Call them."

She rose and went to knock on the door and one of the soldiers came in. Daviir turned his head and spoke quickly in their own language.

The soldiers nodded and one of them ran out while the other helped the doctor to ease Daviir to his feet and they supported him as they hurried out of the back door of the guardhouse and into the block where Daviir had his living-quarters. They laid him on his bed and Rivkah repositioned the pillow to try and make him more comfortable as he lay awkwardly, the wings protruding from his back pinning him down on the bed.

Hurried footsteps came to the door and the second soldier came in, a bag in his hands which he held out to the doctor. She smiled. "Thank you. Can you hold him?" She pointed to Daviir and mimed holding him down and went through the motions of the operation she wanted to perform. To her relief, they understood and went to the bed, one on either side and held him down as she opened the bag and took out a selection of instruments. One looked like a hacksaw and she knew that would be the best. She positioned herself, balanced the saw in her hand to feel the weight, and began to work on cutting through the stem of the first wing. She almost expected it to be soft like the bones of a bird. It was not, it was hard, like human bone.

Daviir writhed and howled in pain as the bone broke as the first wing was severed. He hardly had time to draw breath before she began on the other. He knew she must think it better to carry on than to let him rest and he agreed with her. He wanted this to be over. Pain hit him like a surging wave and sweat streamed down his face as Rivkah began to clean and pack the open wounds. Voices were heard and he weakly lifted his head. "They heard me. They must not see this. They *cannot* find you here."

Rivkah shook her head as she pushed the wings under the bed with her foot. "They will not think anything of it. I know how the prisoners are used." She waved at the soldiers. "Go now, before they get here. Thank you." She smiled at them again as Daviir repeated the words.

"In the cupboard there is a dress. Don't ask, just put it on," Daviir said, seeming to have the same idea in his mind. As captain of the guard, he could take whatever woman he chose from the prison. The fact he had a woman's dress handy told her he had done so before.

Rivkah knew it was the only way. If anyone found her here under any other circumstances she would be back in her cell and she could not risk losing her freedom, not with Stephen MacAlpin to tend to. And Daviir would suffer. It was clear he did not want anyone to know what had just happened. She grabbed the dress from the cupboard and changed quickly. The dress fit well enough and, even as she hurried, she could see it was dark green and went nicely with her dark hair and olive skin.

The dress hung from a clasp on one shoulder and fell to her mid-thigh. As the door was pushed open, she had just enough time to run and sit on the edge of the bed. As the soldiers came into the room, she put her hand on Daviir's face.

The soldiers ran in and pointed their weapons but fell back as Daviir pushed himself up on his elbow. "Since when do you just enter my room without my permission?" he rapped. "Leave at once!"

"Sir, we heard you crying out. We thought..."

"You thought what? It must be a long time since a woman pleased you!"

The soldier blushed so deeply that Rivkah felt sorry for him—almost. She hoped the soldiers would leave soon as she did not want them to see that Daviir was in pain. If they came closer, they would see the purple stains on the bed where his back had bled when he lay down to create their tableau.

"It is the Earth woman from the prison," one of other soldiers said.

Daviir rolled his eyes. "And that is my right," he said, glad that she did not understand Tamoran. "Human women are exciting, and I may take who I choose, I am Dayelh's son." He waved a hand. "Go!" He slid his hand under Rivkah's hair and leaned in as though he were about to kiss her.

The soldiers almost bolted from the room and Daviir collapsed back in the bed, his face white.

Rivkah slid off the bed and rummaged in the bag to find a strong pain killer. She administered it quickly and then deftly repacked the wounds and wound strips of clean bandages around his body as she had intended if they had not been interrupted.

Daviir smiled slightly as he felt the sheets being tucked around him. "You don't need to go back to your cell. Now they believe I have chosen you, you will not be chained up or blindfolded any more. You are still our prisoner and must obey orders, but you will be allowed to attend to your duties in the hospital and you will not be challenged. It is accepted that if you are chosen by me then you do not wish to escape; once you are my woman you will be treated better. Keep the dress, it will serve as a badge—my gift. Forgive me, I would never treat you that way, but they must believe it to be so for you to be safe."

"You do not need forgiveness—you have done nothing to offend." She smiled. "I felt I could trust you, right from our first

357

talk in the shuttle. You opened up to me, and I saw the real you. And then at the hospital, I saw who you truly are. A product of these sadistic people, suffering, year after year, something you could not change. Don't apologize."

He was watching her face and then smiled, the frown of pain easing out of his forehead for a moment. "But I *am* one of them—we killed and tortured your people."

"But you are different. You offered to help me almost at once. And you were telling the truth; it was not a ruse to throw me off guard. You told me things you would not wish me to know—things about your parentage. And you are terrified of the Tamorans finding out." She smoothed the sheets and sat on the edge of the bed. "I will ask your soldiers to take me to the hospital to check on Stephen. You need to rest and then what? We go to meet the shuttle?"

Daviir's eyes were beginning to close as the painkillers took effect. He shook his head. "They landed hear the mines. Because of what has happened to me, we will be too late. It will not be long before they are discovered, and they will be killed or taken prisoner."

Rivkah nodded, knowing that things were moving too quickly for her to stop them. She stood up and went to the door where she was met by Daviir's trusted soldiers. Despite the Tamoran tongue being extremely hard to master she managed to say the word she had learned for hospital and they escorted her there quickly. Once there, her first task was to dispose of the wings and her bloodstained clothes. She slid her feet back into her boots and went to wash her hands.

•

Ross stepped down from the shuttle as the door slid open under his touch of the release pad. He looked around at their surroundings as the rest of the team joined him. The shuttle stood in a clearing, as close to the edge, as possible to be protected by the treeline. The trees stood tall and still. There was no breeze stirring their leaves. It was not hot, but there was a closeness in the air which reminded Ross of an approaching storm on Earth. He looked up at the dark sky with the trees silhouetted against the broad expanse of the cloudless sky. He turned to his companions. "Could almost be Earth," he said. "Even the air is breathable, there's no need for the respiratory equipment we brought." He wished he could send a status report, but they had to maintain radio silence to conceal their arrival for as long as possible. Ross was not so foolish as to believe they were undetected. The Tamorans were not stupid. They would be watching for any move on their part, however small. They would have detected the shuttle by now, but he could only hope their actual position could be kept a secret for a little longer. Every minute they remained undiscovered meant a better chance of success. He checked in his holster. "We'll find somewhere to make a camp. There should be somewhere among the trees. We can lie low and make a move at first light."

"We're not staying with the shuttle, sir?"

"No, that's the first place that will be searched. We were probably detected, and we can't leave that to chance."

They grabbed their things from the shuttle and headed for the dense treeline to the right of where the shuttle rested.

•

President Dayelh frowned at the soldier who had presented himself at the palace, asking to see him. It was the soldier who had alerted Daviir to the appearance of the shuttle on the radar. Daviir's insistence that he would take care of the situation and then the lack of action on his part had raised concerns with the soldier. Daviir was a dedicated soldier and led the Tamoran army with loyalty and courage. He had never hesitated in responding to a threat to the planet.

The soldier attempted to get answers but had found the office in the guardhouse empty. He had tried the door to the colonel's private room but found the door locked. "Dayelh, he did not want me to tell anyone—he said he would deal with it. But he has not. I was concerned. Concerned for what this could mean for Tamora. What this could mean for our people. We must survive."

Dayelh looked at the soldier. "You forget, Daviir is my son. You imply he betrays us?"

The soldier looked scared for a moment and then shook his head. "I do not mean to imply that, but he can be odd sometimes, and he has been in pain." He had been watching Daviir for a few weeks. "He has always been loyal and that is why I was concerned."

Dayelh nodded. "I will deal with Daviir. Take the squad yourself and find where the shuttle landed. When you find the occupants, bring them to me. Do not kill them unless you have no alternative. Once Captain MacAlpin realizes they are taken, he will send more until he has to come himself. Then we will have the numbers promised and we can finish rebuilding Garion." He looked searchingly at the soldier. "Tell me the truth, is he truly loyal?"

"You know he is, President."

"And yet you disobeyed his order to leave this for him to deal with? Why would you disobey him if you thought there no reason?" His eyes glittered, challenging the soldier. "Is the commander of my army to be flouted in such a fashion?"

The soldier almost gulped. "No, President Dayelh, I just thought this was a situation that should be dealt with immediately and not delayed. Daviir was, um, busy. I saw a woman enter his room in the dark. She was there a long time."

President Dayelh laughed, sounding almost relieved. "And since when has he not been allowed a moment of personal indulgence? Go, do the task as I have ordered. I will deal with Daviir should he reprimand you." He turned away, signifying the meeting was over.

The soldier left, hurrying back to the barracks. He selected twenty soldiers and they armed themselves and, opening their wings as one, flew off into the darkness.

48

Captured

All was silent in the camp under the trees, but one of the *Invincible*'s team stirred uneasily. She sat up in the darkness, wondering what had disturbed her. Had it been a sound? Or was it the sudden feeling of oppression in the air, almost like something was pressing down hard on her. She leaned over and gently shook Commander Ross' arm.

Ross woke at once and rolled over onto his side. "What is it?"

"I think I heard something."

Ross sat up and listened. It was all quiet. He was about to say so when he heard it too. A soft rustling; like the sound of air on feathers, and the gentle sound of something landing quietly on the ground. It seemed to come from all around them and he felt a chill run through him. They had been discovered and surrounded.

Bright lights suddenly shone in a circle around them, directly into their faces. Ross flung up his arm to try and shield his eyes and tried to see past the searing light, to see who was approaching them. He saw nothing but dark shadows; shadows which were closing in on them. His hand went to the weapon on his lip. "Close up," he whispered as he heard the others stirring.

They never got a chance to draw their weapons and defend themselves. The shadows were upon them so quickly. A foot on his back pinned Ross on his face in the dry grass and leaves. He heard his companions cry out and tried to turn his head but could see nothing in the dark but could only hear the sounds of their bodies being dragged away. Hands grabbed his arms and pulled them behind his back, and something was wrapped tightly around his wrists. He was pulled to his feet, strong hands gripping his arms on either side and he was dragged, struggling, to the other side of the trees where the faint outline of their shuttle could be seen. With a start, he felt his feet leave the ground and heard the sound of large wings beating and he knew these beings were carrying them away. He looked down and saw a blinding flash under them and a plume of fire shot into the air and he felt the heat on his face. They had destroyed the shuttle.

As the sky lightened, Ross was dragged into what seemed to him to be a square, an area between tall white buildings. He was pushed to his knees, his back to a stone pillar and his wrists bound around the back of the pillar and his ankles were bound in place too. A strap around his neck held him upright against the pillar. He turned his head awkwardly and saw his team being dragged into one of the buildings around the square. He was concerned that they had been separated. "Where are you taking them?" He yelled this with difficulty as the strap around his neck was very tight.

"Where you will all go in due course. To rebuild Garion," one of the soldiers who had dragged him to the pillar told him. "Don't worry—they will not die. Not yet."

Ross struggled as his eyes were covered, leaving him feeling suddenly afraid and more vulnerable than he had even while lying in the ship's hospital waiting for his prosthetics to be fitted. He heard footsteps going away from him but did not know if there was anyone around and he was fighting back the rising fear. He was a very brave man, but it was hard to be courageous when bound and blindfolded, and knowing his crewmates were captives and in danger. He had to keep his head and think, although he knew from trying that he could not get free. He went over everything in his mind, storing the details and trying to remember the few words the Tamorans had said. What was it they had said? They were going to be used to rebuild Garion. What was Garion again? Oh yes, the sister planet that was supposed to have been laid bare by some tragedy. So the Tamorans were repopulating their damaged world with people taken from other planets? Or was that the experiments? It had to be. Tested and mutilated, to augment the Tamorans, to make them able to survive the desolate world. He heard a soft sound behind him and felt a searing pain in his arm and flinched. They had removed the transmitter. How did they know? He remembered what they had thought about the doctor when her signal had suddenly died. They had learned their communication secrets and were removing them. He closed his eyes behind the blindfold. *What would happen now?*

•

On the *Invincible*, Lieutenant Zeal looked across the bridge to where Captain MacAlpin sat. "Captain, their signals have gone. All of them; one after the other. Just like the doctor's did." His eyes were wide with shock. "What shall we do?"

Tiberius gnawed his lip and flicked the comms switch on the arm of his chair. "Ross! Come in." He paused and then repeated the words. "Come in, please! *Kirbie!*" Tiberius was on his feet, pacing back and forth on the bridge. He did not even try to hide his anxiety.

Ross' eyes closed as his heart sank. The receiver had not been removed from his ear and he could hear Tiberius as he tried to make contact. Unable to respond, he struggled although it was futile. Hearing his commanding officer's voice like this made him realize just how alone he really was.

•

The bridge was a flurry of activity as everyone tried hard to locate their missing crewmates. They had identified there was no longer any trace of them close to the shuttle, and the latest scans and images showed the shuttle burning fiercely.

Tiberius turned as he was asked for directions. "Scan the city—that seems to be the only real area of activity. If they are prisoners, then it is likely they are held here—there are no other large buildings. It stands to reason that the prison and laboratories will be reasonably close to each other."

Heads bent over instruments again as they busied themselves. Each of them wanted to get the answers the captain demanded. After a few moments, Popovych looked up from his computer. "Captain, I have enough of a signal to try and pinpoint a location."

"Is it enough to see who it is?" Tiberius demanded. His heart pounded painfully. If it was just one lone signal, could it be Ross? He thought it was likely the team would be split up and Ross would be kept apart from the rest of them.

Popovych shook his head. "Sorry, sir. It is too faint. I don't want to say I can do it." He swung back to the computer for a moment, his forehead creased in a frown of concentration. His fingers darted over the screen and he seemed to be comparing two lists and then slipped earphones in for a moment or two and then slipped the buds from his ears. "Captain, I am almost certain it is Ross' signal. I think they may have removed just one part, unlike the total loss of the other signals, and the doctor's; perhaps they did not realize its strength, or perhaps they mean us to trace them."

"Pinpoint it. I want a deep scan, as close as you can get. Close enough to see him if he is in the open." He strode back to his chair and punched one of the buttons on the chair arm and a section of the window turned into a screen. "I want to see it here—whatever there is to be seen, I want it on the screen." Moments later the screen flickered and lit up. Tiberius leaned back in his chair and fixed his eyes on it as the scans were made and the screen filled with images of the Tamoran city. "Zeal, keep trying to raise the Tamorans—I want answers." He knew it was futile however, they had tried the same with the doctor.

The tall white walls of the city seemed to roll across the screen inch by inch, and everything looked quiet and peaceful. Popovych tapped his screen and intensified the scans. There was something about the peace that was unnerving, and he was not about to be fooled by it. They knew something was going on and in moments, the scene flickered and changed before their very eyes. The white walls gave way to reveal a square in the centre. A lone figure knelt in the centre of the square, bound to a metal pillar. A dark cloth covered the eyes, but the uniform and the lower part of the face was enough—it was clearly Commander Ross.

Tiberius sat very still. He had let them go into this danger and now they were prisoners, or worse. This was proof only that Ross was alive—if he were—they could not tell from here. Tiberius wondered if they were meant to see Ross like this; a deliberate gesture to him and the crew of the *Invincible*. As they watched, in shock and horror, there was a movement at the top left edge of the screen. A door opened and a woman appeared, looking around quickly. She wore a short dark-green dress, fastened on one shoulder, and her long wavy dark hair was knotted low in the nape of her neck and the long end lay across her bare olive-skinned shoulder. Tiberius caught his breath. Even out of uniform, Doctor Malachi was instantly recognisable.

•

Barefoot, Rivkah Malachi made her way across the square, aiming for a building at the other side. She hurried across but stopped when she reached the centre. The last time she had crossed here to check up on Daviir, there had been no-one there;

364

the pillar had stood there, bare. She saw the uniform and went straight to the man fastened to the pillar and knelt, her hands holding his head up, relieving some of the strain of the strap around his throat. "Kirbie, what happened?"

"Rivkah? Go, don't let them find you here," Ross responded with difficulty as his mouth was dry.

She glanced up at the burning sun and sprang up, disappearing for a moment to returned with a little dish which she held to Ross' lips and awkwardly helped him to drink as he couldn't move his head. She knew she would be watched by the Tamorans but she could not just go past him without doing something to help him. "I'll get you out of here. We have an ally here. Are you brave enough to trust me?"

Kirbie Ross did not feel brave right then. Unable to move or see, he was afraid. He felt her hands on his cheeks again and knew she was looking at him and he struggled. "Don't leave me here. I'm scared."

"I have to—you know that. I won't be far away, and I have people who will help us."

He was struggling again, fear rising, and he wrenched at his chained arms as Rivkah straightened up.

Her hands still on his face, she stooped and kissed him on the cheek. "Don't be afraid, I will come back for you." She turned away and heard him call her name as he heard her footsteps heading away from him.

•

Tiberius punched the arm of his seat. He glanced at Ross' empty chair and wished he were there; right now he needed his advice. They had all watched the screen but had no idea what had been said. He took a deep breath and turned to Popovych. "I need you here; you have to take Ross' place for now. We need to get down there and save him, and the others. I don't know what part Rivkah is playing in all this, but she seems to be free to move around the buildings alone—she must be trusted in *some* way. So, we need to get Dayelh up here—split their defences, and we can use him if necessary. We're supposedly here to negotiate for access to the wormhole so, let's negotiate! Get that meeting set up and get him and his entourage into the meeting room. While they're with me, you can lead the rescue mission."

Popovych had come over and taken Ross' seat as Tiberius was talking. "You intend to hold the Tamoran' president here?"

"You saw that?" Tiberius waved at the screen. "We know what they do down there—what they did to Xander; how they killed my father and his crew. Rivkah is a prisoner and we've lost contact with seven crew members and Ross is being used as a goad. I know that is what they are doing; they have him chained up like that, knowing we will be watching and will see him. They are trying to get us down there—for us to leave the ship. They want us all alive down there. They're not going to kill him, or the others—they want us alive. And they want us off the ship. They didn't get everyone from the *Wryneck*—they need us. They need this number of people for whatever sick plan they have. We're in danger, but not of death. Not at first—but the danger of torture and experiments. We were sent here for this." He turned and saw Popovych staring at him. "Why are you still here? Get moving!" He knew he shouldn't have snapped at the science officer—he had still been talking and had not dismissed him. The image of Ross chained up in the Tamoran square had got to him more than he had realized, and he felt sickened to know that if he did nothing, Ross would be killed to make him act. "I'm sorry. I didn't mean to bite your head off," he said as Popovych headed for the door.

The science officer turned and nodded. "I understand. We are all worried about him." He stepped through the doors and they slid shut behind him.

Rivkah Malachi stopped at the door of the barracks and looked back across the square to the kneeling figure in the centre and she felt sad. He had been trembling when she held his face between her hands, and she had wanted to stay beside him to protect him from danger. The fear he was forcing himself to hide had been evident when she touched him, and her heart had almost broken when he cried out after her. But she had to go. She needed Daviir to be on his feet, to rouse the soldiers loyal to him; to help her rescue her people and to put a stop to the experiments and torture. She could not do it alone. She looked back once more and then entered the barracks and hurried to Daviir's room. She found the Tamoran struggling into a sitting position and hurried to the bedside and put her hand gently on his back to check the bandages. "You have stopped bleeding, which is good." She peeled the bandages off and examined the wounds before strapping him up again. She sat on the edge of the bed and told him about Ross. "Do you feel up to leading your army? We need to save them."

Daviir slid his arms into the sleeves of his all-in-one uniform and grunted as he eased it over his shoulders. Without him having to ask, Rivkah leaned forward and helped him with the fastening, and he nodded. "It is tight enough to be comfortable," he said, sitting upright and holding himself stiffly. Swinging his legs over the edge of the bed, he pulled himself upright and limped to the window and looked out. His window looked out into the square from the second floor. He turned back and met the doctor's eyes. He saw the anger and sadness in them, and he shook his head. "They will not kill him yet; he is a guarantee—to keep Captain MacAlpin back. They know he will not endanger Ross' life."

"Are you that sure? Can you be absolutely certain they will not kill him?"

Daviir nodded. "He is too precious to us alive. They will be sure Captain MacAlpin will not do anything to get Ross killed, he's more likely to negotiate to try and save him. I am ready. You asked me if I was on your side—if I would turn on my own people to save yours. I will. I cannot be a part of this anymore. I was experimented on as a child and I suffered until you removed my pain. I owe more to you than to Dayelh and my mother. You have not been afraid of me when your people usually are. Look at our appearance, we fill others with fear and loathing. Look at me and tell me truthfully that we are repulsive to you."

Rivkah's hair slid forward over her shoulder as she shook her head. "Most of us do not think like that anymore—everyone is different and is accepted, and humanity has thrived on its diversity. Think about it. It is not because of how you look, but how you *are*. You—as a people—have tortured and murdered countless people—*that* is what makes you repulsive to us."

Daviir smiled suddenly. "I believe you. Now, we need to decide what to do. Remember, if we make any sudden move, he may be killed."

"You are still the commander of the president's guard. That surely will buy us time?" Rivkah paused and added, "Why did they remove his wrist transmitter? His arms are chained behind the pillar—he could not speak into it?"

"You said it yourself—torture. To cause pain and fear. To know he cannot contact his ship even were his hands free. He is lost without that communication, in pain and alone. Our methods are not just to cause physical pain, but psychological too. Plus, we do not know how you activate them. It could just be your voice that does it."

She nodded. "Of course." As Daviir turned from the window she followed him through the door and into a long room with a table down the centre.

"Don't protest at anything," he said quietly as they walked in. The room was full of soldiers and he pushed the doctor to her knees at his feet and took the thick tail of her hair in his hand, not roughly but enough to hold her still and give an impression of dominance over her.

Rivkah understood. If she stood beside him, she would be seen as an equal; a soldier like himself. But she was a prisoner and only allowed this relative freedom because he had chosen to imply that he had chosen her for his pleasure. Had this been the case she would have felt sick, but he had never touched or hurt her, and going along with the illusion meant she was not locked away in her dark cell. They used her for her medical skill to protect their greatest bargaining tool—the centrepiece of many of their genetic reproductive experiments. The old man who had been the captain of the *Wryneck*, and who now lay badly injured and useless to them without her skill. They would not harm her for this reason, but if they knew she was at the heart of an insurrection among the army, led by President Dayelh's son, they would kill her and the rest of her captive crewmates as revenge. If she gave them no cause for concern Ross would not be harmed. Pinned to her knees, by the hand twisted in her hair, she listened to Colonel Daviir speaking in his own language and she could only pray she had not led herself into a trap.

•

Tiberius barely heard the buzz of activity around him as he stood in the hanger deck as the doors opened to allow the strange winged Tamoran craft to land. It was as though all sound had ceased as he stood, watching as the wings of the Tamoran ship folded back along the fuselage that tapered away like the body of a dragonfly. Fists clenched at his sides to hide the trembling; Dayelh must never see the rage coursing through him. This was the part of their mission that called for all his diplomacy and courage. He had always seen himself more of a soldier than a diplomat, even though their role in space was for the defence of peace not the waging of war. Peace between all peoples was something they all wanted, and worked to maintain but, for Tiberius, he could not let go of the hatred he felt for the

Tamorans. The people who had killed his father and destroyed Xander Galen—the man who had been like a father to him through his teenage years. The blood of an entire ship's crew was on their hands. Taking a deep breath to calm himself and to remind himself that he was not alone, he put his shoulders back and raised his chin just a little. *I can do this.*

The door of the Tamoran ship swung back and President Dayelh and High Lady Delmaa stepped down, their long cloaks sweeping the deck around their feet as they walked forward to where Captain MacAlpin stood waiting, alone. Only two of the President's Guard accompanied them and Tiberius realized they did not feel threatened and knew they gambled on his having seen Ross chained in the palace square. If they believed he would do something, they would have brought more soldiers with them.

Tiberius swallowed his feelings and bowed his head slightly. "Welcome." *Welcome? That was the last thing they were.* Again he pushed his inner thoughts aside and made a gesture towards the door. "Thank you for coming. I saw no reason to delay our talks. After all, this is why we are here." He ushered them into the palatial meeting room which was used for such meetings as this—a room fit to engage in diplomatic talks. "We have been sent by Earth's government to negotiate for the right of access to the Tamoran wormhole. Talks that have been delayed for too long." That was the closest he would get to mentioning the visit of the *Wryneck*. He waved his visitors to comfortable seats at the table and took his place at the head. Behind him, a door slid open and a woman in uniform came in with a tray bearing drinks which she brought first to President Dayelh. "My aide, Ensign Harsant," Tiberius said. "Please, be my guest." He nodded to her after the Tamorans took their glasses and he reached for his own.

Ensign Laura Harsant took a seat at the opposite side of the table and tapped her tablet screen. Tiberius nodded to her. "Thank you." He glanced at Dayelh and added further explanation. "My aide attends all meetings, to log the proceedings." He had seen the expression on the Tamoran's face and guessed the president had not expected anyone else to be present. He smiled slightly. "Normally I would be accompanied by my first officer, but he is preoccupied." He only hesitated slightly and kept his eyes on Dayelh's face and saw just a flicker of something in the Tamoran's eyes and knew he understood that the human knew exactly where Commander Ross was and how he had last seen him. He rested his hands on the table and forced his face to relax as he launched into the talk about the treaty. It felt so wrong to be here, talking over the diplomatic reasons for both worlds to share access to what lay beyond the wormhole when Ross and other crew members were prisoners below on the planet. All the time in the back of his mind he was turning over plans for how to keep Dayelh and his wife onboard the *Invincible* for hostage purposes if everything else failed. He knew this would not be practical and that whatever move he and the crew made, had to be made before the Tamorans left the ship. Beyond the idea of keeping Dayelh away from the planet, he had no real plan. It was at times like this that he missed Ross at his side. Someone he could run his ideas by—someone who told him straight if he was being crazy. Ross would probably tell him he was crazy this time; imagining he could hold the Tamoran president hostage, he could almost hear his voice telling him to think about what he was doing. Ross would be wrong this time. He *was* thinking, and he was not crazy. He was protecting his people, basing this on the assumption the Tamorans would not endanger their leader. Resolutely, Tiberius went on with the discussions, going over everything that would benefit both worlds. In a way it was good he had this to occupy his time—it made his focus his mind. Dayelh was not an easy person to negotiate with and it was clear he did not intend this to be easy.

49

"Aloha!"

Xander Galen walked down the hospital steps, his hand held firmly by Serenity. He had spent nearly a month under observation after the fainting incident in the briefing and he was determined to get back to work, but he had promised Doctor Jessup that he would take it easy and allow Serenity to monitor his condition daily. The hospital had expressed concern over the latest episode and warned that many more like this could leave him helpless. He leaned on Serenity as they left and felt her squeezing his hand. He knew how worried she was every time he ended up in the hospital and how she hated to see his distress when enduring the injections he loathed. His hand and arm were bruised from the multiple needles that had been used this time.

Serenity's real concern was with him going back to work. He was supposed to be working closely with Kehoe, but she could not bear to see the pain this caused him; to know the admiral was responsible for the death of his crewmates must get to him often. "Are you sure you are ready for this?" she asked as she helped him down the last few steps and into a waiting shuttle-cab. His once strong stride was slower now and he was showing his age more than before although he was not that old.

Xander leaned back in his seat and closed his eyes for a moment before turning back to his Android wife and smiled at her. "I'm going to be okay," he told her and squeezed the hand which was still in his.

She reached up and stroked his face gently, looking into his eyes. "I am concerned about you. Every day in her office, you are in danger. She knows you know, and she has tried to have you killed. She will not rest—you are the only one who can tell the truth and she knows that. Her fear of exposure will keep you in danger."

Xander put his arm around her and bent his head to kiss her. "She will also be careful. She knows I can ruin her, and you know I do not know the full truth. I do not know what happened to Stephen and there are ten years of my life which are blank—nothing but pain and darkness."

"Don't talk about it," Serenity said, holding his face between her hands. "You're not going back just yet. Remember, you promised us a honeymoon since you were still so ill when we got married?"

He nodded, watching her face.

"Well, I went ahead and booked a trip as soon as I knew when they were discharging you this time. I want to give you two weeks in the sun—with no Leandri Kehoe to make your life a misery. No work, and rest outside of the hospital will do you the world of good." She reached into the bag she carried and held up a pair of tickets. "I arranged it all before I came to collect you. We're going to Hawaii; to the island of Maui. We'll watch the whales coming through the Au'au Channel and see that Haleakala sunset you have told me about. You can lie in the sun on the beach and get some colour back. What do you think?" She was watching his pale, tired face and smiled when she saw his brown eyes light up.

"I love you," he said, simply. No other response felt adequate.

"We'll stop at your apartment and pack a bag. I have my things already but was not sure what you would want. I packed some bits earlier, we just need to finish."

He ran his hand through her hair and caressed the back of her neck. "I have always wanted to see Maui. Stephen and I planned to take Bethany and Tiberius when we got home; we talked about it a lot."

She looked up. "Don't be sad; I won't let you be sad. You talked about this so much that I wanted to make it happen."

They reached Xander's apartment and Serenity's idea of him packing was to get him lying comfortably on the sofa with a blanket tucked around him as she packed his bag. He was content to lie there and listen to her talking to him through the open bedroom door. While she was out of sight, Xander sat up slightly and pulled his tablet computer off the table and hastily concealed it under the blanket. She had said no work, but he was concerned about what might happen when he was away. He could hear her still, busy opening and closing drawers and he pulled out the tablet and checked some files and then slipped it out of sight again.

He was just in time for Serenity appeared with a small bag. "It will be hot, so we don't need anything bulky," she said. She looked around and picked up Xander's antique Bible and prayer book and smiled as she put them into the case. He took them everywhere and ignored the ridicule he sometimes faced for refusing to work on a Sunday whenever possible. She did not understand the way some people clung to a faith or religion but knew it had been a source of comfort to Xander in the long dark days in the hospital. When he was tired or feeling unwell, he read for hours, or when he was really bad, he would ask her to read to him from the Psalms. The words meant little to her but seeing how he would lie still, listening until he fell asleep, gave her comfort too. She turned and held out her hand. "Ready? I think we have everything."

He pushed himself up, tucked his hand in her arm and they made their way to the door and out into the waiting shuttle-cab. At the shuttle depot, they transferred to another shuttle for the long trip to Hawaii. The last rays of the setting sun were fading against the dark sky as the shuttle came into land at Maui's airport that had served the island in the days of aircraft, long before travel by shuttle became the way forward.

Serenity had arranged assistance so Xander did not have to stand around waiting for their luggage and a young NCO had come with them to see them settled at their hotel before taking the shuttle back to base. They disembarked and the young man went to collect their luggage while the Android and her human husband moved slowly toward the shuttle cab that had come to meet them. Serenity had thought of everything.

The NCO shortly appeared in the door of the shuttle with their bags. "Here you go, Admiral Galen, Mrs Galen. Do you have everything you need? I've called ahead to your hotel with your ETA. They will show you straight to your room and have drinks ready for you."

Xander smiled. "Thank you, Petty Officer. I've recommended you for acceptance into the officer's training programme on an accelerated entry. When I return, if you work hard, you will be halfway to ensign."

The young man stared at him. "I don't know what to say. Thank you, sir."

"You are a good lad. You'll make an excellent officer," Xander replied. "Your grandfather will be so proud."

The NCO blushed and his face stretched into a big grin. His grandfather had served as an admiral around the time of the *Wryneck*'s mission but had resigned when the ship was lost. He had two sons, one of whom had been assigned to the *Wryneck*, the other was the young man's father. He stepped back from the shuttle door and saluted. "Have a good trip, sir."

Xander leaned back as the cab moved off and Serenity looked at him. "That was kind."

Xander opened his eyes and smiled. "Those that are good and loyal at this time must be rewarded. I have not known who to trust for so long. He will do well."

When they arrived at the hotel, they were greeted by staff members in traditional dress who welcomed them with a cheery "*aloha!*" and leis were placed around their necks. Xander reached for Serenity's hand as they were escorted into the hotel, a young boy running ahead with their luggage. After they checked in, a smiling girl with flowers in her dark hair showed them to their suite. She opened the door onto the balcony and indicated the sun chairs. "Your welcome drinks will be here in a moment."

Serenity leaned on the railing and looked out to sea. "It is beautiful." She looked around with a smile and saw Xander settling down on one of the sunbeds as a young man appeared with a tray with a selection of drinks. Xander chose something non-alcoholic as he could not drink with his medication and Serenity took a cocktail—out of interest as she did not need to drink and was certainly fine to take alcohol which did not affect her. "What is this one?"

"A Cuba Libra," the waiter told her. "It is rum and coke with lime. You will enjoy it, it is a great favourite."

When the waiter had gone, Serenity knelt beside Xander's sunbed and leaned over to kiss him on the lips. "Happy honeymoon, my beloved husband."

Xander smiled as they kissed. "It is perfect, my darling. Thank you." He had never imagined he would be so fortunate as to marry. His thirties had been lost; his forties spent mostly in the hospital until he recovered. In his fifties, he had gone back to active service until the recent events occurred and made him swap active duty with a posting behind a desk. He did not care about the censure of those who were surprised or shocked that he had married an Android; that he had fallen in love with a robot. But it was exactly that which made him feel comfortable and safe, and she cared for him just as though she was human. He knew she had enhanced her programming to try and learn to feel what being human meant; the last thing she would have expected was to actually fall in love and marry a human. He watched her as she stood up and walked back to the balcony, leaning her elbows on the rail. The warm breeze from the sea played with her hair and gently rippled her long skirt around her ankles, the evening sunlight showing the shape of her legs through the thin material. No-one would ever guess she was not human, he thought, as she sipped at her cocktail. Kehoe had tried to stop him enjoying this, and that made him even more determined to stop her from destroying any more lives.

When darkness had fallen, Serenity's sharp eyes spotted a light, like fire, out at sea and she scanned the horizon for a moment and then called Xander to come out and join her. "Look, you'll have never seen this before, prairie boy," she said softly, remembering Xander telling her about his childhood in Missouri. "There's a volcano erupting out at sea. It was not there earlier, that tremor we felt earlier must have been this spawning."

Xander came out through the sliding door and slid his arm around his wife's waist and smiled as she leaned into him. "You're right, I've never seen this. I've seen tornadoes and serious lightning storms out in the wide-open spaces, but no volcanoes." A shower of fiery sparks showered up into the black sky and he smiled. "I think it's far enough away that we're not going to be affected by any fallout from it, they'll be watching for signs of a tsunami, but the tremors weren't too big, and this looks like a baby eruption at the moment." He kissed her on the cheek. "Are you sure you didn't arrange this as fireworks for me?"

Serenity smiled and nestled her head into his shoulder. "I can't make volcanoes happen, silly," she said, enjoying the feel of his fingers on her waist. She knew he was happy, and it pleased her. She wanted nothing more than to make him happy.

50

Honeymoon

The rays of the early morning sun streaming through the window of the suite woke Xander. He opened his eyes and lay propped up on the pillows looking out at the sky, tinged with pink and orange above the blue sea glistening with the golden shards of sun rays scattered over its surface. When they had gone to bed, he had stopped Serenity from drawing the blinds. He had spent so many years in darkness that being woken by the sun on his face was still special and he did not want it shut out. She had smiled and tucked him in with a kiss and then slid under the sheets beside him and curled up. He glanced over and saw her still lying curled up beside him. A machine did not need to sleep, but she could, well, not exactly switch off, he thought, trying to think of the best way to describe it. It was more like she put herself in 'sleep mode' like old computers used to have, only she was able to 'wake' immediately if he called her name. Knowing that felt good, and he settled back to watch the colours of the sky changing, gradually becoming blue as the sun climbed above the horizon. He woke again later, hearing a buzzing sound and felt the bed move as Serenity got up. He listened drowsily and heard her speaking to someone and then smelled fresh coffee. He rolled onto his back and opened his eyes as Serenity's footsteps approached the bed and saw her holding out a steaming cup.

"What would you like to do today?" she asked. "Beach? We're taking a boat trip to watch the whales in the evening when it is cooler."

"The beach sounds nice," Xander replied, sipping his coffee. "What are you going to do? I don't suppose Androids sunbathe?"

Serenity smiled and stroked his leg through the sheet. "No, but I have booked a surfing lesson. I can enjoy that, and I understand that humans find such sports exhilarating. Do you want breakfast here, or shall we go down?"

"Here, on the balcony," Xander replied. "It looks lovely out there."

Serenity passed him a t-shirt and shorts and then went to call for breakfast to be brought to the room. She followed him out onto the balcony, and they sat at the table together and watched the sea glittering under the sun, and then after breakfast, they headed down to the beach. Xander lay on a lounger, pulled on sunglasses, and covered himself in sunscreen. His skin was very pale and unused to being exposed to the sun and he promised to find shade if he got too hot, but he wanted to enjoy it while he could and get some colour back. He watched Serenity head off down the beach to her surfing class and smiled to see her mirroring the movements of other women in the group. After a while, he felt drowsy and moved the sunbed under the beach umbrella they had rented from the hotel. His eyes closed moments after he lay back down. A touch on his shoulder a short while later made his eyes flicker and then open and he looked up to see Serenity standing beside him, water dripping from her hair and trickling down her arms. "Did you enjoy it? I saw some but then fell asleep."

"It was just as exciting as I thought," Serenity replied. Picking up a towel, she scooped up the wet ends of hair and twisted them into a towel turban, and then sat on the sunbed next to Xander's. "I fell off less than the humans because I have better balance. I had to fall off a couple of times for the experience though."

Xander chuckled. Serenity's thirst for human experience never failed to amuse him.

That evening, they dined in the hotel's outdoor restaurant under the stars, and they made a point of dressing up for this luxurious meal. Xander wore a linen suit and Serenity wore a long white backless dress which hugged her figure, her long dark hair falling down her back. She wore the simple pearl and chain necklace Xander had given her for their wedding.

Xander smiled at her as they walked out of the hotel and along to their private cabana, close to Wailea Beach, escorted by a young staff member. "I feel like I am with a princess when you are beside me. You are quite the most beautiful woman here tonight," he told her.

Serenity laughed softly. "You are an old romantic." She tucked her hand into his arm. They did turn heads, she noticed with interest, as they followed the waitress to their cabana. She had caught a glimpse of herself in a mirror as they walked down the stairs after getting ready and knew what Xander meant. Perhaps people thought they were movie stars—they were looking at them like that. Humans were funny in the way they idolized people who spent their time pretending to be someone else to entertain others. It was an interesting concept and she felt it would be a good topic to study; it was clear from the way people looked, that they had no idea this woman they were staring at was not a real woman. Xander was a handsome man—she was not the only woman who noticed that, but he never seemed conscious of the fact that despite all he had endured, his advancing years were not that obvious. His greying hair just gave him a distinguished, sophisticated air.

They took their seats in the open cabana and looked out across the sea as the sun was setting, stars beginning to twinkle in the darkening sky. Their waitress brought champagne, but Xander asked for sparkling water instead and nibbled on the canapés which were brought with the drinks. They did not need to place an order as they had already chosen a menu which had been put together for them as part of their romantic experience and they were looking forward to it—even Xander whose appetite was not particularly good over recent years.

Serenity looked across the table as Xander began his seafood starter. "It is nice to see some colour in your face again. Are you feeling better?"

Xander raised his eyes, a grilled prawn speared on his fork. "I am feeling rested. It was nice to lie in the sun and the peace I have longed for is becoming easier to find. I realized that when we went to watch the whales and then sitting with you watching the sunset."

She reached over and rested her hand on his arm. "I am glad. You needed a break from the vicious circle of work and hospital."

Xander put the prawn into his mouth and laid down the fork so he could put his hand over hers. "If I did not have you, I would be dead by now. I know that. I would have died when I was abducted from my apartment. When you began to look and wouldn't give up, they knew they could not kill me because you would demand an enquiry. That is why they tried again in the

378

hospital and tried to make it look natural. But they could not contend with your tenacity and your love. Thank you."

Serenity smiled but said nothing as their plates were cleared to make way for their salad course. When their fresh plates were set in front of them, she looked up, meeting her husband's eyes. "You do not need to thank me," she said softly. "I love you and I would have done anything to help you, and to save you. And I always will." For the rest of the meal, she persuaded Xander to talk about his family and childhood, so that they did not talk about anything connected with work, or what he had been through.

Xander heaved a sigh of satisfaction after taking the last mouthful of his tropical fruit vacherin; a meringue cup filled with pieces of tropical fruit served with a cold pineapple and mango sorbet and a lilikoi—a tropical passion fruit—consommé. He laid his spoon down in the plate and leaned back in the chair and closed his eyes and smiled.

Serenity smiled. "Was it too much? You have not had much of an appetite."

Xander shook his head. "No, my dear, it was enough." He reached across the table and held her hands. "Thank you, I know why you planned all this, and I love you so much. I have been too ill to be of any companionship to you, and I had always meant you to have a honeymoon after we married. I am sorry."

Serenity's silvery eyes seemed to sparkle as Xander looked into them. "I do not regret any moment of the time I spent at your bedside. You are much better now and will continue to recover. You do not need to apologize for it."

They sat for a while, finishing their drinks, and then wandered, hand in hand, down to the beach and walked barefoot on the still warm sand, carrying their shoes, and listened to the surf rolling onto the shore. They stopped and looked across the shining water as the moonlight caught the tops of the rolling waves and made each movement of the water dance and sparkle. Xander put his arm around Serenity, and she rested her head against his shoulder as they stood together in silence, only moving when a wave broke over their feet. "Tide's coming in," Xander said. "Time to go in."

They walked slowly back toward the lights of the hotel and made their way to their suite. They walked out onto the balcony and stood looking out to sea; it was as though neither wanted to bring this peaceful evening to an end but then Serenity looked up and saw, in the moonlight, that Xander was looking drawn and tired. "You are tired." In her heels, she was as tall as him, but barefoot she tiptoed as she cupped his face in her hands and kissed him. She hugged him and then led him back into the luxurious room. It was a bright, modern room but had some old pieces of furniture from many centuries before, such as the writing desk, a coffee table, and a *chaise longue*. A thick cream carpet covered the floor, and a Persian rug was the centrepiece of the lounge area. In the bedroom, the bed faced the window so the occupants could look out to sea if they wished. The linen was crisp and white, and an aquamarine throw across the foot of the bed matched the cushions on the chairs and the colours in pictures on the walls.

Serenity went into the large bathroom and ran a bath for Xander. She helped him in and let him lie back, his head resting on the marble surround, the hot water relaxing his tired body. She busied herself getting his nightclothes ready and then washed her hair before going to call for room service for a hot drink to be brought for him.

Xander was tucked up in bed and Serenity was sitting beside him, preparing his medication for his injection, when a knock at the door heralded the arrival of a waiter with the hot milky chocolate Serenity had ordered. She gave Xander his injections and then settled him back to sip the hot chocolate before he lay down to sleep. She kissed him on the forehead and then sat back on her heels to watch him fall asleep.

The sun was rising when Xander stirred and woke. The pink in the sky had almost faded so it was not early; he rubbed his eyes and rolled over to look at the time. It was 08:00, much later than his usual waking time, but he had been tired. Serenity was not beside him in the bed and he guessed she had gone to sort out breakfast, leaving him to sleep. He sat up and pulled on his dressing gown and went through into the lounge. He picked up his tablet computer and curled up on the sofa to scan through his communications. Serenity had told him no work, but he was a senior officer who knew something was going on, and he had to check. He gave his ID when the computer requested it and then asked for his messages to be opened. Kehoe would not keep him up to date but, before they had left, he had asked Troy Franklin to let him know what was going on. Franklin had refused at first, saying Xander needed a proper break but had then relented, understanding. Xander was too involved to be kept in the dark. He was wrapped up in a reading and did not hear the door open and Serenity's footsteps across the thick carpet. He gave a start and looked up almost guiltily when she sat on the arm of the sofa and ran her hand through his hair.

"Oh, Xander, I thought I said no work," Serenity chided softly. One glance at the screen had told her what he was doing.

"I am just reading, I'm not going to do any work."

"That's what you always say." She leaned down and kissed the top of his head. "I know you are worried about Tiberius and the crew, but there is little you can do. Just the same as the others, all they can do is watch her. We don't know what move she will make, or what orders and communications she will send. All of us are as prepared as we can be."

Xander looked up. "I am afraid of what might already be happening. She may have had this all planned in the tiniest detail—I think she was planning it for years. Why them though? Why the same type of ship? Any ship and crew would have done, surely?"

Serenity shook her head. "Theatrics? A sense of power, knowing what happened the first time, and having it happen again—just as before. An identical ship, most of the crew connected somehow to the *Wryneck*. I think somewhere in all that, she finds enjoyment." She ran her hand lightly across his greying hair and he shifted slightly so he could lean back on her as she sat on the arm of the chair. "What does Commodore Franklin say?"

"He's sent me notes of the last briefing. They don't say much." He scrolled down the screen, touching it lightly with his finger. "Not a thing. But he adds a note at the end, saying Kehoe says that everything is prepared and ready to set in motion. All she is waiting for is acknowledgement. Serenity, they could all be dead." Xander looked up at her again. His brow contracted with a frown of concern and his eyes were dark with anguish. "They should never have been sent, they were never even given proper orders. I should have stopped the launch."

"None of us knew that, my darling," Serenity said softly, her hand still smoothing his hair. "Would stopping the launch have done anything? She would have sent them anyway. There was no proof. Don't get stressed about it, it is not good for you, and will not help matters at all." She worried too, and especially about how it was affecting Xander. When he got stressed or agitated, he would generally take a bad turn and she could see it coming.

Taking the tablet computer from his hands, she pulled him up gently and led him through into the bedroom and persuaded him to lie down on the bed and rest. "I'll go down to the pool for a swim, and I'll bring you some coffee when I return," she promised, stooping to tuck him in. "And you must promise to stay in bed. You can reply later when you have calmed down." Her fingers were on his pulse and he knew she was worried. The last time he had got agitated he had passed out and ended up in the hospital.

He cuddled down against the pillow and closed his eyes. A few moments later he heard the door close, and he rolled onto his back and opened his eyes, lying looking up at the white ceiling. Sunlight streamed through the open window and fell across the foot of the bed and warmed his feet as he lay thinking over everything and he gradually relaxed and enjoyed the peace and stillness of the quiet room. The surf rolling onto the shore and voices from the pool were the only real sounds that came to his ears. He smiled. Serenity had been right that this holiday—their honeymoon—would be good for him. He had not felt this relaxed in years; perhaps not since one day in 2783—the day before they reached Tamora and were taken prisoner.

51

"You came here to die!"

Commodore Troy Franklin entered Admiral Kehoe's office when she pressed the button to open the door after her security system scanned the officer approaching and told her who was there. He strode up to the desk and saluted. "Good morning, ma'am," he said, taking the seat she pointed to. "Your message said I was to come at once. I apologize for the delay. I was in the gym and I did not think you would appreciate my arriving dressed for a game of tennis and covered in sweat."

Kehoe laughed. "Perhaps not. I will excuse you." She tapped the screen set into the desk and a door at the other end of the room opened and an android entered. "Coffee, and breakfast. Bring the baked eggs that I like."

As they waited for the android to return, they talked of nothing in particular; the admiral asking how his game of tennis had gone and the like. Troy Franklin was an athletic man, and despite being older than many of the other officers at HQ, he was well able to give them a good game and won from time to time. As a young man, he had represented the Fleet at tennis and won many a trophy. It was the admiral's way to provide breakfast if she asked her staff to attend in the morning and, after a strenuous game, Commodore Franklin was looking forward to breakfast.

The android re-entered with a tray and nothing more was said until after they finished. Their coffee cups were refilled, and the android left.

Admiral Kehoe leaned back in her chair. She was a very small woman, and there were jokes that she sat on cushions behind her desk to give her a little height—jokes they made sure she never heard. Her grey hair was tightly braided and twisted into a tight bun. She was a buxom woman, and the left breast of her uniform tunic was covered with ribbons; she was one of the most highly decorated officers in the entire fleet. She wore little if any makeup, and her tanned face, clearly showing off her black and white ancestry, showed her to be a still striking woman. Now though, there was something ugly in her eyes; Franklin could not quite pinpoint it—anger perhaps, or hatred. But something guarded too, something was being concealed. "Well, Franklin?" she was saying.

Franklin quickly focused on her, instead of scanning her face as he had been. He hoped she had not noticed. It was hard not to, everyone tried to work her out, and it was difficult to even think that years ago, she and Xander Galen had once dated. "Sorry, ma'am, was miles away."

"I noticed. Have you heard from Galen?"

Franklin forced himself not to show surprise. He had been thinking of him, it was though she had read his mind and he pushed the thought aside that perhaps she could. "He's on leave. I told him not to even think of contacting me about work." He smiled. "He sent me a picture though. Part of their honeymoon package was a photoshoot." He took out his personal computer and tapped the screen for a few minutes and then passed it across the desk.

Kehoe took it and her face hardened, her eyes glinting like steel. "He looks happy," she commented, scanning the photo.

The shot showed Xander and Serenity standing on the beach, sideways on to the ocean. They were barefoot and Xander wore shorts and a bright Hawaiian shirt. Serenity wore a white swimsuit and a long sarong. She had flowers in her hair which was being gently rippled by the breeze from the sea and they were holding hands and looking into each other's eyes, as though the camera was not there.

"You would not guess she is a machine," Kehoe remarked. "And you can barely tell he has been ill." Her voice was harsh and bitter, and it took an effort to hand the tablet back to Franklin.

The look on her face told Franklin that had it been an old photograph she would have ripped it in two. He reached out and took the tablet from her. "I'm glad he is happy and having a good time. He deserves it after everything he's been through." He slipped the small computer back into his pocket and looked at her. "I am sure you did not ask me to come here solely to ask me if I had heard from Galen." His tone was cool and formal, and he did not like the look in her eyes.

"When you served on active duty, you were a communications officer and later a communications chief on three separate vessels, am I correct?"

"Yes, ma'am, that is correct." Franklin was wondering where this was leading.

"I have been in communication with the Tamoran President and his responses have ceased abruptly. You will look into this and see if there is some reason why they have stopped. Perhaps something is blocking his transmissions. Galen was quick to have his android set up security on his computer terminal to prevent anyone from hacking. Perhaps it also tampered with my system before they left."

Kehoe's voice was stiff and cold with suppressed anger and Franklin noticed she did not even attempt to refer to Serenity either by name or by the words applicable to the gender she had chosen. She had called her 'it'.

"I can take a look, ma'am," Franklin said. "Will you give me security access? I need to be able to get into the background areas of your system to see if there is anything." He waited, wondering. It all came down to trust. Would she trust him enough to give him access? Did she know he was a close friend of Xander's and was totally on his side; if she believed him to be on her side then he could accomplish so much more. He knew he was playing a dangerous game. Xander's many hospital stays, the sudden death of his doctor—all these told him to back off, but he had promised Xander he would do everything he could to get to the bottom of what was going on. He came around to her side of the desk. "If you would allow me to look in the settings—I can see if there has been any suspicious activity."

Admiral Kehoe moved her chair aside slightly so he could access the computer. She got up after a moment to answer a call that came through in her earpiece.

Franklin took those few moments of privacy to check out the last few messages sent to the Tamoran president. They were encrypted and he quickly entered a code, sending a copy to his personal computer. Just in time, he looked up to see her coming back to the desk. "It's all clear, ma'am. There must be some other reason why he has not yet responded."

•

There was a reason for it. Dayelh was on the *Invincible* and, under the captain's eyes, he was not able to contact Kehoe.

Tiberius sat opposite President Dayelh and wondered how much longer he could legitimately keep the Tamoran away from the planet. A flashing light caught his eye and he tapped the screen to acknowledgement the transmission.

Lieutenant Zeal, the communications chief, appeared on the screen. "Captain, you asked for this shot." The angle of the screen changed and showed the courtyard in the centre of the Tamoran palace.

Tiberius' jaw clenched even though he knew what he would see. Ross knelt there still, bound to the stake in the centre. He could not tell if he was conscious, and his heart pounded with rage as he looked at the Tamoran. "What do you want with us? What do I have to do to stop this?" Swinging the screen around, he pointed at the bound figure in the centre of the screen. "We came here to negotiate a trade deal and rights of access to the wormhole."

"No, Captain MacAlpin, *you* came here to die."

Tiberius felt the blood drain from his face as he met the cold eyes of the alien sitting opposite him. "No, *you* will release my crew, unharmed." His voice was like ice.

Dayelh laughed, harsh and grating. "*You* are in no position to dictate to me what I choose to have done on *my* planet." He stood up, his long purple robe falling in loose folds around him. He towered over the seated human.

Tiberius rose to his feet in a futile attempt at appearing as tall as the alien. At a couple of inches over six foot, he was a tall man but was nothing in comparison to the Tamoran who stood at least a foot taller. He knew that, by standing up, the Tamoran was intending to intimidate him, and he felt it working as the fear rose cold inside him, icy hands clutching at his vital organs. With a great effort, he kept the fear out of his face. He was not afraid for himself, not really. But he was deathly afraid of what the Tamorans meant to do to Ross, and the others of his crew they held prisoner. It was pretty clear they had no problem with the idea of killing them for no reason. He glanced back down at the computer screen and looked at the image of Ross, a lonely figure in the centre of a wide courtyard. Nothing else moved except for dust from the ground being whipped up by a breeze. He did not even want to try to imagine how alone Ross felt. Clenching his teeth, he slowly looked up and met the Tamoran's cold eyes. "Get the *Hell* off my ship!"

Dayelh scanned the angry face of the *Invincible*'s captain and laughed in a way that made Tiberius itch to slap him. "You have signed their death warrants," he responded. "And you will watch Ross die." He strode out of the door as Tiberius motioned to the security detail on the door to stand aside.

As the door slid shut, Tiberius slumped back into his chair. *What have I done?*

52
Fire

Tiberius stood on the bridge, his face like flint. The call came from the hanger deck, requesting authorization for the Tamoran's request to leave the ship. He took a deep breath and responded. "It's okay, I told him to leave." He turned to face the window and stood still, waiting. It was not long before the elegant, streamlined craft passed in front of the *Invincible*. It slowed and came to a stop and swung around to face the much larger vessel. Tiberius stiffened. "Battle stations!" he rapped, unsure whether the Tamoran ship was preparing to fire on them. The bridge crew sprang into action and alerted the crew to possible attack.

Lieutenant Zeal turned from communications. "Captain, he's hailing us."

Conscious that this was panning out to be similar to the setup of the dreams he had been plagued with at the outset of his command, Tiberius nodded. "I am not afraid of facing him face to face. Put it on the screen." A touch of a button turned the bridge windows into a screen through which visual communications could be received, as well as having the ability to run scans of oncoming craft, as an extra level to the scope of the ship's scanner array. "I'm listening, Dayelh." Tiberius' face did not give away his feelings as the Tamoran president appeared on the screen. "We are not afraid of you, or your threats. Your abduction of *Invincible* crew is an act of aggression. Let my people go in peace, or we will respond with war."

Dayelh laughed. "Fighting talk, Captain MacAlpin? What will it take to get you down to the surface to put your threat of war into action? Or will you sit up here on your ship, hiding from danger? A coward like your father."

A clenched jaw and a tic in Tiberius' cheek were the only signs that he was affected in any way by the Tamoran's words. "Do your worst, Dayelh. If you hurt *any* of them, I will destroy you. You will wish you had never embarked on your genetic experiments. When I have finished with you, what you have put your victims through will be nothing to the pain you will endure."

President Dayelh smiled, showing crooked teeth. "Watch the square. Do you know how long it takes a human to burn?"

The screen flickered and went dark, and Tiberius almost slumped into his chair. He clenched his fists to hide shaking fingers and it was a few moments before he could touch the intercom button on the arm of the chair. "Prepare my shuttle—have it ready for immediate take-off should I give the word." He turned to Zeal. "Keep every scanner on the square." He leaned back, heart pounding. He wanted to do something but knew Dayelh was trying to force him into making a move. If he did, then every member of his crew being held would be executed—he knew that for sure but he hoped desperately that Dayelh was simply playing mind games and calling his bluff.

•

President Dayelh jumped from the shuttle the minute it landed. His long purple cloak streamed behind him, raising a cloud of dust as he strode towards the presidential palace. The door slammed behind him and he shouted for the commander of his guard as he went into his office. Footsteps came hurrying along the corridor and a soldier hurried in. "Colonel Daviir is not here, President Dayelh. He is away to the other side of the planet, there has been trouble at the mine. He left me in charge. What do you need, President?"

Dayelh turned from looking out of the window. "Close the door."

Shortly after, the officer came out of the palace with a small group of soldiers behind him and they strode into the square courtyard where the lone figure of Commander Ross still knelt. They surrounded him and unlocked the chains that held him to the post and dragged him to his feet. He sagged in their grasp for a moment as the blood began to come back into his thighs and he began to struggle as his ankles were shackled and something like a horses' bit was slipped between his teeth and buckled behind his head, stifling any sound he tried to make. With his eyes covered he could only make out faint sounds as whatever was happening was being done quietly. After what seemed ages, the hands gripping his arms began to drag him forward and he was forced to mount steps. It was difficult with his ankles chained. Guiding hands turned him around and his back touched the metal post again and he heard chains being moved and his arms were pulled behind the post and cuffed tightly as a chain was crossed over his body and held him rigid. He tried to kick but his legs were locked in place too and a chain around his neck held him completely still. His pounding heart sounded loud in his ears and he was frightened—more scared than he had ever been in his life. He tried to call out but no sound except a muffled cry deep in his throat escaped him. The footsteps of the soldiers who had bound him moved away and he could hear them descending the steps. He strained his ears and heard faint voices and then one louder voice giving an order. A crackling sound and a sudden smell of smoke told him the truth of what was happening. They were burning him at the stake, like in ancient Earth history. He hoped it would be quick but knew from experience of these people that it would not be. He had read once that it could take between one and two hours to burn a human to death if the fire were controlled. The fact that the fire was crackling and not roaring meant it *was* being controlled and he would be made to suffer as long as possible, in perhaps the worst death he could imagine.

President Dayelh stood facing the stake, his arms folded. Captain MacAlpin had to do something to save his first officer from this agonizing death. He ordered the soldiers to let the fire burn quickly to reach his legs as there was no point in trying to cause him pain when his legs were prosthetics; he would not feel the flames until they reached above his knees. Once it was high enough to touch flesh, they would bring the fire back under control to prolong the torment.

Ross felt the heat of the flames getting hotter and he was frantically trying to struggle against the chains, denied even the release of screaming, as the first of the flames began to lick at the skin on his stumps were the prosthetics were attached.

·

The silence on the bridge of the *Invincible* was deafening as they watched the fire beginning to take hold and saw Ross' desperate efforts to get free. Tiberius' face was white and his hands, gripping the arms of the chair, were shaking.

Dayelh turned to look in the direction of where he knew the *Invincible*'s scanners would be directed. He made a gesture to the soldiers and some more wood was thrown into the flames. He slowly held up his hands, one finger at a time. Ten minutes, that's all he gave Tiberius to decide what to do.

Everyone on the bridge was looking at the captain, and they all looked sick. Tiberius looked up and turned to the intercom. "Get my shuttle ready—departure in two minutes!" It would take almost the whole of the ten minutes allotted to reach the courtyard. The last minutes in which he could save Ross' life. He left the bridge without a word—not even taking the time to give command over to the second officer.

Lieutenant Commander Kiana Yoshizaki, chief tactical and second officer, did not need to be told what she had to do and swung around from her station, calling for a tactical officer to take her place, as she took her seat in the captain's chair. She glanced back at the tactical station as her replacement hurried onto the bridge. "Lock weapons on Commander Ross. If that fire takes hold, kill him." The idea of shooting the first officer was horrible but she could not even begin to imagine the agony he was in as the fire slowly burned him. She would rather hold a gun to his head herself and pull the trigger.

As Tiberius reached the hanger deck at a run, two of the ship's security team restrained him. "You're not going down there, sir! They will kill you and Ross will die anyway. We're taking a team down; we'll save him and the others." Tiberius felt numb as they pinned him against the wall until the shuttle took off. When they let him go, he slumped and sank into a squatting position against the wall, his face buried in his hands. They were right, he knew it, but he could not get the image of Ross in the fire out of his mind.

•

The fire flared as the wind caught it and the flames rose a little higher. It was slow and painful as the strong wind blew the flames away from the prisoner from time to time which would only serve to prolong the agony. The metal bar strapped in his mouth stopped him from screaming but his legs were in so much pain that muffled squeals of absolute pain were being wrenched from him and he never gave up the struggle against the chains holding him to the stake. The stake itself was burning hot as the fire heated the metal. He longed to just pass out so the pain would be over but the wind was blowing the smoke away so he could not even be suffocated and put out of his pain. *Why did no-one come*?! That was the question running through his mind. He was going to die, and no-one was trying to help him. An anguished screech deep in his throat was wrung from him as he felt the last part of his prosthetic legs drop away and the flames began licking hungrily at the stumps. The fire was getting hotter, and he knew it was beginning to creep higher. *Why are they not coming*?! He had heard Dayelh, the *Invincible* could see this. *Help me, please!*

•

A message from one soldier loyal to Daviir had reached the commander of the guard who was in hiding with his band of rebels and Doctor Malachi. Daviir's face was grave as he turned to the doctor. "They are burning Commander Ross at the stake, we're going in. Dayelh is there, watching him burn." He picked up his weapon. "Arm yourselves. You too, Doctor. I know you do not wish to kill, but I think you must be able to defend yourself." He shrugged himself into the top of his skin-tight black uniform; he had been allowing the doctor to dress the healing wounds on his back. He threw a uniform across to her. "Wear this and you will blend in. I think it will fit, you are slim like we are." He eyed her lithe, long-legged physique. "Running and fighting will be easier than in the dress."

Knowing they had no time to lose, Rivkah began to pull on the uniform. She smiled as her companions turned away, giving her privacy—a consideration she had not expected. She refused the weapon Daviir held out but picked up the bag in which she had stored the medical supplies she had taken from the hospital to treat Daviir's wounds. "I am happier with this in my hands than a gun," she said. "My defence will be Krav Maga—martial arts. That can be just as effective, especially at close quarters. I can incapacitate while keeping my oath to do no harm—even to my enemies."

They were not far from the city. Not as far away as the mines, sorting out trouble, which was the story they had left in case they were missed. Rivkah glanced in the direction of the city and the plume of smoke rising from the centre was clearly visible and her heart sank as she imagined the scene and could not bear to think how Ross would be feeling—alone and suffering.

•

Ross could hear nothing now but the crackling of the fire as it grew louder as the Tamorans fed it a bit more and the sudden surge of heat told him that the wooden platform and steps had gone up and were burning fiercely. He wrenched and twisted his wrists as the smoke and heat rose around him. He knew it was futile, but he would not stop fighting to survive. A gust of wind blew the smoke in his face and he choked and hoped this was the end, but another gust blew it away again.

On the *Invincible*, weapons were locked on Ross, ready. Yoshizaki held up her hand. "Hold your fire, don't make a move until it is too late—not while there is a chance." The screen showed the shuttle circling above the palace. "They may be in time." The faces of the crew around her were set and strained. It was hard to sit there and watch Ross alone and suffering what would be an agonizing death if they could not get to him in time. Many of them were remembering that Kiana Yoshizaki and Commander Ross had been close at one time, and possibly still were but they had always kept any relationship discreet, and were perhaps simply good friends and, at a moment like this, no-one would have brought it up.

Lieutenant Zeal suddenly jumped to his feet and pointed at the screen. "Look!" he yelled.

As everyone followed the pointing finger, the courtyard wall behind the fire suddenly became a black mass as dark figures appeared on the top and scrambled over. "What's happening? The shuttle hasn't landed—who are they?!" cried the navigator, almost jumping out of her seat.

•

Daviir sprang from the wall with his soldiers behind him. Ninja-like, in their black suits, even their faces masked with black balaclava-like hoods, they sprang into the courtyard and rushed toward the fire. Weapons drawn, they rushed forward and pushed the soldiers back and formed a circle around the fire. "Go!" Daviir shouted and two of the hooded figures ran towards the flames and began to try and grab at the burning wood— thinking to drag as much away as possible to bring the flames down.

"It's no good!" Rivkah shouted. "We need to get him down." *No mean feat.* A glance had shown he was chained so could not easily be cut free. She saw the ladder behind the stake which would have enabled the soldiers to secure him, and she ran for it and shinned up. Now she was close behind him she could hear the stifled screams of pain and relief shot through her as she saw the shuttle landing behind Dayelh and the soldiers. She leaned off the ladder a little and began to wrench at the padlock that kept his wrists locked together. The heat was terrible, and the flames were beginning to lick around the back of the stake and the metal was hot. She needed the key but knew the last thing the Tamorans would do was hand it over at her request. She bit her lip and forced herself to take a moment to look closely at the chains. They were all linked to that one padlock and there was only one thing she could do. She reached into the bag fastened around her waist and pulled out a syringe. She took hold of his arm and pushed the needle quickly into the vein and pressed the plunger. In seconds, he passed out and the desperate struggles stopped. Slipping her hand back into the bag, she pulled out a knife with a long thin surgical blade. She leaned as far as she could off the ladder and put her arm around him, just under the chest, to support him, despite the flames which were roaring higher around him and were creeping higher up towards his waist. With the knife in her right hand, she cut along the join of his stumps and prosthetic hands. As she sawed through the last piece, the hands dropped away, and the padlock and chain fell with them. The chains around his neck and body fell loose, and he slipped a little way down the stake. With a superhuman effort, Rivkah heaved so that Ross slid around, away from the fire. The ladder slipped, bringing them both down behind the fire. As they fell, Rivkah prepared herself for hitting the ground and landed beside Ross. As soon as she felt herself hit the ground, she knelt up and was unbuckling the gag. She glanced up as running feet approached and two of the security team from the shuttle were beside her with a couple of special blankets which they wrapped around Ross. "You brought oxygen?" she demanded.

"There's a full medical kit, Doctor. We didn't know what you might need."

She nodded. "Help me get him to the shuttle before he wakes; his body will go into shock, I need to get oxygen into him. Hurry, while they are fighting!"

Two of the biggest of the security team lifted the inert body and hurried towards the shuttle, skirting around the pitched battle which had broken out between Dayelh's soldiers and those who were loyal to Colonel Daviir.

Rivkah pulled a couple more blankets out of the medical kit and rolled Ross onto them. She hunted through the kit and saw it was well-supplied with necessary items. She prepared a syringe of pain medication and put it aside until she needed it and got busy getting an oxygen mask strapped over his mouth and nose and opened the valve on the oxygen tank. "We should get him back to the ship, but I don't know if we should go yet—the others are still here, and I have a patient in the hospital." She wondered what everyone would say when they knew the identity of the sick man she had been tending for the Tamorans. She picked up the syringe and slipped the needle into Ross' arm again. She did not want him to regain consciousness and be in pain; it would be better for him to be out of it until he was in the *Invincible*'s infirmary where she could attend to his burns. She thought of the old man who lay sick and a prisoner in the Tamoran hospital and her mind ran on what Tiberius would say when he learned that his father was alive. She had vowed to stay at his side and make sure the Tamorans did no more harm to him, but she realized that he was in a safer place than Ross. "Take us back to the *Invincible*," she said urgently. "I'll get him stabilized, and then return to the planet. The rest of you stay here and help the rebels—they are fighting for us. Don't let Dayelh's soldiers reach the hospital." She knelt back over Ross and was running her medi-reader over his chest, recording his vital signs. Her face set with determination as one of the security team got into the pilot seat and prepared to take off while the other grabbed a weapon, jumped from the shuttle, and ran back to help his comrades and the Tamorans who had turned against their own people; not because they hated them, but because they hated what they had become.

The Tamorans were armed with strange-looking weapons, a peculiar combination between an old crossbow and a laser pistol. Daviir and his black-clad troop weaved in among the soldiers, cutting and stabbing with the long thin daggers they carried in a sheath on the underside of their arm. They were swift and deadly, as deadly as those they faced, and many fell on both sides, the ground growing dark with the shed blood mingling with the dry dust that blew across the courtyard, the cries of the dying mingled with the roaring of the fire which blazed furiously. Daviir glanced over his shoulder and saw no figure among the flames just as the blaze roared upwards. Had Ross still been there, there would have been no saving him now. He turned back and pushed through the figures milling around, determined to reach Dayelh before the president escaped from the battlefield. If he could force him to surrender, the others would throw down their arms and the fighting would be over. As much as he loathed what they had become, and the circumstances of his own birth, these were his people, and he did not want to kill them. He wanted to stop what they did and make Tamora the nation she had once been.

The smoke from the fire blew black across the fighters, and then cleared for a moment and Daviir found himself face to face with his father, the Tamoran president. His two closest soldiers were at his back as usual, and they closed in, daggers drawn and ordered Dayelh to surrender as the fighting swirled around them.

•

The hanger deck doors were open ready for the shuttle and a medical team was waiting with a wheeled stretcher and a trauma kit. As they lifted the unconscious first officer onto the stretcher, the doctor and her team worked at great speed to stabilize him there and then before rushing him down to the ship's state of the art hospital where he was taken immediately into the intensive care section and surrounded by a team of highly skilled and trained nurses and two of Doctor Malachi's junior doctors. She gave terse instructions as they worked. Knowing she could trust her staff to do everything they could, just as she would, she pulled off her gloves and surgical gown after seeing he was stabilizing. "I have to go back down, my help is needed by others. Keep him sedated and you know what you need to do if he begins to go into shock." She pulled off the cap which kept her hair up and it tumbled onto her shoulders. She reached into her desk drawer and pulled out one of the ties she used to keep her dark locks in order. She quickly tied it back and hurried out, running back to the hanger deck. In the shuttle, she touched the intercom and told the captain that Ross was alive although in a critical condition and he was being tended in the IC unit. "I'm going back—there are prisoners in the hospital."

Tiberius slumped in his chair and hoped she did not expect a response. He had watched the scene unfold for as long as he could bear but had finally covered his face and had not seen the doctor's heroic rescue of the stricken first officer. To hear he was alive was nothing short of a miracle. He took a breath and was shocked to find he had been holding it. Now the breath came in a whoosh that almost left him breathless. "Riv...Doctor...the prisoners—bring them on board."

"Most will not survive the journey home, Captain. They don't have four years left. The things they have suffered, and the slave labour..."

Tiberius heard the pause and guessed what she was going to say. "We can take them as far as we can. One of our outposts will be able to care for them as much as they are able. The alternative is leaving a medical team, and I don't want to leave anyone behind when we leave." He turned and looked at the screen.

President Dayelh was being faced by a small group of the black-masked figures and had raised his hands in surrender. Tiberius closed his eyes a moment as relief shot through him. Could this be an end to it all? Now Dayelh had surrendered, would he give up the prisoners without hindrance? Would he allow the *Invincible*'s crew down to the planet to assess the extent of their experiments? He needed a report to take back as proof. Without evicence, Kehoe would be able to deny her part in any of this. They needed unequivocal proof that she had been more than minimally involved in the sale and torture of innocent and frightened people. That she had been the cause of his father's death and Xander's illness, and the cause of the loss of an entire ship and crew. Watching, Tiberius saw the soldiers who had been defending their leader were all sprawled on the ground. Dead or immobilized, he neither knew nor cared, as he watched one of the black-masked rebels binding President Dayelh's arms behind his back, making sure the bonds were positioned in such a way that the president would be unable to unfurl his wings. He was then marched, stumbling, out of the courtyard and in through the entrance door to the presidential palace.

As Tiberius watched, the shuttle landed and Rivkah Malachi jumped down and ran at speed to the other side of the courtyard and disappeared through a door which led into the big white building Tiberius had decided must house the hospital and laboratories. He leaned back in his chair and tapped the intercom and called for the chief engineer to present himself on the bridge. He looked up with a smile as the engineering appeared a few moments later. Kohane Akina was an excellent engineer and was sometimes known as a miracle worker because it always seemed that for whatever was asked of him, no matter how impossible, he had a solution. "How quickly can you turn two of the cargo holds into emergency medical wards, Chief?"

Akina did not bat an eyelid. "How quickly do you need them, *Kāpena*?" he asked, using the Hawaiian for 'captain'.

Tiberius grinned. With a crew drawn from every nation on Earth and some who were born in space, everyone kept, even in this century, some semblance of their cultural identity especially in the use of words from their own languages. He liked this, to keep links with the past and the historical identity of nations despite the changes over centuries. "As soon as possible," he responded. "There are a lot of prisoners down on the planet who need medical attention. Many of them may die anyway but we need to do what we can for them, even if it is just to make their last days comfortable."

"How many?"

"Not sure; a hundred maybe?" Tiberius looked up again. "Do whatever you can, use whatever you need from anywhere to fit them out. Doctor Malachi will need all the room she can get for them." He dismissed the engineer with a nod and turned to make a note in his log of the orders he had just given and to record a note that Ross was still alive. "Although in what condition I do not know," he commented. "I am assuming critical." He curtly recorded a brief account of the scene and then switched off the recording. Even going over the scene in his mind as he recorded the words tightened the knot in his stomach. Watching the fire take hold around Ross and being powerless to help him had been the worst feeling. He bit his lip and turned back to the screen to watch any developments down on the planet.

53

Finding the Records

Rivkah Malachi hurried along the dark corridor of the hospital, heading for the room where Stephen MacAlpin lay injured. She pulled one of the gowns from the shelf as she passed and scooped her hair up into a cap. Lightly running her fingers over the touchpad by the door, she turned the lights up a little so she could see what she was doing and bent over the injured man. She touched him gently on the arm and he turned his head towards her, his eyes still covered with the dark cloth the Tamorans insisted on.

His wrists were still cuffed to the metal rails at the sides of the bed, but he seemed comfortable enough breathing with the help of the oxygen apparatus she had set up to ease the pain of the crush injures as his lungs expanded against the broken ribs. He mumbled something as he turned his head and coughed weakly. "I thought you weren't coming back," he said as the doctor removed the oxygen mask so she could monitor his progress better.

"I was never going to leave you" she replied. "I know you must have been scared, not knowing why I didn't come to attend you." She glanced at his hands and saw they were trembling. "I need to get your hands free first, that will make you feel a bit better. You've been left a while—did no-one help? I assumed they would, they made a fuss about you being injured."

"Only with drinking water. Nothing else, no-one helped me with the toilet, or keeping clean." He sounded ashamed and she understood. Injured and in pain, with his wrists chained, he was unable to help himself with any personal hygiene.

She looked around for something to use to unlock the cuffs. There was no sign of any keys but found a thin piece of metal that would do the trick with a bit of work. "Do you think you will be okay with the light on if I uncover your eyes?"

"If it's not too bright." He drew a breath and winced, coughing. He struggled for breath for a few moments and was relieved when the doctor put the oxygen mask back in place.

Rivkah gently unfastened the blindfold and removed it slowly, so as not to startle him with the light. "Close your eyes; let the light in gradually," she said. Thirty plus years in almost complete darkness was hard to comprehend. Many of the prisoners would be close to completely blind with the inability to focus their eyes after being kept in the darkness of the mines, or in cells with no windows. She smiled when she saw him close his eyes and keep them closed. He would open them when he was ready and would be able to sense the light through the lids. Her next task was to use the metal tool she had found to slip the locks on the handcuffs. She opened the cuffs and lifted his thin wrists out and laid them on the blankets and watched him move them weakly as though surprised he could move. She wondered how long he had worn chains. The scars and raw sores on his wrists told the story of being kept under restraint for many years—years where he must have fought against his chains before accepting the futility of struggling. "Are you okay with me cleaning you?" she asked, fetching soap and water and some cloths. "I'll get you comfortable and then we'll get you transferred to the shuttle—I will be better able to attend to you once we're on the *Invincible*."

He nodded consent. He was too weak and ill to refuse her assistance in any case even had he wanted too. The injuries he had sustained in the mine accident had left him unable to feel anything from his waist down, maybe even from the chest down and he lay quietly, his eyes still closed. He had not tried opening them yet, as though afraid to risk hurting his eyes in the unaccustomed light.

Rivkah worked quickly to clean him up and treated him with quiet respect. A man humiliated and forced to go naked for more than thirty years, she was not about to add to that by lacking in any respect due to an older man, and a senior officer. She pulled the blankets back down and tucked them in. "I'll prepare you now for the transfer to the shuttle. There are some things I need to get first—the laboratory records, and there is supposed to be an antidote to the virus they built. I have to take that back home." She sorted out a syringe and turned his arm over and scanned it. He had been subjected to a lot of injections and invasive procedures—the scars told a clear story. She found an area that was not badly scarred and saw him flinch only slightly as the needle slipped into his skin. "It's only a sedative, just to keep you comfortable while we move you. I do not want to cause you undue pain." She patted his hand as she rested it back on the blankets.

"Does Tiberius know?" His voice was beginning to get drowsy as the sedative worked. He took some wheezing breaths and moved his head from side to side, coughing.

Rivkah checked the oxygen and rested her hand lightly on the mask covering her patient's mouth and nose. "Take it easy," she said. She coaxed him into relaxing his breathing and counted the breaths gently. "Gentle breath in, slow breath out. Steady." When he was calmer, she propped his head up on another pillow and made sure he was comfortable. "Your son doesn't know yet. I did not want to tell him until I was sure you were going to pull through the first few days. Now, breathe steadily and you won't be in pain and you will fall asleep." She held his hand and squeezed it gently. "You can hold onto me until you're asleep. I don't mind." When his head fell slightly to one side, she laid his hand down and tucked the blankets around him so that they would be able to lift him on the mattress and keep him covered. She pulled straps across and buckled them tightly so that when they moved him, they did not run the risk of causing further injury. She left the room and hurried back to the entrance door and shouted for two of her comrades from the shuttle. She waited for them to run up and then took them to the room where her patient lay. "He's ready for transporting to the shuttle. He has severe crush injuries and internal damage. I've strapped him down but try not to jolt him if you can. I have to hunt for the records and some medication." She watched them wheel the bed out of the room and down the corridor before she rushed off to search through the offices. Daviir had told her they kept detailed records of every "treatment" they had given their prisoners and she knew it would help Xander Galen's doctors to treat him once they properly knew about the disease. Finding what she was looking for in one of the offices, she put the medicine into the bag she still carried at her waist and scooped up the books and found a bag which she filled with as many files as possible. She looked around, checking she had not missed anything and hurried out, leaving the hospital behind. She made for the shuttle but paused when Daviir approached her.

He held out a bag. "All the records—the trades and transactions, Dayelh's reports to your admiral, his request for new blood. They are all here along with the footage of the torture of the one we released. There is also footage of one of the laboratory specialists describing the work and the reason for the experiments. Take it. You will need it for the inquiry."

Rivkah took the bag, slinging it over her shoulder, along with the other bag. "Thank you for all you have done. Will you leave with us?"

Daviir shook his head. "No, my people need a leader now. I am Dayelh's son, nominally, and I must take his place. They need someone to help them move on from this. I will not erase what we did from our history, but we will learn from it." He put his hands on her arms. "Thank you for trusting me." He met her eyes. "Leave now—you can do no more for anyone. Dayelh already ordered the execution of the prisoners, there is no-one left alive in the mines. And the officers who came with Commander Ross—they were killed as soon as they were separated from him. I saw their bodies while you have been with your patient. Each one of them had their throat cut. I am so sorry."

Rivkah felt her chest tighten and the colour wavered in her cheeks leaving her very pale. "Dayelh said they were going to be sent to Garion." She thought about how Tiberius would feel; he was very protective of his crew and the cold-blooded, unnecessary murder of his crew members would incense him. She was not looking forward to breaking the news. "Can we take their bodies home?"

Daviir nodded. "I am so sorry," he said again. He turned to two of his soldiers and said something before turning back. "Will the captain come down to the planet at all now? It is safe for him. You can speak to him from Dayelh's office." He pointed to the door. "You will come with me?"

Rivkah passed her bags and the record books to one of the *Invincible*'s crew and told them to stash them carefully in the shuttle. Then she turned and followed Daviir into the palace. It was cool inside as she followed him along a corridor, and she noticed at once that it was very grand in comparison with the plain walls on the outside. She saw him holding open a door and she passed him and went inside. She looked around and found herself in a large room, laid out in formal boardroom style, with a long rectangle table with chairs along its full length. Off the room, was a smaller room, and this must be the president's office.

Colonel Daviir sat at the desk for a moment and tapped at some keys and gave a single word, spoken clearly. A password, no doubt. He stood up and indicated the chair. "The frequency is correct. Call them."

The *Invincible*'s communications officer answered the hail and listened for a moment before turning to from his station. "Captain, Doctor Malachi wants to speak to you privately."

Tiberius nodded and tapped the button on the arm of the chair and opened the connection, linking it to his earpiece so only he would hear the conversation. "Doctor, is everything okay?"

"Captain, everything is clear down here, but I think you need to come and see some things for yourself. All the prisoners are dead, except for one. They executed them all on Dayelh's orders. That includes our crew members who went with Ross. They were murdered at around the same time they were separated. I'm so sorry, Captain—I should have been able to save them."

54

Landing the *Invincible*

Tiberius gasped and his voice caught in his throat as he responded. "*All* of them?" Rivkah tried not to imagine the pain and fear as they bled to death unable to help themselves or each other.

"All seven. They cut their throats," she said. "I thought you would want to oversee bringing them back to the ship." Her voice shook a little too. It was impossible to serve alongside so many people and not think of them as family.

"I'll give orders for the *Invincible* to land," Tiberius replied. "There is an area large enough just beyond the city wall." He slammed the intercom off with the flat of his hand and the sound made everyone on the bridge look around in surprise. They were used to their commanding officer having little flare-ups of temper, but they had never seen an expression like that on his face. Anger and pain were written there, his eyes blazing and glistening with tears. He glanced around and saw them looking. "They killed them—all of them. Ross is the only survivor, and I don't even know if he will live. Kehoe must pay for this—as surely as if she held the blade that slit their throats, she murdered them." His voice was oddly calm but had a fragility about it that everyone knew the captain was grieving deeply. His crew had gone into danger willingly when he was forced to remain in safety, and he was so angry he was keeping it together with an effort. He took a deep breath, and his fists were clenched as he stood up. "Kiana, take over and land the *Invincible* on Tamora." He pointed to the screen, indicating an area to the north of the wall surrounding the palace. "There's room here, let's bring our people home." He left the bridge and headed down to the infirmary to see how Ross was doing.

404

As he entered the bright and sparkling clean infirmary one of Doctor Malachi's team of nurses hurried over to see the captain. "Commander Ross is in surgery."

"How is he?" *Silly question, he's obviously critical—you saw what they did!*

The nurse looked him right in the eyes. "He's barely alive. We are keeping him sedated—if he regains consciousness the pain may be enough to kill him."

Tiberius watched her face as she was speaking but he barely even saw her. The image of Ross burning was one he could not forget easily. He must have wondered why no-one came to help him until the doctor got there. He wondered if Ross even knew by then that he was being rescued. The pain and fear would likely have stripped his reason from him, and he could not imagine how Ross had managed to remain conscious for so long—the doctor had told him Ross was still conscious when she had been fighting to free him. He realized the nurse was still speaking and he forced himself to concentrate on what she was saying and then followed her to the door of the operating theatre. He looked through the window and watched the medical team at work around Ross. "You're not allowed to die. I can't bear to lose anyone else." He watched for a while and saw the team were working at speed and his keen eyesight could make out the vital signs on the screen beside the operating table. Although low, Ross' life signs appeared to be relatively steady and that was a comfort somehow. A slight jarring movement of the ship made him drag himself away from the window. The ship had landed, and he had to go down to the planet's surface, to be faced with the corpses of some of his crew. He headed towards the door and told the nurse to open up the ship's mortuary; the bodies would be held there in cold storage until they reached Earth. They were not going to be buried on Tamora, or in space. They should not be dead, so he would ensure their bodies were returned to earth where their families could bury them.

He ran back to the bridge and thanked Lieutenant Yoshizaki for landing the ship. "I'm going to meet the doctor, you're still in command till I get back," he told her. "I'll take one security officer with me. The Tamoran threat seems to have been destroyed, and the doctor has three with her already." He paused a moment and then smiled slightly. "Don't worry, I think I can do this." He did not know what else awaited him; a shock even greater than being faced with the bodies of his dead crew. He was about to come face to face with a man he had never met and had believed dead for so many years. Had he known this, he would not have felt ready at all. He headed to the very bottom deck of the ship and walked down the gangway that had been put out for him. He paused a moment and looked around, taking in the surroundings, and looking to spot the doctor.

Doctor Malachi was at the main entrance into the palace courtyard, watching for the captain's arrival. She took one look at his face and put her hand on his shoulder. "Are you sure about this?"

Tiberius nodded. "I'm sure." His voice was taut and overly calm, but it was the only way he could manage right now. He gave the doctor a weak smile. "I'm okay. I need to see it. Is it bad? Would it have been quick for them?"

The doctor shook her head. "Five minutes maybe, but that would feel like hours when you're suffocating in your own blood. It's a mess in there." She scanned his face and frowned. "I see anger, pain and grief—that is understandable. But I see guilt too. Do not blame yourself; you are not the cause of their deaths."

"I'm responsible for their safety."

"They volunteered to go. If anyone should be held accountable it should be me. If I had not spoken out of turn, Dayelh would not have invited me down. I disregarded your order not to bring up the subject of the experiments. I think we will all feel the pain of losing some of our own. We're a family but beating yourself up over it is not going to help, Captain." She put her hand through his arm and drew him towards one of the buildings set into the wall. She opened the door into a room off the corridor and looked over her shoulder. "Ready?" She moved slightly and let him step past her.

Tiberius pushed the door wide and stood looking in. The seven bodies lay face down in a pool of thickly congealed blood. Arms bound behind their backs, they were in the various positions of their last struggles as they died. "I'm so sorry—I will avenge you," he said, his voice as hard as iron. "I'm not going to let them get away with this." He leaned on the doorpost and put his hands over his face for a moment. A hand on his arm drew him away and he heard the doctor's voice speaking to someone else and then he was led outside where he leaned on the wall, breathing heavily. He glanced around and saw the doctor standing with some of her team and she was directing them to do something, and he guessed they had the unpleasant task of retrieving and preparing the bodies for return to the ship. He looked up as the doctor came back to his side. "I'm sorry, I nearly lost it in there," he said. "I don't think anything you could have said would have prepared me adequately."

"I'm going to shock you some more," she responded. "Remember I told you that they left one prisoner alive?" She began to tell him briefly about the importance the Tamorans gave to this man, and why, and how he had been injured in the landslip in the mine. "They needed my help because he's human and the injuries were critical." She paused and then said, "He's an old man and has been used very badly and has suffered a lot but he never allowed them to break his spirit."

This time it was a longer pause and Tiberius looked at her curiously. "Who is he, Rivkah? He sounds strong to have been able to stand up to these people."

"I asked his name while I was tending to his injuries. He told me his name is Stephen MacAlpin. Tiberius, your father survived."

Tiberius never heard her finish. A sudden roaring in his ears made his head spin and he slumped back against the wall and slid into a sitting position, his face buried in his hands. His heart was pounding, and his legs had just given up under him. His father had not died?! He had survived all these years, despite everything the Tamorans had put him through? The beatings, the experiments, the slave labour, and the abuse—how had he found the strength to go on day after day? More than thirty years as a prisoner, a lab-rat, and he was still alive? He was going to meet him, the man whose voice he had heard talking excitedly about the news of his son's birth in one of the few logs that remained. He looked up at a gentle touch and saw the doctor kneeling beside him, her hand on his shoulder. "He's not dead?"

Rivkah shook her head. "He is badly injured from the accident, but he is holding on—he is a very strong-willed man. He's in the shuttle now with one of my medics. Do you want to see him now? Or when we get back to the ship?"

"Now," Tiberius replied. "There will be a lot for me to do when we return to the ship. My report has to be made while all of this is fresh in my mind and I don't want to wait—not now I know." He took the doctor's hand and let her pull him up. They walked to the shuttle and he paused only a moment as they passed the remains of the fire where the Tamorans had tried to burn his first officer to death. "It all went out of control—Kehoe intended us all to die." He went on and ducked his head through the shuttle door as he followed the doctor in. His eyes were drawn straight away to the stretcher and the still figure lying there wrapped in warm blankets, the only sound being the gentle hiss of the oxygen as he was assisted to breathe.

Rivkah knelt beside the stretcher and touched her patient lightly on the shoulder. "Feel up to meeting someone?" she asked softly. "My commanding officer—your son—is here." She saw his eyes flicker and open. He squinted and she looked across at one of the medical team. "Can you dim the lights a little? It's a bit bright for him."

The lights dropped a little lower, and the sick man opened his eyes a bit wider. "Tiberius is here?"

"Yes, he's here. I think you can manage without the oxygen for a little while but lie still." She busied herself sliding his arms out from under the blanket and removing the oxygen mask. "It's okay. Take a moment and it will be easier." She put her fingers on his wrist and then smiled as she turned to look up at the captain. "He's ready."

Tiberius took a deep breath and then knelt beside Rivkah at the side of the stretcher. "Hey, dad." The words sounded odd; he had only ever spoken of him as 'dad' but had never imagined actually being able to say those words to his father.

Stephen MacAlpin looked up into the face of his son and his eyes filled up. The young man was around the age he had been when taken prisoner by the Tamorans and it was like looking into a mirror of the past. Tiberius had his face, his eyes, his hair. He reached up and gripped Tiberius' arms weakly. "Tiberius…my son." The tears were rolling down his thin cheeks now.

Tiberius reached out and gently wiped the tears away with his thumb and smiled. "It's okay, dad. I'm taking you home." He moved his hand and rested it on the grey hair. "Go to sleep now. I'll come and see you when we get you into the ship's infirmary." Very gently, in case he hurt him, he slid one arm around Stephen's thin shoulders, and they hugged briefly. The effort was too much for Stephen and his arms dropped limply. Tiberius moved aside so the doctor could attend to him, slipping the oxygen mask back into place. He took one of the thin hands and squeezed it. His father's eyes flickered open for a moment and they twinkled with a faint smile before they shut again.

As the doctor straightened up, she looked at Tiberius. "How do you feel?"

"Happy, despite everything else," Tiberius replied. "I can hardly believe it. It's a miracle."

Rivkah smiled. "Seeing you will have helped more than you can imagine. We'll take him to the *Invincible* and get him comfortable." She glanced out of the door and saw Daviir standing there. "Captain, this is Colonel Daviir. He was our ally here."

Tiberius stepped out of the shuttle and faced the Tamoran soldier. "Thank you for what you have done. Doctor Malachi says you were her ally and you helped save Commander Ross' life. I am grateful. Will you be leaving Tamora with us?"

Daviir shook his head. "No, I will stay here and help my people turn back to what we once were. I will claim the presidency in my father's stead, and he will pay for what he did; after he has made a full confession as to what happened here. You came here to get trade rights to the wormhole. I will, of course, grant your people this to try and offer some reparation for what we have done; the suffering my people have caused." He held out his hand.

Tiberius shook it without speaking for a moment and then said, "I wish you all the luck in rebuilding your world and retraining your people. I was prepared to ensure that every one of you was punished but I think some of you had no choice."

Daviir nodded. "As commander of the guard, I know who carried out experiments willingly and those who were involved in torture. They will be punished. Before the disaster that destroyed Garion, my people were not like this. It was this situation that turned them to find ways of repopulating the dead planet. We went wrong somewhere in the desperate race to save ourselves—I was against this, but I include myself as I am Tamoran."

Tiberius turned to the doctor and told her he was heading back to the ship to make his report. "Tell me when you have my father settled and I'll come down and get a full report from you, and to see him and Ross."

Rivkah nodded. "Are we taking Dayelh with us? He will need to stand trial?"

Tiberius paused and looked at Daviir who nodded. "I will grant you that right," he told Tiberius. "What he has done has harmed your people more than mine—your world must punish him. I will have him delivered to your security officers."

Tiberius motioned to two of the security officers and they followed one of Daviir's soldiers into the palace to reappear a few moments later leading President Dayelh between them. His arms were bound, and his eyes were covered with a black cloth just as he had done to his prisoners. He stumbled between the soldiers as they hurried him out of the courtyard and to where the *Invincible* rested. Tiberius watched them head through the gateway and a sense of relief washed over him knowing the Tamoran president would be secured in the *Invincible*'s brig. A few moments later he headed back to the ship himself, going directly to his quarters. He sat at the computer and began to record his official log and report of the events he had just witnessed. He talked about the burning of Ross, the execution of seven crew members, the murder of all the prisoners by sealing them into the mine, and the discovery of the identity of the only prisoner to be spared and, finally, the arrest of President Dayelh. Despite the strong feelings that were surging through him, he kept his tone calm and clear as he recorded and ended with a recommendation for the arrest of Admiral Kehoe and her three most senior officers who had been associated with her when the *Wryneck* was destroyed. When he tapped the screen to end and save the recording, he leaned back in his chair and exhaled deeply. Then he leaned forward and tapped something out on the keypad before getting up and heading to the bridge.

Once on the bridge, he sat in his seat with a deep sigh, mostly of relief—being on the bridge felt normal after the recent events and he felt like he could cope if he had some normality. He gave the order to lift off the planet's surface and he closed his eyes as Tamora faded from sight. That chapter was over.

55

Xander Makes a Move

Xander Galen looked up from something he was working on when his computer gave the incoming transmission signal. He was back at work now, after returning from Hawaii a couple of days earlier. He felt rested and much better than he had for a while. Sitting up straight, he asked the computer to play the message. He smiled when he heard Tiberius voice, but the smile died as quickly as it had come as he listened to what the *Invincible*'s captain was saying and he listened with growing horror as he heard the events being related. As the log concluded, with Tiberius recommending Kehoe's arrest, Xander took a long, deep breath. "Computer, restart message and pause." He leaned back in his chair and closed his eyes, his hands gripping the arm of the chair.

In the adjoining office, Serenity realized there was silence from the main office and stood up. She had heard sounds earlier; fingers tapping the keypad, a cough now and then, a voice from a recorded message. Always being concerned for Xander's welfare the silence worried her and she went through and saw him sitting with his eyes closed. She went over and touched his shoulder. "Xander? Are you okay?"

Xander opened his eyes and smiled faintly when he saw his wife standing beside him. "Sure, I'm okay. Just in shock. Listen to this. Computer, replay message."

Serenity listened in silence but, as the message went on, she slipped her hand into his and held it tightly. She could hardly believe it when she heard Tiberius' voice stating that Stephen MacAlpin was alive. When the message ended, she looked down at Xander. "What are you going to do?" She was wondering what emotions were running through him, hearing his old friend and commanding officer was still alive.

Xander returned the squeeze on his hand and then pushed himself up, leaning on the arms of the chair. "I'm going to do what Tiberius recommends and have Kehoe and her senior staff arrested," he said calmly. "Once that is done, I can process the rest." He raised his wrist and alerted security, a detail arriving shortly after. "Come with me," he said, turning to the officer in charge of the team. The group headed to Admiral Kehoe's office and Xander knocked at the door and went in, motioning the officers to follow him closely.

Admiral Kehoe looked up from her desk as the group entered. Taking one look at Xander's face, she guessed at once what they were there for and her face hardened. "Well, Galen? What is it?" She stood up, folding her arms.

"You're under arrest," Xander replied. "You will be taken to prison where you will be formally charged for your crimes against me, against Stephen, against the crew of the *Wryneck*, and now the crimes against the crew of the *Invincible*. Further information and evidence has come to light and there is nowhere left for you to hide." He turned to the security team. "Take her." He stepped aside and watched in silence as one of the officers cuffed Admiral Kehoe's wrists behind her back before leading her from the room. The rest of the security team went to three other offices and arrested the senior officers who had worked closely with Kehoe back when the *Wryneck* was sent to Tamora. Under the shocked eyes of the officers and men and women who worked at HQ, the four senior officers were led out under armed guard. They were bundled into a security shuttle and taken off to the prison where they would be charged and held until their courts-martial could be arranged.

The security OIC remained behind to speak with Xander who handed over a copy of the log transmission from Tiberius and requested that the case against Stephen MacAlpin be re-opened with the new evidence that had been uncovered by the pieces of missing logs he and Serenity found in their searches along with all the suppressed evidence, such as the full recording of his hearing.

Xander knew parts had been removed and it was clear that he had been put under pressure so they could state that he had condemned his friend and commanding officer. "Stephen MacAlpin is not dead," he told the security OIC. "Kehoe manufactured the whole situation and intended that none of the crew of Stephen's ship would live to tell what happened." When the officer left, Xander sat down in Kehoe's chair and rested his elbows on the desk while he collected his thoughts. Then he sat up straight and gave his access code when the computer prompted him. "Connect me with Fleet Admiral Caden-Zhu Morgan's office."

In moments, the face of the Fleet's supreme commander appeared on the screen. "Galen, what is it? You are well?" Like most of the senior officers, he liked Rear Admiral Galen. Xander was a well-liked and respected officer, and most had even greater respect for him for having survived his ordeal on Tamora and how he fought to maintain his position at HQ despite ill health.

Xander took a deep breath and then told Morgan what had happened and how he had ordered the arrests. "There is irrefutable evidence that Admiral Kehoe had a major part to play in the events that led up to the loss of the *Wryneck* and the things that have occurred since." He listed the numerous attempts on his life and then told him about the message from the *Invincible*'s captain. "There needs to be a full investigation now, sir. Enough is enough."

Fleet Admiral Morgan nodded without speaking for a moment. "I will order the investigation, and it will be thorough." He paused again and said "I need someone to take Kehoe's place. Someone I can trust to run things efficiently."

Xander nodded and recommended a few of his fellow officers but Morgan shook his head. "I want you to take her place, Galen. No, don't look shocked. Had you not been so ill, and with anyone other than Leandri Kehoe in command, you would have been in a position like this before now. Oh, and if you had not so stubbornly refused to let go of the captaincy of the *Victorious*. Your promotion to full Admiral will be made official within the hour. I know I will have your full cooperation with the investigation; I do not know who, beside Commodore Franklin and yourself, are not connected to anything Kehoe has been involved in. There could be a larger scale of corruption than you realize, and not just with the Fleet. What about who gave the original orders for the Fleet to assist Tamora in this way? That came from the government surely. You will give orders, on my behalf, that all HQ staff fully cooperate with the Judge Advocate General's officers. They are to have full access to everything they require."

Xander nodded. "Of course, sir. I will leave nothing out." He thanked the admiral and then leaned back in his chair as the screen went black. He pulled himself together and headed back to his own office. He went through to Serenity's side office and put his hand on her back. "My dear, will you help me?"

Serenity looked up quickly. "Are you ill, Xander?" She stood up and took his hands, scanning his face intently.

Xander smiled and shook his head. "No, I feel fine, Serenity. I just need your help to move my office—our offices. I spoke to Fleet Admiral Morgan and he has promoted me to Admiral and has ordered me to take Kehoe's post immediately and to assist the investigation into what has been going on."

Serenity squeezed his hands and tiptoed to kiss him. "You deserve it," she said. "Now, go and sit on the couch and I will get everything moved and sorted for you." She touched a button on the desk and some orderlies appeared. "Admiral Galen's things are to be moved into Kehoe's office." She began to direct the move.

Xander did as he was bidden and sat watching them working to transfer the contents of this room to his new office. He tapped his fingers on his knee, deep in thought, and then called for Commodore Franklin. He looked up a few minutes later as his friend came into the office.

"You're leaving?" Troy Franklin observed, looking around the partially cleared room. "Is everything okay?" He shot Xander a look of concern. "You would tell me if your health had deteriorated, wouldn't you?"

Xander stopped him with a shake of the head. "No, it's nothing like that, Ben. Kehoe has been arrested and I've been asked to take her place. I've been promoted and I'd like you to be my chief of staff."

Franklin smiled. "I would be delighted to accept. I am so pleased for you, Xander. You should have been promoted long ago." He looked around the rapidly emptying room. "You're getting bigger quarters. This room going spare?"

Xander chuckled. "Yes, it goes with the post." He paused and then looked at his friend. "I have to speak to the rest of the staff, will you stand beside me? It has been some time since I was permitted that authority, and some may resent it."

Franklin nodded and stood up. "I am entirely at your service, Admiral," he said. He held out his hand and helped Xander to his feet under the guise of a handshake.

414

They walked along the corridor to where the admiral's office was and paused to smile slightly at the plaque on the door which now read 'Admiral A.Z. Galen—Officer in Command, HQ'. "It looks good," he said, running his fingers across the plaque. "I hope this means an end to the problems. That I can sort out the mess and find closure for the families." He pushed the door open and then looked again at his companion. "Ben, Stephen isn't dead."

"*What*?!" Franklin stared at Xander. "He survived?"

Xander nodded. "Yes. Somehow, despite the odds, he survived."

"Just as you did. You're both fighters—you were never going to let them win. Now look at you—you've got one of the top jobs and the one who betrayed you is in prison. And, to top all that, Stephen is coming home." He put his hand on Xander's shoulder. "Let's go and tell the staff and get this investigation underway."

They made their way to the briefing room and saw the HQ staff officers already assembled around the table, the empty chair at the head of the table conspicuous by its emptiness. Xander felt all eyes on him as he walked to the head of the table and sat down in Kehoe's chair. Everyone gave him their attention—his face was grave and there was an air of absolute authority about him. He looked around and then folded his hands on the table in front of him. "Effective immediately, I have been placed in command of HQ—on Fleet Admiral Morgan's orders. Admiral Kehoe has been arrested and will be held in custody pending investigation."

"Can she be held without charge?" one of the officers asked.

Xander smiled slightly. "No, but she will be charged today. We have proof, and further evidence has come to light, of her involvement in the destruction of the *Wryneck* and the subsequent imprisonment and torture of myself and the captain, Stephen MacAlpin. She will be charged with crimes against humanity—and with treason. The three officers who were close associates of hers have also been arrested."

"You say there has been further evidence. What is this evidence?" the same officer demanded.

Xander met her eyes. "The same order she gave which led to what I endured and have continued to suffer, and which led to the death of my crew, and the destruction of our ship—the same order was given and signed by her to have the crew of the *Invincible* enslaved and held for genetic experimentation, as I was—as Stephen was. Commander Ross was used in an attempt to force Captain MacAlpin to hand over the ship. He now lies critically injured in their infirmary. The Tamorans attempted to burn him at the stake." There was dead silence around the table, and he scanned their faces and saw the look of horror dawning in their eyes as they realized what had been going on at the top. He took a deep breath and was about to say something else, but Commander Franklin leaned over and whispered in his ear.

"Don't give them all your information. Keep that bit to yourself for now."

Xander looked at him and wondered how Franklin knew he had been about to tell them that Stephen MacAlpin was alive. He nodded and looked around. "The official orders of my promotion and posting will be sent to each of you by the fleet admiral's office." He pushed down with his hands on the table to help himself up—the only sign of weakness he showed just then. Commodore Franklin put out his hand as though to steady him but did not touch him—it would be the wrong thing to do just then.

Xander went back to his new office and lay on the sofa, pillowing his head on the cushion. He closed his eyes and was thinking about his new role and the investigation, but most of all, he was thinking of the news that his best friend and old commanding officer had not died on the planet that had become their hell. He opened his eyes a moment later as he heard a footfall and felt a gentle hand on his shoulder.

"You are weeping," Serenity said, her fingers touching the damp streaks on his cheeks.

Xander sniffed and wiped his eyes. "I didn't realize. I was thinking about Stephen. I thought ten years in that place was the worst thing—sure that everyone I cared about was dead. Blown up on the *Wryneck* or tortured to death in a cell beside mine. We heard each other's screams as they tortured us. And now I know he lived and suffered so much longer at their hands than I did."

Serenity sat on the edge of the sofa and took his hand and squeezed it. "He will be happy to know you lived too. Despite it all, you both clung to life and would not let go. Not even at the point of death." She looked into his eyes. "You weep because you have grieved so long, and now you do not need to. But you grieve also for the lost years. I understand."

Xander smiled. "I could not have faced these last years alone, without you. I feel better now." He wiped his eyes again. "I can

416

face the enquiry now without being distressed by their questioning—although I do not look forward to their asking me to talk about my experience." He smiled again when Serenity leaned forward and kissed him on the forehead. "I think I will sleep for a bit; I am tired." He closed his eyes again and drifted off as she stroked his hand. He needed his strength to face the investigation.

Serenity re-entered the office an hour or so later and stooped over the couch and gently shook Xander, wishing she did not have to disturb him.

He stirred with a soft groan as he began to wake. "What is it?" he mumbled, rubbing his eyes.

"An officer of the Judge Advocate General's office, he wants to interview you." Serenity took Xander's hand in her strong grasp and helped him up. "I'll send coffee in," she added, watching him go to the desk and settle in the chair. She removed the blanket from the couch and plumped up the cushions. She stowed the blanket in the cupboard before going to the door. She stepped into the corridor and crossed to the bench where a young man in uniform bearing the insignia of the JAG department. "Admiral Galen can see you now. I am Serenity, the admiral's aide." She deliberately played to her android status. If she were seen initially as a machine and not the wife of Xander Galen, they would not be influenced by her relationship with Xander. "Please follow me." She showed the lawyer in. "Commander Isaac Quinn, from the Judge Advocate General's office, Admiral."

The young man saluted and quickly said, "Don't get up, sir," as Xander began to get up, holding out his hand. He leaned over the desk and shook the older man's hand.

Xander smiled. "Please, sit down. I understand you wish to interview me."

Quinn nodded. "I am aware some of my questions might be hard for you to answer as they will awaken memories you do not wish to have stirred up. You can stop me at any time, but the more you can tell me, the more it will help. Your wife can stay with you if you prefer." He had done his homework beforehand and knew exactly who Serenity was.

Xander smiled as Serenity brought a tray of coffee. "I think I can manage, she will be in her office if I need her. And I think you will wish to interview her too." He took a sip of his coffee and let the lawyer begin with his questions.

56
Heading Home

The *Invincible*'s bridge crew took it in turns to take the command shift, giving the captain time to spend in the infirmary. None of them even thought of saying that his place was in the command chair. His place was just as much at Commander Ross' bedside, or at the bedside of the man they had rescued from the planet. The entire crew had been shocked and amazed to hear that it was Stephen MacAlpin, their commanding officer's father—the man he had idolized for so long but had never known. They had a lifetime to make up for and no-one would imagine telling the captain his duty was on the bridge right now. They were heading home, and the bridge crew were more than experienced enough to take the day to day running of the ship.

Tiberius sat beside Ross' bed. Ross was still in the medically induced coma he had been placed into two years ago after being pulled from the midst of the fire that was meant to kill him. He looked up as a footstep sounded beside him and saw the head nurse Asher Graham coming over to the bed. "How is he?" he asked.

Nurse Graham looked at the screen over the bed and then turned to his commanding officer. "As well as could be expected," he said. "You know we had to put him into a coma to reduce the risk of shock. The burns have healed well and there has been no risk of infection for some time. Doctor Malachi believes we can try to bring him around and see how he does with recovering naturally. It will be some time before he is well enough to consider refitting his prosthetics."

Tiberius nodded. "Can you try?"

The nurse nodded and busied himself at the bedside for a few minutes. "Easy," he said softly as Ross moved his head. He touched a button, raising the head of the bed a little, so his patient was not lying completely flat. "The captain's here. You up to seeing him?" He carried on talking gently as he worked, even though Ross was groggy from the drugs that had kept him unconscious. "There, that'll help you feel a bit better," he added, attaching another drip to the cannula in Ross' arm. He moved aside and told Tiberius to go easy and to call for one of the nursing staff if Ross was having difficulties in any way.

Tiberius stood up and moved closer to the bedside. Ross' eyes were closed and his face very pale. Oxygen tubes were still in his nose and the monitor by the bed made a soft beeping sound which Tiberius found reassuring. He smiled and gently touched Ross on the shoulder. "Hey," he said softly. "They say you're making great progress."

Ross' eyes opened slowly, as though his eyelids were heavy and it was a moment or two before they focused on the man by the bed. His lips moved but no sound came. He was heavily doped up and it was taking a while for his head to clear.

Tiberius smiled. "You recognize me, don't you?" he asked.

Ross gave a tiny nod and summoned enough strength to say, "Yes, sir." After a few moments he seemed to rouse a little more and his eyes opened again. "How long?"

"Two years; we're halfway home."

Ross looked along the bed and saw the frame holding the sheets off his body and enough of a memory came through his foggy mind. "I didn't die?"

Tiberius shook his head. "They were trying to make me choose between your death or the surrender of the ship and the loss of the entire crew."

"And?"

"I wasn't going to let either happen." Tiberius briefly told Ross what had happened.

Ross shuddered suddenly as the memory of the flames around him began to come back. Tiberius put his hand on his shoulder. "It's okay, take it easy."

"I'm okay," Ross responded, bravely. "Tell the doctor I need to get back to the bridge. You need me—I need to be there."

"I need you to get well first. You'll be back beside me before we get home, I know it. Doc says you're making good progress, and now you're awake it will be even better." Tiberius glanced up and saw Doctor Malachi heading over. "Here she is. He wants to be back on the bridge, Doctor," he said, turning as she came up.

Rivkah Malachi smiled and nodded. "Of course he does, and I'm going to get that to happen as soon as possible." She looked down at her patient. "How are you feeling?"

"Groggy," Ross responded, the drugs making him slur his words a little. "But I don't feel sick." He seemed to suddenly become aware of the straps that held him down so he would not move and injure himself and he went into full panic as the memory of being bound and burning returned.

Tiberius was almost shoved aside as the doctor made a sign and a team of nurses ran to the bedside and began to work on calming Ross.

Ross lay still and quiet after a sedative was administered and he looked very pale. "I wanted to be ready," he mumbled, looking at Tiberius. "You need me."

Tiberius moved closer to the bed again as the nurses moved away. "You'll get there, you've only just woken up. You're in the right place—let them do what they need. Work hard and do everything they tell you and you'll soon be back on the bridge. We're on the way home, you can take your time." As he left sickbay, he met Doctor Ravello, the ship's psychiatrist, coming in. "When Ross was injured back on Tycho, you said the mental scarring would go deep. What is *this* going to do to him?"

Doctor Ravello looked at him in silence for a moment and then said "I don't know. It was tough on him after Tycho. He is strong and very brave, but this time? I don't know. We will be with him every moment; we will do everything we can. That is all we can do—much of it relies on him and how well he can cope with what has happened to him."

Tiberius nodded and went out. He would pop back later to visit his dad. It still felt odd, knowing his father was alive and on his ship. After all these years, Stephen Michael MacAlpin was coming home. He smiled, there were many years to catch up on, but the brief weak hug Stephen had managed on the planet told him that his father had been happy to see him and to be able to touch him. Perhaps it had made it all seem real—he must have dreamed that one day the ordeal would be over, although even in his wildest dreams he could have never imagined it would be his son's ship that rescued him. He wondered what his mother would say. Ten years ago, she had finally married again. There had been no reason not to. Stephen had been officially declared dead years before, and after all this time there had been no reason to even imagine he had survived. The hearing had been final, and Xander Galen's testimony had been proof enough. Stephen MacAlpin was dead. Bethany MacAlpin had accepted it, but she had not been able to move on for many years and now her son wondered who would take the news the hardest. Tiberius understood, and he understood why his mother had chosen a man who was not in the Fleet, or any branch of the armed forces or the police. She wanted the security of knowing her husband would come home at night and not die on a battlefield somewhere, or perish on a distant planet, in a galaxy she had never heard of. He did not blame her in the least. But it would be a shock to her to hear the news.

•

The docking bay doors loomed nearer, and Tiberius leaned forward slightly in his chair as though by leaning thus he could hasten their arrival. A glance to his right put a slight smile on his face. He had missed having the first officer at his side. Others had stood in for him admirably, but they had all been relieved when Ross had walked back onto the bridge six months ago. Recovery and the fitting of new prosthetics had been harder because of the burns he had suffered but when they eventually healed it had not been long before he was well enough, physically and mentally, to undergo the operations to fit his new prosthetics. He was still under strict medical observation, but everyone noticed that as soon as he was back in his rightful seat at the captain's side, he had brightened up considerably and that aided his recovery without a doubt. A member of the medical team visited him daily on the bridge and he had regular meetings with Doctor Ravello so he could talk over his experience but besides that, he did not talk about what he had been through.

In the hanger deck, the security chief, Commander Jackson Rae, was putting the security detail through their paces as they were to carry the coffins of the seven murdered crew members down from the ship before the rest of the crew disembarked. "You'll follow a drummer down," he said. "Captain MacAlpin will be there with Admiral Galen and a bugler will greet you. It's the best we can give them now."

Ross glanced across at Tiberius and saw him watching the docking bay doors opening and the lights of space dock flaring out into the darkness of space. The captain looked very serious, and Ross wondered what he was thinking of, but he did not interrupt him just then. Instead, he gave the precise heading to the navigator and helm that he had just received on his screen. He glanced back. "You okay, sir?"

Tiberius started and turned at the first officer's voice. "Sorry, did you say something? Forgive me, I was miles away."

"I noticed," Ross said with something like his old grin. "Anything I can help with? Or are you just…um…moody?"

Tiberius could not help but smile before his face clouded again. "I'm just thinking about what to say to the families of your team."

Ross met his eyes. "You know it would have made no difference. Even if you had chosen surrender or allowed me to die, they were dead already. Nothing you could have done would have saved them—the Tamorans did not need all of us to further their project. They only needed fresh blood; they would have chosen a few who fit their requirements and the rest would have been tortured and then executed." He went on as Tiberius looked down at the deck. "Yes, as captain, you are responsible for the lives of all on board, but you're not responsible for their deaths. They sign up knowing there is a level of danger involved. What happened to us was because of betrayal. All you need to say, if you feel you have to, is that you are sorry for their loss and that you will avenge them by seeing justice done."

Tiberius let out a sigh, almost of relief. "I missed you—your counsel is always good."

Ross chuckled and then looked serious. "It's going to be fine. You can get through this. Once the coffins have been brought out, you can get out of everyone's gaze for a while. You need to get a rest before any debriefing. Xander will understand."

Tiberius did not reply as the officer at the helm turned just then and informed him that docking was complete. "Thank you." He tapped the screen on the arm of his chair. "Standby for disembarking." He paused and then said "Commander Rae, is everything ready? I'll go down first, with Ross."

Rae looked around and saw the row of coffins, each covered with a flag, with security personnel standing ready to lift each coffin onto their shoulders and carry them off the ship while the ship's lights were dimmed as a mark of respect and the steady drumbeat leading them slowly. There would be silence from the ship as their comrades made their last journey from the *Invincible*, and there would be silence among the officers waiting to greet them, each silently standing to attention and saluting as the coffins passed by them. "We're all set, Captain."

As Tiberius and Ross stood with the senior officers who had gathered to welcome them home, there was silence all around. A welcome home after an eight-year voyage could wait when that homecoming was tinged with the hovering mantel of death. Tiberius could not get the image of their murdered bodies out of his mind, no matter how hard he tried. He knew it was because he did not want to forget. The column of coffins slowly passed him towards a row of shuttles waiting to take them to their final destination before the funerals were arranged. As the beating drum faded from earshot, a single bugle played the 'Last Post' and Tiberius bowed his head. That bugle call never failed to stir all kinds of emotions and the images of his dead crewmembers rose up before his eyes again. He looked up at the touch of a hand on his shoulder and he saw Xander beside him.

"You okay, Tiberius?" the older man asked.

Tiberius nodded. "Just thinking there are some things as captain I never want to get used to."

Xander nodded. "Losing members of your crew never gets any easier, no matter how long you are in command." He paused and then asked, "Can I see him?"

Tiberius nodded and a smile spread over his face. "Yes, Admiral," he said, a little cheekily. "I'm glad you were promoted, it suits you."

Xander glanced at the rank braid on the sleeves of his dress tunic. "I was honoured to be asked." He followed Tiberius up the gangway and into the *Invincible* where they passed crew preparing to leave the ship, all of whom immediately snapped to attention and saluted. Xander returned the salutes with a smile and a gentle nod which was his way. As they neared the infirmary, he paused. "Is he very ill?"

"Four years of care is making a difference," Tiberius replied. "But it's going to be a long struggle. I think Doctor Malachi is planning to try and get him up and through some physiotherapy. She's good; she brought Ross through both times. I thought I would miss the *Victorious*'s doctor, but we struck lucky with her."

The doors to the infirmary slid open and they were greeted by one of the nurses who took them to the doctor's office. Rivkah Malachi stood up when the nurse showed her commanding officer and the admiral in.

Xander made a gesture. "No need for ceremony, Doctor, we're in your domain."

Rivkah smiled. "You don't want to sit talking, you want to see him. He is doing much better and has made great progress. I hope to start helping him to walk again, and his breathing is getting much easier. Sleep and good food have done more for him than anything else. He still has a long way to go, but I'm glad you did not have to see him as he was when we first brought him aboard."

Xander nodded. "Thank you."

"I'll take you to him now," she said, waving his thanks aside. "It's my job and I love my work. To see him making such good progress is thanks enough."

Xander and Tiberius followed her to the far end of the general ward to where there were a few private rooms. She tapped the entry panel and the door slid open and then she stood back to let Xander go in.

Xander paused at the door and stood in silence for a moment, looking at the man lying in the bed.

Stephen MacAlpin's eyes opened as he sensed someone was there. His eyes fell on the man in the doorway and his eyes opened wide. "*Xander*?!"

Xander reached the bedside in two strides. "Stephen!" He grasped the hand that was weakly reaching out to him. "Stevie…"

Rivkah tapped the panel again and the door slid shut. "We don't need to be here just now, they don't need us." She turned to Tiberius. "I have something. Remember Daviir, the Tamoran who helped us? He showed me the records and I could see a detailed account of every stage of what they did to Admiral Galen. There was mention of a medicine they used to bring him around and alleviate the symptoms of the disease that was afflicting him before giving him the virus again. I have thought I should test it and see if it will help, if not cure him. They were looking for the effects it had on the human body. If he had been able to fight it the way they wanted for people they would send to Garion, he would have been cured."

Tiberius nodded. "I'm glad we're far away from that hellish place. What they did to my father, to Xander, Ross and the crew we lost—and killing all their prisoners, just because they could. If we hadn't left then I think I would have found a way to destroy the entire planet."

She looked sympathetic. "I understand, but what about putting that anger to good use, and seeing the one who sold both crews into that hell is brought to justice?"

Tiberius drew a deep breath and nodded again. "You are right, she must pay for what she has done." He followed the doctor back to her office and went over the notes she had taken from their unexpected ally's translation of the experiment records.

•

Xander stood up as he saw Stephen's eyes closing and knew the medication was making him drowsy. "I'll come back later." The grip on his hand tightened for a moment, but Stephen was still too weak to fight against the drugs. The pressure relaxed and the hand dropped to the sheets. Xander tucked Stephen's arm under the sheet and slipped out.

Tiberius glanced up when he saw Xander pass the office window and made to stand up. The doctor's hand on his arm stopped him.

"Give him time. They both believed the other dead. He will not want to talk to anyone. Not yet, and not even you." She smiled. "Remember how you wanted to be alone when you were able to see Ross for the first time after both those incidents?"

Tiberius leaned back in his chair, nodded. He knew exactly what she meant.

Xander took a shuttle down to Earth from the space dock. He sat in silence during the relatively short journey and strode into HQ without meeting very many people. He reached his office and sank into the chair at his desk. He rested his arms on the desk and let his head rest on his arms. He had hardly dared to believe it was true until he had seen Stephen. He sat still, all his emotions jumbled together as he tried to piece everything together. Against all odds, they had both survived.

57

"I will conduct my own defence"

Six months seemed to drag by, at least Tiberius felt so. Endless meetings with senior officers, and lawyers from the Judge Advocate General's office, endless going over the same details, endless interviews that dragged on and on until they seemed like interrogations. Ross was interviewed with both Doctor Malachi and Doctor Ravello present because they were concerned that the questions about the burning would affect him too much. He managed to get through the interviews without having to take very many breaks and without being too distressed by having to relive the trauma.

The interviews with Stephen MacAlpin took longer as he was still far from well, although making good progress. They were only permitted a short time with him when the doctors judged him comfortable enough. After any session with him where they talked about the first days of captivity, they then cross-examined Xander to see if their stories matched. These accounts were then checked against the official records and with the bits of logs they had access to. There was a lot of material still encrypted and Kehoe would not give in to the JAG officers' demands for access. They had a team working hard to try and break through the encryption codes. Kehoe's defence lawyer had even pointed out that her constant refusal to give the access codes looked bad for someone claiming to be innocent of the charges upon which she had been arrested. She knew her colleagues at the JAG office held her in some contempt for accepting the defence brief. The story of the loss of the *Wryneck* and her crew, and the stories being learned now of the torture and slave labour Stephen MacAlpin and his first officer had endured resonated with many and defending Kehoe was something none of the JAG officers wanted, despite everyone, whatever they have done, having the right to justice and a fair trial. She knew her client was guilty, but Kehoe did have the right to be defended. She called at the prison to talk over the upcoming trial and to try, once again, to get the access codes, and she was troubled to find Leandri Kehoe in good spirits.

"They cannot convict me without proof. Everyone knows Xander Galen's testimony was that of a sick man who had endured ten years of torture and genetic experiments. He would have said anything. It is even debatable whether he was in his right mind at the hearing," Kehoe told her.

Lieutenant Commander Jalila Ahmadi looked at her with almost undisguised disgust written across her face. It took all her willpower to bite back the response she felt rising within her. This woman, almost at the pinnacle of a long career, had no remorse—no compassion towards the people whose deaths she was accused of causing. She took a deep breath and placed her tablet computer down onto the table and folded her hands on top of it. "You are not making my job easy; you are supposed to be giving me a reason to defend you. You have been charged with conspiracy to enslave and murder; they are holding you responsible for all the deaths, as well as the various attempts to murder Admiral Galen."

Kehoe looked at her then. "*Rear* Admiral Galen," she corrected, laying stress on the first word.

The young attorney shook her head. "He was promoted on your arrest." She jumped a moment later when her client slammed her cuffed hands onto the table and made a move to get up.

One of the guards entered the room immediately, and the prisoner leaned back in her chair with a mocking smile. "I should have made sure they finished the job. He should never have survived."

Jalila Ahmadi pursed her lips. "You realize that every time you open your mouth it makes my job harder?"

Kehoe leaned across the table. "Do you think I care?! I've seen the look in those pretty dark eyes—you know the law means I have a right to defence, but you don't believe I *should* be defended. You know I am guilty and you're going to make sure the prosecution wins!"

Jalila's face darkened for a moment. "I will do my job, but the prosecution has a better case—because they have proof of your guilt. Whatever I say, whatever reasons I give for what you did will be shot down in flames by my prosecution colleagues, however hard I try for you." She stood up and picked up her tablet, slipping it back into her briefcase. "I feel sorry for you. You have had a good career and should be looking forward to your retirement. Instead of which, you have come to this. In prison, awaiting trial for murder. Are you aware that you face a life sentence on a penal planet? For a woman your age, this is as good as a death sentence—life will really mean life. It is not one murder, but over four hundred, and the unethical experiments and torture to which Admiral Galen was subjected to. Things will go better for you if you plead guilty instead of persisting in this charade." She closed the briefcase and turned away.

"I'll dismiss you," Kehoe said quietly. "I will conduct my own defence. I can clearly see how you feel." It was the first time the arrogance had died out of her voice and when Jalila looked back over her shoulder, the mocking smirk had left her face. It seemed as though the lawyer's words had finally sunk in and made her realize exactly what it was that she faced. "You have tried to do your best, but you have strong ethics, I don't suppose I am in any position to expect you to lay yours aside. I was wrong to think you would be the same as me."

"I think that is the most honest you have been with me," Jalila responded before turning again and nodding to the guard who unlocked the door and escorted her out. As she reached the end of the passage she paused and looked back and saw Kehoe being led back towards the cells. She watched until they rounded the corner and then hurried out of the prison, as though she could not leave fast enough. Hearing her ex-client speaking about what she had done with no shred of remorse had really got to her.

58

The Trial

The morning of the trial dawned and there was an air of just how big a day this was. Xander had lain awake most of the night, his nerves getting the better of him. The fact he would be called on to testify was getting to him and how it would invoke painful memories that he did not want to talk about. He got up and pulled on a dressing gown and stood on the balcony, watching the dawn breaking over the city. He turned as he heard a footstep behind him and saw Serenity with a mug of coffee which she held out to him.

"It's 05:00, Xander. You've been restless all night. Are you worried about the trial?"

Xander took the mug and nodded. "Yes. Mostly worrying about what they will ask me; what memories that will stir up."

"It will be worth it for this to be over." She rubbed his back and smiled.

Xander gave her a look that told her what he was thinking even if he couldn't put it into words. He sipped the coffee and sighed. "I wonder how Stephen is feeling. Kehoe doesn't know he's alive, that he's home. There'll be an uproar when he is called on to testify—if he's well enough."

"It is hours before we have to be there, you should have a bath and relax. It's all going to be fine, you'll see. Don't worry about Stephen—I believe he will find the strength he needs to finish her. His personal testimony will be more powerful than anything the prosecution will present."

•

In his old apartment, Tiberius had not slept much either; going over everything he wanted to mention when called upon. When they had left for their voyage, Ross had let out his apartment, so

Tiberius had invited him to stay with him. He gave him the bedroom, not just because he was the guest but also because it would be more comfortable with his prosthetics than trying to curl up on the couch. Ross was taller than him, so he took the couch. He lay, his head pillowed on a cushion, and thought about the day ahead and how this would be an end, not to the suffering of the people who had endured pain and grief, but an end to one who caused it. Tiberius had never so badly wanted anyone to pay for their deeds as he did right now.

•

Stephen MacAlpin slept fitfully, dozing in and out of the drugged sleep that kept his pain at bay. He was still hospitalized but was making a lot of progress. The injuries to his chest and back had healed slowly, and he had begun to get feeling in his legs again which had prompted the medical team, under the care of Doctor Malachi who had insisted on being his lead physician, to begin an intense course of physiotherapy. His feet had been damaged by years of broken bones as he had been constantly barefoot in a mining situation and had undergone extensive reconstructive surgery to try and aid his walking again. He worked hard, often collapsing in tears of pain and frustration, but he was determined to be able to stand up without fear of falling when he was called on to testify at the trial of the woman who had betrayed him and his crew and condemned him to a living hell. He wanted to stand there and look her right in the eyes and tell her, "You did not destroy me." He knew he was being kept a secret; she would not know until he was called to the stand. He yawned and stretched, enjoying the feeling of absolute freedom of movement. He had always slept chained to the wall of his tiny cell. Now that he was recovering, he could enjoy the feeling of waking up in comfortable, clean bed and having access to the decanter of water that stood on the cabinet by the bed, beside a bowl of fruit which was kept fresh every day. He reached out and took a handful of grapes and leaned back on the pillows to eat them.

•

At 10:00, people began to assemble in the courtroom. There was an air of solemnity as though even the building itself knew the unprecedented nature of today's trial. The trial of one of the Fleet's most senior officers, for a crime that spanned almost four decades and affected two generations of serving officers and crew, their families and friends. Everyone began to take their places before the JAG officers entered and took their seats at the prosecution bench. The defence bench remained empty, and Tiberius leaned over to Ross. "She's not being defended?" He was surprised.

Ross shook his head. "I heard she dismissed her council. I believe she intends to defend herself."

"That will do her the world of good," Tiberius said sarcastically. "She has nothing with which to defend herself." He glanced up and saw Xander and Serenity taking their seats. "You okay, Xander? I was thinking about you last night, it's going to be a tough day."

Xander smiled. "I'll be fine, I've been through worse. And this has to be done."

"Have you seen dad?" Tiberius smiled as he said that; it still felt strange to say that strange, but in a nice way.

"I went to the hospital this morning. He's doing well, and I think he'll manage. The questioning will be tough, but we've been interviewed in depth so I think they will keep it relatively simple; it's going to be more of a case for the prosecution to present facts and the proof. It's her court-martial rather than a standard trial. She's guilty, they do not have to determine that." Xander smiled and appeared much younger for a moment as he relaxed. "I have to confess that I can't wait to see her face when she sees Stephen, his testifying is more for the drama and seeing her condemn herself as no doubt she will." He reached for his dress cap that Serenity was holding and set it straight on his head. "I'll be glad to get back into normal uniform, dressing up isn't my thing."

Tiberius grinned. "It suits you, and you deserve every chance to wear that uniform. By rights, you should be on the bench."

Xander shook his head. "No, because I have to testify—I'm too involved." He smiled when Serenity slipped her hand into the crook of his arm. He was about to speak to her when the door to the left of the dais opened and the senior officers who would preside over the proceedings entered and took their seats, the elderly but still imposing and authoritative Fleet Admiral Caden-Zhu Morgan in the centre. Everyone had stood up when they entered and there was silence except for the rustle of a roomful of people re-taking their seats. The room then fell completely silent as military police brought in Admiral Leandri Kehoe, their red caps standing out in contrast to the grey uniform caps around the courtroom.

For her court-martial, Kehoe was back in full dress uniform in place of prison overalls. Everyone was fully aware this would likely be the last time she would wear the uniform—a picture of a long and highly decorated career—detailed by the rank on her collar and the many medal ribbons on her left breast, showing how much she had gambled with and how much she had lost. Decades of hiding what she had done had finally been uncovered, leaving her life and career in ruins. But, because of the story and what she had done, there was little, if any, sympathy in the room and there was absolute silence as she took her seat. As she sat down, she turned her head and looked around the room and her eyes locked on Xander. There was such hostility in her expression that Xander almost looked away, but he did not break the gaze and it was she who looked away.

"She hates me so much," Xander whispered to Serenity and felt her hand squeeze his.

"She can't hurt you, she's finished," Serenity responded. "However much she hates you, it's over." She stopped speaking as the old ship's bell on the judicial bench was rung three times to start the proceedings.

Fleet Admiral Morgan looked across the room to the empty defence bench and Commander Isaac Quinn at the prosecution bench stood up. "Admiral, the defendant has waived her right to defence and intends to conduct her own defence."

Morgan nodded. "Begin," he said, leaning back in his chair, resting his hands on the arms. No-one was expecting the trial itself to take long; Kehoe's guilt was already established by the undeniable evidence and on her own admission—which she had later retracted, stating she planned to plead 'not guilty'—to the last she was playing the game her way. No witnesses for the defence had been recorded and Kehoe stated to the court that she would be making her own defence and closing argument. Morgan nodded. "That is your right," he said, giving no sign of what he really thought of her decision. They all knew she was guilty but entitled to a fair trial.

Commander Quinn stepped out from behind the bench and began his opening statement with a brief description of the events surrounding the loss of the *Wryneck* and the subsequent imprisonment and torture of Admira Galen. "The whole event was masked in what transpired to be the greatest cover-up on our in our history, which included the attempted murder of Admiral Galen when he attempted to bring certain facts to attention, to assist and protect Captain Tiberius MacAlpin and his crew in their mission on the new ship, the *Invincible*, which was ordered to go to the same area of space to discover, allegedly, what had happened to the *Wryneck*. It became apparent later on that this was not really the purpose of the mission. The charges against the defendant are treachery, conspiracy to enslave, and crimes against humanity—namely the subjection to genetic experimentation, torture, and degrading treatment. Add to that, the attempted murder on several occasions of Admiral Galen in an attempt to obtain his silence, the intended murder of the crew of the *Invincible* and the execution of Doctor Tierney—the physician treating Admiral Galen."

Evidence, in the form of the hearing where Xander was almost forced into condemning Stephen MacAlpin as the traitor, and the mission logs which had been examined and now the incriminating sections were projected onto the screen, clearly outlining Captain MacAlpin's concerns and the proof in Kehoe's logs of her involvement. Quinn called Xander, Tiberius and Ross to testify. Ross found the questioning difficult as the memories were still too raw, but he got through it, and then Serenity gave her account beginning the day Xander was abducted from his apartment by Admiral Kehoe.

All this time, Leandri Kehoe sat in silence—every word that was spoken, every piece of evidence, making her defence more and more worthless. The crowning blow came when two of her associates, with the promise of a lighter sentence, testified against her. When the second of the two took the stand, that was the only time she spoke. She looked him right in the eyes and said, "*Et tu, Brute?*" The military police took two paces closer just in case she thought of trying anything.

The tension in the room deepened as Fleet Admiral Morgan turned to Kehoe and told her to make her defence.

Kehoe stood up and that was when everyone saw for the first time that her wrists were cuffed in front of her. Generally, an officer would not be restrained at their court-martial, but no-one wanted to take any risks with someone who had shown they were not averse to murder with little provocation. Everyone listened in growing disbelief and disgust as she attempted to justify the betrayal of Stephen MacAlpin and his crew. When asked how she justified the loss of life and the treatment of Xander by the Tamorans, she shrugged. "They knew the risks when they enlisted; besides, they were worth a lot."

"The risk of going into the unknown is an accepted fact," Quinn told her. "But not a price they expected to pay at the hands of a senior officer who conspired to sell them into slavery—their deaths saved them from suffering as Galen did; and for what? The repopulation of Tamora's sister world—of what importance was that to you?"

"Genetic research," she responded. "My father owned research laboratories and left them to me—I found them to be very lucrative businesses. The crews of the *Wryneck* and the *Invincible* were not the only crews I sold. There are not many worlds known to us who escaped, and there are few to challenge me."

"You are challenged now by those here who suffered because of you."

"By Xander Galen and Kirbie Ross? We know they work with psychiatrists, their testimonies cannot be relied on in court, surely?" She could not mask the sneer.

Fleet Admiral Morgan folded his hands together. "Maybe not, but they certainly give the court a clear insight into their suffering. As for a challenge, how will a ghost suffice?" His face was inscrutable but there was a gleam in his eyes.

"A ghost?" Kehoe frowned. "A phantom will be even less of a credible witness."

59

A Ghost Gives Evidence

The door at the back of the room opened and two medical orderlies assisted a cloaked figure slowly down towards the front of the room. There was silence but for the sound of the slow, dragging footsteps, accompanied by the 'tap tap' of crutches.

Everyone's gaze had shifted to the witness stand as the figure was helped to sit. Only a handful of those assembled knew who it was. Morgan turned to face the new witness. "Whenever you are ready, take your time."

The orderlies helped their charge off with his cloak, the deep cowl of which had shielded his face; and a man in the same dress uniform, including peaked cap, was revealed. His head was bowed, his face hidden from view until he placed his hands on the rail of the stand and pulled himself shakily to his feet, raising his head at the same time. Despite the ravages of time and suffering, everyone instantly recognized Stephen MacAlpin and the courtroom fell silent as he stood, leaning on the rail for support. How he managed to keep his breathing steady, he never knew, but he could feel his heart racing and his legs felt like jelly. He had wondered what he would feel, facing her this way. Now he knew. Terrified.

Leandri Kehoe's colour drained from her face and her cuffed hands gripped the rail around the dock. "You're supposed to be dead!" she hissed. "Dayelh told me you died—that's why Galen was released—because he was no use to them when you had been!"

Xander gripped his wife's hand tightly; so tightly that had she not been made from a titanium alloy he would have crushed her fingers.

Veritas: The Captain's Redemption

"Dayelh lied to you, Leandri," Stephen said, speaking for the first time. "He found I was of more use than as a sacrifice to fit in with your story that I had destroyed my ship, and my crew. Yes, I left instructions for the ship to be destroyed if *absolutely* necessary. I did not want the rest of the crew taken prisoner and tortured as Xander and I were. You got away with it this long only because of your so-called trade agreement you made with the Tamorans where you had him released. You bought his silence for years." He broke off and someone fetched him a glass of water.

Commander Quinn stood up. "I have questions for you, Captain MacAlpin, but you may sit down; the court is fully aware you are still under doctor's orders."

Stephen let the orderlies help him to sit and he clasped his shaking hands tightly on his lap. "What I went through is too horrific for me to want to talk about, but I will answer the questions you put to me to the best of my ability. I may take my time to answer, please bear with me."

Quinn nodded. "You may request I stop any time you need to take a rest. We're not going anywhere. Now, in your own words, and taking your time, could you tell the court about the meeting with the Tamoran president, Dayelh, and when you first realized something was wrong?"

Stephen nodded and began, slowly and rather shakily at first, but his voice grew stronger as he talked. He described the meeting, which they had still believed was to do with obtaining access and trade rights to the Tamoran wormhole. "I first realized something was perhaps wrong when they took Xander—I mean Commander Galen—away. When they brought him back, he seemed okay but was a little subdued. It was that night when I woke to find him with some kind of a fever and his left arm was swollen and painful. I examined him as best as I could in the dim light and could make out what seemed to be the marks of needles in his arm." He took a sip of water and went on to tell how they were separated, and how he lay awake at night and heard Xander screaming as they experimented on him. He described some of the experiments that were performed on himself. "As I did not understand their language, I was unable to communicate with our captors; Dayelh was the only one who seemed to speak English and I never saw him after the first meeting. I gathered from the nature of some of the tests that they were conducting experiments for genetic reproduction. I prayed every night that we would die. I stopped hearing Xander's screams after a time and hoped he was at peace." He broke off again and looked across to where his friend was sitting and then went on slowly. As the full details of what he had been used for, and how he had suffered years of forced labour in the mines, the silence in the room deepened and when Stephen paused for a rest, a pin could have been heard to drop.

Morgan nodded at the JAG officer, and Commander Quinn smiled at Stephen. "Thank you, sir, the court has heard enough from you. You may stand down."

Stephen raised his hand slightly. "If I may continue?"

Fleet Admiral Morgan nodded. "You may."

Stephen took a sip of water from his glass. "I lay the blame entirely with Kehoe and the Tamoran president. The Tamorans may have followed a barbaric practice, but it was on the orders of their leadership and they were encouraged to believe it was the way to save their people. Kehoe must bear the worst of the guilt, however, for she sold us. My crew and my son's—two entire crews sold to Tamora to feed their experiments." He paused and took a deep breath, raising his hand again to signal he was not finished. Now that he had gathered the strength to go through with this, he was going to say his piece. Another sip of water, and then he looked up again. "What kind of sick and depraved mind can come up with this plan and accept payment for it? Her hands are stained with the blood of hundreds…" He had to break off there and sat down, his face buried in his hands.

"You may stand down, Captain," Fleet Admiral Morgan said, gesturing to the medical orderlies who helped Stephen up and assisted him to an empty seat beside Serenity.

After Stephen took his seat, Quinn called Doctor Malachi to the stand and she was invited to tell her part of the story, which she did, starting with her being invited down to the planet. She talked about the operation she was forced to perform on a female prisoner and how she had been ordered to tend Stephen after the collapse in the mine. She hesitated a moment before beginning on the events surrounding Commander Ross' traumatic ordeal.

"Thank you, Doctor," Quinn said. He paused as she returned to her seat and then turned to face the bench and began his closing speech. He covered every relevant detail from the evidence and the witnesses' testimonies and pointed out the pre-meditated nature of Kehoe's crimes. "Admiral Kehoe showed a wilful disregard for the lives and safety of fellow officers and crewmen and women. She knowingly sold an entire ship into slavery—and would have condemned every one of those 460 souls into the same torments MacAlpin and Galen suffered. It was only the cautionary nature of Captain MacAlpin's orders to destroy the ship should anything go wrong that ultimately saved them, although tragically meaning a massive loss of life. These events were then deliberately manipulated to create the false story of MacAlpin's treachery which dogged his son his entire life. Questions about his father were met with silence and he was told his father was a traitor and a murderer; enough to destroy that boy. But no, he resolved to serve and clear his father's name. Ultimately, this led to the promise to the Tamorans of another ship with a large crew—referred to as 'cargo' in one of Kehoe's logs. For over thirty years this story was maintained, and it was only when Tiberius MacAlpin was handed his new command that her involvement began to be questioned and her refusal to comply with requests for details began to appear suspicious. This is when she began the attempts on Admiral Galen's life." Quinn paused and glanced at his notes. "I spoke with Kehoe's defence attorney before the defendant dismissed her and even the defence team could not come up with anything to say in defence. They knew her to be guilty beyond any reasonable doubt, just as the prosecution does and I believe that everything we have seen and heard makes my argument for me, and I submit that only a sentence of the death penalty will suffice today in the court." The silence was shattered by one or two gasps. There was not much now in society where a sentence of death was given and very few reasons one would be requested—the last court authorized capital punishment had taken place centuries ago, but it had not been erased from law. All the charges against her came under the death penalty—it was either that or a life sentence to a penal colony. Quinn continued, his words intended to stir up many feelings. "It has been the humane way to preserve a life even when that person has committed murder, and they have been sentenced to life imprisonment in a penal colony as far away from Earth as is possible, with no hope of ever being released or seeing their home and family again. In this case, considering the nature of her crimes against humanity, and the manipulation of an alien world into conducting these experiments in order to continue funding her businesses, I can say, with conviction, that she is, without a doubt, the worst mass murderer we have seen in centuries. If she had not been exposed, she would have killed again. Her hand was not the one to enter the self-destruct code, but she caused it without any thought of the people and their families she condemned to death or a living hell. It is only right that she should forfeit that which she sought to protect for decades. Her life. You have heard and seen everything in this courtroom. I rest my case."

The fleet admiral reached forward and rapped the bell three times. "This court will adjourn until 14:00. Clear the court."

The courtroom emptied and Commander Quinn joined Xander and the others who had been escorted to a private room. There was maximum security around them because there was a belief that supporters of Kehoe would attempt some form of demonstration or attack on those officers who accused her.

Commander Quinn turned to Stephen MacAlpin and asked how he was feeling.

Stephen smiled softly. "I am okay, thank you," he said. "It was hard but not as bad as I thought it might be. Once I faced her, I knew I had no reason to keep anything back. Do you think they will act on your recommendation?"

"The death penalty? I don't know. No officer has been executed for hundreds of years, but then there has been no officer who has done such terrible things." Quinn looked around at the others and then looked at Xander. "What do you think? She had you abducted and locked in stasis while your illness was made worse. She wanted you to die to protect her, and she wanted you to suffer. All she needed was one injection and your life would have been over. How do you feel about the possibility a death sentence will be pronounced?"

"I cannot believe she has gone beyond the point where her rights and humanity cannot be considered. A life sentence will give her years to think about what she did, but she is the kind of woman who will plan revenge. None of us here will be safe as long as there is any chance that she can communicate with any of her supporters." Xander paused and looked down at the floor and Serenity put her hand on his arm.

Commander Quinn nodded. "Do you want to go back in for the sentencing?" He smiled when they nodded. "You want to face her to the last? I understand. I'll come and call you when it is time to return. Go and have some lunch. It has been a long morning for you."

Tiberius thanked the lawyer and came to help his father up, supporting him on the short walk to a nearby restaurant where they ordered a light meal.

"She won't get away with it, dad," Tiberius said. "You're the greatest piece of evidence the court has. You and Xander. Your survival against all odds condemns her."

Stephen nodded. "I know. I am not worried that she will go unpunished." He looked at the dish of beef stew and rice that had been set in front of him. Today was the first time he had ordered something solid; it had taken a long time for his stomach to acclimatize to anything other than the scraps and dirty water they had been given. Enough to keep them alive, but barely.

Tiberius nodded and watched Xander helping Stephen with salt and pepper. It still felt strange, getting used to having his father around. He had gone through his whole life without him, but it was good to get to know him and to see him getting a little stronger every day. He was surrounded by people who cared about him, that could do nothing but help.

They were just finishing their meal when Commander Quinn appeared. "It's time." He led them back into the courtroom and they took their seats as the senior officers entered and took their places at the bench. Fleet Admiral Morgan rang the bell again and turned to the military police. "Bring her back in."

If the tension and silence in the room had been heavy before, it had deepened and there was an air of something about to happen. Tiberius clenched his fists on his knees and was breathing hard. He had waited all these years for answers to the mystery surrounding the disappearance of his father. He had never dared to hope—there had been no reason to—that his father was alive. He had just expected to find out the truth of his death.

The police returned with Kehoe between them and stood right behind her when she was brought into the dock. Her face was set hard and, as she looked across at the seats where the MacAlpins and Xander sat, there was an expression in her eyes that showed her true feelings. It was one of pure hatred.

Stephen MacAlpin turned his head and met her eyes full on and held her gaze without flinching. She had killed his entire crew—his friends—and he had lost, in a sense, his own life, more than half his life being spent as a prisoner; a lab-rat.

Xander could not look. He kept his head down and clenched his hands tightly. He felt Serenity's arm around his waist.

The bell was rung again. "After considering all the evidence and the testimonies; taking into consideration the impact these events have had on a generation, it was not difficult to come to a unanimous decision. Leandri Kehoe, stand up."

Leandri Kehoe made no move, and the military police officers took her arms and pulled her to her feet. She looked straight out in front of her and made no eye contact with the bench.

Morgan continued. "Admiral Leandri Kehoe, you are, with immediate effect, stripped of rank and all honours and decorations." He made a gesture with his hand and the police officers tore her rank braid and pips from her collar and sleeves, and the medal ribbons off her chest. When they were done, he went on, putting on his cap which had rested on the desk in front of him for the duration of the proceedings. "The verdict of this court is that you will be taken from this courtroom and returned to prison where you will be held to await transportation to a penal planet. You are not granted a right to appeal, and you will not be told the exact date set. You will experience the same uncertainty you caused your victims." He met her eyes then as she finally turned to look at him. There was no remorse in her face, and he saw she was laughing. "Take her down!" he said, disgusted by her reaction.

As the military police took her out, she was still laughing.

60
Epilogue

Xander turned from drinks cabinet in the living room of his apartment and smiled. He held out a glass to Tiberius and one to Ross and then sat down on the couch beside Stephen who, like Xander, was not drinking alcohol because of its interference with the medication they were both on. Serenity and Doctor Malachi were sitting on the opposite couch with their drinks and there were plates of food on the coffee table.

Stephen leaned back on the cushions and closed his eyes as he breathed in the scent of the Columbian coffee Xander had made. "I did not realize how much I missed this," he said. "I can hardly believe that all this is over and that she's gone and cannot hurt anyone again."

They had received official confirmation that morning that Kehoe's transportation would be within a year of sentencing, and Stephen had been discharged from the hospital that morning too. Xander and Serenity had offered him their guest room until he was fully recovered.

Xander looked at him. "How do you feel?"

Stephen opened his eyes and turned to look at him. "I don't know," he said, but he smiled. "I suppose I feel free for the first time. It is a feeling I could not describe and if someone asked me what freedom felt like I could not explain it."

Xander nodded. "Everyone talks of freedom and what it means to them, to their nation, to their people—but only those who have worn chains know the true meaning of freedom." He took a sip of his coffee and reached for a sandwich. "What do you think of my being married?"

Stephen looked across at Serenity. "She's perfect for you, and you are obviously happy. If you had not told me that she was not human I would not have known otherwise."

Xander smiled. "I never thought I would find someone to care for me after everything I went through." He paused and then said, "Have you seen Bethany?" He wondered how that would have gone, with Bethany finally remarrying.

Stephen sighed. "She came to see me in the hospital. I totally understand. She waited a long time; not because there was any chance after all this time that I was alive, but because it took that long to move on. I would not ask her to leave her new husband because the unthinkable happened. He appears to be a kind man who loves her and that is enough for me. I was dead for a long time, I am surprised she waited so long. She was young, and it cannot have been easy to raise our son alone."

Tiberius leaned forward. "Perhaps that was because of me. I was a difficult child and she often called me a monster. It was only when I was older that I found out more about you and tried to be what I thought you would like me to be. That is why I enlisted against her wishes. I wanted everyone to know that what they said about you was not going to make me hide. I just wish I could have stopped Ross from getting hurt—especially the second time. Dayelh gave me the choice of saving Ross by surrendering the ship."

"You could not have done that," Ross responded, taking a sip of the cold beer Xander had given him. "And I would not have allowed you to do so. My death would have been better than the loss of the entire crew, even if I was not exactly looking at it that way at the time." He smiled slightly and then added, "Some good came of it. It brought about the end to all of this; Kehoe was finally exposed and we're getting closure. She can't hurt anyone anymore and you get the chance to build a real relationship with your dad. You proved everyone wrong by sticking to your faith in him all these years."

Tiberius grinned. He got up and went to the window and looked out across the city and then turned back. He glanced at Ross and the doctor who were sitting on the sofa together. He couldn't quite tell, without it being obvious that he was looking, but it did look like Rivkah had her hand on Ross', and he wondered. All that time together, working on Ross' recovery would have brought them close. She had saved him from a terrible death, and he owed his state-of-the-art prosthetics to her.

Veritas: The Captain's Redemption

He smiled and said nothing, but just hoped. "Here's to the future—good health and happiness for my friends and family, and here's to routine missions—don't want any more like that one." He raised his glass. "I never believed what they said. I knew there was something more we weren't being told. Welcome home, dad."

Lightning Source UK Ltd.
Milton Keynes UK
UKHW010632220522
403341UK00001B/65

9 781782 011002